Broken

J. Matthew Nespoli

Published by World Audience, Inc.
(www.worldaudience.org)
303 Park Avenue South, Suite 1440
New York, NY 10010-3657
Phone (646) 620-7406; Fax (646) 620-7406
info@worldaudience.org
Edited by Kyle David Torke
ISBN 978-1-935444-48-0

© 2010, J. Matthew Nespoli

World Audience (www.worldaudience.org) is a global consortium of artists and writers, producing quality books and the literary journal *audience*, and *The audience Review*. Our periodicals and books are edited by M. Stefan Strozier and assistant editors. Please submit your stories, poems, paintings, photography, or artwork:
submissions@worldaudience.org.

Inquire about being a theater reviewer: theatre@worldaudience.org.
Thank you.

Broken

by

J. Matthew Nespoli

January, 2010

A World Audience Book

New York, NY (USA)
Newcastle, New South Wales (Australia)

This novel is dedicated to all the beautiful women who inspired it;
especially my beautiful bride, Rea.
In the end, when we die,
if we've loved and been loved,
we will die having lived an important life.

October 1996
Skye Garucci, 17

Some women whored their orifices for drug money. After my childhood trauma, I swore I'd never use sex for money. Sex was a consequence of getting stoned. I didn't care about it, and couldn't remember the last time I'd had it. So, when Momma Honey revealed that I was pregnant, I was shocked. My insides knotted. I felt like I might die. An hour later, Momma Honey was between my legs helping me push out a little baby girl. I took her. She fit in the palm of my hand.

She was dead.

Momma Honey cut the umbilical cord, separating my dead baby from my dead soul. I couldn't peel my eyes off her body. I wanted to cry but I was dried up inside. Momma Honey tried to take my baby away so I didn't have to look at her, but it wouldn't matter. I knew I'd see my dead baby girl, my little Tara Jane, in every smoggy-red Los Angeles sunset, and every night when I closed my eyes, I'd see her in my dreams.

Life on the streets of Los Angeles was tough. Simple things such as finding food and a place to relieve my bowels were problematic. I'd get so hungry I'd become delusional, and the hot sun would look like a Little Debbie snack cake I could pluck from the sky and eat.

"You're going to be something special," said Momma Honey, her throaty voice reminding me of a retired Jazz singer who'd smoked too many cigarettes.

"Yeah, right," I replied.

Momma Honey smacked her lips, "you will," she said.

I wanted to believe her but had no reason to.

Momma Honey looked 120 years old, but she was only half that. Her matted hair resembled dirt stained snow after it had been plowed to the side of the road, and her green-hued skin made her ethnicity indeterminable. She smiled often, and her toothless mouth reeked of decay when she pushed out a laugh. On her left breast, she always wore the same heart-shaped broach, which was missing a few of its red stones. She had penetrating Mona Lisa eyes, never evasive and never revealing. Sometimes I saw my future in her eyes, and it terrified me.

Momma Honey didn't mess with drugs, and though she tried to help me stay clean, I didn't. Most of the homeless were junkies or crackheads. For me, drugs were a thick gray storm that I hoped would wash away my pain. I didn't have a drug preference and would binge on anything; my only goal was to forget. With a couple dollars in my pocket, finding decent drugs was easy. But when I was broke and desperate, I'd be forced to resort to rat poison, spray paint fumes, gasoline, glue, or whatever else I could get my hands on.

Give me anything then give me more.

Drained of the baby who'd wanted to become my daughter, I felt an emptiness inside me that would never be filled.

I killed my baby by abusing drugs, and I hated myself for it. I wrapped Tara Jane in my Ramones souvenir concert T-shirt. Momma Honey put her in a discarded Pick Up Sticks take-out container and we buried her under a palm tree in the Santa Monica knoll that overlooked the pier we slept under.

What happens to the souls of all the babies who never see the world? Are they lost in some parallel universe? Do they go to heaven? Are they on the other side waiting to get their vengeance?

The only way I could make myself feel any better was to get high.

Drugs were my slow-metered suicide.

T.J. Martini, 23

This is going to hurt.

My body was airborne, hurtling toward a brick wall.

I needed a weekend escape from my boring-as-hell accounting job at a bank in Bunker Hill, Oregon. Even more, I wanted a mini-vacation from my roommates, who also happened to be my parents.

I called, Craig, an old college buddy from Pittsburgh, and we planned a weekend getaway, in Miami, to see the Steelers battle the Dolphins. Neither of us geniuses gave a thought to Florida's latest hurricane warning.

We had lousy seats way up in the nosebleeds. However, the stadium was nearly empty due to the looming hurricane and freezing cold, so we snuck down to the lower level on the fifty-yard line. Then we proceeded to drink ourselves silly in an attempt to get warm.

"These seats are great!" Craig yelled over the loud rain that was pelting the empty bucket seats surrounding us.

"They sure are!"

After the game, we hit South Beach in search of female company.

Over the course of the next twelve hours, as is typical, women were throwing themselves at Craig. He had movie-star good looks, rugged but warm, like a young Robert Redford, and a mellifluous voice that had women swooning when he said hello. He was my best friend.

I hated his guts.

I was having much less success than Craig. And by less, I mean zero. I tried everything from simple introductions, to tossing out cheesy opening lines, to sending drinks to a table full of girls like you see in movies. Nothing was working. Everytime I struck out I felt more pitiful and became more desperate. At one point I became so pathetic that I resorted to scare tactics. I told one girl that the hurricane was getting dangerously close and that we should evacuate to my safe house. She laughed at me and then told her friend what I'd said, and the friend laughed at me too. Our weekend getaway was doing little to cheer me up. I'd yet to even get a girl to speak to me... unless you count the girl who called me creepy and told me to stop smelling her hair... I tried to tell her that I wasn't smelling her hair, that I had a case of the sniffles from sitting in the rain for three hours at a football game, but she wasn't hearing it.

Anyway, we moved on to yet another bar, and by four a.m., Craig and I found ourselves in a club that played loud trance music accompanied by irritating flicking lights.

"I'm gonna have a seizure. Let's leave!" I said, fifteen minutes after getting inside. Craig had already met some ladies.

"Are you crazy? We just stood in line for an hour."

"Yeah, but I can't handle this music. The bass is making my balls clang together."

"That's the most action you've seen all year," said Craig. "Enjoy it!"

Craig's new girl returned from the bar and handed him a drink. They talked while bopping their heads to the music like teenage lovers on speed.

I made my way to the bar and ordered two beers, one for each lonely hand. I downed them quickly and ordered another beer and a shot of Jaeger. Then, something rammed into me from behind.

"Shit!" I spilled beer down the front of my shirt.

A large, meaty hand clamped on my shoulder. "Sorry, buddy. I didn't see you," said the owner of the hand.

My eyes, which were still adjusting to the flickering lights, began to focus on the man's face.

Holy crap, it's Jerome Bettis!

This was going to be a pivotal moment in the life of this diehard Steelers fan. I'd say hello, and he'd say hello. He'd assume I was just another irritating fan, but I'd surprise him. I wouldn't say stupid things like some star–struck groupie. I'd ask the right questions. We'd talk, and I'd dazzle him with my knowledge of football, life, and women… Well, maybe not women.

"Jerome! Great game today!"

"I fumbled twice, and we lost by eight. What was so great about it?"

"You fumbled with pizzazz."

What the hell did that mean?

Jerome didn't respond.

I tried to start some conversation, "umm, hey, what do you think about–"

"Hey, buddy, I owe you a drink. Hey Bartender!" Jerome said. The bartender tended to him in about two seconds, which is about half an hour less than it would have taken me to get served.

"Hey Jerome, I wanted to tell you something about me you probably don't know. I mean, of course you wouldn't know it, because you don't know me. Well, I just mean that–"

"Good meeting you." Jerome slid me a beer, slapped me on the back, and then left to go upstairs to V.I.P. where all his teammates would be partying with beautiful women who never talked to guys like me.

I had to get up there…

"Kicker coming through," I said to the large bouncer guarding the red velvet rope.

The bouncer, whose forearms were the size of my head, didn't acknowledge my presence. So, I stepped over the rope. I took two steps forward before Popeye dropped his humongous forearm on me. I crumpled like an empty can of spinach.

"Punter?" I said, looking up at him.

He didn't smile. The guy had the personality of a cheese sandwich.

Back downstairs, I began to suffer an unbearable headache from the pulsating lights. I closed my eyes, but I could see them flashing through my eyelids. The thumping music worsened the pain, so I tore off the ends of a napkin, rolled them into tiny balls, and stuck them in my ears.

A sexy girl pushed through the crowd to get to the bar. I stood firm to make sure that I could get some good brush up action. She wore a skimpy tube top made of material so thin her nipples pressed through. Whenever the lights pulsated, her large breasts cast a shadow over her diamond-studded bellybutton. A chain ran from the belly stud and disappeared under her tube top.

Wow.

The girl's friend tried to squeeze between us to get to the bar. She wore one of those J. Lo dresses with a plummeting neckline that miraculously manages to stay on.

I maneuvered myself to get some brush up from her as well. She squeezed past me, brushing her rotund buttocks up against the front of my jeans; sadly, it was the best part of my night.

"Having fun?" I asked her.

J. Lo wanna-be flared her nostrils. It reminded me of the way a puffer fish blows up to scare away its predators — a factoid I learned on the Discovery Channel.

She waved to the bartender who ignored the other four thousand customers to come take care of her.

"Hey Larry," she said to him. Then, J. Lo wanna-be leaned over the bar to kiss him, revealing a clear view down her dress to the South Pole.

Suddenly, from out of nowhere, a plan materialized. "Hey, ladies. You fan's of the Steelers?"

"What's a Steeler?" asked J. Lo wanna-be.

"It's a famous and wealthy football player."

In 1980, Bobby Bonds set a single-season MLB record with 189 strikeouts. Although I'd already broken his record tonight, I decided to take another swing.

"My good friend, Jerome Bettis, asked me to come down here from V.I.P. to escort you ladies upstairs."

"Really?" said bellybutton-nipple girl.

The three of us headed upstairs. With an arm around each girl, I looked Popeye the bouncer dead in his eyes and said, "Can you please unhook the rope? My hands are full."

Popeye unhooked the rope.

It's rare when beta-male personalities like me get to be arrogant to gorilla-sized men like Popeye the bouncer and live to tell the tale, so this was pretty cool. However, seeing the look on Craig's face, watching me as I walked into V.I.P. with two incredibly sexy girls, was even better.

There were about forty people in V.I.P. and at least fifteen of them were Steelers; the girls ditched me in about two seconds. Drunk and happy, I helped myself to the appetizers and alcohol lining the tables and started chatting with players. I did a few shots with the three-hundred-pound captain of the offensive line, Dermonti Dawson, who found me humorous for some reason. We chatted for maybe half an hour and did a few shots together.

After the fourth shot of Tequila, I made my way to the dance floor. "Hey, wanna dance?" I asked a particularly lovely young lady.

"Su-ure," she said, stretching the word into two syllables. She was probably the only person there more drunk than I.

We danced. We grinded. We shook, jiggled, and bounced. We could really freaking dance. Everyone watched, wishing they could dance like us.

"Hey, pal, you're dancing with my girl," some guy yelled over my shoulder. His strong, alcohol-soaked breath wilted the hairs on the back of my neck.

I ignored him. My partner and I continued to dazzle and amaze everyone with our sensational skills. We went from the bump and grind to the robot. Actually, I did the robot, and she was jumping up and down and head banging. She built quite a bit of momentum, and I worried her thrashing head might fly off her shoulders.

"Uhh, like, why do you have those napkins in your ears?" she shouted.

"What?" I asked, and then–

Boom!

I'd been blindsided, vaulted toward the wall.

Splat!

I hit the wall, stuck to it for a second just like a cartoon character, and then gravity pulled me to the floor. I immediately sprang to my feet and assumed combat position. The large man who'd hit me laughed. Embarrassed, I lowered my head, and escorted myself out of V.I.P.

This type of humiliation was nothing new; in fact, it's pretty much the standard for beta-male losers like me.

Defeated, I rejoined the common folk downstairs.

"How'd it go up there?" Craig asked.

"Shut up."

Jackson Rockenberger, 28

"Joanna, get my pills," I said.

I felt a pop in my neck when I hit the little punk. When I sat down, the room started moving around me. I became lightheaded, and my nerves felt like raw copper wires dipped in acid and plugged into a nuclear power plant.

I'd survived thousands of collisions with three-hundred-pound linemen, but they'd worn out my body. My joints were frayed, and my muscles moaned with a permanent ache. Years of using steroids to build strength and shorten healing time had, ironically, left me weak and unable to heal from minor injuries. I was hurt nearly every game; every injury lingered into the next game, and then I'd tack on another.

My neck had been surgically repaired two years ago. Now, after six years as a linebacker for the Pittsburgh Steelers, I'd re-injured my neck hitting some pasty, pot-bellied dork in a bar.

I knew I'd just ended my career. And I'd done it by getting territorial over a girl I'd been sleeping with since high school that I didn't even like that much.

Amber Johnson, 19

Kimberly pulled nourishment from me until she got her fill. I lifted her from my breast and laid her down. Anxiety overwhelmed me as tears flooded my eyes.

I'd failed my daughter, Kimberly.

And I was sorry. Sorry I screwed up my life, sorry for destroying my mother, and sorry the love of my life, my daughter, would someday learn she was the product of my most horrifying moment.

Kimberly would turn two soon, and I feared not being able to provide for her much longer. I didn't have a job, and black high-school dropouts don't have employers banging on their front doors.

Kimberly began crying, bothered by her teething. I rubbed Nyquil on her gums.

"Momma, book?"

"Yes, love." I smiled and picked up my dirt and blood-stained copy of *Beloved.*

Kimberly couldn't understand the story, but the sound of my voice soothed her. And despite the constant parade of police sirens roaring past our apartment, she eased into sleep. *Beloved* is about the invincibility of the mother-daughter bond. Believing in that bond has always comforted me. I hadn't spoken to my mom in four years.

Kimberly and I had just moved to Compton, and I didn't know anybody yet. I had only nineteen dollars left to my name, and couldn't afford a sitter. Needing work fast, I set a worn blanket on the floor in the closet and laid Kimberly on it. I prayed, "God, Buddha, Mohammed, Allah, Jesus, and anyone else who's listening, please take care of my baby."

If anything happens to her, I'll kill myself.

I kissed Kimberly and locked her in the closet. It was a stupid thing to do, but it was the only option available. Reluctantly, I left her and hit the dark streets. The type of work I qualified for could be found most easily at night.

I kept a brisk pace while passing crackheads and whores, and in my haste, I bumped into a prostitute.

"Watch it, bitch!" she growled.

Startled, I jumped. She and the two hookers with her laughed at my reaction. Laughing feels good. My laughs have been few and far between. I wondered how these prostitutes would feel when their laughter stopped. I wondered if they were as scared as I was.

It was the time of year when my most horrible memories felt as fresh as yesterday. I was constantly on edge. I knew I'd never escape him, and one day he'd be the shadow on my grave.

Tell anyone, and I'll kill you, he'd said.

So I didn't tell. I wrote Mom a note, left home, assumed a new last name, and began a new life. I lived in constant fear. At nineteen, a legal adult, I still behaved like a kid. I couldn't go to sleep without a nightlight because, in the dark, I was back in the barn in Naples where my innocence was murdered. I feared men, the dark, and failing Kimberly. My biggest fear was some day he'd learn about my daughter and come after her.

I saw it happening all the time. I'd see him during my bath, when I slept, and while grocery shopping. Over and over again, in slow motion, I saw that green T-shirt, the dark shadowy outline of his body, his hand extending, snatching Kimberly, and disappearing.

Compton was the newest in a long line of cities we'd squatted in since leaving Florida. Kimberly and I arrived there with a backpack, four changes of clothes, a couple of books, and six hundred dollars. I got the money in Tucson by pawning diamond necklaces I'd stolen from Mom's bigoted boss in Naples. Though Compton was rough, it was the only section of Los Angeles where six hundred dollars would cover rent plus security deposit.

Minutes after bumping into the prostitutes, I met their pimp, Tyrone.

Besides pimping, Tyrone dealt drugs. He carried a lot of pent-up anger on his two-hundred-and-fifty pound frame. Word on the street was he'd framed his little brother for a murder Tyrone himself had committed.

Tyrone approached me. "I'll take good care of you," he said, grabbing my arm.

I stepped back. "I'm not here for that kind of work," I said. My knees felt wobbly.

"Everyone is here for that kinda work." He smiled. His yellowed teeth were chipped and splintered with spider web fractures.

Tyrone's phone rang. "Wait," he said and answered it.

I waited because I was scared not to.

Tyrone screamed into the phone, "You're a fucking dead man!" He hung up. Tyrone looked down, cussed under his breath, and then looked at me. He picked at a scab on his bald black head and spoke to me. "My boy bailed on an important delivery. The job's yours," he said. I hadn't even said I wanted work.

Without waiting for my answer, Tyrone pulled a pen out of his back pocket, grabbed my arm, and wrote an address on the back of my hand. "You're going to this address to pick up some shit. I'll kill you if you steal from me."

So I had a job.

Becoming a drug runner in a dangerous neighborhood wasn't going to win me Mother of the Year, but it paid the rent and was better than letting my child starve to death. Besides, it was temporary. I'd save money, move Kimberly and I to a better part of town, get my G.E.D., and send myself to nursing school.

All I had to do was make sure I didn't get us killed before all the good stuff could happen.

May 1997
Skye

After my baby Tara Jane died, I'd dreamt frequently of her, inside me, singing happy songs. And every time I woke and realized she was dead, I wished I could trade my life for hers.

Last night, I set up shop and performed on the Santa Monica Promenade. I had a territory carved out for myself that was located between the Mexican Michael Jackson impersonator and the teenage break dancing squad. Holding a territory was a constant battle, and any night it could become a life or death fight. This night was a busy Saturday night; the streets filled with chatty Asian tourists toting cameras and wearing Mickey Mouse ears. I played guitar and sang stupid cover songs as my new friend, Adaku, a Kenyan immigrant turned Santa Monica vagrant, played bongos. To maximize our earning potential, we tried to look pathetic and cute. Looking pathetic was easy; cute was much more difficult; Adaku pulled it off easier than me.

Adaku's drumming was off the beat; she hadn't played well in weeks. After an hour of performing, she disappeared. When I took my break I found her in a restroom filling her syringe with toilet water. She saw me looking at her.

"Don't look at me that way," Adaku said. "The sink isn't working, and security won't let me in the mall."

"You're out of control."

"Hypocrite."

"Whatever," I said. I left Adaku to her vice. She was beaten. The dope got inside her, grew like a weed, and choked the music out of her.

The next morning, when I woke, I found Adaku lying next to me beneath the pier.

"You ready to play?" I asked.

Adaku didn't respond.

"Get your bongos."

Nothing.

I shook her. She didn't budge. Then I noticed the needle sticking in her purple foot.

"Wake up, Adaku!"

I shook her harder. She was cold. I rolled her over. The back of her head was dark red from dry, crusted blood.

My friend, Adaku, died two feet away from me as I slept, in the same spot that I'd lost my baby, Tara Jane.

I lost my baby and my best friend. There's no coping with this grade of tragedy. I did the only thing I knew how. I dug through her stuff, found the dope that had killed her, and cooked up the biggest shot I'd ever had. I was determined to numb the part of my brain responsible for my pain and suffering—permanently.

Amber

Six months after going to work for Tyrone, I'd managed to save a little money, but not quite enough to leave Compton. We were still at least five months away from being able to afford a move. Nights there were the worst. Gunfire kept me awake with worry that a stray bullet would find its way to my daughter. We had to get out soon.

When blessed with a night free of local gang activity, our neighbor's rap music kept me up. Our paper-thin walls vibrated like giant woofers as *fuck, shit, pussy,* and *bitch* seeped through them. Their music, like their gunfire, was another way for the gangs to flex their muscle.

Kimberly and I were neck deep in the trenches of these noise wars.

And I feared if Kimberly grew up in that neighborhood, she'd end up like the rest of them.

Tonight, like every other, I read *Beloved* to Kimberly. I loved books. When Mom and I lived and worked as housemaids, in Florida, I spent much of my time in the personal library of Mom's boss. Surrounding myself with characters in books helped me feel less alone.

Kimberly fell asleep, my babysitter showed up, and I left to pick up the cocaine from one of Tyrone's grunt workers. He gave me two fairly big bags of cocaine, which made me immediately nervous, and he instructed me to make two deliveries near the beach. I arrived at the bus stop about ten minutes early, a situation I typically tried to avoid because sitting alone under the dim yellow glow of the street's single light terrified me.

This night was cool; the streets were quiet; the air was thick and held an acrid smell of gunfire and gasoline. There wasn't a single star in the sky.

The bus arrived, I got on, and it belched a thick plume of smoke as it pulled out. I sat in the back across from an elderly Mexican lady. Her head bobbed with palsy, which agitated my already unstable nerves. An oddly familiar looking middle-aged white guy with long dreadlocks sat two rows behind me. Every time I looked at him, he was glaring in my direction.

"Why you be lookin' at me?" I asked. I wasn't raised to talk way, but using street lingo helped me blend.

"I ain't looking at you," he said.

We had no more dialogue, but he kept staring. When the bus stopped, the Mexican lady got off. I considered going with her, but the next bus to Venice Beach wasn't for another forty-five minutes, and I didn't want to sit alone in the dark. When the bus pulled back into traffic, the white guy got up and approached me.

I kept my eyes focused straight ahead. He sat down next to me and put his hand down his pants, digging at himself.

"Hey," he said.

"Hey."

"So. You gonna share?" he asked.

"Share what?"

He pointed over his shoulder at a black guy wearing a backward cap. "You see guy back there? He's a cop."

"Fuck off," I said. I hoped he was lying, but I didn't necessarily want to find out.

"Give me half of what you're holding, and I won't rat."

I was screwed. If I got busted and went to jail, I'd lose Kimberly. But if I gave the guy half of the dope, Tyrone would kill me.

"I ain't got shit," I said.

"Is that so?"

"Yep."

The guy stood up, and walked toward the cop.

"Wait," I said.

He came back, sat down, and grinned. I hesitated, considering my options, and then discreetly opened my purse and slipped him one of my two bags. Asking for only half my stuff was smart. With me holding the other half, he knew I couldn't go to the cop.

Eventually, I made it to Venice, which was quiet and peaceful at night. The ocean's fragrance typically calmed me, but tonight I'd passed the point of being pacified by simple pleasures. I went to the customer's home, which sat on Ocean Front Walk. I knocked, and he let me into his beachfront paradise. I gave him his drugs, he gave me nine hundred dollars, and then he asked me to stay and party. I declined politely and left.

I skipped the second drop in Santa Monica because I didn't have the second bag.

On the bus back to Compton, I grew more and more nervous. Tyrone would cause me serious harm if I shorted him on the cash. I'd flee, but he had enough information about me that he'd be able to find and kill me. I had only one option.

I stopped in at my place to check on Kimberly and grabbed my hidden stash of moving money; the money I'd earned from all these months of working, the money that was going to get Kimberly and I out of this life. Then, I walked the dark streets to Tyrone's beat-up, dirty house in the absolute worst section of Compton. He lived in the kind of neighborhood where the colors you wore could get you killed. Tyrone could've afforded a nice house in Baldwin Hills, but he liked his thug life and gang-infested neighborhood.

"What up, Nigga?" Tyrone asked.

I handed him the eighteen hundred dollars he expected, nine hundred from the first customer and nine hundred of my own. It was the only way he'd let me live.

Tyrone snatched the money out of my hand. "Larry called," he said. Larry was the customer I'd skipped. I was fucked.

"Tyrone, I gave you all the mon−" Tyrone punched me in the face before I finished. I dropped.

"You fuckin' nigger junkie bitch! You stealin' from me? Huh? You fucking cunt!" He cocked to hit me again.

"No, I'm not, Tyrone! I−"

"Fucking bitch!" Tyrone hit me again; his punch sent a pulsating ring through my head. He picked me up by my neck and slammed me against the wall. "You fucked me, now I'm gonna fuck you! Or maybe I'll kill you, then fuck you!"

Tyrone had me pinned against the wall with his hand wrapped tightly around my neck. I tasted blood as I gasped for air. Tyrone raised his fist again. I kicked him in the balls. He doubled over. I couldn't believe I'd done that. In shock, I somehow managed to get my legs under me and run.

Tyrone quickly jumped to his feet and gave chase. "You're dead!"

I cut through the night air as fast as I could, but I couldn't outrun my fear.

"You're fucked, bitch!" he yelled. The sound of his voice became softer, I was out-running him. I kept running, too scared to look back. Though I was losing him, he knew where I lived, and he'd surely be there soon.

I ran deeper into the dark, passing landmarks I knew were there but couldn't see. I burst into my apartment and grabbed Kimberly. The babysitter looked startled.

"Leave!"

She bolted without question.

I grabbed the very little bit of money I hadn't given Tyrone, slung Kimberly over my shoulder, and ran for at least twenty minutes without stopping. With Kimberly's added weight, my knees felt like two sandstones grinding together. Kimberly screamed the whole time, and my pulse sang in my ears.

I'm a horrible mother.

Finally, I stopped to rest. My breaths were short and painful, and my legs were numb. I wanted to cry together with Kimberly, but I couldn't. I had to be the parent.

"Shhh, love, don't cry. Momma's gonna make everything okay."

"I scared, Mommy." Her words broke my heart.

"Don't be scared, love. Mommy will take care of you."

I started running again. It took all my effort to make it to the woman's shelter. Once there, and before one of a volunteer named Beth, could tell me all the house rules, I collapsed on an empty cot. After Beth left, I sat up just long enough to shed my shoes and peel off my socks.

"Mommy, you feets bleeds."

"I know, love. It's okay. Mommy's okay."

But I wasn't okay. My bloody feet were the least of my worries. I was a scared and battered nineteen-year-old kid with a baby and no place to go in the morning.

Men who hit women know where the shelters are. We had to move before Tyrone showed up.

But where would we go? And would Tyrone find us?

Jackson

I'm no homophobe.

I'm comfortable with my sexuality. So the massage didn't bother me because he was gay; it just bothered me that he wasn't a woman…

"How's your neck?" Joanna asked. She stood behind me, massaging my neck, the ocean breeze blowing her hair into my face.

"Same as always," I said. "It hurts."

My pain is incurable. I've tried acupuncture, chiropractic, metaphysical healing, reflexology, suction cup therapy, heat, ice, yoga, meditation, reiki, chakra balancing, tantra, colonics, physical therapy, hypnosis, DNA intuitive healing, and everything else anyone has ever recommended. Nothing worked. Pills and massage were the only temporary reliefs I'd ever found.

Today, I was out on my forty-foot trawler, about twenty miles east of Catalina Island, fishing for swordfish with friends. Joanna brought four of her beautiful actress friends; they were all sunbathing, naked. I should've been having a great time, but I felt guilty about leaving Mom with a sitter on the day of the week we typically spent together. Guilt, combined with my regular smorgasbord of pain, gave me enough reason to pop a few extra OxyContin.

I was as stoned as can be when I finally got a bite. I yanked the rod hard. Too hard. Cold white light shot up my neck and into my eyes. The pain would inevitably get worse, but I'd deal with it after I conquered my fish.

Fight! Beat him! Destroy!

And I did. I fought the fucking fish to his death. It took two hours, but I did it.

By the time we headed back to dry land, pain had its merciless claws in my flesh and was grating my raw nerve endings. My head was pulsating; I felt a dull rusted handsaw cutting the cords that rooted my eyes to my head. So I popped pills until the pain quieted to a soft murmur just loud enough to let me know it was there.

Two hours later and closer to shore, I was finally able to get a cellular connection. I called for a massage. Wendy, my masseuse, had magical hands and always made me *happy* at the end.

"Hello, Jackson Rockenberger here. I need Wendy. Now."

"Wendy's not in today. I can fit you in at five thirty with Dave."

"No."

"How about Louise at six o'clock?"

"Umm. fine."

Once home, I showered the fish stink off me. I put on jeans but no underwear, this strategy helps me communicate to the therapist that I want her to make me "happy" at the end. Then, I threw on a Steelers T-shirt so Louise could place my face, which also usually helps.

By the time I climbed on my Harley, the effects of the pills had worn off. Lightning was shooting up and down every nerve throughout my body, and there was a roaring thunder in my brain. When I arrived for my appointment, I was in so much pain I could barely hold up my head.

"I'll be with you in a couple minutes, just let me wash up," said some dude.

"Oh, no, no, no. I'm here to see Louise."

He gave me a goofy grin that was missing a tooth. "I'm Louis. There's no Louise."

"Oh. I'll sort this mess out." I approached the receptionist. "I need a female masseuse."

"I'm sorry, but nobody's free."

"Tomorrow?"

"We're closed."

My only options were to stay in severe pain until Monday or get massaged by Louis. I examined him. He had good posture, but it wasn't overly perfect. He wore jeans and sandals, nothing too fashionable. His remaining teeth were bad, and gay guys have perfect teeth.

"Okay, Louis, give me two minutes. I forgot something." I shook his hand; his grip was firm.

I went to a clothing store across the street and bought a pair of boxers. I strapped on the cotton armor, which would be the only barrier between Louis and my penis.

Back at the clinic, Louis escorted me into the massage room, and I did my best to focus on pain relief.

Ten minutes later, Louis did something seriously wrong. He ran his hands up and down my thigh to squeeze out the tension, but he went too high, and the back of his hand grazed my scrotum.

Was that on purpose?

While I contemplated, it happened again.

I rolled to my side. "Could you focus on my ribcage area?"

"Sure," Louis said. He took my hand in his, which seemed odd, and then, even worse, he rested the back of his hand on top of my crotch! I'm 100% positive that the back of a man's hand doesn't fall unknowingly into another man's crotch. I yanked our hands north, and scratched an imaginary itch. I was about to put an end to the massage, but before I was able to speak, the most horrible thing in the history of my life happened. My little Jackson, in defiance of me, got a little bit chubby — not a lot — but enough that I couldn't pretend it didn't happen. I jumped off the table, practically threw Louis across the room, hopped into my pants, and fled.

"What happened in there?" I screamed at my penis, speeding away on my Harley. "How could you do that to me?"

Okay, calm down. Analyze the situation; there's got to be a logical explanation. Maybe my penis and brain weren't communicating. Maybe my penis thought it was a woman's touch. Maybe I got so relaxed by the massage I fell asleep and was dreaming. Yeah, that's it. *No, I couldn't have fallen asleep.* I wasn't relaxed. I'd never been less relaxed! Louis was gayer than a dozen sweaty naked men in the YMCA steam room.

So *now what?* How does life go on? I'm not gay. I played professional football. I know I'm not gay. *I'm positive I'm not gay!* It must've been a random event. Yeah, that's it. My mini-erection and the ball grazing were two separate, unrelated events that coincidentally happened at the same time.

The Laws of Randomness applied, that's all that happened. Shit happens. I swallowed this pseudo-Buddhist philosophy with a shot of Rockenberger Rum and three Vicodin. Then, I took a scalding hot shower. The rum, Vicodin, and shower were to combat my neck pain; they had absolutely nothing to do with the fact I got an erection after a man grazed my balls. I was fine with it because it was all just complete randomness.

Case closed.

Later that evening, I met up with friends for drinking and male bonding during the Lakers' playoff game. The testosterone was flying. We shot the shit about football, fishing, and sexual conquests, but despite all this manly activity, I couldn't seem to get Louis and his toothless grin out of my head.

I needed a woman to set me straight.

Beth Crawford, 21

Birthdays suck my fat, white butt.

While I was on summer break from Santa Monica Community College, my high school boyfriend — whom I stayed faithful to despite never seeing him — dumped me the day he came home from Princeton.

I'd made a pathetic total of only two college friends, and they had both returned to their respective hometowns for summer. I didn't want to spend my birthday celebrating with my two dads, and I couldn't stay home on my birthday. Though I rarely drink, it was my twenty-first birthday, so I felt obligated. I went stag to the nearest bar, Double Dribble, in Santa Monica.

The dank sports bar reeked of flat beer and stale pretzels and had more televisions than patrons. One TV was tuned to a surfing show, and all the other TVs were showing some basketball game, the Lakers maybe. The bar stools had red vinyl coverings, and the stool I sat on had white stuffing peeking out of a torn hole in the vinyl. I examined the rows of liquor lining the shelves; I didn't recognize most of them. I knew vodka, gin, rum, and tequila, but their brand names meant nothing to me. The bartender was gorgeous and hateable. She was tall and busty and wore a tank top with strategic tears that made it look like she'd been attacked by a clawed animal or a gang of horny men.

Just once I'd like to be attacked by men.

I ordered a Long Island Iced Tea because it was the first drink that came to mind. I sipped it and tried to make a sound of deep satisfaction like men make when drinking a cold beer after working in the yard. I wanted to like my drink, but it was strong and nasty.

Two attractive girls were sitting next to me. The one girl blabbered about her *wonderful* boyfriend, their *incredible* weekend at Lake Tahoe, the *splendid* people they met, and the *exciting* places they made love. Her friend *oohed* at the appropriate places in the conversation. Brats.

"He gave me this goooorgeous tennis bracelet," the brat said, extending her decorated arm at her friend. "I love him."

Though she was a ditz, she was an excited ditz. I wanted to be excited about something like she was. I searched my heart and mind. There was nothing. I lack passion.

I finished my drink faster than I expected. I tilted my glass, tapped the side to get the last of the ice from the bottom, and got up to use the bathroom. As I passed a table of four guys, I noticed one in particular was very handsome.

But, as is typical, I was having a horrible hair night.

Jackson

She gave her hair a flirty flip as she came out of the bathroom. She was practically begging for it.

"Guys, you'll have to excuse me," I said to my three dorky friends.

My buddy asked, "You're leaving us?"

"Yeah."

"Good, your cologne is starting to irritate me."

"Who you leaving us for?" asked buddy number two.

"Her," I said, pointing.

"Oh. She's kinda cute in a Rene Zellweger/Bridget Jones sort of way," said number two.

Buddy number three chimed in, "Dude, you can do better."

"It doesn't matter if I can do better, which, of course, I can. What matters is she's lonely and needs me to cheer her up. I'm a philanthropist if nothing else."

The truth was I needed to re-establish my manhood after the massage incident.

"What makes you so confident she wants you?" asked dork number two.

"It'll be like taking candy from a baby," I said.

"I don't know, man. She looks like she really likes candy."

Beth

I stood to order another drink, and when I sat back down on the stool, a fart noise came out of the chair's hole. The two girls looked at me.

"Umm, it wasn't me. It was the stool."

Neither of them responded.

"Never mind," I said.

I sucked down another Long Island Iced Tea and made as much noise as possible to drown out the babbling girls.

"Sex under the pier was just soooo, like, amazing," said one of them, drawing out the O in an annoying, loopy-O way.

I looked at the handsome guy by the bathroom again. He was the dark Italian type, or maybe he was half black. Regardless, he was beautiful. His face was sculpted and manly. He had a rugged five o'clock shadow and a cleft chin that was big and strong like two marbles in a sack. And his body was just as macho and sexy as his face. He had a thick muscular torso, broad shoulders, and confident posture.

He approached the bar. I wanted to talk to him, but knew I wouldn't.

I wished I was one of those girls who always has something snappy to say, the girl with the witty comeback or the clever putdown. I want to be the chick at the bar who makes all the guys laugh with her cute little jokes.

But I'm not that girl. In fact, sometimes I don't feel like a girl at all. I don't feel like anything. I'm invisible. I could walk down the street wearing only panties, singing the Star Spangled Banner at the top of my lungs, while pulling along an alligator on a leash and nobody would even see me. I have no heartbeat; I breathe no oxygen; I'm nothing to anyone; I'm not real. And yet I'm cursed with a brain that won't rest; it torments me.

The beautiful man sat between me and the annoying girls. "Hey, gorgeous. Why so sad?" he asked the girl next to me.

She ignored him. Irritated with her cool disposition, I gulped my beverage.

"Yeah, that was a lame line. Let me try again. Hi, I'm Jackson. I couldn't help noticing such a lovely girl sitting all alone."

Huh?

"Excuse me, did you hear me?"

Holy crap, he just touched my shoulder. Okay, don't say anything stupid, don't say anything stupid, don't say anything stupid.

"My boyfriend dumped me."

"He must be an idiot."

"Why?" I asked.

"Umm. Because. Never mind. I was trying to give you a compliment."

"Oh. I'm sorry. Please, compliment away."

"Well, you're very pretty."

"You think I'm pretty?" I nervously twirled my hair.

"Very. May I join you for a dri—?"

"Yes."

"Okay, then, what are we drinking?" he asked.

"Long Islands."

"That's a stiff drink."

"I'm alone on my twenty-first birthday. I need a stiff one."

Jackson

I bet you do honey.

I called the sexy bartender over. She wore a torn up shirt exposing the perfect amount of cleavage and belly. "Can I get two Long Islands?"

The Zellweger birthday girl was already drunk; I almost felt bad about buying her another drink.

Almost.

"I was having a bad day until I saw you looking at me. Fans always cheer me up," I said.

"Huh?"

"I said I love my fans."

"Fans of what?" she asked.

"Umm… you didn't recognize me, did you?"

"I'm sorry, no."

"Oh. I'm Jackson Rockenberger," I said and waited for a response. None came. She didn't recognize my name. I'd hit a dead end. Louis and his gay massage had won. In a single moment I'd lost my entire manhood. I went for the easy, sure-thing to boost my ego, and it completely backfired. I couldn't even score with a lonely chubby girl on her twenty-first birthday.

"Never mind. I'm sorry I bothered you."

I tried to stand up, but Zellweger pulled me back into my seat. My manhood could still be salvaged. She began some small talk. We conversed for the longest half hour of my life. Her name was April or Tammy or something. She was in college, blah blah blah.

I should've hit on one of the two babbling idiot blondes sitting next to her.

Beth

We talked for a few minutes and had good chemistry. Jackson played professional football for the Pittsburgh Pirates or something.

"It's getting pretty late, and I have to be up early, so I should get going," he said.

"No! I mean, awe, that's too bad. Do you have to leave? It's only eleven, and it is Saturday night."

"Well, on Sundays I get up early to take my sick Mother out for breakfast," Jackson said. "It was nice meeting you. Enjoy the rest of your birthday, but make sure you don't drive."

"Actually, I'm going to get going. I have to, umm, work tomorrow," I said.

Offer me a ride, offer me a ride, offer me a ride.

Open your eyes and uncross your fingers, stupid!

"Do you have a way home?"

"I'll catch a cab," I said, trying to be nonchalant.

"I drove my Harley. I could take you if you're okay with bikes."

"Yes!" I blurted.

Half an hour later, I was on my back at Paradise Beach in Malibu. The bright moon sat on the horizon and cast long shadows across the white sand. It was right out of one of those cheesy romance novels that has a bare-chested man with long blond locks on the cover. I was completely taken.

Jackson's body was nothing but tight cords of muscle on thick bones. I don't think I'd ever even seen a body as perfect as his, let alone touched one. He was way out of my league; his chiseled body pressing against mine made me feel even fatter than usual. He kissed me for about a minute and then slid off my panties and tried to insert his manhood.

"Oooh, no, no, no. Not there," I said. I assumed his bad aim was not intentional.

"Sorry," he said, then regrouped.

Jackson was like a cheetah going after his prey. He was fast and strong and moved inside me with precision and expertise and an obvious goal. I tried to find pleasure with him between my legs, but I couldn't.

Jackson was only the second man I'd ever slept with, and guilt was killing my good time.

He doesn't think I'm a slut. He'll call me tomorrow. *Stop thinking!* Relax and enjoy this beautiful man. But what if he doesn't call? What if he's using me? Stop thinking! Freaking enjoy it!

Jackson rapidly pumped in and out of me. I wanted to be kissed again, but after my panties came off, he was all pelvis. Jackson put his hand in the back of my hair and pulled tight, making me his prisoner for a moment.

"Ouch."

"Sorry." He let go of my hair but continued to hammer away at my insides. It'd been a long time since I'd been with a guy, and my little flower had all but shriveled up from a lack of use.

Relax. Breathe. Enjoy.

So what if the sand in my crotch is painful? Enjoy the fact this incredibly perfect guy, who'll probably never speak to me again even if I literally run into him, is making love to me on this beautiful *SANDY* beach! Enjoy it! *Enjoy! Enjoy! Freaking enjoy!*

"You're amazing," I said to Jackson, trying to talk myself into the mood.

"You aren't too bad yourself, kiddo."

Kiddo? What the hell does he mean? Forget it. Stop thinking! He's probably being playful, that's all. Why can't I have fun? Have fun. Have some f-ing fun!!! *Fun! Fun! Fun!*

Was that a raindrop?

"I'm gonna come, Becca!"

What? Who the hell is Becca? And it's only been three minutes! How can he come so soon? It's my freaking birthday!

"You're never going to call," I said, not meaning to say it out loud.

Jackson

I erupted in a volcano of manliness, proving my semi-erection and Louis' massage were separate, unrelated, random events.

"It's starting to rain. We should go," I said, pulling on my pants. Luckily, the rain killed the potential for post-coital snuggling.

There's truth in the old maxim about sex and love; men use love to get sex, and women use sex to get love. Neither is wrong or right; they just are. I love all women, including this one. Being attracted to women purely for physical reasons is not adolescent. It's natural.

"I'll call you," I said.

"Ummm. Yeah. Okay," Becca replied.

I grabbed paper and pen out of my Harley. She scribbled her name and number.

BETH, it read, in big letters.

Whoops.

The next morning, in a comfortable state of semi-consciousness, the haze of the sleeping pills wearing off, I felt good. Then Joanna started barking in my ear, questioning me about the previous night.

Joanna was residing in my guesthouse while contractors remodeled her place. She'd have preferred to stay with me, but that would feel too much like being married. On some nights, I'd stay with her because I was too tired to put my clothes back on and walk to the main house.

My house is an odd, one-of-a-kind mishmash of world history. There's a theme room of ancient Egyptian kings, an Italian Renaissance art gallery, and one room dedicated to historical navigators of the sea. There's an all-purple smoking salon, even though I don't smoke. There's a kitchen with bisque marble flooring and stainless steel appliances, and there's another kitchen that's just for show. It has teak wooden flooring and valuable antique appliances.

Somehow when my dad had this home built, his interior designer convinced him the historical theme was a clever idea. To me, it feels like I live in a museum.

From outside, the architecture makes my home appear to be an old castle from some extinct kingdom. I'm surprised they didn't build a damned moat around it.

After I got Joanna to chill out, I went to check on Mother. She hadn't been out of bed in six weeks. My maids help with her, but I take care of most of Mother's needs. I bathe her, feed her, and dress her. I empty her catheter and wash her soiled bed linens. I take her coffee and cake every morning and tuck her in every night. I make sure her electric wheelchair stays charged in the event she wants to go anywhere, which she rarely does. I do everything I can for Mother because I can't bear to watch other people do for her.

Sometimes I wonder whether my actions come from a place love or if they're because I need her to know that I'm taking care of her.

People who visit my house are blown away by its size. Six bedrooms, eight bathrooms, indoor and outdoor pools, a two-lane bowling alley, a full gym, two Jacuzzis, a steam room, and a dry sauna. It's got cathedral ceilings, marble floors, spiraling staircases with crystal railings, three balconies, and a steeple tower above my dad's old prayer room, which I now use for storage.

Mom's depression and confusion had gotten worse since her stroke. Sometimes she didn't recognize me; sometimes she'd confuse me with Father and shower me in obscenities. The doctors said anger is part of her dementia.

But what about my anger?

The landscaping on my estate is postcard-worthy. Tall rare sago, howea, and coccothrinax palms form an expensive organic fence around my property. A rare orchid garden, a vegetable garden, and my father's empty horse stable fill the landscape that runs all the way down to our beach.

"Mom, I got your coffee cake." I put the cake under her nose for her to smell. No reaction. "Mom, wake up." Nothing. I tickled her feet. "Mom, time to get out of bed." Still, she didn't wake.

Is she dead?

Sadly, the thought gave me relief, but only for a brief moment.

I felt for a pulse. She had one.

I wanted to tear down the whole gaudy house and construct something normal, but Mother says the house makes her feel like she's in a fairytale, and she likes that. For me, it's more nightmare than fairytale, but living oceanfront in Malibu does have advantages.

In the morning, the sun greets my property with the first color of day; I sit back and enjoy the morning storks as they dive through the fog, disappear beneath the ocean's surface, and emerge with breakfast. At sunset, I numb myself with painkillers and lie in my hammock with a glass of wine, watching the purples, pinks, and oranges reflect off the clouds as the sun dips under the ocean. It's the singular peaceful thing in my life.

"Mom, wake up. You can't sleep all day."

"Leave me alone," she grumbled.

I shook her. She lashed out and caught the side of my cheek with her fingernail. It took some flesh from my face and it stung.

I'd become used to my parents hurting me. When I turned twelve, my dad told me I was too old to hug. When I was fourteen, my Jewish father told me I was too black to be his son.

I play a lot of golf; it's a good distraction from thinking. I have a cigarette boat, a fishing trawler, scuba gear, water-ski equipment, and a few jet skis. I inherited my father's hotel empire and sold it, then I made even more money playing professional football which I parlayed into Rockenberger Rum. Later, I opened Rockenberger Records with my on and off girlfriend, Joanna.

I have every luxury imaginable, I own acres of land, and have enough money to buy the moon were it for sale. Though people think I have everything, it sometimes feels like my possessions own me; towering over me and reducing me into a small bundle of insignificance.

Blood trickled down my cheek; a sliver of my flesh was beneath Mother's fingernail. I left her room, called the Board and Care, and made arrangements to take Mother there tomorrow. Though I wanted to be the one to care for her, it just wasn't worth it when she was no longer aware of the sacrifices I made for her. Over the past few months she'd become 100% demented, and there was no longer any validation of my effort.

I sorted through my thoughts in my Italian art gallery. Looking at a Rembrandt, I remember Father telling me a painting from a famous dead artist is more valuable than money. Father painted. He thought when he died his paintings would become valuable.

And then he died.

And Mother threw all his paintings away.

My light skinned Jewish Father was dead; my black Catholic Mother was confused. That made me 50 percent black, 50 percent light skinned, 50 percent Jew, 50 percent Catholic, and 100 percent messed up; guilt comes at me from all over the place.

I love you Mother, and I'm sorry I'm sending you away.

Would my child so easily discard me to a place to wait for death?

August 1997
Skye

Adaku's drug stash wasn't enough to kill me.

Momma Honey found me the following morning in a puddle of

my own vomit. She begged some Japanese tourists to take me to the hospital. There, when I woke, my first words to the doctor were, "Give me drugs. Take away my pain."

But they wouldn't.

Had the windows not been sealed, I wouldn't thrown myself out one. Had I the strength, I would have gotten out of bed and darted onto the 405 during rush hour. I didn't want to continue on with life, and I made life hell for the healthcare team that was trying to help me. Then, I met a nice bath nurse named Flora. She was full of life and fun to talk to. She made me smile for the first time in as long as I could remember. The two of us shared long conversations about music. Layered in our conversations, I felt some pain that had been buried deep within her. Her pain helped me to feel less alone.

After about a week, they released me from the hospital. The doctor recommended I go to rehab, but I didn't listen. I was a legal adult and could make my own decisions. I went right back to the streets. My talks with Flora re-ignited my love affair with music, and awakened my passion to pursue it. I thought about what Momma Honey had said, how I would be something special. I don't believe in omens, but maybe my cheating death had been one.

I decided to try to prove that theory right.

I put on the cleanest outfit in my backpack and went to an overcrowded shop on the Promenade. I took five outfits into the dressing room, put them all on, and then put my original outfit back on top of the clothes, to hide them. Then, I walked out the front door, and ran like hell when the alarm sounded. After eluding the short-lived and uninspired chase of the mall security, I grabbed my guitar, headed south, and hit up every coffee shop from Santa Monica to Venice in search of a job.

Two days later, I was hired to bus tables at Steaming Steve's on the Venice boardwalk.

I didn't care for the work, but sometimes on lunch shifts, my manager let me play a set to entertain the customers. And though Steve's was only a coffee house, and though I was usually stoned, I rocked those sets like I was playing a sold-out show at the Forum. Being paid for performing, regardless of how little I was paid, made life tolerable.

Then came the break of my life. Jackson Rockenberger, owner of Rockenberger records, and producer of one of my favorite bands, Shag Carpet Treasures, came into Steve's. I knew his face from his picture in *Rolling Stone* magazine. I begged my manager to let me perform, and he gave me the go ahead to play a three song set. I gave that set everything I had. Mr. Rockenberger never took his eyes off me, and I was feeling good about my chances, but after he finished his coffee, he got up and left. I chased after him.

"Mr. Rockenberger!"

He turned.

I summoned up the most manipulative smile I was capable of producing, introduced myself and told him I was a big fan of his label. His phone rang.

"Hold on, hun," he said, then answered his phone.

As he talked, I stood there, waiting, watching him, and trying to be as casual as possible about the whole thing. I was failing miserably at this task. Jackson got a look of irritation on his face and I hoped it was because of whomever he was talking to and not me. He hung up the phone and smiled at me.

"My one o'clock just cancelled. You want to go grab a drink?" he asked.

I hadn't finished my work shift, but I didn't let that stand in my way. This was the opportunity of a lifetime. So, I left with Jackson. If I got fired, I'd deal with it tomorrow. Today, I was chasing my destiny.

"I'd love to, Mr. Rockenberger," I said.

"Please, call me Jackson."

We went to a nearby joint for drinks. Jackson ordered for us without even asking me what I wanted, which I wasn't sure what to make of. We each had a couple drinks and spent an hour there together; he flirted with me the entire time. It was obvious he was more into my body than my music. I used that to my advantage and touched his hand or knee as often as possible.

And then, an hour after we sat for drinks, he signed me.

That was two weeks ago. Tonight, one of Jackson's smaller bands canceled a gig at the last second because their drummer got arrested for a DUI. They were scheduled to play at a tiny venue, and Jackson asked me if I'd fill in.

My first real gig.

"Don't be nervous. Just kick ass," Jackson said, backstage at the Prince O' Whales in Playa Del Rey.

"I'll try my best."

"After the show, we're going to a little party. You should join us," he said. Then he left me there, alone and with my vices, before I took the tiny stage.

I bent over my Jane's Addiction, *Ritual De La Habitual,* CD. Traditionally, I always do my blow off this CD case before I play in public. I relate to the two women on the cover; they're naked, hard, and afraid, just like me. I put the straw to my nose, sucked in, and filled my lungs with soft white powder. I felt ready.

The curtain pulled back, and I announced my musical birth to the world. It didn't matter one bit to me that the place was nearly empty, in that moment, I felt alive and ready to take the world by storm. I ripped a wicked guitar riff and then let loose on a love-hate song about street life, the life I was about to leave behind. I pushed out the lyrics with the ferocity of a priest exorcising demons from the possessed. The lyrics burned as they left my mouth. It was a cleansing.

Inside a song has always been the one place I'm most at home. Music never abused me, never made me sick, never tried to kill me. Music is the one thing I can't afford to lose.

Jackson

Skye finished her first song. The sparse crowd applauded politely.

"This won't sell," my business partner and part-time lover, Joanna, said.

Joanna was the only girl I'd had sober sex with in the last ten years. Sober sex used to be my barometer for whether or not I liked a girl, but I hadn't been sober in years, so the barometer no longer applied.

"I think she's great," I said.

"She's too tragic, too 1990. People don't want to hear depressing bullshit anymore. They want to party."

"She's sexy. Sex sells."

Joanna scowled. "Is that why you signed her? Do you have to fuck every bitch on the label?"

"I didn't sleep with her," I said.

Joanna turned her back on me. "So you signed her because she shot you down and you can't let one get away."

"She didn't shoot me down."

"So you did fuck her!"

"No!"

"If you fuck her, I'll kill you!"

"Relax Joanna! And why do you have to swear everytime you get mad? It's really unattractive."

"Fuck you!"

Joanna took in deep a breath and tried to calm down. "Her voice isn't bad. If we could make her more Britney and less post-rehab Courtney Love, then we might have a chance. Otherwise, forget it."

"Well, we advanced her a year's rent, so she better work out."

"You shit!" Joanna pounded my chest. "Stop thinking with your dick!"

Amber

The bible says the meek shall inherit the earth.

When the hell is this supposed to happen?

For the first few years of her life, Kimberly and I shared beds in dirty, roach-infested apartments across the country. We lived in the kind of places that always smelled like cat piss, even after they were cleaned.

In St. Louis, we lost our hot water because I couldn't pay the bill. Nothing hurt me worse than the sound of Kimberly's cries when I'd wash her in a cold bath on a cold night.

So no, I do not feel ashamed for how I make my living now.

Most of our money went to rent, the rest to food, just the basics: milk, bread, jam, peanut butter, noodles, tomato sauce, eggs. In Dallas, our electricity was turned off; we couldn't refrigerate our food, and it all went bad. Without lights we were forced to use candles. It felt like constant nighttime in our apartment, but not in euphoric bedtime kind of way.

So no, I do not feel ashamed for how I make my living now.

Rarely did we have money for clothes or medicine. Kimberly grew fast, and buying her new outfits was pointless. I usually bought her used clothes. But then *used* became *vintage*, and those also became too expensive.

In Atlanta, our situation was so bad I had to beg for money. Old white ladies would look at Kimberly and say to their husbands, *What a little doll. Black people have the cutest babies.* They talked about Kimberly like she was a puppy. They'd give her a couple dollars and smile. Their proud smiles made me feel small.

After escaping Tyrone, we moved to Culver City. Our rent tripled, but at least we were able to sleep without being disturbed by gunfire.

I got my G.E.D.

Then I discovered my G.E.D was worthless.

Tonight, I watched my beautiful Kimberly sleep. Such a pretty and perfect child. She didn't have a single mark on her lovely face. Kimberly was the kind of pretty that caught the eyes of strangers and made them feel happy inside.

I knelt and kissed my baby. My eyes met the medallions hanging above her bed. I'd grown to hate those medals. I wasn't able to give Kimberly a father, so I invented one for her. I bought the medallions at a garage sale and told Kimberly the army had awarded her father the medals for saving another soldier's life. I lied because, more than anything in the world, I wanted Kimberly to be happy.

I gave her one more kiss goodnight.

Kimberly awoke. "Hi, Mommy." Her sweet breath tickled my nose.

I picked a stray eyelash from Kimberly's cheek. "Make a wish," I said, holding it between two fingers.

Kimberly scrunched her face into a tight ball, held her eyes shut, and concentrated on her wish so hard I could nearly hear it. Then, she opened her eyes and blew the lash away.

"What'd you wish for?"

"Can't tell," Kimberly said.

"Yeah, you keep it secret. I love you, baby. Goodnight." I stood to leave.

"I's dream of bikes. I get bike, Mommy?"

"Someday, baby."

"Tomorrow?"

"Soon."

I was tired of talking to Kimberly about the *someday* when we'd live in a big house with a dog and lots of toys. We wouldn't make it to *someday* unless I took us there. So, last month I finally took charge of our situation.

A year ago we were practically homeless. Months ago I was slinging dope for a gang banger and worried about getting shot. Or worse. Now, I make good money in a relatively safe environment. Soon,

Kimberly will have a bike, and I'll have money to put myself through nursing school.

I take off my clothes and dance for men.

No, I do not feel ashamed for how I make my living.

Anyone who looks down on me needs to take a walk in my shoes.

Beth

Plus for positive. Minus for negative.

The next minute would set the course for the next eighteen years of my life.

I pulled down my panties and peed on the little white stick. I wiped, flushed, pulled up my panties, and put the stick face down on the counter. Then, I ran into my bedroom and buried my face in a pillow.

My phone rang. I hoped it was Ed McMahon calling to tell me I'd won ten million dollars. Or maybe it was Jackson calling for a second date. It'd been about ten weeks, but maybe he'd been busy until now.

"Hello?"

"Beth, you're crying. Does that mean—"

"I don't know yet."

"You can't avoid this forever, Beth."

"What am I going to do if I'm pregnant? I've got no money, no job, and no man. I'll have to get an abortion."

"No! Having Kimberly was maybe the only good decision I ever made. You won't get an abortion. I'll help you through this," Amber said.

"It won't feel right without Jackson."

"Beth, you don't need some misogynistic asshole ordering you to get him another beer while he lounges in his recliner watching some stupid televised sports thingy."

"But I. I waaaaaant hiiiiiiiiiim," I said, hyperventilating.

"Beth, calm down—Shhh. Stop crying. C'mon baby, you can do this."

I threw my favorite pillow, the one with the silky white tassels. It hit the wall with a soft thump; it didn't have enough oomph to convey the anger and fear I was fearing. I needed to smash something significant. I picked up the bedside lamp, and then put it back down. I'm just not that person.

"But you don't understand. I'm scared. What if I can't do it? What if I'm a terrible mother? What if I resent my baby?"

"You're getting all worked up for nothing. I bet you're not even pregnant."

"I'm-soo-scaredrightnow."

"I'm coming over. Don't do anything until I get there."

Amber hung up, and I went bonkers.

I met Amber at the woman's shelter where I volunteer. I heard someone frantically knocking on the door, I opened up, and there was Amber, panting and sweating, with her daughter slung over her shoulder. I gave them a bunk. I liked her and her daughter immediately and really wanted to help them. Later, when I checked on them, I found Amber leafing through Toni Morrison's *Beloved,* which is my favorite. I felt an instant connection with her and used that common thread to strike up conversation between us. We talked about the book, which led to other things, and by the end of the night we were instant best friends.

I'm slightly older than Amber, but her life experiences make her more mature. She became somewhat of the mother figure I never had. My dads' various lady friends always fussed over me and taught me girlie things to try to fill the gap of my motherless childhood, but none of them made any real difference in my life. Amber, in addition to being my best friend, has been as much a mother to me as anyone else. I don't care how silly that seems.

Besides growing up without a mother figure, with two gay dads, I didn't exactly have a strong father figure either.

If I have a baby boy, I won't have a clue.

On top of everything, I didn't know my genetic birth parents or anything about the potentially defective genetics I could be passing on to a growing fetus inside me.

I got up and went to the kitchen, fixed a pot of coffee, returned to my cluttered room, and tried to drown my anxiety in caffeine.

My body has an odd relationship with caffeine. Unlike most people, I find my nerves are eased by the chemical; without it, I'm a bigger neurotic mess than usual.

After polishing off the last cup, I cuddled with one of Amber's old sweaters, and for whatever reason, I felt slightly better.

Amber

Part of me wanted Beth to be pregnant so she'd need me.

I sound more like a drug dealer than a friend.

I ran to my apartment, where Beth was camped out. I was a sweaty mess by the time I got there. Before I even went in, I could I hear Beth weeping through the bedroom window.

I followed a trail of tissue paper from the downstairs bathroom to the bedroom where I found Beth lying across the width of the bed. Her limbs were flung out like a fallen ballerina, her pudgy, pinkish feet were sticking out from under the down comforter, her head dangled over the side, and her brown hair looked knotted and greasy. But even in her tousled condition, she was beautiful.

Beth's a little bundle of love. Barely five feet tall, she has the heart of an eighty-foot woman. Her porcelain white face is soft and round. Some people would say Beth's overweight; those people are the same idiots who think the anorexic, pill-popping supermodels in *Cosmo* define beauty.

I lay next to her. "Beth, honey. Hey, baby." I get no response from her. "Beth! Give me a hug!"

Beth sat up and hugged me. She squeezed me and started crying. She had me in an embrace that made it difficult to breathe. "Be. th." I said, forcing out her name.

"Am. ber." She replied in the same cadence.

"Beth. let. go." I felt faint. Beth released me, and I sucked in air. Nobody besides my mother had ever hugged me like that.

Beth's nose was bleeding. I pulled a tissue from my purse and wiped it.

"Thanks. That's been happening since second grade."

"Wow, really?"

"It's not that big a deal," she said. But then she seemed to reconsider. "Except once, in seventh grade. I went to a party at Mike Coppermen's house. I never go to parties, but I had a huge crush on him, and my only friend talked me into going. When I got there I saw Mike playing spin the bottle with all the cool kids. I'd never played a game like that, and went completely out of character and joined in. It was Mike's spin and I wanted it to land on me so badly that I probably had my fingers crossed. Well, I got my wish; when the bottle stopped spinning it was pointing at me. My stomach got all queasy and excited and I felt like my heart might explode out of my chest. I got the kind of butterflies a girl gets before her first kiss. He leaned in to kiss me and I closed my eyes. I had no idea how to kiss a boy. I think he was just going to give me a quick peck, but when I felt his lips, without opening my eyes, I grabbed his arms and pulled him in, held him tightly, and kissed him until he kissed me back. It was my very first kiss."

"That's so cute."

She smiled, momentarily losing herself in the sweet memory. Then, her disposition changed and she continued with her story.

"After the kiss, Mike sat back down, and I was horrified when I saw what I'd done to him. Tommy Mansour stood up, pointed at me, and yelled, *Period Face!*"

"I'm so sorry, Beth."

Beth began sobbing again. For some reason, at that moment, she was vulnerable and cute to me, like a little school girl with a broken heart. I almost smiled, but then I felt bad about it. This was traumatic and obviously still painful to her.

"The next day at lunch, Tommy got all the kids to chant it. They were pounding their first in cadence and chanting to the beat, *Per-i-od Face! Per-i-od Face! Per-i-od Face!* I ran home and told my dads. I wanted to quit school, but they wouldn't let me. They told me that fighting through things like this is how a person grows."

I put Beth's head on my shoulder and became a human tissue for the mucus pouring out of her face.

"I'm sorry, Beth. That sounds terrible."

"What am I going to do if I'm pregnant?"

"Things will be okay."

"Things won't be okayyyyeeeee." Beth sustained the last syllable so long it became a sentence by itself. "I don't do well with stress. I freak out, get a nose bleed, and run to my parents!"

"I'm going to help you."

"Thanks, Amber, I appreciate that. But if I have a kid, I'm going to need a whole lot of help."

"You and I are screwed up losers, but if we combine our strengths, then we should be able to raise a couple of harmless little kids, don't you think?"

Beth smiled. "I love you," she said.

Beth often told me she loved me. She meant it, but never in the way I wanted.

"Now go pee on the little white stick," I said.

"I already did."

"And?"

"And I haven't checked it. I'm too scared."

"Do you want me to do it?"

"Why would I want you to pee on it?"

"Do you want me to check it?" I asked. Beth let out her bottom lip and nodded her head up and down like an adorable little girl. I couldn't help but smile. "Everything will be okay, I promise."

With Beth leaning on me like this, I felt important and needed, and I wanted Beth to always need me.

I'm the mother kangaroo who doesn't want her baby to leave the pouch.

T.J.

I couldn't handle another day in my father's perfect house. I didn't want to be an accountant anymore; I didn't want to marry some pale homely girl from Bunker Hill, Oregon, and have two point five pasty, white, homely children. I didn't want to be Tacey Jonco Martini anymore. In fact, I never really wanted to be that guy.

I started introducing myself as T.J. in college, but Dad didn't like that, so I was still Tacey back home. I'd been living my whole life to please my father, and it made me miserable. Because of Dad, I played basketball instead of football, majored in accounting instead of film, and went to Pittsburgh University, his alma-matter, instead of Florida. I couldn't be what my father thought I should be anymore. I decided I'd start living for myself even if meant fucking up my life.

So, for the first time, I stopped thinking and acted on instinct. The spontaneity made me feel free. I quit my job at the bank, emptied my account, packed some clothes, kissed my mother goodbye, shook my father's hand, and told him I was moving.

Where? he asked. *I don't know,* I said. *You're in over your head. You won't make it six months.*

I drove to the airport. I wanted to be somewhere warm and busy. I narrowed it down to Miami and Los Angeles and ended up choosing Los Angeles. I chose L.A. partly to pursue my dreams in Hollywood, but also because it wasn't too terribly far from home, just in case.

A week later, today, I had yet to find a job and I barely had any money. If the day ended without my landing a job, I'd have to call my father to ask for a handout. I didn't want to do that, and luckily I found work. I got a night job in communications that paid well and kept my days open for auditions.

My new employer gave me one day of training and then threw me to the wolves the next night. I wasn't thrilled about my new line of work, but it was better than calling my father and begging for a handout.

The phone rang. My first call. I answered. "Hey big boy, this is Myron," I said, punctuating my voice with the stereotypical lisp my boss trained me to use for my phone sex customers. "What can I do for you tonight?"

"I'm Steve. I want you to strip. I'm gonna tie you to a tree with my belt. Then, I'm going to coat your cock in peanut butter and creamed corn and watch Bruno go at you."

Click.

I quit immediately. I went straight home, took a hot shower, and drank myself silly. Regardless of how much I drank, I couldn't fall asleep. Everytime I started to feel even the slightest bit of relaxation coming over me, that phone call replayed itself in my head. For months I had nightmares about what Bruno was.

I awoke the next morning feeling very stressed, worried that maybe my father was right; maybe I couldn't make it on my own. I knew that I needed to find some way to relax, or I was going to completely fall apart. I decided to spend the day trying to relax and unwind. In a day or two, I'd look for new work and panic about calling my father for money. But today I'd explore my new city, unwind, and try to forget about Bruno. I headed to the infamous Venice Beach. A crazy old Middle Eastern dude in a turban was rollerblading toward me while simultaneously playing electric guitar with an amplifier strapped to his back. He caught up to me, put weight on his heel brake, and did an interesting rendition of Hendrix's *Purple Haze*. I tried to walk away, but he followed me, still jamming. Somebody gave him a dollar, and then I realized he'd continue stalking me until I did the same. After I paid him, he moved on to his next victim.

Five minutes later, in an open-faced beachfront store, I saw a postcard of the Middle Eastern Hendrix. Apparently, he was a bit of a local celebrity. This was encouraging, and I felt a new surge of confidence moving through me. If the turban-wearing Hendrix could make it in L.A., then I could. I bought the postcard and a stamp, addressed it to my parents, and wrote, *I love you, but I'm staying here forever. I fit in with the other misfits.*

I took a taxi to Beverly Hills. The cab dropped me off on Rodeo Drive, which sounded familiar, though I couldn't decide why. I did some window shopping and stumbled upon a cool art store with a beautiful blond girl working the register. She looked like she should be in paintings rather than selling them. I went inside and pretended to examine some pieces while working up the courage to speak to her. At random, I grabbed a Picasso lithograph; it was three simple pencil lines on a piece of paper that seemed to have been put there without rhyme or reason. I didn't understand the litho, but I thought I'd look smart if I purchased it. I carried it to the counter. The girl made eye contact with me and her big, beautiful, brown doe eyes dilated.

"Hi," I said.

"You aren't supposed to take those off the walls," she said.

"Oh, it's okay. I'm going to buy it."

She looked me up and down. It made me nervous and excited.

Is she actually interested in me?

"How much?" I asked.

"Umm, twenty-two."

"Cool. I'll take it," I said. I fumbled with my wallet and dropped it like a total dork. I bent to pick it up.

"Really?"

"Yes, I'll take it."

"Okay. Well, what's your social security number?"

"Why do you want that?"

"It's just policy. I need to check your credit before we can put you on a payment plan."

Odd, a payment plan for twenty two dollars? They're nicer in this town than people say.

"Oh, I'll just pay cash," I said.

I pulled twenty two dollars from my wallet and pushed it across the counter. She smiled big.

She actually does like me.

Her smile got bigger and bigger until her mouth couldn't contain the tickle in her throat, and she broke out into laughter.

"Umm, what's so funny?"

"The. Sketch. Is. Twenty—" she was squeezing out words

between cackles. I was embarrassed, but wasn't sure why.

"What's so funny?" I said, joining her in laughter.

She put her hand over her mouth, closed her eyes, took in a breath through her nose, and spoke. "It's an original Picasso. It's twenty-two thousand." Suddenly, I remembered why Rodeo Drive sounded familiar. "You're not from here, are you?" she asked, still laughing. Mortified, I shook my head no. "Welcome to Los Angeles, love," she said, then patted me on the head like I was twelve-years-old.

In a cab, on my way home, I realized my father was probably right when he told me I'd be in way over my head in Los Angeles.

I hate when he's right.

Dylan Slade, 21

Standing outside my place, on Ocean Front Walk at the quiet end of Venice Beach, I watched women blow by on bikes, rollerblades, and skateboards.

"Hey," one girl said as she passed.

She was pretty enough to fuck, but girls like her don't fuck guys like me. They like to tease.

I wasn't always this crass. Allison made me this way.

I first saw Allison six years ago, as a high school sophomore, in English class.

I stared.

I forgot my name, forgot what I had for lunch, forgot what planet I was on. I couldn't avert my eyes, not because Allison was the most beautiful girl, but because she was so interesting to look at. She had big brown eyes and awkward eyebrows that made her appear to be deep in thought. When she walked, she was moonlight on legs lighting up the faces of everyone she passed.

For the first time in a long time, I felt sure about something; I wanted Allison to be my girlfriend.

And as my first and only overachievement in life, I made that happen.

Our first year as a couple was bliss. The conversations were nearly as good as the sex. Once, during our junior year, we snuck out of a class taught by Allison's dad and made love in the back of his van. Afterward,

Allison fell asleep on my shoulder, and I watched her sleeping until my arm went numb. I carefully slid my arm out from beneath her and rolled onto my other side. Without waking, Allison instinctively rolled toward me and slung her arm around me.

That moment was the only true love I'd ever known.

A month later, Allison hit me with the news: "I have to break up with you."

"Why?"

"Because you've become a weirdo."

And that was the end of us.

I knew I was a weirdo, long before Allison's revelation; this wasn't news. Years prior, while my classmates at Lincoln Middle School in Weirton, West Virginia, tried to decide whether to pledge their allegiance to Def Leppard or glam rockers Poison, I spent my nights alone in my room listening to the Stooges, Velvet Underground, and MC5. While the popular kids spent their weekends in the Pizza Hut parking lot mastering the skill of shooting tobacco juice between their two front teeth, I hid out in my bedroom and read the bible because I wanted to dissect it and find its contradictions. But what I really loved was literature. My favorite was Anthony Burgess' *A Clockwork Orange*. I read it over and over until I'd memorized it. Soon after, I started writing my own stuff; I hoped to pen the next great American novel.

Part of me wanted to be like the other guys at school. I wanted to be simple. People who do less thinking tend to be happier. I wanted to play football, talk about pussy in the locker room, drink beer in the back of somebody's pickup truck, and take target practice on empty Budweiser cans with the hunting rifle on the gun rack. I wanted to be like the other guys because the other guys were having more fun. But I couldn't be like them because I hated everything they stood for.

The first time I put on make-up was Halloween of my junior year. Allison dressed as a butterfly, and we went to a party hosted by one of her popular friends. I didn't have a costume so I raided Allison's make-up and did the Goth thing: black eyeliner, black lipstick, and black mascara on top of white foundation. I used almost an entire can of hairspray to spike my hair, which I dyed pink. I wore Allison's fat sister's black denim skirt, a fishnet top, and army fatigue boots. I won two hundred dollars for best costume, which was nice, but the self-discovery I made was even more valuable. I felt like a different version of me in those clothes.

I started dressing differently on some random weekends, which soon became every weekend, and then a few weekdays when the urge struck. I mixed it up; Goth, eighties glam rocker, or sometimes I'd throw on an old muumuu and a wig just for the fuck of it. I wasn't what most people call a goth; in fact, I hated their music. I wasn't gay, and I wasn't dressing all weird just to be anti-conformist. I dressed differently than most people simply because I liked it. I felt comfortable in my own skin for once.

Some people, like Allison, pretended to know things about me because of the way I dressed. People have always liked to label other people; labels comfort their simple minds.

Jock, Nerd, Goth, Weirdo, Preppy, Fag, Cheerleader, Brain, Skateboarder.

I like wearing make-up and dressing up, so I'll always wear a label given to me by society. I have no idea what my clothes say about me, but I know they don't define me.

The first high school party I attended after Allison dumped me was horrible.

"Hi," said Sara, the head cheerleader.

"Um, hi," I returned, shocked she'd spoken to me.

Her alpha-male jock boyfriend, Chad, got so pissed testosterone practically shot out his ears. "Hey, fag!"

"I have pink hair and mascara. Is fag the best you can do?"

"Fuck you, faggot!"

I wanted to say— *You're nothing. You're less than nothing; you're an abyss; a waste of molecular energy.*

But instead, I said, "Fuck you, too."

The crowd looked at me like I was on drugs.

I wasn't, unless you count pot as a drug, which I don't.

"You're a dead man, fag boy," Chad said. He tore off his t-shirt, which read *1. God 2. Family 3. Football.* Chad was so hairy I couldn't tell where his pubic hair ended and his belly hair began. He pounced on top of me and started punching.

"That doesn't hurt because I can't feel it. Because you're nothing!"

Chad rolled me over, straddled me, put my arm behind my back, and mashed my nose into the floor. "Say *Uncle* or I'll break your arm!"

The agro-locker-room-towel-snapping-ape was calling me a fag, yet he wanted me to call him Uncle while straddling me.

Interesing.

"Uncle," I said.

Things like this happened to me frequently throughout the rest of high school. I couldn't have cared less about those people, so it didn't really bother me. But I did care about Allison, and when she judged me, it hurt.

Today, after watching a few dozen beautiful women blow by on rollerblades, ignoring me, the weirdo, I went inside. I washed off the weird purple eyeliner, took off my weird outfit, combed out my weird hair, and got ready for work at my very normal job.

At work, I found myself surrounded by Prada bags, Versace suits, and shoes that would cost me two paychecks. Every car was a Jaguar, Lexus, or Porsche with stupid vanity plates the owners felt were clever. All the men had perfectly manicured hands, and the women could identify each other's designer labels from a hundred yards away.

Inside, they dip their lobster in melted butter, chew their steak with bleached teeth, and wash it all down with a two hundred dollar bottle of wine. They pretend to enjoy each other's dull conversation — the same conversation that's happening at the table next to them and the one next to that. They check their Rolexes to make sure they're not running late for their red-eye to Paris. Then they excuse themselves to the bathroom to pop antidepressants and snort coke.

Nobody's impressed by anybody else because they're all too consumed with trying to cover up their own shortcomings. Here, at Crustaceans, in Beverly Hills, is a microcosm of our world of lazy moral ideals and social indifference where every man is trying to convince himself he's a king.

Two couples entered. "Reservations for four for Rockenberger," said one guy.

"Follow me, please."

I escorted them to a table.

The guy who made the reservation was a big, athletic looking, black guy in a fitted suit. His date wore a full-length red dress that would've been considered extravagant at the White House inauguration dinner. She looked familiar. I'd seen her in some movie or something. Joanna something, I think. Whatever.

The couple with them was equally obnoxious. The woman had that rich, white-woman, anorexic look. The diamond on her finger was so huge that it wouldn't have surprised me to see a moon revolving around it. An elaborate string of emeralds hung around her neck and disappeared into her cleavage. I imagined her to be the type of person who defined herself by her clothes and jewels; she was nobody without them.

"Do you think he spent more money on her tits or the jewels around her neck?" I asked the other host, Nate.

"The jewels. The tits are real," Nate said.

"There's no way they're real. You're stoned."

"Yeah, but so are you," he said.

"These pompous assholes are gonna make me lose it one of these days."

"Lose what?" Nate responded. "You've got nothing to lose."

"Lose my mind. I still got that... I think."

Now seated, the athletic black guy talked loud enough for the entire restaurant to hear. "So, I told him I'd just buy out his company and fire him." The others laughed in a mechanical cadence.

I went to the bathroom and took a drag off my one-hitter; the weed was smooth and full. I took another hit and then returned to my station. I'd only been in the bathroom for a minute.

"Where were you?" my manager, Stephen, asked.

"Disneyland."

He didn't even acknowledge my witty retort. "I saw you come out of the bathroom."

"Then why'd you ask?"

"Listen, smart-ass, you're not scheduled for break for another hour."

"Dude, I had to piss. I could've done it here, but I figured you'd prefer me to do it in a urinal."

"You were in there for ten minutes. I had to seat two tables during the time you weren't doing your job. You only got this job because I went to high school with your father. Don't make me fire you." He stepped closer and whispered, "No more pot."

"Okay, I won't smoke if you don't," I whispered back. And with that, manager Stephen was off my back.

The woman with the giant diamond ring laughed hard about something. She clapped her hands, kissed her husband on the lips, and finished chewing the fat piece of lobster in her mouth. He smiled and touched her hand.

"I hate rich people," I said.

If I ever get to the point in life where I judge myself by the amount of money I make, how many people work for me, or what kind of purebred lapdog I own, then I'll do the world a favor and jump from the highest building in L.A.'s financial district.

"I can't do this job anymore. I'm not a restaurant host. I'm a writer."

"Yeah, well, I'm an actor. Combine your earnings from writing last year to my earnings from acting, and we still couldn't afford a cup of Top Ramen soup," Nate said.

He was right. And that's why I'd gotten stuck in Crustaceans, working the kind of job unsuccessful writers work.

Another idiot got out of his obnoxious SUV with a long-legged gold digger perched in the passenger seat.

"He must have a little pecker. Why else would a guy living in a city that never snows buy an SUV?" I said to myself, but loud enough to be heard.

The guy handed the valet his keys and approached me, holding hands with his expressionless mannequin. "Table for two," he said.

"It's a forty-five minute wait for walk-ins," I replied.

He gave me a look that suggested he might throw out the infamous, *Don't you know who I am?"*

I knew who he was, everyone knew. So what? It was Bruce Willis, maker of some truly awful films.

The actor approached my manager who would likely give him the best table in the house. Everyone in the restaurant watched him while trying to appear like they weren't.

Bruce chatted with my manager, Stephen, who looked at me. I'd probably be fired later; and to be honest, I was okay with that. Every second I spent working this job was wasted life I'd never get back.

Stephen escorted the actor and his long-legged, large-breasted, tan, slim, blond groupie to a table.

Celebrities suck... but I wouldn't mind having groupies.

Kelly Dampier, 24

I was exhausted. It had been a miserable day and I was ready to go home and crawl in bed. I thought my workday was done. But little did I know that my day was just starting. It would be the luckiest day of my life.

The kind of day that an average Joe like me only gets to experience vicariously through his cooler, and better looking, friends.

I had just switched off the overhead lights and started to leave, when my fax spit out another doctor's order.

Maria Orlando: Half-hour breast massage, three times a week for four weeks.

Two seconds later, a well-endowed, beautiful young woman poked her head through the open door.

"Hi. I'm Maria Orlando. I have a four o'clock appointment… Are you open?"

My eyes teetered from the order to her and back.

Wow.

"We're open."

She had perfect posture; long, wavy brown hair; a smooth and tan complexion; high sculpted cheekbones; eyes as big as golf balls; and thick pouty lips. Her expression was slightly vague, but not an empty vague like a supermodel in a perfume ad.

She approached me.

"Are you here for the brea— umm, are you Maria?"

She cocked her head to the side, and her large silver hoop earring kissed her shoulder. "Didn't I just say that?"

"Yes, you did. Pleasure to meet you, Maria."

"You, too." Maria smiled; her mouth turned up at one corner and down at the other. Her beautiful crooked smile was like Melanie Griffith's, in *Working Girl*, before the plastic surgery.

I flipped the light switch back on. The light reflected off the freshly waxed linoleum floor, creating a mirror effect, and I could see the dark outline of Maria's inner thighs up her tiny brown skirt.

Stop staring, idiot!

"Have a seat. I'll be with you shortly. I just need to make a phone call. I'll be right back," I said"

Maria sat in the middle seat of our three plastic blue bucket chairs. She picked a *Cosmopolitan* magazine out of the rack, sat it on her lap, and turned pages while her other hand fiddled with the marble-sized pearls around her neck.

She looked up at me and I realized that I was still standing there, staring.

I retreated to my office and called Maria's doctor.

A receptionist answered, "Hello, Dr. Nudelman's office. May I help you?"

"Yes, umm, hi. This is Kelly Dampier, PT. I just received an order from Dr. Nudelman that I have a question about."

"The doctor's busy. Would you like his voicemail?"

"No, that won't help. The patient's here and I'm slightly confused."

"About what, Mr. Dampier?"

"Well, it says I'm supposed to massage her breasts."

"And?"

"So, umm. Okay, I'll be frank. I've only been working here for two months, and I've never heard of this before."

"No problem, Mr. Dampier. We'll send the patient to our sister clinic up in the Valley."

"NO! Err, no, that won't be necessary. Why don't you just brief me? I mean, I'd hate to make the patient drive all the way up to the Valley during rush hour."

The receptionist let out a heavy, annoyed breath. "I'll put you on with a nurse. One moment please."

The nurse picked up the phone, "How may I assist you?"

"I need a crash course in breast massaging."

"How sad," she replied.

"I meant I have a patient whose post-op breast implants, and I need to know the proper technique."

"It's simple. You start around the nipples."

Thank you, Jesus.

"Massage gently in small circles, gradually working your way outward. The idea is to gently break up the scar tissue. When you finish the massage, lay a foam cylinder under her spine, have her spread her arms out at her sides, and gently stretch them toward the ground. Hold for thirty seconds, relax, repeat. That's all there is to it. Got it? … Mr. Dampier? … Mr. Dampier?"

I'd stopped listening after she said *nipples.*

"Huh? Oh, yes." I realized my free hand was inside my shirt rolling my nipple between two anxious fingers. I yanked it out. "Thank you. You've been helpful," I said and hung up.

Ninety-five percent of the population hates their careers. I'd lied my way into a dream job working for the Motion Picture and Television Fund, and I would've been willing, at that moment, to sign a lifetime contract. Unfortunately, I had a feeling my fraudulent resume would eventually catch up to me.

Maria Orlando, 18

My breasts felt like giant water balloons one droplet away from exploding. The implants were exactly what I wanted from Daddy for graduation, and I thought I'd feel sexy after getting them. But I didn't. I felt bloated and fat and I couldn't wait until I could start jogging again to lose weight.

I took off my clothes, put on the robe, and called out, "I'm read—"

"Okay, let's get started," he said, ripping open the curtain before I could finish my statement. His mouth hung open and his eyes bulged out of his head; he looked like a handicapped trout.

"Don't worry, I'll be gentle," he said. He sounded wiry. "I'll start around your nibbles. Umm, excuse me. I, uhh, went to the dentist at lunch and my tongue is still a little numb. Anyway, I'll start around your niPPles, and work outward. Let me know if it becomes too painful."

"Okay."

I lay on my back, lowered my gown, and waited. So many people had poked and prodded my chest in the past few weeks I'd become desensitized to it.

"Is there something wrong?" I asked.

"Wrong? No, I'm just sizing things up."

Curious choice of words.

"Okay, here we go, and please, call me Kelly."

Kelly began massaging me; soon he was sweating like a heavyweight prizefighter. The massage eased my pain, but I couldn't relax. I was worried about Daddy. He was having a *meeting* with Toni Scalesci at our restaurant. Daddy never told me much about his work, and for most of my pampered childhood in New York, I assumed he was just a successful restaurant owner. I was probably about thirteen when I started to notice how other men acted around him. Dad was fat, and he wasn't tall or muscular. However, he had a large presence; he could intimidate the most dangerous men with a simple smile and a wink.

We moved to Los Angeles when I was fourteen, and Daddy climbed the ladder rapidly. I'm sure the climb was bloody.

I worried any day could be my father's last, his life ending in violence.

Kelly

"I know some day you'll have a beautiful life
I know you'll be a sun
in somebody else's sky"

Stuck in gridlock on the 405, after work, after my glorious day of massaging breasts, I sang into the unplugged microphone that I keep in my ride. Mr. Eddie Vedder belted the lyrics to *Black,* Pearl Jam's masterpiece.

I had to drop off my Saturn for its 125,000 mile check-up. Typically, I'd rent the cheapest car available, but after the breast massage, I was riding a high, and by renting a Jaguar convertible, I was able to keep the momentum going.

"But why? Why? Why-y, can't it be?
Why can't it be-e-e-e miiine!"

Black. I love that damn song to the point of pain. Eddie grabs my heart and twists it into a big meaty knot every time. The outro reminds me of my mother. I forced her out of this world on my way in; she died birthing me. She is the sun in the sky I can never have.

While singing, I noticed an incredibly sexy woman in another convertible singing along with Eddie and me. I smiled at her and we all sang together, *"Do-dah-doot-doot-do-dah-do,"* She smiled back at me as the song was ending.

Typically in a situation like this, I'd blush, and then nervously stare straight ahead until traffic started moving again.

"I like your microphone," she shouted over the loud engines of the idling cars.

I couldn't believe she was showing an interest in me. This really was my lucky day.

Is smog some kind of aphrodisiac or something?

"Thank you. Your harmony complimented Eddie and me nicely," I said.

"I'd say you and Eddie complemented me nicely," she countered.

Okay, Kelly, now say something witty.

She beat me to it. "We'll probably be stuck in traffic long enough to get through *Jeremy*. Wanna try?" *Jeremy* was the next track on Pearl Jam's *Ten*. This knowledge made her even sexier.

"I'd rather spend the time trying to get your phone number," I said, doing my best impersonation of a cool guy.

"Oh."

"Oh what?" I asked.

"We had a good moment going. But you ruined it. Too bad."

Her car began to inch forward; mine was stuck behind one of those sixteen wheelers that take forever to start moving. I had to regroup.

"Clearly I remember pickin' on the boy," I sang with conviction, both hands wrapped around my microphone, my knee tending the steering wheel. She took my bait, and sang with me:

"Seemed a harmless little fuck

Ewwwe, but we unleashed the lion

    gnashed his teeth and bit the recess lady's breast,

    how can I forget?"

Her phone rang. She answered. I couldn't let the call come between us; this was the closest thing I'd had to a date in months. I turned the stereo up a few notches and sang louder, trying to drown out whoever she was talking to.

"Then he hit me with a surprised left

    ewwwe, my jaw left hurtin'

    dropped wide open, just like the day

    ewwwe, like the day I he—eard!"

Her lane stopped moving. She tried to ignore me, but the lyrics were trying to tickle their way out of her mouth. I turned the volume up even louder.

"Turn that shit down, asshole!" yelled some guy in a Mercedes. I turned it up full blast. Chatty Kathy continued with her phone call, but now she was smiling at me.

    "Daddy, didn't give attention, no

    to the fact Mommy didn't care—air

    King Jeremy, the wicked, ruled his world."

My freeway lover girl pulled the phone from her ear, put it in front of her mouth, yelled obscenities into it, and hung up. Then she joined me in song, *"Jeremy spoke in cla—ass today."* We continued through the entire chorus. A few others stuck in traffic joined in. It was a block party on the 405.

I mentally rehearsed a witty comment while we sang the final chorus. I was going to say, *We're quite a team. Maybe we should go on tour.* As I was about to deliver my line, her car pulled ahead of mine.

"Shit."

She moved, three, four, and then five car lengths ahead. I pounded my steering wheel.

"Shit! Shit! Shit! Fucking truck! Go!"

This cat and mouse game continued for a few miles. I pursued her, at about five miles per hour, with my hands glued to the steering wheel, leaning into the windshield, eyes peeled open. I was supposed to get off on Culver Boulevard, but she didn't, so I followed.

Pearl Jam made it through *Oceans, Porch,* and then *Garden,* and I still hadn't caught her. I worried she'd met some jerk with a better voice and a sweeter car. We hadn't even exchanged names, and already I was acting like a paranoid jealous boyfriend. Then again, that's my M.O.

Finally, as *Deep* began to play, I caught up to her. "Hey, remember me?"

"Oh my God! Are you Eddie Vedder, the lead singer of Pearl Jam?"

"Can I have your phone number?" I asked. My desperation was obvious.

"I don't give my number to guys I meet on the 405. You could be a stalker!"

"C'mon, do I look like a stalker to you?"

I was already stalking her— *duh.*

Her lane sped up. "Yeah, you do, but it kind of works for you. Meet me at Gold's Gym in Venice Beach for racquetball. Eight o'clock!" she yelled from two car lengths ahead.

"What time?"

"Eight! If you beat me, I'll give you my number!"

Irritated drivers were honking. She hit the gas and stuck her hand in the air to wave goodbye. I put a hand in the air to wave back.

Crash! Pop!

The airbag exploded in my face as I rammed into a truck.

"Shit! Shit, Shit, Shit!" I pounded the steering wheel. The front end of the rented Jag was mangled.

"Shit!"

Reece Brooks, 29

"Go screw yourself!" I yelled and then hung up on Isaac again. "Where is this guy already?"

"How much longer you gonna give him?" The plump front-desk girl asked.

I looked at the clock. "Until eight thirty."

"I never stick around for a guy for more than five minutes. Especially on a first date," she said.

You'd be lucky if you got a date to show up five days late, I thought.

"I hope he shows," she said.

He showed up, but not until eight forty-five.

"Is this guy for real?"

He wore blue sweatpants so tight I could see his bulge, and he was heavier and shorter than he seemed sitting in his Jaguar on the 405. His headband matched both his sweats and the blue bandage across the bridge of his big nose. And to top everything, he carried a tennis racquet.

"Hi. We didn't exchange names. I'm Kelly."

"Reece," I said and shook Kelly's hand.

"Sorry I'm so late. Thanks for waiting."

"I wasn't waiting. I just finished a match. I'm on my way out," I said.

"Well, you don't look like you broke a sweat. Maybe you've got one more game in you?" Kelly asked.

"Maybe. What happened to your nose?"

"Crashed the Jag," Kelly replied.

"Oh my God. Are you okay?"

"Yeah. I smashed my nose, and I have a headache, but I'm okay."

"I'm glad it wasn't serious," I said.

"Me too. So, you ready to play?" He swung his tennis racket at an imaginary ball.

"I'm ready, but you're not," I said.

"Huh?"

"We're playing racquetball."

"And?" he asked, completely clueless.

"You brought a tennis racquet."

"Oh… yeah, I know. I just had this in the trunk and I didn't want to leave it behind in the Jag with the triple-A guy. You can't trust people these days."

"You were okay with him towing your Jaguar, just so long as you got your precious tennis racket out of it first?"

"Let's just play," he said, a competitive gleam coming across his face.

"Beating you is going to be too easy," I said.

"I don't think so."

"Wanna bet?" I asked.

"Sure," Kelly said, then dug his pinky finger halfway down his ear hole and twisted it. "Okay, here's the bet. When I win, I get your number. If you win, you get mine."

I put two fingers under his chin and directed his gaze from my chest to my eyes. "Why would I want your number? What I want is for you to buy dinner for my girlfriend and me at Crustaceans."

"You want your girlfriend to come on our date?"

"No. I want you to send my girlfriend and me to dinner. You stay home and watch Survivor."

"Oh."

"But if by some miracle you win, then you can take me there for a friendly date."

"Fine. But if I win, we have our date tonight," Kelly said, again to my chest.

"Deal."

Kelly

"Ouch!" The racquetball smacked me in the back of the neck.

"You did that on purpose."

"Interference on you. Fourteen to thirteen, my lead. Game point," Reece said.

Reece made up rules as we played, and she played dirty. She wore a tank top without a bra, and she made sure to wiggle and jiggle as much as possible to distract me. The technique was pretty effective.

"Timeout," I called.

"Awe, what's-a-mattah? Tired, stinky, sweaty boy need a little breaky-poo-poo?"

"No, I just need time to strategize and exploit your weakness."

I took a swig of Gatorade. What I needed was a tall glass of steroids.

"My game has no weakness," she said.

Reece hadn't even broken a sweat, and she'd been casually chomping on a piece of gum the whole match. "However, your super tight, Richard Simmons-style sweatpants is somewhat distracting."

A plan hit me like a Mike McCreedy guitar riff. I pulled my sweatpants up to my nipples and tucked in my Dodgers tank top.

"Time in," I said and then I served.

Laughing, she whiffed.

"Fourteen— fourteen. My serve," I said.

Reece stopped laughing and put on her game face. I served, Reece returned, I placed it short, she charged the ball, and her foot caught a sweat slick from where I'd fallen earlier. Reece skidded, missed the ball, and crashed into the wall.

"I win!" I said.

She got back to her feet and brushed herself off. "If you're actually going to take point, then you're less of a man than the little bulge in your sweats suggests."

"You'll never see what's in there if you keep insulting me. And yes, I'm taking point. I win!"

"No, you don't. The game ends when someone wins by two."

"What? Since when?"

"Since forever."

"Fine! My serve, game point."

I peeled my sweats out of my butt crack and served the ball. Reece returned, I hit it back as hard as I could, it lined hard to her left, she made an athletic dive for it, and her left breast popped out.

And I swear that I heard a chorus of angels.

Oh, that's lovely. Forget it. Watch the ball, watch the ball.

Reece, ignored her bare breast, and sprung to her feet. The ball came back at me slowly; I delicately laid it back on the wall in the area of my sweat slick, hoping she'd fall again. Reece charged the front wall, her boob bouncing. She hit the ball hard off the side wall.

Watch the ball, not the boob.

The ball went to the front wall, to the side wall, and back at me.

Oomph!

I hit it as hard as I could.

"Ow!" I'd hit Reece in the back of the neck, the same place she'd hit me; only I hit her harder.

"Ooo. Ouch. That looked like it hurt. Are you okay?" I asked, trying not to smile.

"No. Ow. Mother F-er!" Reece tucked in her breast and rubbed the back of her neck. She had a welt the size of a cow's teat.

"I'm sorry, Reece. I didn't mean to do that. I'll get you some ice."

"Forget it. Let's finish the match."

"The match is finished. That was interference on you. My point. Sixteen— fourteen, I win."

"Interference is bullshit!"

"It's your rule."

"You're seriously going to take victory?" she asked.

"If I say no do we still go to dinner?"

"No."

"Then I seriously am."

"Fine. I'll honor the bet, but I promise I won't enjoy a single second of it." She forced her racquet into its carrying case.

"Fine, then I won't enjoy it either." I smiled.

Reece looked at her watchless wrist. "We can't go tonight."

"Why not?"

"There's no possible way we'll get a table at Crustaceans this late without a reservation. Besides, they won't allow us close enough for a whiff in these clothes, and we don't have time to go home and change."

"We look sexy like this. Just shower and put on what you have handy. I'll handle the reservations."

"You're unbelievable."

"Thank you," I said and made for the showers.

I had no idea where the hell Crustaceans was. I considered suggesting we go somewhere casual, but because that wasn't the bet, it would give Reece an out. I knew Reece wasn't really into me, and she'd blow me off if we didn't do it tonight. This was my only chance. I just had to go with it and hope that my lucky day continued on for a few more hours.

I got in the shower, and without realizing it I had begun to fantasize about Reece. She was running her long tanned fingers through her blond hair, working up a lather. The suds fell from her hair into the curve of her lower back, around the swerve of her buttocks, and then disappeared between her thighs.

"Hey, buddy. Stop that," the guy showering next to me said.

"Sorry," I said, then removed my fingers from my nipples.

I've got to stop that.

Dylan

"Holy shit. Look at these two," I said.

"They look like they came straight off the beach." my co-host replied.

I wondered why such a laid-back couple would come to Crustaceans. The woman walked straight to the bathroom. People don't just walk in here dressed like these two and expect to be seated without a reservation. The guy had a look of anarchy in his eyes, a hell-raiser, one of my own.

"Hey, I don't have a reservation. What are my chances?" asked the trouble maker.

"You don't meet dress code."

"I know. My bad. Is there anything we can do to make this happen?"

He reached for his wallet. I found that to be a bit pretentious, but I took it anyway.

"Why should I help you? I mean, I could lose my job."

"Let me just level with you. I'm here, on a date, with a woman who is way out of my league. The circumstances are complex, so I won't waste your time, but if I don't make this happen tonight, it never will. So, can you do me a favor and help make my miserable life just a little bit better?"

"I don't know, dude," I said.

"Okay, well, thanks anyway… Can I get my twenty back?" he asked.

"I'm just messing with you." I handed him a jacket.

He smiled.

"But no, you can't have your twenty back."

Reece

When I came out of the bathroom, Kelly was sitting at a table adjacent to Bruce Willis' table!

I'm pretty intuitive about men, and I had a good feeling about Kelly, but now I knew for sure. Kelly was an important man.

Why does he drive a Jaguar? It must be his second car.

The restaurant had a unique smell, a mixture of garlic, seafood, and heavy perfume. It smelled expensive, and I liked it. I ordered lamb chops and a nice bottle of red. Kelly ordered a salad. He said his stomach was upset from racquetball.

Halfway through the bottle of wine, the food came.

"So, Kelly, what do you do for a living?"

Kelly leaned in and whispered, "C.I.A. Don't tell."

I laughed. "Cute. But seriously?"

"Professional bull rider."

"Bull riders are sexy," I said. Kelly laughed. "What do you do when bull riding season is over?"

"I'm a physical therapist."

"Oh. Where's your clinic?"

"Our operation, the Motion Picture Television Fund, has four branches. My office is at our home branch off of Pico."

Holy crap! He owns the MPTF empire!

Kelly

Regardless of how we'd dressed, Reece was the prettiest girl in the restaurant. She didn't need an expensive dress to look good.

Girls like Reece live in a different galaxy than guys like me. I needed an angle. So I embellished about my work and some other things. I may have gone to far when I told her I donated a kidney, but for the monetary damage this date inflicted, I had to pull out all the stops.

The busboy cleared our plates. The salad didn't touch my hunger. I was about to walk away from a hundred-fifty-dollar meal with an empty stomach.

Would it be tacky to eat Reece's scraps?

The waiter came back. "Dessert?" he asked.

"I'll have the crème brulée," Reece said.

"Nothing for me, thanks." I couldn't afford their freaking coffee.

After dessert, I paid the bill, and we stepped outside. It was oddly cool for an August night. I shivered.

"Thanks for dinner," Reece said. She was being surprisingly flirtatious. I hadn't expected that and didn't really know what to do with it. Rejection, I'm good at dealing with. Flirtation? Not so much.

"Maybe we could do it again?" I asked.

Reece handed the ticket stub to the valet. "I don't think so," she said.

"Oh, okay."

"My husband, Isaac, gets jealous. And he can be a little psychotic sometimes."

"Huh?" I looked at her finger. No ring.

Reece saw me looking. "I don't wear my ring when I play racquetball."

I'd been scammed. The contrast between the cool night air and my red-hot face must've been obvious.

"Don't give me that look. This was your idea," Reece said.

"But you didn't say you had a husband."

"I didn't know I had to. The terms were for a *friendly* date."

I'd been had on a technicality.

"Well, nice meeting you," I lied.

"You, too." The valet pulled up in Reece's car. "Bye, Kelly." Reece got in, pulled forward about two feet, and then rolled down her window. "Hey, want to get a drink? I know a place in Playa Del Rey where a good band is playing."

"Huh? I thought—"

"This is a one-time offer."

Is Reece affair shopping? Is this a game? I shouldn't.

"Sure, let's go," I said. Reece was way too smokin' hot to say no.

I got in her car, and immediately began to plan where I'd try to take her after the bar. I couldn't take her to my grimy place; she'd think I was broke. I'd have to get a hotel.

I can't get a hotel; I'm broke.

Beth

Amber was downstairs doing my laundry. I was exhausted, nestled under my 700-thread count silk sheets. I'd had the lights off and the blinds drawn for days, so my eyes had adjusted to constant darkness.

Amber came upstairs. I'd been camped out at her place. "Beth, you've been lying around all week. This ends now." She flicked on the lights.

"Ow!" I got the kind of blinding pain you get from looking directly at the sun. "Turn it off!"

"Your Daddy Gerrie called to ask me why you haven't been home in a week and why you aren't returning his calls. It's not my job to tell your parents you're pregnant, but if you don't call them soon, you'll force my hand."

"I'll tell them. I'm just not ready yet. I need some time. Turn off the lights."

"How much time, Beth? Another six months? You've started showing a little this week, you know. I love you Beth, but you can't stay here forever. Are you going to come home from the hospital with a baby and then explain?"

"Don't be a hypocrite. You ran away from home without telling your mother a thing," I said. I felt horrible as soon as the words escaped.

"That was mean," Amber replied.

I'm a self-absorbed brat.

"I'm so sorry, Amber." I put my hand on her shoulder. "You've been wonderful to me. I shouldn't have said that."

"Yeah, I have been wonderful, and you're a bitch for saying that. But you're right. I ran, and I shouldn't have," Amber said.

"You were just a kid."

Amber leaned in, put her hand on my belly, and massaged it gently. It felt nice.

"Yeah, but that doesn't make it right," she said. "You know what we need? We need to get out of here and go have fun. Get up; we're going to go celebrate!"

"Celebrate what? I don't have anything to celebrate."

"Yes you do! You're going to celebrate being pregnant! It's time to crawl out of your ravine of pity and embrace the life inside you. Get showered. I'm taking you to Crustaceans."

"Crustaceans? Amber, you can't afford that."

"I can."

"How'll we get a table?"

"I met this guy, Dylan, at Barnes and Nobles a few weeks ago; he's the host there. Besides, if we can't get a table, we can sit at their bar. Now get showered. You stink like a hermit."

"I am a hermit."

Amber

Beth got up and showered. She emerged from the bathroom looking flushed and refreshed. A towel was entwined with her hair in an elaborate tower atop her head.

I held up Beth's favorite dress; I'd picked it up from her parent's place. It was a strapless yellow gown patterned with yellow flowers of a different hue.

"I can't get into that anymore," Beth said. "I'm pregnant."

"Yes you can. You've barely gained a pound." I poked Beth in the stomach and she giggled. I tickled her until she agreed to try on the dress.

She relented and attempted to try it on, but got stuck half way. "It doesn't fit! I'm huge! I'm a cow!"

Crisis.

I pulled at the bottom of the gown as Beth shimmied, wiggled, and squirmed. Once it was on, Beth held her breath, and I tried to zip up the back. I tugged at the zipper with little success. Beth's mouth quivered; she was on the verge of tears. Her mental health depended on getting the metal teeth of the zipper to kiss each other all the way to the top of the dress. I continued to tug, and forty seconds later Beth's face started turning purple. I took in a breath, closed my eyes, and yanked the zipper. I expected to hear a rip, which would have completely killed Beth's spirits, but miraculously the mouth of the dress closed all the way. Beth let out her air and grabbed at more to catch her breath.

"Thank you," Beth said, but she didn't look happy. Her victory was nominal compared to the disheartening struggle. Fatigued, she plopped face down on her bed.

She rolled onto her back, then to her belly. Beth looked me over, head to toe. "How do you stay so thin?" she asked.

"Anxiety. I burn a gadzillion calories a day just by thinking too hard."

I thought my response would elicit a laugh, but Beth buried her face back into her pillow.

"We're going to have a blast, I promise," I said, trying to convince us both.

Beth

We sat at the bar at Crustaceans. We weren't important enough to get a table, and Dylan, Amber's friend, couldn't swing one.

The restaurant was filled with happy, wealthy, married people who probably had perfect kids at home. I appreciated Amber's attempt to cheer me, but it wasn't working.

"Chuck, get me a Seven and Seven," Dylan ordered.

"It's against policy for you to drink here."

"I'm off duty, besides, it's probably against policy for you to smoke a fat bowl in the parking lot during your shift." Dylan whispered into Chuck's ear. Chuck put a glass under the bar and made Dylan's drink.

"Can I get a vodka soda?" asked a lanky Asian girl. Her huge augmented breasts atop her wiry frame made her look like the Asian Jessica Rabbit.

"Absolutely." Chuck mixed the drink and gave it to her. She tried to pay, but he pushed her money back at her and winked. "On the house."

Men never stop thinking of sex.

"Did you see the rack on her?" Chuck asked.

"Yeah, nice. She had a cute face, too," Dylan said.

"What face?" Chuck laughed. "Hey, Dylan, if she was a vampire she'd be—"

"dRACKula," Dylan said, finishing Chuck's joke. "I bet you in high school she ran—"

"tRACK," Chuck said. They giggled like fifteen-year-olds. "If she were a dinosaur she'd be a—"

"Shut up. You guys are breast-obsessed pigs," Amber said, directing a nasty glare at Dylan.

"teraRACKdle." Dylan said. Chuck's body started convulsing as he tried to hold in his laughter. It was too much to handle, and a thimble full of water shot out his nose.

"Gross," Amber said.

"Look at that guy. He walks like a prick," Dylan said.

"Which guy?" I asked. "And how does one walk like a prick?"

"Just like that," Dylan said, then pointed directly at— Jackson!

"Oh my God! O-ma-god, omagod, omagod, Oh! My! GOD!"

"Beth?" Amber asked.

"That's him."

"*Him* him?" Amber asked.

"Yeah, *him him.*"

"The black guy?"

"Yeah. Wait. What? Black? I thought he was Italian. Forget that. What the hell do I do? Hide me!" Acidic bile ascended my esophagus.

"Beth, get a grip! Go tell him."

"What do I say? Hey, Jackson, that night on the beach was nice. How've you been since? Oh, that's nice. Me? How kind of you to ask. Not much, really. Hey, I'm pregnant. It's yours."

"You have to talk to him," Amber said.

"He looks wealthy," Chuck said.

"I can't do it."

"He's leaving. If you don't talk to him, I will. And I won't be as nice as you," Amber threatened.

"Okay, Amber, you do it. Chuck, give me a stiff one," I said.

"Isn't that what got you in this situation in the first place?" Dylan asked, laughing.

Amber slapped him. "Jerk!" She yanked my arm, and I dropped my Shirley Temple. It shattered on the floor, and I considered impaling myself on one its shards.

Amber dragged me toward Jackson.

"He looks like he's in a hurry. Maybe another time," I said.

"You're going now!" Amber pulled. I dug my heels into the ground, resisting like a little kid. Dylan followed behind us; his smile gave away his enjoyment of the situation.

Outside, Jackson was at the valet post with a gorgeous tall blonde on his arm.

"Look at his date; she's an actress. Umm, Joanna something. I can't compete with her!"

Amber yelled, "Jackson!"

Jackson turned, looked at Amber, and then he looked at me. He had an expression of vague recognition.

"What, you don't remember her? She's Beth, you jerk. Remember the beach in Malibu?" yelled Amber.

"What's she talking about?" Joanna asked.

"Tell her what I'm talking about, Beth."

Weak in the knees, I had to sit on the valet stool.

"Umm, hi, Jackson," I muttered.

Jackson

Joanna was pissed. She gets this way every time we run into some girl I've seen naked. I guess in casual-sex relationships that last for more than a decade, like Joanna and I, frequent tiffs are inevitable. Joanna got in the car and left with our friends.

"I would've called, but I lost your number," I said. Truth is I didn't know her name until her friend said it, and I couldn't place her face to save my life.

The angry, sexy black chick stepped between us. "You wouldn't have called if the number was tattooed on your forehead, you stupid ape!" she said. Thick veins stuck out of her neck like angry snakes.

"Amber, you aren't helping," Beth said to her friend. Then she turned back to me. "Jackson, I need to talk to you."

"I'm sorry I didn't call. Things got hectic with my mother, and—"

"I'm pregnant."

Thinking, thinking, thinking. "Is it mine?"

If there were a television show called *When Mad Black Women Attack,* the next sequence would've played with the opening credits every week. Beth's friend darted at me like a cocaine-fueled Lawrence Taylor going after a quarterback who had spit on him the previous play. It took all three valet guys to wrestle her off me, and by then she'd torn three buttons off my shirt and pulled some hair from my chest.

"Crazy woman!" I shouted. I bent to pick up the scattered buttons. "I'm freaking bleeding, you psychotic bitch!"

Like one of those trashy chicks on *Jerry Springer,* she charged again. I sidestepped her; the valet guys caught her, held her, and hollered for the skinny, pale, gothic-looking white guy to get her. He was balled up in a corner laughing.

"Beth, I'm sorry. Look," I said, looking at her wild-eyed friend, Amber, "can we go get a drink and talk about this?"

"She can't drink, you stupid monkey! She's pregnant!" She tried to come at me again. The laughing guy held her back. "Let go of me, Dylan!" she yelled.

"Beth, let's go somewhere ALONE and talk."

"Okay," Beth said.

I always wanted a child, a little me who played sports. I'd high-five the parents of the weaker kids when little Jackson scored a touchdown. But I didn't want a kid right now, and I didn't want one with Beth *ever.* If the kid was mine, she'd have to abort it.

The valet pulled up with my car, and Beth and I got in. I had no idea what to say. I still couldn't place her face. But knowing myself, I'm sure I had sex with her during some pain killer haze.

My conversation with Beth went something like this:

"Abortion."

"No."

"You sure it's mine?"

"Yeah."

"How?"

"Only sex I've had."

"You should get an abortion."

"No."

"I don't want to be a dad."

"You don't have a choice."

"I'll pay child support."

"Yes, you will."

"But I can't be a dad."

"You're a jerk."

It was kind of like that, except it was a two-hour conversation with a lot of tears and several punches.

Kelly

We were at Moe's, a dinky bar in Playa Del Rey, when this guy dressed in an eagle costume flew into the bar on a wire, flapping his wings and gawking. I learned later he was the bar's owner, and he does this sort of thing often. He landed on stage, and introduced the band. "Put your hands together for Empty Nest!"

Empty Nest was terrible. My old college band, Christmas Party Junkie, would've blown them away. Regardless, Reece and I had fun. We drank and laughed, and we played this game where we made up life stories about other people in the bar. Reece pointed out two guys sharing a booth, and I pegged them as tag-team serial killers whose next victim would be the transvestite playing pinball. I pointed at a couple sitting at the bar, and Reece decided the guy was a senator with a bestiality fetish on a date with a crack whore.

We had fun, and despite the annoying little fact Reece had a husband, I figured she and I still had a slim chance to end the night in a hot, sweaty, fleshy mess. But she was married, and I should've had some sort of moral issue with it.

I should have.

A few drinks later, Reece decided she'd had enough. "The alcohol's giving me a headache. Let's get out of here," she said.

"Yeah, I have to work early tomorrow. I should call it a night," I replied.

Reece popped a fresh piece of gum in her mouth and said, "That's not what I meant."

It may not be possible to feel your own pupils dilate, but I did. "Where should we go?"

"My place," she offered.

"What?"

"My place."

"Umm. Your jealous husband?"

"He works the night shift. If you're gone by seven a.m., we'll be okay."

"But I—"

"What?"

"Are you sure it's safe?" I asked.

Reece started laughing. "I've been messing with you. I'm not married."

"Huh?"

"I'm not married. But you thought I was, and you were still going to try to sleep with a married woman. You men are pigs." Reece blew a bubble, and it popped in my face.

"I knew you were kidding."

"Liar. Well you ready?"

"But you just called me a pig?"

"Awe, I'm sorry, did I hurt your feelings?" she asked, patting me on the head.

"No, I just didn't think you'd... nevermind. Let's go," I said.

I jumped in her car before I could say something to screw it up. On the drive to her place I tried my best not to smile more than fifty percent of the time.

At her apartment, Reece led me by the hand to her couch. She didn't bother turning on any lights, and before I was able to get my bearings, she'd straddled me and began kissing my neck. We nestled in the feathery couch cushion, beneath an open window, and moonlight came through the thin flapping pink curtains, pink light falling upon us. Reece pulled away and looked at me with intimidating, sex-starved eyes. She ran her manicured fingers beneath my shirt, up my belly to my chest, and out the top of my neck hole, resting her soft hand against my face.

Then, with her mouth wide open, Reece moved in for the first kiss.

Conventionally, a first kiss consists of a few soft pecks, a brief touching of tongues, followed by the calculated parting of lips, a passionate stare into one another's eyes accompanied by a smile, and followed by the big kiss.

Reece wasn't conventional.

Reece's pointy tongue darted deep into my mouth like she was trying to clean out the corners of a snack-pack pudding box. It tickled, and it was ridiculous, and I wanted to laugh. I covered my mouth with my hand to hold in my laugh. Laughing would ruin my chances. I removed my hand from my mouth, tucked my laughter in behind my tongue, and smiled at Reece like, A*www, we just shared our first kiss.* I took in a deep breath of air, knowing Reece wouldn't let me get another one for a while, put my mouth back to hers, and tried to match her wild style.

Tongues were flailing, darting, tickling, teasing, and protruding further than Gene Simmons in his most glorious moment. Fiddling, dancing tongues, saliva running down my cheeks. I was catcher to her pitcher, and I desperately hoped she didn't make a wild pitch and poke out my eye. Our heads turned left, right, up, down, and every time I looked at Reece her eyes were wide open and looking back at me. The kissing carried on for fifteen minutes or so, then *kaboom*, we were in the bedroom.

We fooled around for a while. Eventually, Reece was naked and had her perfect body on top of my soft belly. I slid my hand down to take my boxers off, but she hit me with the, *I don't have sex on the first date.* She rolled off me, and said goodnight; intentionally leaving me with a burning pain in the root of me.

How cruel!

I lay there, disoriented, for an hour, too agitated to sleep. I contemplated going to the bathroom to unload the internal pressure that had built inside me, but I worried she'd wake up and catch me. Eventually, I was able to relax and the warm embrace of sleep took me. It was a good sleep; it'd been many moons since I'd felt the flowery warmth of a woman nestled next to me.

I woke at dawn. Reece lay naked in my arms. The morning star rose over Reece's windowsill, declaring a new day and bathing her creamy white flesh in warm August sunlight. I lightly blew on her nose; she wiggled it, and I blew on it again. Reece scratched her nose, causing the sheet to fall off her shoulder, tormenting my already tortured libido. I can't remember feeling more happy than I felt at that moment.

I lay there for quite a while, admiring her beauty. But as dawn turned to early morning, I started looking around. I noticed her walls and furnishings were curiously bare, like someone had just moved in or someone was moving out; I hadn't noticed this at night.

I could've lied there forever next to Reece, but I smelled ripe, and I wanted to freshen up before Reece awoke. I got up to shower where I found about twenty different kinds of body washes, shampoos, and conditioners. I used a little bit of each. I scrubbed my back with her falafel or loofah thinger. I'm not sure of its name, but it's a hard spongy job on the end of a stick, and it gave me the sensation of someone else scratching my back. I made a mental note to buy one.

Beneath the sound of the water pelting the opaque shower door, I sang the first verse of *I'm Just a Girl* before I realized what I was singing. But I was too pent up with agonizing sexual energy not to sing, so I changed my tune to Pink Floyd's *Us and Them*.

After showering, I dried off, put on a robe, and tinkered around in Reece's medicine cabinet. I found an antibiotic that I hoped was not cause for alarm. Then I found her birth-control pills, and for some reason, this gave me hope that I'd eventually have sex with her.

I poked my head out; Reece was still sleeping. I didn't want to wake her, so to kill time I started playing with her many perfumes. I sprayed a little of each in the air, and sniffed at them. The scent from one reminded me of scented love letters my mom had written my father when they were dating. I remembered sitting in our basement curled around those old yellowed letters, reading them by flashlight for hours. My parents love was a real deal. Like an old black and white starring Humphrey Bogart and Ingrid Bergman.

My dad never blamed me for Mom's death, but I knew that my presence, on a daily basis, was a painful reminder to him that the love of his life was gone.

I killed my mom by trying to be born.

Reece awoke. "Kelly, what are you doing? Take my robe off. You're stretching it out."

I plopped on her bed. "Good morning to you, too."

Reece rubbed the sleep from her eyes, opened her mouth, and let go of a yawn that pushed her morning breath over the shelf of my upper lip and into my nostrils. It smelled sweet like baby's breath. Then I noticed she was chewing gum. She'd fallen asleep with her gum in her mouth and had automatically begun chewing it as soon as she woke.

"Why does it smell like the perfume section of the mall in here?"

Reece asked.

"Um, I dunno."

Reece sat up, and the sheet fell down to her lap. *Good morning!*

"I noticed your room is pretty bare. Did you just move in?"

"That's none of your business."

Her defensiveness made me curious. "Geez, sorry," I said.

"No, I'm sorry. I'm grumpy when I wake up. Well, Kelly, time for you to go home."

I was hoping for an early morning antidote for my lingering erection. Reece's nipples were looking at me, taunting me.

"You want to get some breakfast with me?" I asked.

"I don't have time."

"Okay, well, I had fun. See you again?" I half asked and half stated.

"Sure, next time my husband's out of town I'll give you a call," Reece said and winked.

I gave Reece a peck on the lips, left my number on her vanity, and departed. I saw a love-making session with myself in my very near future.

Paul Ritter, 24

The landscape was too beautiful not to be painted. But not by me; it needed to be painted by an artist with talent and impartial eyes. The rolling green hills went on for miles, punctuated by countless brown trees whose branches bowed under the weight of delicious red apples. Nestled between the hills was a meadow containing a smattering of houses and too many people. One of Mother's homes is still there.

I didn't like me, so, recently, I decided not to be me any longer; I'd be someone else; I'd become a mishmash of everyone I admired.

I became a preacher. And I was leaving home; moving to the most sinful state in the union, California. I'd understand people and their problems, and thus, I'd be able to help. Helping would be some kind of small penance for my sin.

The drive from Florida to California was long and sad and quiet. Today I was in Kentucky where I stopped to deal with my demons. Disturbed, yet oddly comfortable, I sat beneath a tree could've been the very same one, and I remembered…

It was about seventeen years ago, almost to the day, when I was here. At seven years of age, I didn't understand the significance of what had happened.

We were picking apples; my mother and sister were putting apples in wicker baskets to bake pies. I roamed around on my own.

"Don't eat the apples. You'll ruin your appetite," mother said.

As soon as my mother was out of site, I grabbed the juiciest and reddest apple I could find, pulled it off the tree, and bit through the apple's skin into its meat. Sweet juices dripped down my cheeks. I ate as fast as I could, hoping Mom wouldn't catch me. While chomping away, I felt a cloth to my chin. I snapped my head around to find an old black lady with a handkerchief.

"You best slow down on that apple; you'll choke," she said. Then she tucked the handkerchief down the front of her blouse.

I swatted at flies buzzing around my head. "It's a good apple."

"I'm sure it is." The old black lady looked around. "Where's your Daddy? You shouldn't be out here all alone."

"My Daddy died a few weeks ago. My mom's over there." I pointed.

The old black lady stared at me. "You poor child."

Father had been sick for as long as I'd known him. I only spent time with him on Sundays and only because Mom made me. I didn't see the point of visiting him; he couldn't talk, and he didn't seem like he listened when I talked. Lying in bed hooked up to machines, my father was more *thing* than dad. I cried at his funeral, but only because my mother and sister cried. Seeing my father in the coffin seemed no different than seeing him in bed, except in the coffin Father wore a suit and didn't have any tubes coming out of him. He looked better.

After Father died nothing really changed.

Until the old black lady pitied me under apple tree.

She looked at me with the saddest eyes I'd ever seen, and I felt pathetic. The sorrow in her dark eyes burned into my brain, becoming a part of me. It made me realize the significance of my father's death; my father was gone forever, and being a fatherless child is a very sad thing.

I didn't understand my feelings and misinterpreted them as hate for that black woman, and what she made me feel. My hatred grew over time.

What I really hated was myself, but I was too stupid to realize it then.

"Paul, get over here," my mother called.

I approached my mom. "Don't talk to people like her," Mom said. "You don't ever talk to blacks when I'm not around. You hear me? It's not safe."

Mother was a bigot.

And, on this day, I became one too.

Years later, standing in the same orchard, I thought about how that singular moment evolved into my greatest sin. And now, no matter what, I see that sin in my bathroom mirror each morning.

Someday, it will catch up to me, the balance of good and evil will be restored, and when I die, God will sort it out on judgment day.

Beth

My parents' house looked a little frightening. The needles on their Santa Rita cacti looked sharp and dangerous. Bark was peeling from the skinny twin dogwood trees making them look like legs of an old witch with eczema.

My anxiety was approaching record highs and I feared another nose bleed. I sat outside on the oak bench, looked at the house, and rehearsed the speech I'd give my dads. The dull red of the house seemed more robust and angrier than usual. Gazing skyward, the clouds' underbellies looked pregnant, distended with moisture. A raindrop landed next to me, but I didn't get up. I wasn't quite ready to face my dads. Lightning streaked across the sky followed by a dull roar of thunder. Thirty seconds later, heaven opened its mouth and dumped a sea of rain on me. I ran for the porch but was soaked before I made it. The awning above hummed under the heavy rain. I knocked. Daddy Gerry opened the door.

"Princess Beth, you're soaked. Get inside and get warm." I stepped in. "Take that wet shirt off." I did. Daddy put a dry blanket around my shoulders.

"Thanks, Dad," I said. I felt Daddy Gerry would be thrilled about my news, but worried Daddy David would get all practical and logical.

We dilly-dallied around, small talking and catching up for probably half an hour, but I can't be sure. Time was dragging, and I was too preoccupied and anxious to concentrate on any of what was being said.

Eventually, we sat to eat. Daddy David stood up with the bread knife and cut through a thick baguette. "We haven't all sat down to eat like a family in quite some time. We've got empty nest syndrome, love. When are you going to give us a grandchild to hold and love?"

My throat clenched into a fist.

"Umm, Daddy, it's funny you mention that."

"Oh my God, our princess is pregnant!" Daddy Gerry blurted.

Daddy David stopped cutting. He let go of the knife, which stood suspended in the hard crust like a saw in a log. "You're not!"

"I am."

"Wow! How far along?" Daddy Gerry asked, dumping a heaping spoonful of buttered mashed potatoes on my plate. My dads have the metabolism of cheetahs on crystal meth. Unfortunately, I don't.

"A few months."

"This shouldn't have happened," Daddy David said.

"But it did."

"Well, you shouldn't have let it," Daddy David said.

"Shut up, you! Come here, baby, and give your dad a hug!" Daddy Gerry said.

Daddy Gerry has always tried to make me feel good about myself. I remembered the awkward looks we'd get as a family. Daddy Gerry always told me people looked because I was so beautiful.

That wasn't true. I wasn't beautiful.

"Who's the father?" Daddy David asked. "I didn't know you had a boyfriend."

"I don't— I slept with someone on my birthday," I said, lowering my head in shame.

"I knew we should've taken you out for your birthday," Daddy Gerry said.

"And you offered, but I'm sure you can understand why I didn't want to celebrate my twenty-first birthday with my parents. That would make me like the lamest person ever, which, as it turns out, I am."

"You're not lame, baby," Daddy Gerry said. He plopped a second helping of turkey breast on my plate. I'd barely touched the first.

"Is the father going to be involved?" Daddy David asked.

"Only financially."

"Oh, baby, we're going to have so much fun. I can't wait to get started on the nursery," Daddy Gerry exclaimed, squeezing me. Though an effeminate man, he possessed the strength of ten mothers in one of his hugs, or so I imagined. I'd never been hugged by the mother who gave me away at birth.

"What about college?" Daddy David asked.

"I can take care of the baby while Beth's at school," Daddy Gerry offered.

"I'm quitting school and getting my own apartment."

"What? Why?" Daddy Gerry asked.

"Well, that's sorta hard to explain."

Daddy David answered for me. "Because she doesn't want to live here and have her baby raised by a couple of fags."

"That's not true. Is it, baby?" Daddy Gerry asked, hurt.

"No, Daddy, that's not true."

"What are you going to do for money?" Daddy David asked.

"We'll give her money, silly," Daddy Gerry said.

"The father, Jackson, is very wealthy."

"You can't count on this Jackson guy for money if he doesn't want to be involved," Daddy David said.

"I'll work part-time."

"What kind of job is a twenty-one-year-old pregnant college drop-out qualified for?"

"Don't be mean," Daddy Gerry said. He plopped another generous helping of buttery mashed potatoes on my plate.

"I'm not being mean. I'm being logical. What kind of job do you think you're going to get? And who's going to care for your baby when you're working?"

"Amber's going to live with me."

"Amber? Your dyke friend? Are you in love with that lesbi-man?" Daddy David stood up from his chair, leaning both arms on the table.

"Dad, I'd think a gay man wouldn't use names like that."

"I don't understand, baby," Daddy Gerry said. "You'd rather have Amber's help than ours?"

"Yes—I mean, no. What I mean is, if I stay here, I know you'll take excellent care of my baby and me. I know everything will be taken care of just like it always is."

"And why would this be bad?" Daddy Gerry asked.

"Because she wants to do it herself like a *big girl*," Daddy David said, sarcastically.

"Don't condescend."

"Well, that's the truth, isn't it?"

"I want to feel like this child is really mine. If I stay, the two of you will take over and be Mommy and Daddy, and I'll end up being big sister."

"It won't be that way, baby," Daddy Gerry assured me.

"You won't intentionally make it that way, but that's how it'll turn out. I don't want to hurt your feelings. I just need to do this. I want you both very much involved as grandparents."

Daddy Gerry squirmed. "Oh my God! That makes us sound so old!" He put his hand on Daddy David's shoulder.

"Shut up, Gerry. Quit being such a fag. So how will this arrangement work with you and the lesbi-man?"

Daddy Gerry looked at him and said, "Her name's Amber. Don't be such a ass-fucker!"

"Stop it! Both of you! I know it won't be easy, and I know it isn't conventional, and I know I'm going to make a lot of mistakes. I also know both of you have been through circumstances with me that were unconventional and hard, but everything worked out. I'm asking for your blessing. Can you two give me that?"

"Of course we can, baby," Daddy Gerry said.

"Daddy David?"

"Yes, dear, we'll be there for you."

We hugged and then cried a happy-sad cry. Daddy Gerry seemed eager, Daddy David seemed concerned, and I was absolutely terrified.

September 1997
Maria

Sometimes, I'm able to trick myself into believing the illusion that I'm in control of my life.

Hollywood stinks. Yesterday, after screen testing for a new NBC sitcom, my agent said the casting director loved me but felt I was a little too heavy for the part. So, even though I'd already been jogging earlier today, I drove back to the park to run again.

Before getting my implants, I was jogging and lifting weights three times a week. After surgery, I couldn't jog, and my stomach showed it. After bombing yesterday's audition, I knew I needed to be stricter about dieting and exercise if I wanted to make it in Hollywood. So, on top of jogging, I cut my caloric intake to one thousand per day.

Fooling the body into thinking it's full on only a thousand calories can be difficult. The trick is to chew the food until the flavor is gone, then spit it out. Some food slid down my throat, but that couldn't be avoided. In some situations, like dinner parties, the chew and spit technique was hard to pull off, so I turned down most invitations. However, if the host was an important industry insider or a business associate of my father, I had to go. In these situations, I chewed the food so long it was pretty much liquid by the time I swallowed it. This way vomiting after burned less.

Doctors may say I'm anorexic or bulimic, but I'm not. I do this for the work; all actresses do it. But unlike most, I don't use cocaine to suppress my appetite, and I think that gives me a mental leg up on the competition.

I was determined to get back to the weight I was the previous summer when I shot the calendar *Bikini Beauties of USC*. Unfortunately, I was closer to my weight in junior high when I was one hundred twenty five pounds of fat. My father is obese, my older brother is obese, and my mother was obese when she left my dad. Being fat was part of my genetic make-up, and staying thin was a constant struggle.

At the park, I got out of my pink Mustang, laced up my size sevens, plugged my headphones into my diskman, and turned up the volume of Carol King's *Tapestry* CD. Jogging to the mailbox to drop in a few headshots, I sang along with Carol:

> *"Tonight with words unspoken*
>
> *You say I'm the only one,*
>
> *But will my heart be broken*
>
> *When the night*
>
> *Meets the mor—ning sun?"*

I opened the mailbox, made my deposit, and jogged back to my car:

"I'd like to know your love
Is love I can be sure of.
So tell me no-o-w
And I won't ask again.
Will you still love me tomorrow?
Will you still love me tomorrow?"

I stooped to hide my keys in the little magnetic key holder under the car's frame.

"Stupid. Stupid! Stupid! Stupid!"

I looked at the mailbox, looked at the envelopes still in my hand, looked back at the mailbox.

I'd mailed my keys instead of the envelopes.

I'm not an airhead, but sometimes there's too much air in my head, a tornado of words and ideas moving too fast for me to latch on to any singular thought.

I'd have to call Daddy to fix this. I went to the pay phone. "Damn spandex!" I had no pockets for coins. "Stupid!"

"You don't look stupid to me," replied an attractive stranger. He was tall, had beautiful blond locks, brown eyes, and cheekbones that could have cut leather.

"I just mailed my keys."

"To where?"

"To nowhere. It was an accident. That's why I called myself stupid."

"That is kind of stupid."

"I don't have time for this. Do you have a quarter?" I asked.

"Insult me and then ask for money—not the best strategy. I don't have a quarter, but I can fish the keys out if you have a coat hanger in your car."

"I'm locked out of my car, Einstein."

He slapped himself in the head. "Duh. Maybe I'm the stupid one. Oh, wait, actually I think I have one."

"A quarter?"

"No. A coat hanger."

"You have a coat hanger in your car, but you don't have a quarter?" I asked.

"Yeah. Strange huh? Let me run to my car, and I'll help you out."

"Thank you for offering, but I've got to go."

"How? You have no keys."

I walked away.

He called after me, "What's your name?"

"Lexi," I lied.

"Well, Lexi, I presume it's Lexi Maria then?"

What? How does he know my real name?

"My name's Paul, and I can help you if you want."

"How did you know my name's Maria?" I felt frightened. Was he from one of Daddy's rival families? Was I in danger?

"I have ESP."

"Well, then, maybe you can ESP my keys out of the mailbox," I said and started toward the convenience store so I could call Daddy.

"Look, Maria, I'm going to fish your keys out of this mailbox. You can stick around, or you can allow freaky ESP guy walk away with your keys."

I didn't really like either option. "Fine, I'll wait," I said.

"Good. Here's the deal. After I retrieve your keys, you call me your hero, and then I'll give them back."

"Whatever."

Paul

Maria's brown eyes were large and inquisitive. A man could lose track of time while exploring the long open meadows of them.

"Here it goes," I said, then slid two wire hangers into the mailbox. I started aimlessly stabbing at mail, pulling up one harpooned piece of mail after another. I had absolutely no idea what I was doing.

"Hey, MacGyver, isn't tampering with mail a federal offense?" Maria asked. Her voice was long and thick, but grated around the edges. It was a stick of butter rolled in sugar. "I won't be an accomplice to this. I'll watch from my car," Maria said.

"If I get arrested, you'll be an accomplice no matter where you watch from. They're your keys," I said.

Maria started to shiver. "Take my sweatshirt. It's getting chilly," I said. Maria refused, but I insisted. She took it, pulled it over her head and covered up her sinful figure. I immediately regretted giving it to her.

I pulled mail out of the mailbox for ten minutes. When I felt the wire hangers scraping the metal bottom, I knew I had to be getting close.

Seconds later, I hit pay dirt. "I got 'em!" I said. I pulled them out and proudly dropped the keys on top of all the mail scattered at my feet.

Miss *Lexi* Maria jogged over, parts of her bouncing. "Thank you," she said. Maria took the keys, looked at them, hesitated, and then said, "Those aren't my keys."

"What do you mean they aren't your keys?"

"Not. My. Keys."

"Is this some sort of hidden camera television show?" I held the keys in front of her face. "These are keys, aren't they?"

"They're keys, but they aren't mine."

"How is that even possible?" Baffled, I looked at the mailbox. "How can these not be your keys?"

"Look, I appreciate your help, but this is ridiculous. Please leave so I can go to the convenience store and call someone."

"I'm going to get your keys."

"Whatever." Maria walked back to her car and sat on the hood, arms folded in protest.

I continued to scrape the wire hangers on the bottom of the mailbox. Two minutes later, I retrieved another set of keys.

"Hey, Maria, don't get too excited, but I've got another set of keys here."

She walked over, looked at the keys, and gave me a big crooked smile. "Thank you."

I let out a sigh of relief. "And?" I asked.

"And what?" she asked.

Maria

And? What's this pervert expecting?

"And. Come on, you know. I'm your—"

"Oh yeah. Myyy heee-ro." I acted it out over-the-top, like he'd just untied me from a set of railroad tracks seconds before a train, driven by a bad guy, ran me over.

After we finished putting all the mail back in the mailbox, Paul stood there with the other set of keys in his hand. "What should we do with these?" he asked.

"We could try them in every car in the parking lot, steal the car, take it to a chop shop, and sell it for parts," I said.

"Yeah, then we could go rob the house of the people who own the car while they're at work." Paul chuckled.

"Nah, I'd feel bad if we got busted. You're too pretty to do hard time," I said. His eyes lit up when I said that, which made me wish I hadn't complimented him.

Paul dropped the keys into the mailbox. "I'm a minister at the Protestant church in Marina Del Rey. Ministers don't steal cars."

"You seem too big a flirt to be a minister."

"I'm a minister, not a saint."

I blushed. "Well, it's too bad you're Protestant. I was starting to like you, but I'm Catholic."

"Maybe I'll convert—I mean, I'm not married to it," Paul said.

I laughed. "So tell me how you knew my name."

"I told you, I have ESP."

I was nervous about who he could be and didn't feel like playing games. "Seriously, how did you know?"

"ESP."

"This is messed up. How did you know my name? Do you know my father? Did the Coronas send—"

"Shhh—" Paul said, putting his finger to my lips. "Jeez. I don't think I want to hear the rest of that." He looked down at the diskman tucked in the waistband of my spandex. I followed his glance to my hips. *Maria Orlando.* My name was written there in thick black ink.

"I'm an idiot," I said, relieved.

"Well, idiot, before you go, may I ask for your number?"

"No, but you can give me yours if you like." Paul whipped out a pen from his pants pocket faster than Zorro could draw his sword. He scribbled his number on a Subway receipt. "So. you'd be willing to convert for me, huh?"

"Sure, but I could only be a parishioner. I could never be a priest. They aren't allowed to, well, you know."

"Pervert."

"I'm not a perv. Just human."

I smiled, shook his hand, and left. I had a lunch date with a friend. But when I left, I was still wearing his sweatshirt—a good excuse to call him later.

Reece

I went to Spago to have lunch with my new friend, Maria Orlando, whom I met a month ago at a casting call for Slim-Fast. Maria was much younger than me, but we were a good fit. Maria came from a powerful family, and I felt strong when near her. I thought she'd adequately fill the role of the Godmother who spoils her Goddaughter with expensive gifts.

"Maria, I'm pregnant."

"Wow. Really? Wow. Congratulations. What are your plans?"

"Marriage."

"Really? Wow. Are you still seeing Isaac? Is it his?"

"No and no."

Maria blushed. "Oh. Well, who's the father?"

"This guy, Kelly. I've been seeing him for about six weeks. We're just getting to know each other, but I'm positive he'll be a great father."

"Do you love him?" Maria asked.

"No, but I'm okay with him."

"Does he love you?"

"He lusts for me. Men are incapable of loving anyone but themselves."

Maria polished off her glass of wine. "That's not true," she said, then poured another glass. "At least not from my experience."

"No offense, Maria, but experiences with young puppy love don't count."

Maria set the wine bottle down forcefully. "My age has nothing to do with anything."

"You're right, I'm sorry. I can't speak for all women, but for me men are nothing more than simple creatures that need food to nourish their erections so they can give us their sperm. Other than that, they serve no real purpose," I said.

"What's made you so bitter?"

"Men. All of them. But mostly Isaac. I thought he loved me. But he didn't. All I ever wanted from him was a baby, but he wouldn't give me one."

I cooked and cleaned for Isaac. I sucked him every night and swallowed his nasty stuff. I took care of him when he was sick, and I massaged his shoulders after work. I was a great freaking wife.

"How do you know Isaac didn't love you?" Maria asked. She hadn't touched her mud pie dessert.

"Are you going to eat that?" I asked.

"No. Take it."

I pulled her plate around to my side of the table and took a bite. Maria was eyeballing me in a way I didn't like.

"What?" I asked.

"How do you stay so slim?" she asked.

"Anger. Anger burns calories."

"Oh," Maria said. "Anyway, how do you know Isaac didn't love you?" she asked.

"Because he wouldn't have lied and cheated if he loved me. Last year at my best friend's wedding, I caught Isaac with one of the bride's maids in the utility room. Isaac had the slut bent over a washing machine, her dress pulled up over the back of her head."

Maria's richly tanned face turned a few shades whiter. "That's horrible. Why didn't you leave him then?"

"I put in too much time with Isaac to end our marriage before getting a baby out of it," I said.

Isaac cheated on me with half the women in town. He thought I didn't know. I did; I just didn't care anymore. All I wanted from him was a baby. I quit taking my birth control pills without telling him, and I started putting trace amounts of marijuana and ecstasy in his food so he'd get horny enough to screw me.

I didn't tell Maria that part. However, I did share quite a bit, things you don't typically share with a new friend that's half your age. Then again, I didn't have many friends.

Actually, Maria was my only friend.

"I never got pregnant. Then, to top it off, I discovered he'd been married before and had kids he'd never even met."

"Oh my God. You poor thing. How did you find out?" The color had returned to her face. She seemed to be enjoying my soap opera of a life story.

"I was in line at the movies, fighting on the phone with Isaac. The woman behind me overheard. I guess my Isaac sounded like an Isaac she knew. She asked me his last name. I told her. She turned out to be Isaac's ex-wife. Isaac divorced her when he found out she was pregnant with twins."

Maria gulped her wine.

"So, I finally decided to leave Isaac. The divorce was finalized a few days ago. And even though his lawyer killed mine and Isaac got everything, I'm here today, with you, to celebrate my freedom."

"I'm so sorry. It will get better. Not all men are incapable of love."

"All the ones I know are. My father was a drunken wife-beater. It ruined my mother, and she took it out on me," I said. "When he left her, she became dependant on me for love and support. I cared for her night and day until the day she died. In the final week of her life, she told me not to have kids because I'd be a terrible mother."

"Wow. That's about the worst thing I've ever heard. But Reece," Maria asked gingerly, "how can you marry another man when you despise them?"

"I can't raise a baby alone. Love may not be real, but my needs are."

"Reece, you know it's wrong to deceive Kelly, right? Don't you believe in Karma?"

"Look, I'm going to have a daughter, and I'll be happy."

My plan was to tell Kelly I got pregnant because my antibiotics had weakened the effectiveness of my birth control pill. *I'm so sorry, Kelly. I should have thought about that.* Kelly will believe me because he'll want to believe me. He won't want to know the truth.

Maria and I left Spago and went our separate ways. I went home, relaxed for a few hours, and got ready for my date.

Kelly knocked on my door at seven.

Lights, camera, action.

I opened the door, "Hi, Kelly," I said, giving him the smile of my life.

"Hi. You look amazing," Kelly said. Kelly knew that, physically, I was way out of his league, which was good. A man's physical appearance is inversely proportionate to how he treats his woman.

"Thank you."

"Well, let's get going. I've got a big surprise for you tonight," he said.

I coughed to hold back a laugh. The irony was almost funny. "I bet my surprise is bigger."

"You got me a surprise?"

"Well, Kelly. I'm not sure how to tell you this— "

Jackson

I stared in the mirror of Mother's bathroom at the Board and Care, trying to figure out what to say. I couldn't feign concern about the coming baby with Beth; all my thoughts revolved around how a baby would end up affecting me. An abortion would have fixed everything, but Beth wasn't willing.

I'm aware I'm not the best person in the world. I don't like being self-centered, but knowing your faults won't change them. People can't change; we're preprogrammed robots going through the motions. We're the same at death as we are at birth. I've tried to change. I got involved with a charity when I played for the Steelers, but I did it for the positive press and to make my mother and my dead sister, Cheryl, proud of me. I didn't care about those handicapped kids.

I took a final look at myself in the mirror and then walked into Mom's bedroom. "Hi, Mom."

"Hi, Jackson."

I needed my Mother's love; I had nobody else. I'd loved women, but I'd never been in love. I had no real friends, just people who used me. I have no family besides my Mom; I lost my sister and my dad in the same week.

I remember my sister's funeral vividly. Dad yelled at Mother, accused her of slowly poisoning my sister to death.

Father screamed at her, "I suspected it all along, but I didn't know for sure until I found the bottle in the trash can!" Then he spat out unspeakable, filthy lies about things my mom had done to me as a child. I've never repeated those lies.

They screamed at each other for fifteen minutes. I tried to

maintain my composure when he called Mom a "fucking cunt," but when he slapped her, I lost it. I charged across the room and hit him.

Hard.

I was only sixteen, but I was bigger than him, and when I hit him, he dropped. He looked up at me from the floor, I saw fear in his eyes; he knew he could no longer control me. He got up, and stormed out of the house. The next day, police found his mangled body in his wrecked Porsche at the foot of the ocean about a hundred and fifty feet below a sharp turn in the highway.

I looked at my Mom in the bed. "I need to tell you something, Mom."

"I'm listening."

"I don't know how to say this so I'm just going to come out and say it."

"Okay."

"I got someone pregnant."

"Really? So I'm going to be a grandmother? You're getting married!"

Mom wrapped her good arm around me. She was much more alert and oriented than usual. I should've told her the truth; I wasn't getting married, and I didn't want anything to do with the kid. But I couldn't.

I stayed with Mom for an hour; eventually her thoughts became clouded again, and she forgot about the pregnancy. That's how it goes with Alzheimer's, and this time I was grateful.

I kissed Mom goodbye, got in my car, slammed a few OxyContin, and made my way through the city back to Malibu. Downtown Los Angeles is ugly, but once the pills kicked in, my surroundings became invisible.

Invisibility, in a way, is beautiful.

Back at home, the air felt thick and swampy. I wanted it to swallow me up and make me completely disappear. I slogged through its thickness, walking around my property while the sun dipped below the horizon. The orange sky depressed me further, so I swallowed a couple more pills and waited for warm deep purple light to run over me and wash everything away.

When morning came, I stood naked in front of the vanity mirror; I observed the contrast between my dark ashy feet and the white marble floor. It reminded me of the contrast between my mother and father.

I swallowed a handful of pills.

I'll stop eating pills some day, but not today.

The pills took effect slowly and peacefully, moving in me like a warm violet light. The hardness of thought softens, and solutions to problems feel within reach. The effects usually last about three hours, and then I need more.

My cook paged me over the intercom. "Mister Jackson, you're breakfast is ready. Shall I bring it up?"

"Yes, please," I replied. Then I shook Joanna. She reeked of alcohol. "Joanna! Wake up!"

"Huh?"

"Wake up! It's time to go home."

"Leave me alone!" She swatted at me and rolled over.

Normally, I'd let Joanna sleep all day, but today I felt like spending my day in bed, and I didn't want to have to look at Joanna the whole time.

I'd been between Joanna's legs too many times over too many years. I've wanted to end it a thousand times. I hate her in ways, but in others, beside my mother, she's all I have.

Joanna was one of my first sexual conquests. In high school, she was already a budding Hollywood starlet, and I considered myself lucky to be with her. But now, sex with Joanna had become habitual, and I was bored of fucking her rail-thin body. She was the biggest celebrity in a high school full of them, and though she looked curvy on the big screen, she was a skeleton in real life. Her long chicken legs ran straight up into her lower back; she was ass-less. Her ribs showed through her skin, and if it weren't for the saline, she'd have no tits. She did so many sit-ups over the course of a day, she had a better eight-pack than most male athletes, and her abdominal bumps went all the way down to the mound above her vagina.

Sometimes, like today, I want to stop having sex with Joanna because not having sex with her would at least be something new.

So, tonight, after she takes me to climax one last time, I'll tell her we're finished for good. This time I'll make sure it sticks.

I pushed the intercom. "Is the food coming?"

"Yes, Mister Jackson. Two trays?"

"Not today. Joanna's on her way home."

I shook Joanna again, but she didn't budge. My cook came up with a bacon, egg, and cheese sandwich.

I ate, knowing I didn't deserve the food I chewed. I ground the food between my teeth, slowly, letting time flow away. Today I'd sleep. Tomorrow I'd go visit Mom.

I'll love Mom, and she'll love me back.

The pills started kicking in, and I felt a little better. I felt my blood creeping slowly through my veins, taking warm purple light all through me, making my body feel like it does when I lie on my beach and listen to the sounds of the sunset.

November 1997
Maria

They stand in line like heroin addicts at a methadone clinic: pathetically, waiting for their five-dollar grande chai tea lattes and venti blended-mocha-caramel espressos with extra whipped cream.

I wanted one.

But I couldn't indulge because I needed to lose at least five more pounds.

I denied myself a Starbucks treat and assessed the checkout lines at Vons. Tardiness was Paul's pet peeve, and I was late. Again.

Tonight, Paul planned to take me to see Phantom of the Opera at the Pantages Theatre. Until Paul, I had only dated the monkey-brained sons and cousins of my dad's associates. These mobsters-in-training considered a good date to be a day at Hollywood Park betting on horses named Sicilian Slice and Milan Fashion Model. They were egomaniacal misogynistic pigs who paraded me around like an accessory. Paul was the first guy to ever show interest in my thoughts and ideas.

My Paul was cooking spaghetti for dinner before the show. Even though I grew up on pasta, I'm not a fan of it; it's too heavy and spicy, and it burns when I puke it back up. Paul hates spaghetti, too, but he wanted to practice making it before Daddy came over for dinner next week.

"Price-check on the ready-mixed salad," the checker said over the intercom. Her glasses were as thick as the bulletproof glass of a bank's windows.

How thick must glass be to be bulletproof?

"It said $2.79, not $2.88," insisted the old lady. She was bent over like a frail palm tree. She was holding up the line for nine lousy cents. I was running late, and would've given her the difference, but I didn't want to seem pretentious.

They resolved the issue, and then the old lady picked another fight. "This coupon says two for one on milk."

"Yeah, it says two for one, but you're in Vons, and this coupon is for Ralphs," said the checker, whose nametag read "Momma Honey," which was odd.

"But you accept competitors' coupons."

"We accept *valid* coupons. This expired two months ago," Momma Honey said. On her breast, she wore a heart-shaped broach that held large, fake rubies. And just for a second, I was mesmerized by the shine of it. It wasn't beautiful; in fact, it was quite gaudy, but there was something about it that held me rapt. I felt envious of the broach; I wanted to capture attention in the way broach had caught mine.

"I'd like to speak to your manager," the customer insisted.

I would've changed lanes, but I'd already invested five minutes of my time in this one, so I stayed.

Ring. Ring. Ring. Ring.

My cellular phone. I love the convenience of being able to talk to anyone at any time, but I don't appreciate the looks people give me like, *hey, look at the rich bitch on the cellular phone.* Yes, I am rich, and I do have the luxuries of things like cellular phones, but I should not be judged for these things. My things are not me.

I answered my phone. "Hi, Paul."

"Where are you, baby?"

"I'm sorry, Paul. I'm stuck in heavy traffic. I'll be there soon."

"It's already 6:35. Dinner's going to get cold."

"I won't be much longer, honey."

"Price check on apples," the checker announced.

"Busted!" he said, annoyed. "You're still in the grocery store, aren't you?"

"Umm. yeah."

"Hurry up, Maria."

"Okay. Bye," I hung up. "Dammit! Damn cell phone! There's no privacy with these damn things."

"Price check on K-Y Jelly," the cashier announced.

The old, bent-over bitty couldn't have had sex in at least fifteen years. She was probably just buying it because she had a coupon she couldn't stand to waste.

"Can we please speed it up a little?" I politely asked the osteoporotic coupon clipper.

Ring. Ring.

"Hello, Daddy."

"Hey, little meatball." He's always called me names like that. *Little meatball, pork chop, beanie, etc.* "Come to the restaurant tonight, and I'll cook you the best meal of your life."

"I'd love to, Daddy, but I have plans."

"Cancel. I have a special guest coming over to meet you."

"Dad. How many times do I have to tell you I'm in love with Paul before you stop trying to set me up with every Catholic Italian in Los Angeles?"

"Oh, Beaner, you're just going through a phase," he said.

"And what phase would that be, Dad?"

"The, date-a-guy-your-father-hates-just-to-get-under-his-skin-and-slowly-kill-him stage." I could practically see him smirking.

"You haven't even met Paul. How can you hate him?"

"I don't hate him. I just don't like him."

"Yeah, I know. I should *be with a good young Italian boy like Tony here*," I said in a deep tone as I slapped myself on the back like Dad would do to Tony. Then I realized Dad couldn't see my shoulder slap. Too bad, it was a good imitation. "Daddy, I love you. I gotta go."

"I swear, one of these days I'm gonna get through thick head—"

I hung up before he finished.

"Price check on frozen pizza," Momma Honey said.

Kelly

While urinating, I noticed the normal sensation of grit beneath my feet was gone, and the yellowish ring around my toilet was missing.

Strange things like this had been going on for days. The mountain of clothes on my floor had been neatly tucked away into a laundry basket I didn't know I owned. My bed was dressed in fresh sheets that didn't stick to my body when I rolled over.

The décor was new; contemporary paintings replaced my Pearl Jam and Soundgarden posters. Plant life filled the corners instead of the amplifiers and athletic gear I'd kept there. On the mantle in my living room, disturbing little Hummel figurines replaced my old high school trophies. Dusting had revealed that the gray windowsills were actually light brown.

In the five weeks Reece had been living with me, she'd turned my apartment into something that may have actually passed an inspection by the Board of Health. I'd lived in organized man-filth from the day I was born, and though Reece's female touch was another blaring reminder that I'd grown up motherless, she was the joy of my life.

Reece was still mad that I'd misled her into thinking I was rich, but I knew our love would move us past that.

The soft blond hairs on Reece's thigh tickled my leg as we lay in a tangled mass of flesh, still breathing heavy from the love we'd made. We were good together in bed, and our kissing had gotten much better. I never said anything to Reece about her offensive protruding tongue, and over time Reece learned to control it. Our individual styles meshed together naturally into something uniquely ours.

Reece became pregnant on our fourth date because a Cipro prescription rendered her birth control ineffective. This was the biggest blessing of my life. We married immediately, and the five weeks since our marriage had been my happiest. Being loved, for the first time, felt good and warm and tingly just like the movies always made it seem.

I put my ear on Reece's belly. "What are we going to call him?" I asked.

"How do you know it's going to be a boy?" she countered.

"I can hear him rocking out in there. He's going to be a rock star."

"First of all, it's too soon for him to be making any noise. You're hearing things. But if it is a boy, he'll be Theodore."

"Theodore? May I suggest a manlier name?"

"No," she said, joking.

"I get no say in this?"

"Do you want to be the pregnant one for the next seven

months?"

"Yeah, I do. Yeah, let's do that."

"You only say because it can't be done."

"Nuh-huh."

"I'll tell you what, if you carry this baby, you can name it. Otherwise, I'm naming it. Theodore if it's a boy because Theodore sounds distinguished. Xanadu if it's a girl because its artistic and beautiful."

If we had a girl, I'd put my foot down on the Xanadu idea. Xanadu didn't sound artistic or beautiful. It sounded like what it was — a bad Olivia Newton John song.

"Do you want a boy or a girl?" I asked.

"A girl," Reece replied without hesitation.

I expected her to say she didn't care as long as it was healthy.

My ear was still pressed to Reece's belly. He was still rocking out. This little man would play percussion in my band, Christmas Party Junkie, when I called up my college buddies and put the band back together.

I put my mouth to her belly. "How's it going in there, Teddy? I bet it's nice and warm. Enjoy it because in seven months you'll be out here in the real world. Time to get a job. I'm not raising a moocher." I put my ear back on her belly, pretending I was getting a response.

"Please get your fat head off my stomach. I'm sleepy."

I lifted my head and lay down next to Reece. "Goodnight," I said and tried to force myself not to worry. But I knew I'd fail to relax just like every other night since Reece got pregnant. I wanted to believe my mom's death during my birth wasn't my fault, and I wanted to believe I didn't pass the mom-killing gene onto my son. I wanted to believe Reece would give birth without complications.

"Goodnight, Teddy," I said.

"Theodore."

"What?"

"It's going to be Theodore. Don't shorten the name. I hate that."

"Goodnight, Theodore," I said.

December 1997
Paul

My soul felt like my worn-out Van Gogh t-shirt: threadbare and full of holes.

Outside my church, art surrounded me. The flower garden could be a painting; the birds singing atop the steeple could've been crooning a song about love. The homeless man on the corner, begging for change, had lived a novel about loss that needed to be written. Art expresses complex intangible feelings we can't explain any other way. Art is everywhere, art is love; love is God; God is art. They're one and the same, and my job as a preacher is to help my parishioners find art and God within themselves.

"People have forgotten the principle of loving one another. Religion's becoming less about loving God and more about using God as a vehicle to tell other people how to live their lives. We need to change that," I said to my congregation.

But I was a hypocrite, and I knew it; my faith was weak. Vincent Van Gogh, my idol, was one of the best painters to ever live and a man with strong faith, and he was a genius, and I wanted to be that guy. My faith wouldn't let me, and my talent paled in comparison.

Van Gogh went crazy and died. I feared that fate would be our only similarity.

Though I'd only been seeing Maria a short while, she inspired my sermons, no matter how weak my faith. Seven days ago, I delivered one of my best messages ever. Words came from my mouth like divine oral ejaculations. I read from the book of Matthew like Jesus was speaking through me.

I wonder if Jesus would like me if we met.

Recently, I'd noticed dark circles around Maria's eyes, and her body was shrinking. Her skin looked unhealthy, her beautiful long dark hair was thinning, and her knees became knobby, like softballs wedged between two sticks. She denied being bulimic or anorexic, but it was a problem.

After the service, Maria came to my private quarters.

"Maria, let's go to brunch today instead of walking in the park."

"Hmm. How about brunch and then a walk?" She bartered

"Deal. Wait here for me, I've got to mingle."

"Okay."

I went outside the church to chat with what was left of my congregation. Usually, it's just a few elderly women who wait to speak with me, most of them wanting to invite me to brunch to meet a daughter or niece.

"Paul, great sermon today."

"Thank you."

"Paul, this may be a sensitive issue, but I want to talk to you about Maria."

"Who are you?" I asked.

"I'm a therapist, and I can help her."

I felt shame. And then anger. Shame that Maria's condition made me look bad as a preacher, anger that I couldn't help her. "I have to go," I said. I shook her hand, said hello to a couple other people, and then returned to my quarters to get Maria.

We went to brunch in the type of upscale place in Brentwood where the waiters wear white gloves and refill your coffee every thirty seconds.

Maria ordered a boiled egg, coffee, and a glass of champagne. Nothing more. She reached across the table for the pepper shaker. The skin, at the point where her arm meets her armpit, was loose and empty. It was gross.

"Maria. You look horrible."

"I'm doing the best I can to get thin. I can't help it if I'm genetically predisposed to be fat."

"That's not what I meant! You're anorexic and sick, and it needs to end now. Today."

Maria started crying. But I didn't feel bad about it.

"Why are you being such a jerk, Paul?"

"Why? Are you serious? Maria, you're so skinny you're barely a person anymore."

Her face crinkled in anger. "You're a jerk!"

Maria ran out of the restaurant. I followed. She got in a cab. I feared I'd never see her again.

Then I thought about her gangster father, and worried for my safety.

I was surprised the next day to learn Maria had listened to me and checked into Promises rehabilitation. The next month was horrific. My loneliness became a cross I couldn't bear. My sermons lost their energy and inspiration, and my nights were filled with nothing but bad memories. I needed Maria around to keep me in the present, keep me happy, keep me full of love, and help me push my hatred aside.

I wallowed, alone, for the next month, in a pit of self-pity.

Finally, thirty long days passed. Maria graduated and checked out of Promises. She'd gained about ten pounds and looked healthy and beautiful.

When I picked her up, the first thing she said was *thank you.* The second was *Do I look fat?*

"No, baby, you look perfect."

Maria's eating disorder was going to be a lifelong battle, but at the moment I was just happy to have her back. I held her for a solid minute.

"I love you, Maria, and I'm sorry."

"Don't be sorry. You told me the truth."

Maria smiled at me, and I knew I'd been forgiven.

In the car on the ride home, I put my pinky on top of Maria's. It felt right. The month without her was like a year, and I never again wanted to not be touching her.

T.J.

I'd yet to land an audition.

I hated my busboy job as much as I hated my first two jobs.

I hated my neighborhood and was afraid of the residents in the projects across the street.

I got a concussion the first time I tried to surf. Running with my board, I tripped on the leash, fell, and smacked my head on the sand before making it to the water.

My roommate was a professional contortionist who chewed his toenails and left them all over our living room.

Through all this, I would not give up my dream of acting.

But the event last month put me over the edge. I came home from work and found some Mexican gangbanger shot up and bleeding to death outside my apartment complex. I tried not to panic. I went inside, dialed 911, went outside and put my pillow under his head and my comforter over his cooling body. I waited for the police, gave a quick report, and left immediately for the airport.

Reality was that I couldn't make it as an actor. I failed and was depressed, and this wounded Mexican was the final straw.

I moved home to my parent's place. Dad was right again.

I hate that.

Today, New Year's Eve, sitting in my parent's attic, I realized how pathetic and lonely my life had become.

Life is all about love. Everything — hate, lust, money, power, death, birth — it all stems from love. If life were put in a giant pot and boiled like a piece of chicken, all the fat would melt away, and what you'd be left with is love. In this huge world, this giant cauldron full of beautiful women wanting love, why couldn't just one spill over into my lap?

For 364 days a year, not being in love sucks. Then, one day a year, New Year's Eve, when it comes time for the traditional midnight kiss, not being in love is about the most painful thing in the world.

I was in my parents' attic at five minutes until 1998. It was an usually cold winter night. It had stopped snowing, but the heavy pitter-patter of small hailstones pounded against the south side of the house. Icicles hung in the windows like prison bars. I didn't feel like watching Dick Clark with my parents, so I stayed in the attic leafing through old photo albums.

I found a photograph from a celebration of my eighth birthday at Skatetown. I skated hand-in-hand with Angela Harding. I had a devastating crush on her that blew my world apart. She's remained perfect in my imagination since she moved away in fourth grade. Tonight, the picture gave me the same ache to be wanted by her I experienced back then.

At midnight, I kissed Angela's picture and closed the photo album. Angela wouldn't be my girl then, and if I bumped into her now, she still wouldn't.

Almost every woman in my shit-hole hometown of Bunker Hill, Oregon, was married, and the ones who weren't were unmarried for a reason. The nearest major city, Eugene, was loaded with nothing but beer–guzzling, granola eating, hippy chicks with hairy legs and pits.

I was depressed. Back with my parents for just over a month, it took exactly one minute into the New Year for me to realize moving home with my father was a cowardly mistake. I needed to go back to Los Angeles, the city of four million beautiful single women, and make it work.

And that's exactly what I planned to do.

Skye

I was backstage at O'Malley's in my hometown of Oakland, getting ready to play my first gig outside of L.A. I stared at the Oakland Athletics baseball pennant hanging in the dressing room. It wasn't long ago that I was a five-year-old girl who loved sitting on the couch with my Dad, cheering for the stupid Athletics. Those first five years of my life were almost normal. Then, my Dad lost his job, and soon after we lost our house. My Dad's casual cocaine habit became a full-blown crack addiction, and we ended up in a two-room apartment in the east side slums. It was the type of apartment where a family might stay, but nobody really lives.

All we had was a microwave, and a television which was always on. Television is a great way to avoid talking to your family. Dad and I spent all day at home watching television. Dad smoked his crack and paced around, sometimes punching holes in the walls. He only hit me once that first year.

Mom became a functional crack user, working twelve to fourteen hours a day to support their habit. At night, she'd come home, and they'd smoke and fight like I wasn't there. Mom didn't leave him. I'll never understand why.

Mom's habit eventually got her fired, and we lost the only source of income we had. So, my parents started locking me in the apartment at night when they went out to make money; Mom would pull tricks, and Dad hustled crack. The size of their habit continued to grow, but their income didn't.

I was about seven years old when Dad started whoring me out to freaks and perverts. I have no idea where he even found these people, but they came from somewhere, and they had money, which outweighed his guilt; if he had any.

Luckily, it only happened a couple times before some junkie informed my mother about the disgusting things my father was doing. Dad was crashed on the couch when Mom came home with a baseball bat. I watched as she came down on his face with it.

Dad didn't move. He didn't even open his eyes. Mom grabbed

me, and we ran. We stayed at a friend's house and went to a shelter for a couple weeks while we searched for something permanent. We never found a home because Mom got arrested for soliciting sex to the wrong guy. I was sent to an orphanage.

I became a traveler of orphanages. I spent my time either using drugs or trying to find a way to get them. By the time I was fifteen I felt forty.

Finally, in 1994, not yet sixteen-years-old, I ran away to Los Angeles to chase my dream of making music. And now, today, backstage at O'Malley's, the Athletics pennant made me think of my dad. To this day, I don't know if he survived my mother's attack, nor do I care. He's gone and I'm free of him, but I'll never be free from what he did.

Nobody's truly free. Everyone is prisoner to a secret, a sin, a lie. It wasn't by accident that, in the *Star Spangled Banner,* Francis Scott Key set the word "free" to a note so high nobody could attain it.

I snorted one last ganking line, grabbed my guitar, and took the stage. "Are you guys ready to rock tonight?" I yelled to the small crowd of about a hundred and fifty people.

Music and drugs were the only two things that dulled my anger. When I'm performing, everything is automatic and easy, like I'm hovering in air that's thick with ether. I stop thinking and let the music out in screams, ripping chords, and angry verses.

I played my heart out. The gig was the last on this little mini-tour, and judging by the general public's overall poor response to me, I didn't know if there'd be another.

I went to the airport to fly back to Los Angeles, defeated.

T.J.

I was in the Oakland airport on layover. I was heading back to the sexy Los Angeles sunshine. This would be my final move.

An Asian girl in a white US Airways button-down, khakis, and a matching headband talked to a slender blonde with yellow hoop bracelets that went from her wrists to her elbows. The blonde was cute, but then another girl crossed in front of her, and she stole my attention.

She had a guitar slung over her shoulder, sexy as it gets. My eyes traced the curve of her buttocks down to the bottom of her tight skirt where the hem dug into her thigh. Then my gaze fell into the crease in the back of her knee, on down to the bubble of her calf, which narrowed into a tight cord at the back of her heel which was enveloped in a black sneaker.

She sat three rows away from me. All I could see was the back of her head. I got up, circled, and sat across from her. Not yet ready for eye contact, I stared down at the worn, grayish carpet where hints of green and red hid beneath muck left by thousands of travelers. I picked up a magazine and pretended to read it while stealing subtle glances of the girl. She crossed her left leg over her right, uncrossed, and crossed right over left. She caught me staring at her crotch, and my eyes ducked for cover behind the magazine. But I couldn't resist for long. Soon I was peering over the magazine again.

She scribbled something in a notebook. I needed to know what she wrote. Had I piqued her interest? Was she writing about me? She looked about eighteen, but could've been twenty-five. Whatever her age, I wanted her. It'd been too long since I'd been with a woman. Somehow, I needed to find the courage to talk to her. Over the years, I'd developed intense crushes on strangers who I never spoke to. I needed to get some courage or I'd never meet a woman; I'd never find love. I'd be stuck going from one innocuous and unrequited crush to another.

"Go say hello," said the large, blue-haired woman seated next to me.

I played dumb. "Huh?"

"She knows you're looking."

"What are you talking about?"

The old woman grabbed my magazine, turned it right-side-up, and put it back in my hands. Then, in a burly voice loud enough for everyone to hear, she said, "I've never seen a guy so interested in *Modern Bride*. Maybe it's more interesting when it's upside down."

The pretty girl hid her face behind her notebook. My face burned with red-hot embarrassment; I became more uncomfortable about blushing, and then I blushed more.

The girl would see my discomfort and her chuckle would turn to a laugh. Everyone would laugh, their giggles hovering around me like vultures. My face would get redder and redder until there was not enough room in my face to contain my embarrassment. Boils would erupt from my face. The girl would get one look at my sickly face and vomit. The vomiting would become contagious, and everyone would vomit. It'd be too much to handle, and I'd become the first person to legitimately die of embarrassment. At my funeral, they'd say nice things about me, but they'd all be thinking of how pathetic I was. My epitaph would read:

Here lies T.J. He died of embarrassment.

I needed to get out of the airport.

I should run.

"Go say hello," the old woman said again, loudly, clearly enjoying herself.

By this point, I pretty much had to go say hi. I sucked in a deep breath, got up, and went in for the score.

As I got closer, I noticed she had the bluest eyes I'd ever seen. They were impossible not to fall into. Lost in admiration, my foot caught the strap of someone's carry-on, and I crashed face-down at her feet. I could feel the eyes of everyone staring at me like I were an obese, transvestite, Eskimo, dwarf. People were laughing. Their laughter sounded muffled and polite, like a sitcom laugh track under water.

I considered lying on the ground until everyone in the terminal had boarded; it was only a half hour away, and I'd just peed fifteen minutes ago, so I was pretty sure I could wait it out. If I didn't look up, then the fall never really happened. I'd be invisible, like a little kid who disappears from the world by closing his eyes.

Or maybe I could get up and pretend I fell because of an old football injury which left me with a trick knee.

Yeah, that's it. I used to play high school football, and I took one too many hits to the knee. I'm crippled now, but, wow, you should have seen me run back in the day. I ran like lightning. The scouts said I'd have gone pro if I hadn't injured my knee. Old men in town still talk about how I ran. *Damn, T.J. Martini was a gazelle.* The cute girl would be turned on by my athletic prowess. She'd want to take me home and nurture my knee and make babies with me so her babies would get my athletic prowess.

Skye

When he fell at my feet, I laughed. But then he just lay there, which was odd.

"Are you okay?" I asked, standing over him. "You need a hand?" He didn't answer me. "Excuse me. Can I give you a hand?"

"Uh, no, actually. It's nice down here. I'm considering leasing this tiny little area of real estate."

At least he had a sense of humor.

"Let me help you up." I extended a hand. He took it, hopped to his feet, and mumbled something lame about an old football injury.

His face was blood red. "Thank you," he said.

"So, you getting married soon?" I asked.

"What?"

"*Modern Bride* magazine?" He had the magazine in his hand.

"Umm, I. Well. No, no, I'm not,"

"You a wedding planner?" I teased.

"Umm. No." He threw the magazine backwards over his head. It hit an old lady. I laughed, but only because was completely unaware of what he'd done. "Look, to be honest, I thought you were cute, and I was looking at this magazine until I could think of something impressive to say to you."

"Your one-and-a-half-twist was pretty impressive."

"It was a full double-twist. I was on the diving team in high school."

"I thought you played football."

"Yeah, I, dove, I mean, I dived, err, I was a diver after football season."

"Oh, really. Is football season before or after fibbing season?"

"I'm sorry, I'll leave you alone," he said. He lowered his head and started walking away.

"I'm Skye."

He stopped, turned and smiled. "I'm T.J. It's an excruciating pleasure to meet you, Skye." Some of the red drained from his face, and a more suiting pale pink remained. T.J. was sort of cute in a nerdy Michael J. Fox *Family Ties* kind of way. "Do you mind if I sit with you for a minute or two while we wait?"

"You might as well."

T.J. sat down. He had a long pointy nose with a bulbous point, light brown hair, and hazel eyes. He was thin, but with a little potbelly.

"What were you scribbling in your notebook?" T.J. asked.

"Song lyrics."

"Really? Wow. So you're a musician. Why are you going to L.A.?"

"Los Angeles is home. I'm going back to record my first album."

"Really? Wow, that's exciting."

"Yeah, I'm happy about it. So, what's your story?"

"I'm moving back to Los Angeles. My degree is in communications, but before I begin a life of boredom, I wanted to take another shot at acting."

"Another shot?"

"Yeah, my first shot failed."

"I hope it works out for you."

"Me too. So, tell me about your music."

"Music's my life. Hopefully it will all materialize into something. I'm not getting my hopes up or anything, but I'm keeping my fingers crossed."

T.J. crossed his fingers and showed them to me. "After you make it big, I can tell all my friends back home I knew Skye before she was famous. You're lucky to make a living doing what you love."

T.J. was right. In making music, I'm able to create something concrete people can put their ears on. I couldn't imagine working every day in a cubicle, punching numbers into a computer. That kind of work is empty. It has no heart. Music's the only thing I love, and it's the only thing that loves me.

We talked for a while. To my surprise, I wasn't totally annoyed. There was something endearing about him, and he wasn't shamelessly trying to get in my pants.

The terminal was packed like it always is around the holidays. If I breathed in hard enough, I could smell the alcohol dripping out of the pores of holiday binge drinkers. One guy had both his shoes off and had been running the toes of his left foot up and down his right leg for the last fifteen minutes. Getting tweaked before a flight when you're about to be trapped in a small vessel with total strangers is hardcore; it's like teasing the gods of paranoia. Thinking about his high gave me the craving. I excused myself and went to the bathroom to do the fat line I'd stashed in the liner of my carry-on.

When I came out of the bathroom, I heard, "Skye Garucci and T.J. Martini, please report to gate 32C." T.J. and I had apparently gotten so wrapped up in conversation that we'd nearly missed boarding. I hustled to the gate, and there was T.J., waiting for me, smiling.

Ron Griffin, 27

This is what I scribbled in my journal on the day I took off for Los Angeles:

'It was my first time flying, and I had mixed feelings. I was happy to be free, but scared about what I'd do with that freedom.'

There's not much to do in prison but journal, so I've filled up quite a few Mead notebooks with my thoughts.

At the airport, watching all the planes take off made me think of all the sad days I spent as a teenager gluing together model Air Force fighter planes. But the goal of today's new journey was to leave all that ancient history behind. I had a two-hour flight to dream up a new life.

> *Me miserable! Which way shall I fly*
> *Infinite wrath, and infinite despair?*
> *Which way I fly is Hell; myself am Hell;*
> *And, in the lowest deep, a lower deep*
> *Still threatening to devour me opens wide,*
> *To which the Hell I suffer seems a Heaven.*
> *O, then, at last relent: Is there no place*
> *Left for repentance, none for pardon left?*

This piece of *Paradise Lost (IV)* by John Milton circled my consciousness. Anxiety plagued my thoughts and dried my mouth.

I boarded. A pretty girl started cramming her guitar into the storage bin above my seat. With her arms extended overhead, her tank top rode up her belly and exposed her navel. It'd been a long time since I'd seen a pretty woman's navel; simple pleasures such as this were the things I didn't realize I'd miss until they were gone.

"Hi," she said as she sat down. She seemed young, but she had a hardened look I'd become familiar with. She pulled out a notepad and started scribbling.

The stewardess explained the emergency procedure and then, minutes later, we took off. The powerful acceleration thrilled me; liftoff made me feel heavy in my seat; objects below us grew smaller as we soared higher into a blanket of clouds so thick that the wing tips disappeared. The last of the white clouds slipped behind us as we broke through into blue air. The plane continued its climb; it seemed to go so high I grew concerned we were nearing the definitive spot where the colorful atmosphere yields to the blackness of outer space.

Eventually, the plane leveled, and the 'fasten seat belt' light turned off. A ray of sunlight came in through the window and ran across the face of the girl with the guitar. Her pupils had contracted, and her eyes filled up with the most spectacular shade of blue. I grabbed my notebook and penned:

Blue like the thick mist of a waterfall.

Blue like the color of lust after it cools.

Blue like blueberries a day or two before they're ripe.

I wanted to talk to her, but my social skills had become rusty. I had no idea what to say. *Hi, I liked your guitar. Are you in a band?*

No good. Maybe I should try to sound young and hip. *Heard the new Coldplay album?*

Or maybe something smart. *Have you read* Naked *by David Sedaris? He's so witty—*

"Excuse me, sir, this may sound weird, but Skye and I were talking earlier in the terminal, and I was hoping to continue our conversation," said some pale-faced dork, trying to butt in. "Could I pay you to trade seats with me?" he asked.

Only rich men behave this obnoxiously.

"What's it worth to you?" I asked. I needed money in a bad way.

"How about twenty bucks?"

"Twenty bucks? Is two hours of engaging conversation with me worth only twenty bucks?" she asked him.

"I think two hours with you would be worth about five hundred," I said.

"Yeah, at least that," she said.

"Your company's worth ten times that, but I only have a hundred dollars," he said.

"Liar," I replied. Then, he opened his wallet and showed me.

"It's a deal for a hundred," I said.

"Deal."

I stood up; he took my seat and handed me his ticket. 32B.

I walked down the aisle. Cute girl in 22A, cute girl in 29C, sexy older lady in 30C. I found 32B; unfortunately; there was a fast talking Oriental in 32C. The Oriental spoke loudly to an elderly stewardess who couldn't understand a word he said. His Chinese-Japanese-Taiwanese-whatever-ese accent was as thick as the hair on my grandfather's back.

To make matters worse, a fat, greasy wetback with blue hair came out of the bathroom, and I just knew this woman, who was big enough to play middle linebacker for the Eagles, would sit next to me.

"I'm 32A," she said , squeezing her fat ass past me. She plopped down in her seat, tilting the entire plane.

"What name?" the slant-eyed Oriental asked, practically yelling as he spoke. "What name?" he asked again.

People shouldn't be allowed into my country until they learn proper English.

"My name's Ron," I said.

"I a Ron Too. Ha Ha. Dat Funny. Nice Hat! It Leather?" He asked, yelling every syllable like each was a sentence in its own right. Then, without asking, he grabbed at my black leather Oakland Athletics hat.

I slapped his hand away, "Don't touch."

Old Blue Hair ripped a fart. "Excuse me."

"Ha Ha Ha Ha!" The yellow man made no effort to hide his amusement.

Blue Hair ignored him. "Ma'am, may I have a margarita?" She asked the elderly stewardess.

I almost rang the call bell to request a seat change, but then something changed. It smelt heavenly.

It smelled like southern jazz in a smoky room.

Like a Sunday afternoon watching football.

Or a freshly opened bottle of Jack Daniels.

The smell was both calming and exciting.

In my periphery, the Mexican lady dug through her Tex-Mex sized purse. Beneath wads of used tissues, *Oprah* magazines, and make-up and creams that couldn't possibly disguise her girth, there lay a stash of folded hundred dollar bills. There had to be at least twenty of them. I swear to God I could smell it. It had that sweet musty smell of money that's been in a dark safe for decades.

My parole ended two days ago, and I was finally completely free. I decided to move to L.A. for a fresh start, but I didn't have any money. I wanted to go straight, but Blue Hair's money taunted me; it gave me the middle finger and stuck out its tongue.

The lady downed margaritas at record pace. Eventually, Old Blue Hair would have to get up to take a piss.

January 1998
Dr. Juan Salazar, 35

Gina was the only thing made me feel connected to this world, and I knew I couldn't keep her.

Tonight, Gina and I met in the penthouse suite of The Standard Hotel in Hollywood. The suite was huge and swanky, and the price reflected it.

Gina, naked, was as beautiful as anything I'd ever seen. I took Gina's hand and sat down next to her on the bed. I inhaled. She always had the same unique scent; a faint musk hidden by the fresh flowers she wore in her hair.

"Let's order room service," I said.

I was thirty five. Gina was twelve. I knew our relationship was wrong, but I didn't understand how society equated my love for Gina with crimes such as murder and rape. Still, as a doctor, I knew my affair with Gina was harmful to her mental development, and my desire for her was a constant mental tug-of-war. Everyday, I hated myself a little more for loving Gina, but I couldn't stop.

Room service knocked. Gina hid in the bathroom when the delivery boy came in with two large, cracked crabs drenched in garlic and butter. Their succulent texture seduced our mouths. The crab was accompanied by steamed asparagus and a bottle of the hotel's most expensive champagne. I only let Gina have one glass.

"Juan. I'm ready tonight," Gina said, after dinner.

"What do you mean?" I asked.

"I want you to do more than look at me. I want to do it with you."

"Gina, I want to so badly," I said, throbbing. "I want it more than anything in this world. But it's not right… It's time for you to get dressed and go home."

In all our meetings, I never let things go further than light petting. Gina was a dangerous young girl, determined to be with an older man, and I considered myself the guardian of her innocence. However, soon I'd be gone.

Staying gentlemanly became more difficult every visit as Gina's moans of pleasure grew more intense. Somehow, I managed to remain stoic. I never touched her between her legs, I never put my mouth on her, and I never exposed my erection. But my urges were getting stronger, and I no longer trusted my willpower.

"I'm not going home. My mom thinks I'm staying at my friend's tonight."

"Really?"

"I want to have sex. I'm ready."

"Not tonight, Gina." I pulled my wallet out and gave Gina five hundred dollars. I'd never given her more than twenty dollars before. Though Gina never asked me for anything, I loved her so much I couldn't stand not to give to her. This is what men do for the women they love.

"Oh my God! Thank you so much, Juan!" Gina's tiny mouth parted to a great big smile. That smile was her gift to me, something beautiful to keep for eternity. "Why are you giving me this?"

"Because I want to. Promise you'll think of me when you spend it."

"I will."

"And, Gina—"

"Yeah?"

And then, for a splinter of a moment, I considered killing her. Not because I wanted her dead, but because I wanted to protect her from growing up. It'd be better for me to kill Gina than to watch the world hand her a slow, ugly death.

But the thought was fleeting.

"You shouldn't take your clothes off for old men like me. It's not right."

Gina didn't say another word. She finished getting dressed, kissed me on the mouth, and left. I cried after she left. Gina was the only real love of my life. I was freeing her, and I would never love again.

Left to my own devices, I stepped onto the balcony and gazed out on the moonless night. Tonight's black had a different tint. A slight breeze rippled through the tall palm trees, and I tried not to hear the demons above me, flapping their rubbery wings, waiting to descend upon me and eat my soul.

I took the bottle of Valium out of my pocket. I'd written a million prescriptions for Valium, but I'd never tried one. I put a few in my mouth and chewed. They had a light, chalky texture. I washed them down with my last sip of champagne.

Three is not enough.

I took three more, chewed them to a paste, and swallowed. Then I composed a note to God. I had nobody else to write:

God, life is too much, too hard. It's not worth the effort to keep clean, to feed my body, to fight infection, to fight my own desires. Life's too much work to justify the anemic payoff. Regardless, my heart continues to beat no matter how badly I want it to stop. I wish you'd made me normal, but you didn't. You made me a beast that lusts after the clean flesh of young girls. Therefore, because you made me this way, I should be spared punishment for mortal sin I'm about to commit. I'm ridding this world of the monster you created. Have mercy on me.

God is a sadist.

On the count of eleven, I'd jump.

"One, two, three, four, five, six."

Dylan

"A lobotomized chimpanzee could do my job. Thinking is completely unnecessary," I said, on the phone with my little sister.

"A hemiplegic golden retriever could do your job," she replied.

"Yup. If I'm still working some lame office job when I turn thirty, promise me you'll put cyanide in my birthday beer and end my misery."

"I promise," she said.

Most men would never leave their homes were it not for sex, food, and drugs. Unfortunately, work is a necessary evil to obtain these things. Very few people are lucky enough to love what they do for a living. I am not one of the lucky ones.

Predictably, I was fired from Crustaceans. In my new job, working for an airline, I spend nine to five in a tiny cubicle that feels like a vise tightening around my skull. The cramped space feels smaller every day, and I fear if I work there much longer my brain will be squeezed out through the open orifices of my face.

Today, in the break room at lunch, I sat next to the water cooler, beneath the motivational poster of the skydiver.

Success: It doesn't come to you. You have to go get it.

Every day, I look at that poster and consider standing on my chair to *get it* so I can take *it* into the bathroom and wipe my ass with *it* after a *successful* shit.

Shortly after I started on my meatloaf sandwich, the rest of the work crew arrived: Lawrence, the speed eater; Monique, the large-breasted fingernail chewer; Brent, the belcher; Stephanie, the fast talker; and Dave and Larry, Monique's breast gawkers. I despised these androids more than my horrific job, so I ate quickly and went back to work early.

"Hello. Thank you for calling Freedom Airlines. This is Dylan, how may I be of service?"

"Money was stolen from my purse on my flight to Los Angeles," cried a woman who sounded fat.

"That sucks."

"Excuse me?"

"I said, how much? How much did they get from you?"

She told me her name was Mrs. Bernadette Salazar. The airline records showed the man sitting next to her was someone named T.J. Martini.

"Ma'am, I'm going to transfer you to security. They'll assist you."

"Thank you."

I had four more hours of work before I could go home and get naked with my new fling, Mandy. Mandy and I were no good for each other, but she was a suitable diversion to the boredom of my routine life.

Dr. Juan Salazar

After being too much a chicken to jump off the balcony at the Standard Hotel, I tried other ways of ending my life. I tasted paint thinner, but couldn't get myself to swallow. I tried to overdose on alcohol and pills while watching an *I Love Lucy* marathon, but I'd never been a big drinker, and was unconscious from the alcohol before I made it to the pill swallowing part. I bought a gun, but I couldn't pull the trigger because the thought of my own blood made me pass out.

I was too big a coward to kill myself. So, to make life bearable, I had to change.

Today, I visited Dr. Scheps for a psychiatric evaluation. We were halfway through the session, and the only thing we'd accomplished was confirming what I'd already long suspected: we, psychiatrists, are a waste of money. We pair our worthless jibber-jabber with powerful medications to fix problems we don't fully understand.

"This analysis isn't helping, Doc. My life is constant self-analysis. I even do it in my sleep. I wish we could just paralyze the part of my brain that does the thinking."

"I want to erase everything I've ever learned and live on instinct."

"Our ability to think and to reason is what separates us from animals. It's what makes us human."

"Well, maybe being human is overrated. I mean, chickens never get depressed. Crocodiles never worry about their sexuality."

He wrote something down; his mannerisms were pretentious. I wondered if I came across the same way to my patients. "Interesting. Tell me more about your sexuality."

"What more do you want to hear? I already told you I'm not gay."

"But you've said before that vaginas disturb you."

"Yes."

"Why?"

"They're unclean," I said.

He shuffled through papers. I picked up his Rubik's Cube paperweight and started aligning colors.

"So how do you know you aren't gay?" he asked.

"Because the penis grosses me out, too. Thinking about ejaculation makes me sick, even my own. I'm so fucked up I wear gloves when I masturbate. I shower immediately afterward, and I always wash my penis exactly eleven times."

"Why eleven?"

"I don't know. I just have to. Eleven. One-one. It's a sharp, clean number."

"I'm sure I don't need to tell you that's a compulsive behavior," he said. He took off his glasses, wiped them, and put them back on.

"I'm aware. I don't know how I ended up like this. I wasn't always such a disaster."

"Juan, you're a psychiatrist. I'm sure if you step away from your situation and look at yourself through scholar's eyes, you'll be able to figure everything out. When did you start behaving this way?" Dr. Scheps asked.

"Believe me, you don't want to go there."

"Have you ever talked about it before?"

"No."

"Talking about it with someone else is the first step toward discovery."

"Well, it hasn't exactly come up."

"Tell me," he insisted.

"No. There's no point."

"Then why did you come here?" he asked. He had a cocky smirk on his face that made me want to strike him.

I didn't want to talk about it, but then my mouth opened, and the words started coming out. "I was thirteen, and my best friend Tamara was twelve. One evening, we walked down to the Santa Monica Pier to drink." I put down the Rubik's Cube that I'd been playing with. "You know, this is stupid," I said.

He scratched his ear with his pencil, "Please continue."

I let out a sigh. I didn't want to talk about this, but knew I needed to. I just needed him to give me a little shove.

"If you won't tell me, I can't help you."

"Fine," I said. "I'll tell you, but it's not pretty. We were at the Pier. There were usually other kids or some homeless people down there, but that night, we were alone. Tamara touched my hand in a way that felt new. Then she kissed my cheek. I kissed her back, and we started heavy kissing." I hesitated to choke back the tears that were about to flow. My lip began quivering so much it blocked the words from coming out.

"Go on," Dr. Scheps said.

"Well, out of nowhere, I felt a kick in my side. I dropped. When I got up off the sand, two drunk white guys were standing over us, laughing at us!" I said, pounding the table with my fists. I could feel the anger rising. "They were probably in their early twenties. *Go on, keep kissing her,* the one guy yelled. I got scared and froze. He kicked me again, this time harder. *Kiss that fucking spic bitch, you fucking wetback!* I kissed her, and they laughed and spit on us."

"What else happened?" the Doctor asked, sounding too riveted. It didn't matter; there was no stopping me now.

"The other guy punched Tamara in the stomach and tore off her dress. *Lick her fucking greasy spic twat!* They commanded. I refused. The other guy kicked me in the back of the head. I was dizzy and scared and confused, and I didn't know what to do," I said, tears streaming down my face.

"It's okay, Juan. It wasn't your fault," Doctor Scheps said.

My stomach knotted. I was sure I was going to throw up. "Again, they ordered me to lick her down there, and I didn't want to, but I was afraid of these men, so I did it. I licked her!"

I put my hands over my face in shame. I didn't want to share anymore, but the words kept coming.

"I remember the taste. The horrid taste. She was having her period that day. I'll never forget that taste. They told me to stop and I erupted into tears and was shaking all over, but Tamara just sat there, expressionless. She didn't even try to cover up. *Now get the fuck out of here!* Tamara and I got up and started running. *Not you!* One guy yelled at Tamara. He tackled her. I never looked back. I ran all the way home," I said.

Dr. Scheps didn't say anything, but he looked repulsed. I disgusted myself. I was less than human.

"Tamara and I never spoke after that. The next day my parents told me Tamara had been mugged. Nobody said anything about rape. But I knew."

"Juan, it wasn't your fault."

"Bullshit. That's such fucking psychiatric, cliché bullshit! It was my fault! I should've been brave. I should've protected her! I shouldn't have run!"

"They may have killed you. Juan, this is the root of all your problems. You've got to forgive yourself."

"Yeah, it's really fucking obvious. I'm a textbook case. So what? Knowing this doesn't fix me! God made me a freak!"

"Juan, surely you're more logical than to blame God."

"Am I? I'm the only thirty-five-year-old virgin in Los Angeles. And it's not because I can't get laid. It's because I don't want to fuck. I don't even like the sound of the word. Making love sounds nice, sure, but it's only different than fucking in name. Fucking is impossible for me because I can't deal with the close-up smells of human breath, body odor, hair, and worst of all, blood. The exchange of saliva frightens me, and STDs terrify me. The mere thought of contracting herpes has set me into an uncontrollable panic attack at least twice, which is two times more than a virgin should ever panic about herpes. And a relationship? Forget about it. I'd sooner put a bullet in my head than have to deal with the filth of a woman when she's bleeding. So, please, tell me, doctor, what the hell does any of this craziness have to do with Tamara?"

"Juan, you already know the answers," he said.

"Right. I associate all sex, the smells and the fluids and everything with my experience with Tamara on her period that day. It's made me some weird asexual being, right, Doctor?"

Dr. Scheps said nothing. He just raised an arrogant eyebrow.

"Well that isn't it! Because you know what? I'm not asexual. In fact, I crave sex. I have wet dreams. And, ironically, in my dreams, the sex is as dirty as it gets! But then, when I wake back up into reality, I have no choice but immediately to wash my sheets because they're stained with my disgusting semen."

He picked a book off his shelf and handed it to me. "Your dreams are similar to the binge dreams drug addicts have when they detox. You dream of sex because your body craves it, but when you're conscious, your phobias overpower the cravings. Read this," he said, extending the book to me.

I pushed his hand away. "You're wrong, Doc! When I'm awake, my sexual cravings don't go away. They just shift to young girls. Little girls are the one thing the sexual impulses of my body and the phobias of my brain can compromise on. But young girls are forbidden to me, and that, consequently, has made me the loneliest person in the world."

Dr. Scheps gave me more worthless advice and explained more things to me I already knew. Typically, a psychiatrist can fool a patient by telling him the root of his problem can be fixed with this pill, that support group, and more psychiatry appointments. They don't tell the patient that the really fucked up people, like me, never get better. They mask their diseases by dousing themselves in heavy narcotics to numb their sickness for years until the peaceful eternal sleep comes and takes them away.

Sometimes, the only thing I want out of life is a comfortable place to die.

February 1998
Beth

I sat at the kitchen table in our small, two-bedroom apartment. Amber gave me my pre-natal vitamins with a tall glass of milk.

"What are you cooking? I'm hungry."

"You're always hungry," Amber said.

"Yeah, I guess. Thanks for cooking."

"A pregnant woman is a queen and should be treated as such."

Since I'd moved in with Amber, she'd been spoiling me with attention no man could match. Amber cooked, cleaned, and shopped. She held my hair when I threw up in the mornings. I wished I could make myself into a lesbian and live with Amber and give her what I felt she wanted. But it doesn't work that way.

Though I was still afraid about having my baby without Jackson, I'd begun to embrace my pregnancy and do the fun things pregnant women do.

"You coming with me later today to pick out some baby outfits?" I asked.

"Wouldn't miss it."

I intended to be the best mother I could to Jonathon.

Amber

Things were finally going decently for me. Beth and I were getting along great, I'd just gotten my daughter a bicycle, and I'd enrolled in nursing school. While waiting for Beth to get off work, I went to the Laemmle Theater in Santa Monica to see an indie flick. Afterwards, rushing to pick up Beth, I wasn't aware of my surroundings as I should be in a parking structure.

"Give me your wallet!" He yelled.

Terrified, I straightened like a soldier. A paralyzing fear ran like a cold chill down my spine. After all this time, Kimberly's father had found me.

"Don't hurt me."

"Give me your purse."

I did.

"Now, lie down and count to thirty."

I did.

He disappeared.

My body was convulsing with tremors as I got in my car. I was both disgusted with myself and relieved. I was disgusted because I didn't defend myself. I let myself be the victim again. I was relieved because I knew it wasn't Kimberly's father. He wouldn't hold me up for my wallet. He would want something much more important to me. He'd want Kimberly.

This incident taught me one valuable lesson. When he did finally find us I may not be able to trust myself to have the strength to fight back. Because of that, my daughter would never be completely safe with me. I had to take further action to ensure her safety.

Beth

I knew something was wrong with Amber while we were shopping. I'd pick up the cutest outfits, and she wouldn't notice or comment. She was unlike herself. That night, I cornered her and asked about it. She withheld, but in the middle of the night, I awoke to her cries..

"Amber, wake up. What's wrong?"

She woke. "Oh… nothing. Just a bad dream."

I knew she was lying. "Amber, it's okay. Tell me."

And she did. She told me about the mugger she encountered this afternoon. It was horrible to hear, but it felt good to be able to help. In our relationship, I've always been the baby bird and Amber the nursing mother.

After she opened up about the mugging, she seemed uneasy. She didn't sleep well for weeks. It felt like she was withholding some information. I mean, being mugged is traumatic, but Amber is a tough girl, and I know for fact that she'd been through far worse. I couldn't believe that getting mugged was what kept her awake during the nights.

For the next couple weeks, Amber was a paranoid mess. She never left the house other than to work. She stayed in and cooked for me every night; cooking was her way to avoid dealing with the real world.

Amber fed me constantly, but somehow almost all my new pregnancy weight was in my round belly. I had the same arms, same legs, same face and neck—and this ridiculous looking belly.

Many nights I'd wake up in a pool of my sweat, actually terrified by the recurring nightmare of giving birth to a basketball.

And almost every single one of those times, Amber was there to take me in her arms and comfort me. It felt, to me, that she'd been awake the whole time, just lying there, watching me. It was obvious that there was something on her mind.

Today, fresh out of the shower, I observed my naked profile in the full-length mirror. I wasn't glowing.

Why don't I have a pregnant glow?

I felt a tickle in my belly like dozens of spiders were setting up a web of flytraps. Then, something wrong happened, and I screamed "Holy crap!"

Amber burst in the bathroom wearing only her white cotton panties. "What?"

"Look at this!"

Amber looked at my nakedness. "Newsflash Beth: I've seen it before."

"No, not that. Look!" I pointed at my belly.

"What about it?"

"Watch," I said, waiting for it to happen again.

"Holy shit! Reminds me of the movie *Alien* when the baby alien is ripping out of Sigourney Weaver."

"Okay, you're not helping," I replied.

"It seems the little crazy man is trying to break out of his padded cell."

"That's not nice. He's my son, not some lunatic."

"Every man is a lunatic, Beth." The mugging had made Amber even more resentful of men than usual.

"Don't talk like that about— Look! He's doing it again!" I said. Then, "Ouch!"

In the nine months I'd been pregnant, I'd been kicked, prodded and punched by my baby. My insides were twisted in every possible direction, and sometimes they felt like they were in a giant knot. Everything my baby could do inside me, he did. But this was a first. I could clearly see a balled up fist move from the left side of my abdomen to the right and back again.

"That's freaky," Amber said.

"Kimberly never did that?"

"No."

I went to my room and put on a maternity dress; it'd been six weeks since I'd been able to wear pants. My belly hung so low that the waistline of all my pants sat only about a centimeter above my vagina; speaking of which, I wasn't even sure if I had one anymore. I hadn't seen it in months, and nobody had visited it since Jackson.

Asshole!

I dabbed powder on my face and grabbed my purse to go shopping. I put on the burgundy Members Only jacket I bought at a secondhand store a few years ago. I'm not sure why I bought it at the time, but now I was glad to have it. During the third trimester I was chilly every morning. Sweatshirts and coats make me too warm; the Members

Only jacket was the only thing that kept my body at the right temperature.

I was tying my shoes when, "Ouch." My first contraction. "Amber!"

Amber came back. "What's wrong, Beth?"

"Contractions."

"Exciting. How far apart are they?"

"I don't know."

"Yeah for Beth! It's starting! Lie down and rest. You've got a long way to go before this actually happens."

"Okay." I laid down, but I couldn't relax. I wasn't yet full-term. My baby was just over eight months. I was a bit terrified. Would he be some kind of deformed preemie? They say at 35 weeks you have nothing to worry about, and I was right about there, but barely. I tried not to think about anything. I tried to just let my head go empty.

But that was impossible.

I stared at the ceiling to try to slow my thoughts. Ten minutes later, I had an intense contraction. "Amber!"

She burst back in. "What?"

"This baby wants out! Look at my stomach! Baby Jonathon's trying to get out!"

"Beth, just rest. Your contractions need to be five minutes apart before we go to the hospital."

"Take me now!"

"Are you sure?"

"I'm f-ing positive!" I snarled.

"Okay, I'll get dressed."

I waited in the kitchen while Amber got ready. She came out with my bag, and we made for the hospital.

We were in the car, fifteen minutes from the hospital, and my contractions were about seven minutes apart. Amber was positive that I wasn't yet ready to give birth. But then—

"My water broke!"

"Stay calm, love. Everything's going to be fine."

"He's yanking at my insides! Why's he so angry?"

"Calm down, honey. You're overreacting."

"Don't tell me I'm overreacting!"

"Don't yell at me, Beth. I love you, but today you will not treat me like I'm the man who got you pregnant."

"Sorry," I said.

"Apology accepted. Don't worry. You're going to be fine."

"Amber, I'm scared. Why did I decide to go through with this?"

"Because at the end of all the pain, they'll hand you a beautiful little baby boy which you get to keep for the rest of your life."

"Oh yeah. Ouch! Ow, ow, ow, ow, OW! OOOOUCH!"

Amber

Beth's pain tolerance is equal to the Catholic church's tolerance for premarital sex. Zero. I worried about her getting through this. I had recommended her to plan for an epidural, but her paranoid dads had her believing that her baby would be born a drug addict; like he'd be born with needles hanging out of his veins.

They wheeled Beth into OBGYN. I called her dads and filled out paperwork. I thought I'd have plenty of time to spare, but by the time I got to her room, the doctor was already between Beth's legs.

"Okay, Beth, you're fully dilated, 10 centimeters, fully effaced, and the baby is crowning. Your baby is going to be in your arms soon. You just have to push through this last bit," Dr. Mikelstein said. I couldn't believe how fast all this was moving. It took half a day for me to birth Kimberly. It made me worry that something actually was wrong. "Relax and breathe, Beth. Now get ready. Breathe nice now, and PUSH!"

"GEEEEERRRAAAAH!" Beth let out a deep, primitive scream. She squeezed my hand so hard I felt the labor pains.

I could see the top of her baby's head being forced out of his cozy home and into the world. "You're doing great, Beth. You can do this," I whispered in her ear.

"Push again, Beth!" Dr. Mikelstein coached.

Beth squeezed my hand again. Her nails clawed into the soft meaty flesh between my thumb and index finger, and I was positive that she'd drawn blood.

"It hurts so badly. Talk to me, Amber," Beth said.

"Remember last year when we took Kimberly to Disneyland? That was so much fun. Just think, next year we can take Jonathon with—"

"AAAWAAAH!" Beth screamed. This time it was one of those

high-pitched screams that shatter wine glasses in the movies.

"Relax. Breathe, breathe, breathe, and push!" The doctor instructed. The nurse was gently rubbing Beth's lower back and encouraging her.

"It fucking hurts! Get your fucking hands off me!"

Beth

"Give me a fucking epidural!"

"It's too late for that now. You needed to plan on that long ago," the fucking bastard doctor said.

"That's bullshit! It hurts!"

"We can't give you an epidural now. You've got to do this. Ready now, push!"

Every time I pushed, it felt like my vagina was going to split in half. The sensation firing through me wasn't pain; it was something infinitely more severe. The pressure in my head was unbearable; I feared my eyeballs would blow out of my head and fly across the room. I'd be an eyeball-less mother.

"Push again!"

And I pushed! I yelled my head off and gripped Amber's hand tighter.

I looked in the mirror and saw fluids were coming out of me like a decapitated fire hydrant.

"Oh God, it hurts! I think the baby just tore me in half!"

And I was correct. I looked in the mirror and saw my vagina was ripped all the way to my anus. And I'd pooped. Had I not been in incredible pain I'd have been humiliated.

The next contraction was so intense that it felt like O.J. Simpson was sticking his knives in my back while a baby whale tried to swim out of my butt.

"Oh my God! I'm going to freak out! I need a distraction. Amber, sing to me!"

"Loosen your grip, honey," Amber said.

"Sing!" I commanded.

"Okay, Beth. Breathe, breathe, breathe."

"Sing!"

Amber started singing my favorite song, one which was completely inappropriate for the moment:

"Lightning crashes, a new mother cries

her placenta falls to the floor

the angel opens her eyes

the confusion sets in

before the doctor can even close the door."

"Push, Beth!" the doctor said. I screamed. Amber sang louder to cover my screams.

"LIGHTNING CRASHES AN OLD MOTHER DIES

HER INTENTIONS FALL TO THE FLOOR

THE ANGEL CLOSES HER EYES-"

"You're singing me a song about a mother dying in childbirth? Shut up!"

"Oh. Right. Sorry."

"Why does it hurt so much?" I cried.

"Because he's a big baby," Dr. Mikelstein said.

Of all the random men in Los Angeles, I had to get knocked up by a freaking 240-pound football player. *Fucking Jackson!*

"Okay, a few more big pushes, and I think we'll have him."

"I can't do it anymore."

"Come on, baby. One more push," Amber said, siding with the doctor.

Bitch!

"EAAAARAAAAH!" I screamed.

"His head's out!" Amber yelled, excited.

In the mirror I saw my baby's entire head. It looked like a big, wet, pointy melon.

I hope he's not deformed.

His face was all wrinkled and wet, he was cross-eyed, one eye looking at me and one at Amber, and his forehead was sloped like a skateboard ramp. I knew this was supposed to be the most beautiful moment of my life, but my son's face looked like he'd missed a couple steps on the evolutionary ladder.

"Push again, Beth!"

I pushed, and to distract my brain from the pain, I screamed at the top of my lungs. Amber put her fingers in her ears, and I tried to scream even louder. I wanted to share my suffering.

"It's going to take one more big push," Dr. Mikelstein said. "Now push, Beth! Last time. Push!"

I pushed as hard as I could. My baby was all elbows and knees and shoulders as he tunneled through me, trying to be born.

"Keep pushing!" I pushed so hard I pushed my colon out through my anus, and then I pushed some more.

And then I was empty.

And Jonathon was a person.

"Give him to me." Tears streamed down my cheeks. I was happy, hurting, scared, and amazed. It was unreal; a human being had just come out of my body. The doctor wrapped Jonathon in a blanket and handed him to me. His skin was pinkish-pale. I was happy he wasn't dark like Jackson. I didn't ever want to think of Jackson when I looked at Jonathon.

"Hi, Jonathon. I'm your mommy."

He had the cutest little fingers, and his head was as bald as a cue ball and wrinkly like an old man. He was that adorable kind of ugly newborn babies are. He was precious and beautiful and handsome and completely wonderful. His mouth was already puckered, searching for a nipple.

"Hi, Jonathon," Amber said. Her hand rested on my shoulder. I put my hand on top of hers and smiled at her, then back at my Jonathon.

"Doctor, is that normal? Will that go away?" Amber asked, referring to his cross-eyes.

"Yes," he said, and we both felt a little relieved.

Instinctively, I started counting. One, two, three. Ten toes, ten fingers.I'd just done the most important thing a person can ever do. I'd made life. At the very instant he was put into my arms, I loved this new person more than anyone but a mother can understand.

Today the galaxy fluxed and left me amazed. And I swear Jonathon smiled at me.

November 1998
Dr. Juan Salazar

Across the street, girls with sun-stained knees played hopscotch, tetherball, and ring-around-the-rosie. A little girl wearing a denim skirt put her foot on the park bench to tie her laces. She had fresh raspberry scratches on the bend of her left knee, and I could tell she was a mischievous sprite. I stopped and sat on a bench outside my apartment complex to allow myself the simple joy of watching. Watching was the one harmless thing I could do to ease my neurosis.

She resumed jumping rope with her two friends, one of whom was a redhead. Her skin was peachy and freckled. The third girl was a little taller than the other two. She wore a knee-length skirt with knee-high white socks, exposing only a sliver of her flesh. She was very thin; her girth had not yet caught up to her height. After she'd jump the rope, on her way down, the air pushed her skirt up above her buttocks, and for a split second her white cotton underwear would peak out.

This is what I do with my mornings before work. It keeps me from completely losing it.

Later that day at work, I finally generated up the courage to talk to Flora, the new girl, and the first woman of age that I'd felt any kind of attraction to.

Flora shut my office door behind her. "I am here, Dr. Salazar. What you want to see me por?" Flora's accent was almost as adorable as her little button nose that crinkled when she smiled.

The Filipinos at the hospital tended to mix their P sounds with their F sounds, and V with B. Also, they often emphasize the wrong syllables, which makes them even harder to understand. I found it to be charming.

"You need see sick lady. He need help," Flora said.

In Tagalog, there's no sex-assigned pronouns, so when Filipinos speak English, they frequently get confused between he and she. Her mistakes were cute, and I enjoyed the way her mouth pushed out the words.

"Take a seat, Ms. Garcia."

"Take seat to where?"

"No, Ms. Garcia. I meant for you to Please-Sit-Down-For-A-Minute-To-Speak-With-Me-"

"I not so good at English, but I not deaf. You not have to yell."

"Sorry, Flora," I said. Then suddenly one of my many nervous ticks kicked in. I started clucking my tongue. Once I start doing this, it's impossible to stop.

"Are you okay, Doctor?"

"I'm fine," I said,

Cluck, cluck, cluck, cluck, cluck.

Disguising my O.C.D. is nearly impossible. There are so many germs in a hospital that I often wonder about my career choice: Chlamydia, herpes, scabies, pneumonia, streptococci. Hospitals are the breeding grounds of the apocalypse. To defend myself, I always wear gloves, and I wash my hands every opportunity I get. I spent years at Brotman Hospital without anyone noticing my O.C.D. I stayed off the radar by avoiding social contact with co-workers.

But I couldn't keep away from Flora.

Flora is tender and beautiful. She has the kind of natural, youthful beauty women spend thousands of dollars trying to attain. Her skin is the color of honey before it's processed. She looks to be about fifteen-years-old, but I checked her file and found out she moved to America from the Philippines eleven months ago, and her eighteenth birthday was a couple weeks ago. With a girl like Flora, I knew my life could be pleasurable instead of something that had to be endured until it was over.

"So, what dis meeting for, Doctor?"

Cluck, cluck, cluck, cluck, cluck.

I couldn't stop. I knew I was freaking her out. "Well, Flora. I—"

"Dr. Salazar, Mr. Rockenberger's on line two," my secretary, Sheila, addressed me over the intercom. "He's calling about his mother."

Sheila was a large, sweaty woman with a hoarse voice that reminded me of a chain-smoking manatee. She was nice, and she liked me, but her frequent advances were tiresome. The thought of being in bed with her huge flabby boobs and trucker's thighs sickened me.

"I'll take it in a minute, Sheila." Her disgusting voice calmed my excitement enough to stop the clucking. "Flora, please sit down."

Flora approached. I felt the kind of butterflies in my stomach I got on the first day of second grade when I found out Tommy Singleton had moved out of town and I'd be sitting next to Alicia Smith all year.

By the time she sat down, I noticed she was emitting a foul bouquet of feces. Shear panic ripped through me. The butterflies in my stomach morphed into mosquitoes with razor blades for wings. I started clucking again, my throat closed up, my palms became sweaty, and I felt faint.

"I sit. Now what?" Flora asked.

My vision blurred, and I feared I'd vomit.

She must've come from cleaning a patient. I hope she washed her hands.

"Are you okay, Doctor?"

"I'm fine, Flora." My hands trembled. In a second or two, I'd be involuntarily humming in a high-pitched voice.

"You no look so good."

My tongue swelled. I had to get rid of Flora. I struggled to make words. "Please-Take-This-Document-To-Nurse-Bowen."

She just sat and looked at me.

"Take it now," I said, trying to remain polite and trying not to choke on my fat tongue.

"You sound punny." Flora opened her hand and reached across my desk for the document. I tried to let go of my end of the document at the exact moment her fingers closed around it. I didn't release in time, and for a split second, our hands held the paper simultaneously.

Flora stood. "Doctor, you too much sweating. Let me wipe you pace." Flora reached for me. The poop smell overpowered me. I vomited a little in my mouth and swallowed it. I stepped back. "No! Thank you," I struggled to say. I put my hand in the small of her back and ushered her out. I wished I hadn't touched her, and briefly contemplated cutting off my arm.

Once Flora was gone, panic had its way with me. With a great sense of urgency, I opened and closed the top drawer of my desk eleven times; I grabbed the pills inside my top drawer, opened and closed the bottle eleven times, downed the prescribed amount, then a couple more, and then a few more after that. Eleven in all, I believe.

I went to the sink and washed my hands eleven times under scalding hot water. I grabbed a sterilize towel and disinfected the chair Flora sat on.

Oh shit!

I'd swallowed my pills before washing my hands! I touched her back! She just cleaned a soiled patient—

I'd ingested second-hand feces!

I got sick all over myself.

Kelly

Had I known where Mr. Rockenberger's proposition could lead, I'd have spit a wad in his face. A good wad, too, one of those nasty globs cultivated from the gunk in the back of the throat.

After one year as the therapist of the Motion Picture Television Fund, management discovered my resume lies and fired me.

Forever gone were my workdays spent massaging beautiful women's newly augmented breasts, cavorting with Hollywood actors, and the ocean view from my office. My new jobs required an hour commute to a landlocked hospital followed by a forty-five minute lunchtime commute to work afternoons at a nursing home.

Today at the hospital, I had a new patient, Ms. Rockenberger, mother of ex-linebacker, Jackson Rockenberger. The deep lines in her face showed her age, but her bone structure suggested she'd been a beautiful young black girl at one time.

"Hi, Ms. Rockenberger. I'm Kelly Dampier, your physical therapist."

"Nice to meet you, Doctor," she said.

"Doctor, wow, thank you, but I'm a physical therapist."

"Thank you for coming to see my mother, Mr. Dampier. I'm Jackson," the linebacker said, as he entered the room.

I shook his hand. Jackson smelled like he'd taken a bath in his cologne. A sharp suit adorned his tall, athletic frame. He had light brown skin and a shaved head; he was a pretty good-looking dude.

Guys like me, with sexy wives, can say things like that without sounding gay.

"It's my pleasure to be here," I said, wishing I were still massaging breasts for a living.

"What time is dinner, Doctor?" asked Ms. Rockenberger.

"He's a therapist, Mom. Mom has Alzheimer's," whispered the handso— her son.

"Today, Ms. Rockenberger, we're going to get you into a chair for half an hour. Each day we'll sit you up longer, until you're strong enough for a stand-pivot transfer to the bedside commode."

"Mom hates hospitals, and the stress of being here will make her sicker. You need to make sure she's getting up in two days so I can take her home."

"I'll do my best," I said.

"If Mother likes you, I'll hire you as her private therapist."

Mr. Rockenberger was going to be one of those royal pain-in-the-ass rich pricks who treats us working class people like medieval peasants.

"Mr. Rockenberger, I'm flattered, but I'm fine with this job."

"I live in coastal Malibu, ten miles north of Pepperdine. It's an hour and a half from here. You couldn't make the drive after working here, so if Mom likes you, we'll hire you full-time."

Hmmm, hang out with some old bat a few hours a day on the beach in Malibu or continue grinding out my days in this morbid hospital?

One old lady or dozens of them?

The smell of piss or the smell of the salty ocean?

Obese, chain-smoking nurses or rich young women jogging on the beach in sports bras?

"I'll consider it," I said. "For now, let's just work on getting this lovely young lady on the road to recovery with as little discomfort as humanly possible. Are you ready, sweetheart?"

December 1998

Ron

Finally, today, after six months of psychological rehabilitation, I was being released.

The wetback, Doctor Juan Salazar, asked, "How will you avoid falling prey to the church again? How will you handle your fears?" He clicked and unclicked his ballpoint pen in an authoritative fashion, and then he pulled a pair of silver-rimmed reading glasses from his lab coat. His lab coat was an extremely clean shade of white. I took out my notebook and wrote:

White like bed sheets in their original packaging.

White like wet chalk.

White like over bleached teeth.

I was a little nervous about being released. I was twenty-eight-years-old, and I'd never worked a nine-to-five. I wasn't built for it. On my first attempt at freedom, I committed a crime on a flight to Los Angeles. Luckily, they couldn't prove I took old Blue Hair's money.

That easy score encouraged me. I began snatching purses from women in parking structures around Culver City. Then, two weeks after arriving in Los Angeles, I got arrested for stealing $200 from an unattended cash register at a deli. Considering my priors, I was facing jail time. So I told the jury the Church of Scientology put me up to it by telling me, *You can save your soul by giving money to the church.* The jury, mostly older citizens, bought my weak story about the cult. I was found guilty of the crime, but given time in a psych ward instead of prison.

God bless our judicial system.

"Dr. Salazar, thanks to your help, I have everything under control. I'll continue with my daily mental exercises, and I'll take my meds."

If anything, my six months at Brotman Medical Center was making me legitimately crazy. Dr. Juan Salazar filled my body with medications like Thorazine, Zyprexa, Xanax, and Zoloft. Giving these meds to a man like me was the equivalent of giving an angry teenager an eight ball of blow and a gun. But the medications weren't even the worst thing about the psych ward. The nights were worse. Nighttime was active; it was when the crazies earned their labels by making as much noise as possible. The screams and cries were hollow and haunting.

It takes the average person seven minutes to fall asleep, but there were many nights here when I didn't sleep at all.

Even worse than the nights were the magnetic anklets they clamped on us like sheep. The anklets made us prisoners, causing stairwell doors to lock automatically when we approached them.

Dr. Salazar asked, "And if your insecurities start to get to you, and you feel like you may do something wrong?"

"I'll call you immediately, just like you instructed me."

This was a necessary dance between patient and doctor. I pampered his ego and answered his inquires in a manner any doctor would expect of a mentally sick patient. But every once in a while, I'd mess with him. *Why do you always wear gloves, Dr. Salazar? What's with that clucking noise you make?* Dr. Salazar was compulsive, and I enjoyed the head games. He always mouthed the number of steps he took as he entered and left my room. Eleven every time. Once, I moved his chair from its normal position to fuck with him, and he leapt to make it in exactly eleven strides.

I heard over the intercom: "Paging Nurse Picastro to the lounge."

Another suicide attempt, the fourth since I'd been here. Nurse Picastro was code for a suicide attempt. Betty helped me break the code. Betty resided two doors down from me; she was schizophrenic. Betty had hair the color of nicotine and a voice like a fork scraping a ceramic plate. If paranoia has an odor, then Betty omitted it. Still, Betty was nice enough, and I liked her.

Betty used to roam the halls, cursing an invisible pig for murdering her non-existent ex-husband. I guess the day she threw herself out of the window of the unlocked employee break room, she'd had enough. She fell two stories. When she landed on the ledge of the fourth floor, the vibration shook the windows on our floor.

Paging Nurse Picastro to the break room. Nurse Picastro to the break room, I'd heard. Betty lay on the ground like a mangled acrobat for half an hour before any help was able to get to her.

"Ron, you've made tremendous progress. I'm proud of the work you've done under my supervision. I don't expect to see you back here," Dr. Salazar said.

"Thank you so much, Doctor. I couldn't have gotten better without your guidance."

Flattery is an underrated weapon.

"Stay out of trouble," he said.

And I wanted to, but I doubted I could exist as the type of person society thinks we all should be. Society builds laws around us to keep us safe, but these rules imprison me in boredom. Crime is exciting. I'm a risk-taker and an explorer.

I'm Christopher Columbus.

I'm the first Thai man to eat a giant cicada.

I'm the kid who dares to enter the witch's house at the edge of town.

How could I go straight?

Dr. Salazar stood and shook my hand with his gloved hand, and security took off my anklet. Free again. I walked down the shiny, waxed linoleum hallway. The heavy smell of lemon and pine disinfectants began to dissipate behind me, and the smell of freedom became stronger. I walked through the doors, and security drove me away.

I needed a drink. And I needed a woman.

Amber

Chocolate or vanilla birthday cake?

Biggie Smalls' *Hypnotize* played in the background while I jiggled my breasts in some jerk's face.

Both. I should get chocolate and vanilla.

I lay down on the waxed stage, arched my back, threw my chest in the air, spread my legs and pulled the waistband of my G-string from my skin to make room for the jerk-off's tip.

Did I send an invitation to the neighbor's kid?

I got back on my feet, put my hands on the floor, and pumped my butt up and down to the beat.

"You gotta beautiful black ass! I wanna taste that chocolate!" yelled a regular.

I took two running steps, jumped in the air, wrapped my arms and legs around the pole, released my hands, and dangled upside down by my legs.

"I'm in love!" said some decrepit black man with a cigar.

I should decorate everything pink; Kimberly loves pink. But the boys may not like it. Maybe baby blue with pink trim.

I slowly slid down the pole, holding on upside down with only my right leg. My left foot pointed heavenward.

"Let me suck your toes!" the old geezer said. He threw a dollar in my direction. "Marry me!"

Don't these idiot drunks realize we wouldn't use fake names if we were interested in them?

"That's all for Cinnamon on stage tonight, gentlemen," announced the M.C. Then he poked his head out his cubicle. "Nice set, Cinnamon."

I hated my stage name, but sexy names that reference skin color tend to pull bigger tips. Onyx, Chocolate, Caramel.

"But Cinnamon's available the rest of the night in the V.I.P," the M.C. added, ducking back in his booth.

V.I.P is where the big money is, but there the pigs get all over you like bacteria.

I went to the bar. "Dylan, can I get a T and T?" Tanqueray and Tonic, my staple drink, gives me the nerve I need to dance. Some of the girls say they enjoy dancing. If so, why are ninety-nine percent of them drug addicts.?

Dylan slid me a drink. I helped Dylan get the bartending job after the airline fired him. He'd been fired from every job he'd ever had and I knew he'd eventually screw up and get fired from here, too.

"Hi," said some guy. His eyes were an impossible shade of green and strangely familiar. They made me both uneasy and curious.

He was alone. The loners are the dangerous ones. They're almost always grabbers and the most likely to negotiate for sex. And I don't do sex.

"Can I buy you a drink?" he asked.

These men all have the same lame pick-up lines. In private, they talk to me like they love me while pretending the lewd crap they yelled when I was on stage didn't really happen.

"No, you can't buy me a drink," I said. I moved as close as possible without touching him. "But you can buy a dance," I whispered. His beer-soaked breath rested on my neck, nauseating me.

"I'd rather just talk," he said.

I knew his type. He was a hero. With him, I'd have to play the role of the damaged girl. I'd make myself pathetic and small and let him believe our three minutes together was all I needed to fix my unbearable life.

"What's your name?" I asked.

"Ron."

"Nice to meet you, Ron. I'm Cinnamon. You're cute for a white boy." They love that black-girl-attracted-to-the-white-guy bull. "But if I get caught socializing instead of dancing, I get in trouble. You wouldn't want that, would you?" I touched his cheek.

Angelica, who was sitting next to me sipping a Jack and Coke and tapping her long fake nails on the counter, tried to contain her laughter. It must have been contagious because I let out a little giggle.

"You make me giggle," I said, covering for myself.

Angelica coughed and a bit of her drink shot out her nose. She got up and walked away, running her long nails across my back as she did. Normally, something like that feels nice to me, but no physical contact in this place ever feels nice.

"So you gonna buy a dance? We can talk all you want in V.I.P."

"How much?"

I pressed myself between his thighs and put my hand on his worn khakis. "Forty for three songs."

"Okay. But I just want to talk."

I've heard the '*I just want to talk*' routine about four million times. Yeah, they want to talk. About my boobs, '*Are they real?*' or about my scent, *'What kind of perfume do you wear?'* The sharp ones will slide in a, *'So, what's your real name?'* As if I'd suddenly forget how nauseating he was and tell him my name. Sometimes, they'll get philosophical, *'It's horrible how society frowns on strippers; it's a beautiful art form.'* They think they're so original. I know what they're going to say before they know. Then, after about thirty seconds of talking at me, they think they've gotten my blood pumping, and they expect me to act like I can't contain my lust for them, like I want nothing more in the world than to rub my breasts all over their face.

What I'd love to do, just once, is stand up and announce the truth—

I'm a lesbian, you idiot!

Ron

I'm not attracted to black women, but for some reason Cinnamon made me want to do things.

We were in V.I.P., Cinnamon had me sit on the couch; it was a typical strip club couch, the kind with extra-long cushions designed to stretch out a man's lap area. The hazy red lighting in the room reminded me of one of those lava lamps frat guys use in their dorm rooms.

I felt extremely horny. Six months in lockup will do that to a man.

"You smell amazing. What perfume do you wear?"

"That's all me, love. 100% Cinnamon." She said softly in my ear, veiling her real voice beneath a raspy, stripper voice. Behind her, a smoldering miasma of cigarette smoke rose from an ashtray full of freshly crushed butts.

Cinnamon bent to press her face against mine. She felt like a warm bath against my rough skin.

She ran her hand across my cheek. "You're going to like this." Velvety sex oozed from her mouth. "Just remember, doll, I'm the only one allowed to touch."

Cinnamon started dancing. She was curvy, sinful, and as mysterious as the tattoo on her back. **B-E-L-O-V-E-D**, it read, starting from the base of her skull and running down her spine to the top of her buttocks. She had a high hairline, and tiny curly hairs melted down the sides of her cheeks. She leaned over me and turned the dimmer switch even lower. Her charcoal eyes dilated in the lessening light. It's said the eyes are windows to the soul, but hers were calloused with indifference.

"What's your real name?" I asked.

An uncomfortable feeling of déjà vu overcame me.

"It's Cinnamon," she said, smiling.

I remembered a poem I'd read before my hospital discharge.

> *Her name is but a name,*
> *A symbol, just a mask—*
> *Concealing what I see,*
> *Revealing what I ask.*

It was by a poet who shared my first name, Ron Carnell. It felt like it fit the moment between Cinnamon and me. I read poetry in prison; I also read a lot of literary fiction. I never let the other inmates know this because it would've shown weakness. Prison locked up my body, but occasionally my spirit was able to ride a poem into a numb oblivion, and there I was able to be free for as long as the poem lasted. I always wanted to live inside a poem, and now, in an odd way, I was.

Cinnamon laid her hand on my inner thigh. Blood left my brain, flowed between my legs, and I became more stupid than I was before she put her hand there. I wanted to believe Cinnamon wanted me, but I knew I was just another customer who helped pay her bills.

Cinnamon grabbed my legs, spread them, and pulled my lap forward. She wedged herself between my legs and began grinding her fleshy ass against me to the cadence of some rap noise. I was so hard it hurt. Cinnamon stood, turned to face me, and danced. My eyes followed her slender black fingers as they traced her shadowy figure. Her fingers ran up her stomach to the underside of her tits, and her left hand squeezed her breast as she passed over it, moving to her neck and up to her full lips. Her right hand descended down her belly, over a mole, past the coarse dark hairs beneath her bellybutton, and down to her panties.

She wore sophisticated panties that disappeared into her rich brown skin. And when she grazed them against me, they felt softer than anything I'd ever touched. It was as if they were made of some new element that existed only in her panties. She flirted with the bow that held her thong in place, and perverted thoughts swam in my head like sperm. I was approaching the point of no return where thinking stops and actions are driven by instinct.

And then she took off her bra.

"You like that?"

"I lub dhat." My lips were two steroid-injected steaks.

Cinnamon's naked breasts were as perfect as her ass.

Her hips moved to music I'd stopped hearing, and her hands wandered the playground of her body. Her dance was so erotic I thought sex with her might be anti-climatic. But even if it were, I still wanted to feel her steaming hot insides massaging my hardness. I'd never slept with a black woman, and in this moment, I was curious.

"Look at me," I said.

"Why?"

"Because I like it."

Cinnamon stared hard. It was uncomfortable, not like it usually is when someone stares at you, but uncomfortable in the way overwhelming déjà vu can be.

Suddenly, I remembered why I was having déjà vu! It was her eyes. How had I not noticed earlier? I remembered her eyes as she walked in the parking garage. I saw fear in them and I took advantage of her vulnerability. I snuck up behind her and stole her purse. And now here she was, grinding on my crotch, to earn back the money I took from her. Ironic.

I felt a tinge of guilt, but I also saw opportunity. This coincidence was good luck. She was an easy target. I'd find her weakness and exploit it.

Amber

After his last song ended, he paid for three more just to talk. We chatted about literature, which is odd conversation for a strip club. Even more surprising? Our tastes were similar; he even liked *Beloved*.

"To me it's about the indestructible bond between mother and daughter," he said. "And that's a beautiful thing."

That's exactly what *Beloved* is about, and that's why I have it tattooed on my back. I'm not sure if he was fucking with me, but if he was, he was doing a good job of it.

Ron tipped me well, and then he left Starr. Talking to him was the first time I ever actually enjoyed time with a customer; still, something about him made me uncomfortable.

I did a few more lap dances, exceeded quota, and packed up for the evening. On my long drive home, my thoughts wandered to Naples, Florida. I try to never think about that day, but every once in a while some small thing will happen over the course of a day and it will trigger that memory. And once that happens, I can't get it out of my head without a good purging. I'm not sure what triggered it today, but something had. I became nauseated and had to pull over. I threw up, twice.

I should have fought back.

This thought rolled around my brain like a two-ton marble.

I had been almost fifteen-years-old. We worked for a family in Naples, which has the highest millionaire population per capita of any city in the States. It's the type of town where rich white women carry purse-sized dogs outfitted in Louis Vuitton sweaters. It's the type of town that needs only one cop on duty at a time. The type of town where the only minorities are the servants for rich white folk.

I was a pretty smart kid with fair grades. Life wasn't perfect. I'd have liked a dad and at least one friend who resembled me, but I was content. Mom and I had a lot of fun together.

But tonight, on my drive home, I wasn't remembering the fun times. I was remembering the way my life changed forever on New Year's Eve of 1992.

I was in the horse stable reading *A Clockwork Orange* to Blossom. Blossom was the prettiest horse our boss owned, and she was my best friend. Blossom always became subdued when I read to her. Tonight, even as the fireworks exploded outside, Blossom remained calm.

The pungent sulfur smell of fireworks drifted into the barn. I stood up to stuff a rag under the barn door, but it swung open. He stood in the dark opening, barely a silhouette, framed by the black of the night. "What are you up to?" he asked. My lamp illuminated him as he approached, and I was able to make out his a party hat, and deep green t-shirt. He smelled of alcohol and had anger in his eyes.

I remember how the pain in my vagina flowed to every part of my body. Each thrust was a rusty railroad spike pounded into my innocence, contaminating me. My face was buried in the deep green of his musty t-shirt. I held my breath the entire time he worked at me. I nearly passed out. Fireworks continued to loudly explode outside the barn, and inside it I cried silently. I wanted to scream and fight back, but the fear was paralyzing, so I just lie there, taking his abuse. Blossom cried for me, but she couldn't help. After he finished, he got up, put his pants on, and said coolly, "I'll kill you if you tell anyone."

Then he left.

And the child in me was dead.

I silently wept until I fell asleep.

And then I awoke. Broken.

For years, when I'd close my eyes to sleep, I'd see the horrible green of his shirt smothering my face while he abused my body. When I smelled sulfur, I'd get sick to my stomach, and fireworks made me cry for years. It took forever to force myself to repress the details, and now, tonight, they were so fresh it felt like yesterday.

Three months after being raped, I realized I was pregnant. I considered abortion. But Mom could've aborted me when my father left her, and she didn't. With that on my conscience, I couldn't end my baby's life. I couldn't talk to Mom about what happened because she would go after my abuser. She'd lose her job, but more importantly, he had warned me about talking, and I knew he was serious. There was only one solution for me. I left Mom a note.

Mom, I can't bear to face you. I was raped, and I'm pregnant. I know you're disappointed in me, and I'm sorry. By the time you read this, I'll be long gone. Please don't look for me. I don't want to be found. I love you. Thank you for being such a wonderful mother. I'm sorry.

Goodbye—   Amber

I was a selfish coward. My mind was filled to capacity with worry that I'd never love my baby, and I didn't have room in my head to think about how my running away would affect my mom.

Sitting in my car, tonight, on the side of the road, I felt disgusted, ashamed, and as afraid as I did all those years ago.

I should have fought back.

Stripping is the closest I've come to being brave. It lets me feel like I have power over that which frightens me — men. But tonight, man won again. The deep green of my customer's eyes made me remember everything. The color was so striking and familiar. I couldn't place it because it was buried under years of trying to forget. But Ron's eyes were the same exact shade of green.

Green like canned spinach, or like cucumbers after they've been soaked in vinegar. Green like the rolling hills of safe places I've never been, and green like the musty t-shirt I'll never forget.

I was a mess, and the drive home was nearly impossible. When I finally got home, just when I thought my life couldn't get worse, I went inside and discovered our apartment had been robbed.

I knew who did it.

Beth's Daddy Gerry had a massive heart attack last night. The last thing I wanted was to be the bearer of more bad news to my Beth.

I called her at the hospital. "Beth. We've been robbed," I said.

"Oh my God! Are you okay?"

"I'm fine. I was out," I said, not letting her know how terrified I was. Not letting on I knew who did it.

"How is the place?"

"It's turned upside down. He got everything."

"Everything?"

"Yep. Including both my stashes."

I kept my dancing tips at home, hidden inside hollowed-out copies of my favorite books. And because of that decision, I was broke. Now I'd have to work more hours instead of using my time studying for my nursing license.

But that wasn't my biggest concern. The person who jacked us was Kimberly's father. And this time I was sure.

My life was in tatters. I was failing out of nursing school, I'd just been robbed of everything I had, and worst of all, Kimberly's father had found us.

Kimberly, Jonathon, Beth, and I would have to move; staying would be suicide.

Ron

As soon as I got home from Starr, I dug out the purse I'd taken from the stripper, and looked for her driver's license.

Her name was Amber.

She lived in a bad neighborhood in Compton.

Strippers tend to have a lot of cash, and they keep most of it at home. No banks, no safes, no reason to alert the IRS. I went to her address and waited half a day, watching one jobless darkie after another heading down the street, doing nothing, just wasting time. Then, after about ten hours, a woman walked up to Amber's apartment and let herself in.

Amber had obviously moved from that address. But that was a minor glitch in the operation. Strippers have cash, and I wanted hers. I could get her address if I played my cards right. For days, I worked on a

137

plan that would allow me to take full advantage of this situation. However, whenever I started planning, I became distracted. I kept thinking about the soft curve of her hips, the sweet smell of her nape, and the naked pain in her eyes. I had Amber on my brain for three days. I couldn't seem to keep myself from wanting her, but I had to get my priorities straight. Love hurts. Women hurt. Money does not. I had to stay focused.

I had a plan, and the first step was to earn her trust. Her sadness and pain made her an easy mark.

Today, three days after our initial meeting, I was back at Starr. Amber moved about the stage in some kind of perverted ballet. Then, she sprung up in the air, grabbed the pole, and swung around it like a tetherball. She let go of the pole and landed lightly on her feet, and then her legs parted to a split. She wore a nearly invisible G-string that practically gave away everything.

The song ended, and Amber gathered the money scattered at her feet and walked backstage. I went to the bar for a drink. Two minutes later, Amber sat next to me. "Oh, hey Cinnamon. Remember me?"

"Umm, yeah. It's Ron, right?" I was surprised she remembered my name; it was a good sign. "Did you want to buy a dance?"

"Actually, to be perfectly honest, I was hoping you'd allow me to take you for a bite to eat," I said.

"Look, Ron—"

"Wait, I didn't mean to sound creepy. Maybe we could just sit in the corner and talk a minute. I'll pay you like last time."

"Listen, Ron. I'm sure you're a great guy. But here's the deal. I'm in a sour mood, my back is throbbing, and my feet ache," she said. There was a visible strain on her face; her lip began to quiver in either frustration, anger, or grief. It was obvious whatever was going on in her life, she was in over her head.

"You seem stressed," I said, trying to sound sympathetic but not invasive.

"Stressed? Yeah, I'm freaking stressed! Not that it's any of your business, but I've been working double shifts all week and I have to get up early in the morning to take a final exam in a class I'm probably going to fail because I can't properly prepare for it with my daughter running all over the house unattended. My girlfriend is taking care of her sick Dad, and I don't know anyone else who can babysit. So as much as I'd like to have dinner with a creepy stranger who pays money to watch me take off my clothes, I think I have more pressing needs."

"Well, I—"

"Wait, Ron. I didn't get to the best part yet. Are you ready?"

I nodded.

"Are you sure?"

"Yeah, I'm sure."

"I date women. And not because I'm kinky and like to mix it up, but because I'm a full-fledged lesbo."

"A lesbian. Wow, I didn't see that one coming."

"You still want to take me to dinner?" she asked.

"What would be the point? But maybe we could go to a sports bar and catch the Thursday night ESPN game of the week." I thought she'd laugh, but she didn't. "Forget that. Listen, I have a good idea."

I had to wing it; her sexual orientation threw a wrench into my original plan, but I wasn't ready to give up.

"Obviously, we won't have a romantic connection, but I'm new to town, and I don't have many friends. I know this sounds pathetic, but we seem to have some things in common, and, well, I'd like to be friends. So, as your friend, I'd like to help you tonight."

"How?" Amber asked.

"You need to study tonight, and I need something to do. You, your daughter, and I can go somewhere public where there are lots of eyes on us, and I'll entertain her while you study."

I didn't even like kids.

"Why would I trust you with my child?"

"You don't need to trust me; we'll be in public. And your child will love me. I'm great with kids. I paid my way through college babysitting." The only time I'd ever set foot on a college campus was to steal rich kids' beer money from their dorm rooms. "Hold on one second. Bartender, can I get a pen?" He handed me a pen, and I wrote:

Contract: Free babysitting services for Cinnamon to be paid back within thirty days via a harmless dinner date.

As I handed her the note, I realized her story didn't add up.

If she's a lesbian, how'd she get a child?

Amber

Ron handed me a napkin. "There it is, a legally binding agreement."

"So let me get this straight. You want to babysit my daughter while I study and then take me, a lesbian, to dinner?"

"That's right."

"Are you a cop?"

"I hate cops."

"So you're a con."

"No. I know it sounds crazy. Maybe I am crazy. I dunno. It's a take-it-or-leave-it offer. No strings."

"I'm not going to sleep with you."

"That was understood when you said you were a lesbian."

"I'm not telling you my real name."

"I thought it was Cinnamon."

"Don't be a smart-ass."

"Sorry."

"Is this some sort of penance for a past sin?" I asked.

"I'm not sure. Maybe. I think I'm just trying to make a friend. Yes or no?" Ron threw up his arms. He was getting impatient and was about to leave.

"Yes," I said.

"Yes?"

"I said yes, didn't I? But later, on the date part, when we go to dinner, I get to bring my girlfriend." I meant Beth, but he'd think I meant *girlfriend* girlfriend.

"I wouldn't have it any other way. I mean, you can't just go to dinner alone with some strange man."

"Don't be an ass."

"Sorry."

"Okay. Look, I'm not good at saying thank you," I said.

"It's not necessary."

"Good. Meet me at the Barnes and Noble on Torrance Boulevard in an hour. My daughter, *Tanya*, likes to hear stories. I'll be studying, but I'll make sure the security guard knows the situation and is watching you."

"Seems reasonable."

I couldn't believe it had come to this. "Okay, Ron, I'll see you there."

I started to leave.

"Wait," Ron said. "Sign the contract."

Cinnamon. I signed on the line.

On the drive home, I felt pathetic. After years of living in L.A., Beth was the only friend I could count on. Unfortunately, because of her father's heart attack, she was at the hospital. I didn't know anyone I could call last minute and ask to babysit, and considering the robbery, I really didn't have any money to spend on anything besides bills and school. I'd gotten to a point in my life where I had no other choice but to trust in a total stranger who frequented strip clubs. It sucked, but to be perfectly honest with myself, I'd put my daughter in worse situations.

At home, I told Kimberly she was, under no circumstance, to tell Ron our real names. Besides not trusting him, I hate my last name. Names in general kind of stink, they're so permanent and suggestive— sometimes they try to define you.

Oh, you're Moon? Your parents must've been hippies. Got any pot?

Nice to meet you, Sebastian. Have you seen the new 500 Mercedes series?

Hey, Shaniqua, you heard the new Puff Daddy album?

Daves play football,

Myrons are dorks,

Cinnamons strip.

My last name is Johnson. Johnson, like all names ending in s-o-n, is a slave name. Somewhere in my family tree, there was a black man working in a cotton field in Alabama or Louisiana for some rich white prick named John who would whip him with a leather rope if he didn't pick cotton fast enough. All of "John's slaves" were John's sons. That became Johnson. Just like Albertson, Richardson, Jefferson.

When we arrived, Ron was already there waiting.

Ron took Kimberly by the hand, and they sat four tables away from me by the Starbucks counter. I asked security to keep an eye on her, and then I casually asked the checker girl at the Starbucks counter to keep an eye on them as well. Ron gave Kimberly ice cream and started reading something to her while I tried to study, but I couldn't concentrate.

After the first hour, I accomplished about ten minutes of work. I looked over, and Ron and Kimberly were laughing about something, and it made me a little jealous. Sometimes I felt I wasn't a very fun mother.

I remember when I was Kimberly's age; some nights, Mom and I would run around in the humid Florida air catching fireflies and stuffing them into Mason jars. I thought fireflies were magical, and I always wanted to keep what I caught, but Mom would make me free them.

I hope Kimberly has fun memories of me.

Focus, Amber! Study!

If he lays a fucking finger on her, I'll kill him where he sits.

Ron

Kimberly was a sweet little girl. I actually enjoyed her company. She was pretty; her complexion was a couple of shades lighter than her mother's. Still, they were black, and I wanted to hate them, but for some reason, I didn't.

It had been three hours, Kimberly's ice cream sugar high was wearing off, and she was starting to crash. My Dr. Seuss reading, performed with riveting voices for each character, wasn't enough to hold her attention. I closed the book and walked her over to her mother.

"Time to go. The store is closing, and your daughter is falling asleep."

"Yeah, I know. I'm screwed. I don't know this stuff."

"Don't worry. I'm sure you'll do fine. Now, here's my address and phone number in the event you need help again. If you don't need my help, I at least expect a call within a month for our dinner date."

She took the note, read it, then turned and fired eyeball bullets at me. The note read—

Amber, your daughter, Kimberly, was an absolute pleasure. Call me. (310) 397-8223."

"Kimberly, I told you not to tell him our names," I heard her say, scolding her daughter.

"Don't worry, Amber. I'm harmless." I was lying. I wasn't harmless. Nor did her daughter tell me her mother's name.

"You better be harmless. Thanks again. I guess I'll talk to you later." Amber shook my hand and left.

I had a plan, and it was coming together. But what I did with the plan was another story. I was feeling drawn to these two girls in ways I couldn't really wrap my head around. However, until I decided otherwise, I'd follow the plan. I'd become her friend, babysit her daughter when she needed me to, and get her to trust me enough to share her shady painful past with me. All strippers have a painful past, and usually it revolves around something a man did. I was guessing Amber's wounds had something to do with Kimberly's father.

After fully gaining Amber's trust, I'd have an associate kidnap Kimberly. I'd have the kidnapping happen during a time I was baby-sitting, I'd bloody myself up to make it look like I put up a fight, and I'd describe the kidnapper as someone resembling the man from Amber's past. The plan was perfect, and whatever money Amber had accumulated could soon be mine.

Amber

Is there anything more pathetic than an aging stripper?

That's what I was thinking as I sat in Burger King having a sundae with Kimberly. Every year, my make-up will get thicker to fill in my growing wrinkles; my exercise routine will lengthen to fight the winless battle against gravity. Eventually, I'll be forced to turn to plastic surgery to remove the loose, wiggly skin under my arms and on my ass.

This is my destiny.

What will Kimberly think of me when she's old enough to understand how I make my living?

Not only am I a pathetic stripper, but now I'm officially stupid, too. I failed my final; I failed out of school.

Now what?

T.J.

You're wasting your $120,000 education. You're not an actor, and you're not making it in Hollywood. Come home and get a real job.

I sat on the 405 North during rush-hour traffic contemplating my father's words. Maybe he was right.

I'd been back in the giant chicken coop of L.A. for almost a year and a half. I still didn't have an agent, and I hadn't even gotten a single audition. But I wasn't ready to give up and settle into some boring accounting job for the rest of my life. So, to survive, I worked humiliating part-time jobs for Coastal Promotions. Last week, I was a gorilla wielding a cell phone for one of the mobile carriers, the week before I was a giant Subway sub, and this week I'm a giant chicken promoting McDonald's new chicken sandwich. I'd stand on the corner, flap my chicken wings, and make chicken noises. *Bawcalk!* I considered myself lucky to be the chicken; the McRib costume was twice as heavy.

I couldn't help contemplating the irony of what I was promoting; why would a chicken be encouraging people to eat chicken? And the McRib promotion made no sense to me either. If the McRib is so damn good, then why do they have to bring it back every year? Why does it go away in the first place?

Getting out of the chicken suit takes about fifteen minutes. Today, because I was in a rush to make it home for the Steelers' Monday Night Football game, I wore the suit in the car to save time. Bad idea. The needle on my gas gage was moving more than my speedometer. It was ninety degrees, and I was hot, sweaty, and dirty. It felt like Crisco was slogging through my veins.

The air conditioner in my crappy '89 Ford Taurus blew hot air, and rolling the windows down was about as refreshing as sucking on a tailpipe. The Los Angeles smog is no joke.

Earlier, I'd devoured three McDonald's chicken sandwiches. Another bad idea. Consequently, while I was daydreaming about driving a convertible on an open Midwestern road, something was attacking my stomach. I probably should've considered my ulcers before eating those sandwiches. I let out strategic intermittent small bursts of air to relieve some pressure. I was halfway home when the force inside me became too great. I muscled my car into the exit lane. The exit was a hundred yards away, and the off-ramp was backed up to a stop. Tiny monsters with ice picks jabbed the inside of my stomach. I bit my hand to create a diversion, and I focused all my energy on holding myself together until I could get to a facility.

But what if I hold it in for too long?

My colon could explode, and the toxins would eat my vital organs. I could die a horrible death if I hold it any longer. I must let it go; I must relieve myself!

But then what?

Go home with soiled pants? My roommate might be having a get-together. Everyone would know I shat myself. They'd run away laughing and tell everyone in sight I shat myself. People would come in off the streets to see the man in the chicken suit who shat himself. Word would spread, and I'd become a local legend. Children would point and laugh, and they'd yell, *Hey, chicken man, hey you, chicken suit pooper man!* I would become known as *chicken suit pooper man,* and I'd never recover. When I died, my epitaph would read, *Here lays chicken suit pooper man.* No! I won't let happen! I can hold it! I can!

I gripped the steering wheel at ten and two and held on for dear life. I made it across the off-ramp and entered the first fast-food joint I found, a Burger King. There was thunder in my stomach, and I moved like lightning to the bathroom.

Accidentally, I pummeled a little girl with a tray of chicken nuggets. I had no time to consider the irony. "Sorry!"

"Jerk!" the mother yelled.

The bathroom was near. *Relief.* My bowels began to relax. *Oh shit!* It was one of those bathrooms that require a dime to enter. As if corporate America doesn't rip us off enough by charging a buck fifty for a fountain soda, they also want to charge us for pissing it back out. I had no change in my pocket-less chicken suit. My sphincter had started to relax, and there was no way to regain control. My bowels were calling the shots now.

"DOES ANYONE HAVE A DIME?" I screamed, scaring women and children. No response. "FOR THE LOVE OF JESUS, DOES ANYONE HAVE A DIME?"

No help. Apparently, heroes don't hang out at Burger King.

I flew out of the restaurant to my car. I fumbled with my keys, grabbed a handful of change, and sprinted back inside. I was in such a hurry I never saw the little brat with the chicken nuggets stick out her leg. She tripped me, I crashed into the floor face-first, did a half somersault onto my back, and watched my keys and change spread like a California wildfire. I bounced to my feet, grabbed a dime off the floor, and darted to the bathroom. Once inside, I slammed the door behind me, got out of my chicken suit as quickly as possible, and with no time to lay down the protective seat cover, I collapsed onto the toilet—just a second or two late. I'd soiled myself...

I was on the toilet long enough to listen to Inagodadavida, the live concert version.— twice. I read every last bit of graffiti on the walls, and then I romanticized about murdering my boss at Coastal Promotions. Then, finally, I'd finished.

I went to the sink, soiled chicken suit in hand, ready for damage control. I had no option but to wash it and put it back on. I began scrubbing, and then, just when I thought things couldn't possibly get any worse, they did.

While I was standing at the sink, naked, the lights went out. *Stay calm.* I set the chicken suit in the sink, put my hands on the wall and walked myself, hand-over-hand, toward the light timer knob. I'd just give it another twist, and I'd be fine. At two or three feet from the switch, the bathroom door swung open, and the light turned on automatically. I was standing with my hands against the wall, my bare ass pointed in the direction of a humongous man who stood in the doorway, looking.

"Ummm, hi. Could you, um, please shut the door?" I asked.

The mother of the child who tripped me walked out of the adjacent ladies room and screamed.

"Dude, close the door," I said, calmly. He did. I looked at the ceiling, "Why God? Are you bored? Does this amuse you?"

I locked the door and finished cleaning the suit. I exited Burger King with my head down, and headed for my car.

No Taurus!

I'd forgotten I dropped my keys when the little brat tripped me. Someone picked them up and stole my car.

Who would steal a Taurus?

I was forced to go back into the Burger King in my chicken suit and beg someone for a quarter so I could call a friend to come get me.

My father was right. I wasn't making it in this town.

Amber

"Mom, look, there's the chicken guy!" Kimberly said.

He was on the payphone.

"Bawk, bawk, bawk, bawk, bawk, chicken!"

"Kimberly, stop that! That man is retarded. Don't make fun."

"Here chicky, chicky, chicky!"

"Stop it!"

"Hey, you! Your little brat is the reason my car got stolen! You owe me!"

The poor retarded man dropped the phone and started walking toward us. I hustled Kimberly into the car and we left as fast as possible.

January 1999
Dr. Juan Salazar

Flora's dark, silky hair spread out on her pillow, lying around her head like a halo.

"You are the most incredible woman a man could aspire to have," I said.

"What is assfire?" She asked. I laughed. Though her English had improved a great deal, she still mixed the sounds of her Ps and Fs as well as her Bs and Vs. "It's pronounced aspire, not assfire, and it means to seek, to hope for, to wish for."

Flora responded, "I assfire you, too."

I laughed and kissed Flora's cheek. Gazing at her, I realized I'd never before seen a woman without a single hair on her face. There were no little mustache hairs, no nose hairs, and no sideburns. Her delicate skin was so soft I could feel the roughness of my own fingers when I touched her. Flora was funny, smart, entertaining, humble, engaging and innocent. She was everything a man could want, and that terrified me.

"Goodnight, Flora."

"Goodnight."

There would be no sex tonight, and I was fine with that. We had sex about once a week, and though I didn't love it, I didn't hate it, either. However, losing my virginity to Flora was terrifying. In the beginning of our relationship, I was only able to make love to her when she was passed out, drunk. We never talked about it, but I think she knew what was going on, and I think she understood. I think she wanted to help me.

Things went on like that until about the eighth week of our courtship. Then, one night, Flora asked me to kiss her vagina. I couldn't do it. Instead, I put my fingers there and massaged her. Aroused, Flora climbed on top of me, and we made love. I was scared out of my mind, but I survived it.

Flora was my only chance at normalcy. With Flora by my side, I believed I could beat anything. In fact, I felt so comfortable with her I was able to tell her about what happened with Tamara and me under the Venice Pier when we were kids. Besides the Doctor, I had never spoken of this to anyone. After telling her about it, I felt like I could become a whole new me.

With Flora in my life, my O.C.D. symptoms weren't as prevalent. I no longer fantasized about little girls. I'd all but forgotten about the young pixie, Gina, and soon I'd even be able to forgive myself. It was only a mistake; everyone makes one or two.

I fell in love with Flora the first time I saw her at work. I loved her more every day, but loving her was frightening because losing her love would be unbearable. I had no choice but to love Flora until death and pray she'd love me the same. But I knew that was unlikely. Flora was much too desirable not to be pursued by other men. I'd spend my whole life butting heads and locking horns with every man who came near her. I'd have to mark her with territorial pissings and lock her away when she was in heat.

I lay awake and struggled with insecurities about Flora as I did every night. My brain never lets me get any sleep.

Ron

I thought about Amber often since I babysat Kimberly, but I never returned to the Starr club to see her. I decided that for the plan to work, I needed to earn her trust at a pace comfortable to her. If I kept hanging around the club, I'd look like a stalker, and it would never work. Still, it had been some time since our last contact, and I hadn't heard from her. Another day or two, and I'd have to go back to Starr regardless.

And, oddly, I missed her.

Just as I was thinking about her, my phone rang.

"Hey, Ron, sorry I never called. I'm a woman of my word, and it's been a month, so I guess I'm ready for the dinner date I owe you," Amber said.

I was genuinely surprised at her call. Apparently, she already trusted me to some degree. We agreed to meet at eight o'clock for dinner at Captain Jack's, on the water, in Marina Del Rey.

I arrived early at seven thirty.

I'd downed three gin and tonics by the time Amber arrived at eight thirty. She looked great in her pink t-shirt; *Girls*, it read in red letters across her chest.

"Hi, Ron."

"Hi, Amber. I'm glad you made it," I said. I couldn't help but notice that she had not brought a friend with her, as was the agreement. This was encouraging.

"Sorry I'm so late. I had to wait for Beth to get home to watch

Kimberly." I felt disapproving stares of white couples looking at the black girl and white guy.

"No problem," I said.

"Ron, before we order—"

"I know, you're a lesbian, and there's no chance of anything happening."

She laughed. "Besides that. I wanted to start by apologizing for being so rude to you at the club and at the bookstore. I was in deep trouble, but that was no excuse for being a bitch."

"No apology necessary. I'm sure you get a lot of creeps in that place. You were just protecting yourself. Anyway, are things better now?"

"Well, I guess I'm keeping my nose above the fray, but things aren't great. I failed the final, and I'm out of school."

"I'm sorry to—"

"A drink for the beautiful lady?" asked the black waiter. His tone was flirtatious, and he smiled at Amber.

"Just water, please," Amber said.

"You sure you don't want a glass of wine or something?" I asked.

"I don't drink when I drive," she said, and the waiter left.

"Okay, I'm going to level with you, Amber. I got here at seven thirty to get us a table with a view. I was nervous about meeting you, and I ordered a drink. I had to keep ordering drinks to keep the table. I'm a little drunk, and I'm probably going to make an ass out of myself."

"Hmm, that's kind of sweet."

"Are you two ready to order?" the black waiter asked. His arm brushed against Amber as he set her water on the table. He was definitely hitting on her. It shouldn't have bugged me, but it did.

"Oh, you have oyster stew; that's great! I haven't had that since I was a little girl. It's my favorite. I'll start with that," Amber said.

I'd never had oyster stew. "I'll have the same."

I don't think either of us said more than ten words after ordering. We sat, mostly in silence, and just stared around the room. It was uncomfortable. I mean, what does a straight white guy talk about with a black lesbian anyway? Ten minutes later, when the stew finally arrived, I was relieved. Eating would help fill the empty spaces.

"Is your stew good?" I asked.

"It's delicious. Yours?"

"Yeah, it's good," I said. The stew looked and tasted like a bowl full of giant boogers in warm milk.

We ate without speaking much, and I couldn't escape the feeling of guilt about stealing Amber's purse in the parking garage. Crooks aren't supposed to have a conscience, and I've never had one before. Every time I looked at her, I felt guilty. How could I possibly kidnap her daughter if I couldn't even get over stealing her purse?

Amber

Ron's eating thoroughly disgusted me. Nothing gets under my skin like a soup slurper.

"You like the stew?" Ron asked.

"Yeah, Ron, you just asked me that five minutes ago."

"Oh, yeah. Sorry." Ron and I struggled for dinner conversation. I was pretty confident that this was the first time Ron had been in this kind of social situation with a lesbian… and maybe the first time he was with a black woman.

"So, Amber, what's it like to be an African American?"

"What? What the hell does that mean?"

"Umm, I—"

"First of all, I'm not African American. I wasn't born in Africa. I'm an American. Do you call yourself European American?"

"No, I was just trying to be politically correct."

"What's the deal with you? Are you the kind of bigot who wants to have sex with black women to dominate them?"

I despise bigotry. I'm not a bigot; I don't prejudge. White men have shaped the opinion I have of them. White men are irresponsible with their power and money. Our beautiful earth is millions of years old, and in a mere five hundred years or so, white people have nearly destroyed it. Another hundred years like the last hundred, and there won't be a living creature left on the planet.

"I'm not a bigot. I've just never had a black friend before."

"That's great, Ron."

"That came out wrong. Look, I'm not a bigot, and, no, I don't want to experience jungle love. I mean, I'd *like* to experience jungle love, bu—"

"Jungle Love? Are you freaking kidding?"

I would've gotten up and left after the Jungle Love comment, but his extreme ignorance was mildly fascinating.

"What I mean is that, like I told you before, I want to be your friend."

"Why?"

"I don't know why. I don't understand myself. "

"I don't understand you either."

Ron played with his stew. "I don't mean *I don't understand myself.* Although I don't. I mean, I don't understand my wanting to be friends with you any more than you understand it."

"Are you two ready to order your main courses?" the server asked, appearing out of nowhere.

"I'll have the lobster. He'll have the *JERK* chicken."

The waiter wrote down the orders and left.

"That wasn't nice," Ron said.

"You aren't nice. And now I'm leaving."

"But you just ordered lobster."

"So chew on it."

Ron's eyes closed. He sucked in a breath, and then spoke. "Please, just give me five minutes to explain everything."

"Why should I?"

"You shouldn't. But would you?"

"Five. Go." I looked at my bare wrist to suggest I was timing him.

"I was raised on the east coast in an Italian family full of bigots. Hearing my mom and dad use the word nigger is one of my earliest memories. I went to an all-white school in an all-white community. The first time I saw a black man, my father said, *look at that filthy nigger.* Before that, I thought a nigger was a kind of nut because my grandmother always referred to those long black Brazilian nuts as *Nigger Toes.* When—"

"If you say nigger one more time, I'm going to beat the shit out of you and shove your jerk chicken down your jerk face!"

"Sorry. Please, just listen. This is hard for me to talk about."

"I didn't come here to give you therapy. Get to the point," I said.

"Okay. Fine. Will you just shut up and listen?"

"That's it!" I slammed my fist on the table and stood up. "I'm outta here." I turned and walked away.

"I saw my mother get raped by a black man!" Ron shouted at my back from halfway across the restaurant. It stopped me where I stood.

All eyes were on me as I turned around, walked back to Ron, grabbed his white hand, and walked him out of the restaurant.

Ron

It was eighteen years ago, but some wounds aren't healed by time.

I was only eight-years-old, a voyeur in my own house, paralyzed by curiosity. At first, my young mind didn't understand what was happening. I just stood there watching him move on top of my mother.

Mom sounded uncomfortable.

"Say one fucking word, and I'll slit you from your asshole to your mouth-hole," the large black man said, and then I knew Mom was in big trouble.

His large, naked black body pinned her frail white figure to the floor. I needed to help her, but my legs were stuck in invisible quicksand. Then, Mom noticed me. The humiliation in her eyes ignited a fire inside me that would stay lit for years. I was filled with rage, an emotion I'd never experienced.

I grabbed the ceramic lamp off the end table; it was heavy, but I was able to lift it quietly. I came in from behind; my mother closed her eyes, and I smashed the fucking lamp into the back of his head!

"Fuck!" He got off my mother and swung around to face me with his knife in hand. He had the biggest penis I'd ever seen. Petrified, I stumbled backward. He raised a fisted hand to hit me, but my mother jumped on his back and clawed at his eyes.

"Leave my child alone you fucking NIGGER!" Mom yelled. Her nails dug in deep; blood squirted from his eye.

"Ahhh! You fucking bitch!" In a single motion, he knocked my mother off him and blindly swung the knife, which caught Mom's left arm. Her blood gushed on the floor, on the man, and on me. Mom dropped to the ground.

I threw an empty beer bottle at him, but he was halfway out the door before it left my hand. I picked up the phone and dialed 911. It took me at least fifteen seconds to calm my voice enough for the operator to understand. When the police arrived, I was holding Mom, both of us soaked in her blood. My thin arms were wrapped around her. Mom's expression was bland, and she robotically stroked my face with her uninjured arm while singing the saddest song I'd ever heard. That song got inside my head and took over.

The way weeds take over a garden.

The way a virus takes over a body

And when I think of her sad song, I still cry.

I never told anyone about this event. It was between me, my mom, and my journal. For whatever reason, I made the decision to make Amber the first person I shared this information with.

After that horrible day, the relationship between Mom and me changed. I did everything I could to avoid her. I played sports, hung out with buddies, and read books. I liked words. I liked how, when strung together in different patterns, they could make something beautiful. I tried writing, but everything I put to paper tied into my layered angst, hatred, sadness, and humiliation. So I quit writing; it was just too painful.

I was no good at sports, so I quit those, too, and took up a hobby, burying myself in the details to occupy my mind. In eight months, I put together models of nearly two-dozen historical Air Force fighter planes in chronological order, starting with the 1941 P-40 Warhawk and ending with the 1963 A-6E Intruder. But my hobby wasn't enough; my mind wasn't busy enough. I fell in with the wrong crew and got involved with some nickel-and-dime crime. I loved it; crime was exciting, and it allowed me to be somebody other than the young white kid who saw his mother get raped by a nigger. Eventually, at the age of fourteen, I ran away.

I took care of myself financially with petty crime jobs. But the petty crimes led to bigger jobs. I got caught and went to prison. It was only a short sentence, but the isolation left me without distraction. All I had were my thoughts, and my mother's rape grew more vivid. So, again, I wrote. I wrapped myself around poetry; it was the one beautiful thing that muted all the ugliness inside and around me. Poetry gave my brain something to picture, so when I closed my eyes, I saw something beautiful instead of my poor mother with the nigger on top of her.

I told Amber this story, staring at my feet the entire time as if the script of the incident were written on the tips of my shoes. It was the first time I'd ever told the story. Why I'd chosen this moment, with this person, I had no idea, but as I spoke the words, something changed within me.

I went on, telling her, "My dad was so sickened by his wife being raped by a black man, he divorced Mom. I've spoken to my mom only once since I left home, and it was only to let her know I was okay. I never bothered to ask if she was okay. I've never stopped being angry with her."

I stopped my story before the part where I became a convict. Once I finished, I was finally able to look up at her.

"I'm so sorry, Ron." A stream of tears flowed from her eyes. I wiped her tears with the cuff of my shirt. "Sometimes, I think we're all living a different version of the same sad story," Amber said.

It was at this moment I realized we were two broken people who needed each other. I couldn't harm this woman; I couldn't take advantage of her; what was beginning here, in this moment, was something too big and too important. My plan for Amber was a million miles away. All I wanted was for her to touch me the way two friends touch. And for whatever reason, for the very first time, I didn't care what color she was.

"Ron, I think we need to be friends," she said. The momentous nature of what had just happened was obvious to her as well.

"I want to be your friend," I said.

"We have a lot more in common than you know," Amber said. "I have to go home to my daughter now. Call your mother, Ron."

Amber handed me a quarter. "Call her now, Ron."

She patted me on the shoulder, smiled, walked to her car, and left. I watched her drive away. I looked at the payphone and got in my car. I turned the ignition, looked back at the phone, turned off the car, and walked to the phone. I put the quarter in and dialed.

"Hello," I heard her say.

"Hi, Mom."

October 1999
Reece

"It's an old injury from my pro football days." *Blah, blah, blah.* "I knew I was taking a big chance, but it obviously paid off." *Blah, blah, blah* "Rockenberger Rum became a huge success for me and led to bigger and—" *Blah, blah, blah.*

I was wearing a stunning Versace gown at the hippest party in the Hollywood Hills, and I was talking with an incredibly rich, incredibly attractive man named Jackson Rockenberger, but I couldn't enjoy it because of Kelly. I never loved Kelly, but that's no excuse for him cheating on me with my ex-friend and godmother of my child, Maria

Orlando.

"Reece? Reece?"

"Oh. I'm sorry, Jackson. I was just thinking. Please, go on."

"That's okay. Sometimes I can be a bore," Jackson said and looked at me expectantly. "Usually, this is the part where the woman says, 'No, Jackson, actually you're quite fascinating.'"

I'm thirty-seven. I'm in my sexual prime. It isn't natural to waste it all on my loser husband, Kelly.

"Reece? Reece, it was a pleasure meeting you." Jackson shook my hand and walked away, irritated that I hadn't been listening to him.

How did I make such a mess of my life? One lousy game of racquetball with a complete stranger, and life changed forever. I was supposed to be a famous actress with a daughter who wanted to be me when she grew up. I was supposed to be married to a successful man, someone like Jackson Rockenberger: rich, good looking, and famous.

Fuck you, Kelly.

I casually walked after Jackson. "Can we get out of here?"

"Where do you want to go?" he asked.

"Your place," I suggested.

"Why don't we get a suite at the Argyle instead?"

Wow. A suite at the best hotel in Hollywood. This could have been my life, but life happened wrong for me.

Dylan

She wore a short yellow skirt, yellow heels, and a yellow tank top under a yellow blazer with huge yellow buttons. She was probably a gullible shopaholic convinced by some young, skinny twenty-something salesgirl on Melrose that the Big Bird look was the hottest new style.

She pointed to her car and handed me a ticket stub.

"I love your sunny outfit," I said.

"Thank you, doll," she responded.

I hated my night job working as a valet, as much as I hated all the others. The customers were the worst. I'd had it with these rich, depressed, trophy housewives who spent their perpetual free time popping pills and shopping for overpriced clothes made by nine-year-old kids in Chinese sweatshops. They shop, they purchase, they get more depressed, and the cycle repeats. They're forever spending their lawyer husband's blood money on ridiculous designer clothes to wear the following Tuesday afternoon on their next shopping binge.

"Thank you, Larry, for bringing me tonight. The benevolence was inspiring. I had an exquisite time," said Big Bird lady.

She could have simply said, *Thanks, I had fun*, but she probably wanted to show off the sophisticated words she learned in her book club.

I retrieved her Jaguar. She got in and turned on her CD player. Britney Spears was her music of choice. I became dumber in the few seconds I was forced to listen to it.

The distasteful music rich people play in their cars is one of the worst parts of the job. Not once had I ever parked a luxury vehicle playing decent punk music. Unless you count Green Day as punk, which I don't. Every once in a while, I'd steal a CD or two, not to keep, but to destroy. I was on a mission to rid the world of bad music, one Matchbox Twenty CD at a time   Another couple approached. They, like most, were pretending to be in love.

Forgive me if I sound jaded. Forgive me if I think the only part of love that's worth a damn is the first few days together. The first look, the first conversation, the first touch, the first kiss, the first fuck, after the novelty of it all wears off, it's all down hill.

After Allison called me weird, broke up with me, and destroyed me in high school, I swore off love and fell into a string of lusty pseudo-relationships. There was Theresa, Erika, Terry, Monica, Susan, and Kim. There was Lucinda, who told me her biggest passion in life was *great sex*. And she backed it up. Nothing about any of these women was unique, and none of them were interesting. They were fleshy playgrounds of tits and ass that gave me orgasms, but rarely provoked thought.

But then there was Melinda. She was an exotic orgy of ethnicities; her parents' DNA blended into something spectacular. I tried to avoid falling in love with Melinda, but she tried that much harder to win it. Melinda pampered my injured heart, nurturing it back to health. Then, once she knew she had me, she reached down my throat, ripped out my heart, and stomped it into a worthless lump of flesh. She rammed my dead heart back into my chest and disappeared, leaving me alone to stitch myself up.

That fucking bitch Melinda ruined me in four weeks flat.

Last month, Melinda visited me, unannounced, while I was working at the Starr club. I was irritable and said something stupid to her. Melinda stormed off, and later I caught her making out with my coworker in the bathroom. I kicked his ass and lost my job.

And then Melinda told me she was pregnant with my child.

"I want you to know I'm with you in this," I said, offering her my life. "I know we've had a rough time, but we can make this work."

"I already aborted it. I'd never have your child," she said, speaking casually as if it were just some worthless thing, like half an uneaten donut she decided to throw out.

Her intention was to hurt me. Mission accomplished.

And now I park cars for a living.

Tonight, I was parking cars at a celebrity charity event. The wealthy buy pretentious art they don't understand and take it home to display like a trophy. I take care of their luxury vehicles while wearing my red linen monkey suit and cap provided by my company. My pay was a paltry eight dollars an hour, so to make the job worthwhile, I stole loose change from their cars.

The rich don't notice missing change.

Tonight's event was for malnourished children in Africa. The cost to put on the party was probably more than whatever money they were sending overseas. The wealthy gather and listen to speeches stolen from embroidered pillows in Christian bookstores. They eat, fawn over the celebrities, get drunk, and hand over a couple dollars so they can go home feeling better about their self-indulgent lives.

But maybe the rich aren't so bad.

Maybe if I had been rich, Melinda wouldn't have aborted my baby.

Fuck Melinda.

Fuck the rich.

Another jag-off handed me his keys. I recognized him immediately. It was the guy that had gotten Amber's friend, Beth, knocked up. Jackson something, I think.

"My Hummer," he said.

I'd had enough, and decided to draw the line with this dick.

"Your truck is right there; you can get it. I'm too slammed right now," I said, standing there, doing absolutely nothing.

"Go get it," his date demanded. She held a cigarette in one hand and a half empty glass of wine in the other.

"Yes, ma'am!" I gave her a snappy salute and skipped off to the vehicle. I climbed into the monstrous global-warming machine, fired up the engine, revved it, slammed it into reverse, and peeled out. Gravel fired off the tires like shrapnel, and dust engulfed the Hummer. I traveled the twenty yards to where my customer stood and tossed him the keys.

"You guys should call a cab. You're both too wasted to drive."

"Excuse me?" he asked.

"I said you smell like a winery. And the car you drive, whose name means blow job, is killing our world with its ejaculatory waste."

"Jackson! Don't let him talk to you that way!" said his date.

He looked at her, back at me, and puffed out his chest. "Show some respect, young man," Jackson said.

"Jackson, Jackie, Jacko. Calm down, relax your tail feathers, get in your environment destroyer, and go the fuck home."

"I hope you can read, buddy. Tomorrow, you'll be searching the classifieds for a new job," Jackson said. He jumped into his Hummer.

"Yes, I can read. In fact, I'm a big advocate of education!" I yelled over the roar of his loud engine. "Here's some learnin' for you; scientists have estimated every time you listen to a Celine Dion song, you lose approximately fifteen hundred brain cells."

"He stole my CDs!" Jackson yelled. "That's it." He got out of the car and stomped toward me, his fingers bending to make fists.

"Lay a hand on me, and I'll own that blow job," I said pointing at his Hummer.

Jackson hesitated. He shook a finger at me. "I'll be speaking to your supervisor." He climbed back in his Hummer and started driving away.

"My name is Dylan! You've met me before, but arrogant fucks like you don't remember us peons. I've been smoking weed all night. Make sure you tell my boss that, too!" I shouted louder as they got further away. The others who had gathered outside were staring. I was about to be fired from my third job in as many months… at least I was good at something.

"And I didn't steal your CDs! I threw them away. I'm saving the world from your shit music!"

November 1999
Kelly

Reece lied about her age when we met, but most women do. Although probably not by ten years. I think Reece would've eventually come clean about her age, but then she got pregnant, and she was probably scared I'd leave her if I knew how old she was. If lying about her age was her biggest crime, I could live with that. She wasn't perfect by any means, but she and Teddy were the best things to ever happen to me.

Unfortunately, until recently, our sexual activity was at a standstill. Things had become so mundane that Reece didn't even bother with excuses for why she didn't want sex anymore. I thought women were supposed to reach their sexual prime in their mid-thirties, but Reece's sex drive died a few weeks after we got married. So did her passion for cooking and cleaning.

I had high hopes that, as the years passed, we'd get more creative in the bedroom. Last night, I addressed my concern. "Honey, it's not like I'm asking for a threesome or anything, but we need to kink it up a little. Maybe a little role-playing, homemade porn, dominatrix stuff. I could tie you up, mutual masturbation, anything."

"Go to sleep, Kelly," was her response.

"I'll settle for a blow-job."

"Gross," Reece said. She hates giving them. She doesn't give them. Of course, she's never had any problem with me going down on her yankee doodle dandy. On our honeymoon, I came up smiling from between her legs, a mustache of wetness on my upper lip. I lay on my back expecting my cunnilingus to pay oral dividends, but Reece fell asleep instead, foreshadowing what marriage would be like.

Reece's sexy friend, who ironically was one of my first breast massage patients at the Motion Picture Television Fund, Maria Orlando, helped me throw Reece a surprise party recently. Reece knew Maria and I were spending time together, and though she never said anything, I think she thought we were having an affair, and she probably felt stupid about that after receiving her party.

After the party, we finally made love. It was the first time we'd had sex in quite a while. After, I wanted to keep the sexual momentum going, but that didn't happen. Reece and I were destined to spend our lives together having sex about once a quarter, doing the standard missionary in-out-in-out, *oh-ah that feels good, ouch you're on my hair, hurry up and finish— Letterman's on.* Our lovemaking sessions were robotic and empty, and our kisses were like carnival consolation prizes.

Today, Teddy was with Reece's Mom because Reece had an important audition for some low-budget film. I prayed she landed the role. A gig for her would equal money and possible celebration sex. However, the prospect of Reece booking the part was grim if it were a speaking role. God blessed Reece with the greatest body and face in the history of wannabe actresses in L.A., but he didn't bless her with any actual acting ability. If silent films ever make a comeback, Reece's Hollywood stock will go through the roof.

Reece's car was in the driveway when I got home.

Odd, she shouldn't be home so early.

I decided to drive down the street to a boutique; I'd buy her a gift and keep the romance moving forward. I bought her flowers and lingerie. Lingerie was the greatest gift in the world for Reece; she could show off, which she loved, and I got to watch her showing off, which I loved. Armed with gifts, I drove home to surprise my bride. I entered the house stealthily.

"Hey, Reece."

Reece's mouth was too full to respond.

"Oh boy," Reece said as she unwrapped her lips from the man-part of my boss, Jackson Rockenberger.

I handed the flowers to Jackson. "These are for you, boss."

Jackson

I used to tell this joke about aging:

Do you know how to tell when you're getting old? No? It's when you stop taking drugs for fun and start taking them because they're prescribed.

I don't want to get old, but no amount of Botox, surgery, creams, or potions can prevent it. The only way to avoid old age is to die young. That doesn't appeal to me either.

When Reece's husband, Kelly, walked in on us, he started yelling about love and commitment. That made me think about my mother; I hadn't seen her in two months. Mom had a major stroke, and I'd been avoiding her since. Yesterday, I'd gotten a call that her situation had turned to critical. I left Reece's, while the two of them screamed at each other, and went home to try to work up the courage to see Mother.

My heart nearly splintered out of my chest when I saw Mom lying in the hospital bed. Her frail body disappeared beneath the heavy blankets. The small bumps in the blankets from Mom's knees and the tips of her toes were the only evidence a body was present.

Mom's face was old and tired and thin, and her eyes were sunk in. There were long grooves in her face, deep enough for pennies to stand in.

160

Her hair was flat and matted and thin. Mom was meticulous about her hair, and if she had any energy, she'd have fussed. Her eyes were barely open, they were yellowed and distant and some greenish substance was caked in the corners. The left side of her mouth hung partially open, exposing an empty space where teeth should have been, and a thick tube hung out of her mouth. There was a bag of urine on the side of the bed. A thick, yellow catheter ran under the blankets and disappeared between her legs. Yet another line went to her heart.

Mom closed the left side of her mouth; drool ran down her cheek, caught a deep wrinkle, and rode it all the way to the pillow. Her drool had an unpleasant stench, that nearly overpowered the smell of feces that hung in the air. I wondered if the feces smell came from my mother or the soiled linen cart outside her room. I hoped it was the latter.

I watched Mom's chest rise and fall. It seemed to stop for a minute, but I couldn't tell for sure.

I should call a nurse. If she's stopped breathing, what can they do? I've never seen anyone die before. How will I know when she's dead? Will she go silently? Will something spectacular happen? Did she die already?

Mom resumed breathing.

She opened one eye. The overhead light highlighted her face like a spotlight, and made me feel like we were in some dramatic theatrical production. It's the final scene; she's alone on stage about to share her thoughts with her rapt audience. She'll say something important, and it will stick with me for the rest of my life.

But Mom didn't say anything. She couldn't. She looked at me and went back to sleep. With her eye slightly open, it was as though she was watching me, which was creepy. I searched for the beauty I'd always seen in her, but it wasn't there, or if it was, I couldn't see it through all the decay.

I wanted Mother to love me again; I wanted to crawl back into my mother's womb, the only place I'd ever been safe.

What will happen when she dies? Who will love me when she's gone?

Dr. Juan Salazar

I entered Mrs. Rockenberger's room; Jackson's face was expressionless.

"Mr. Rockenberger, its okay to be scared… I want you to

consider a few sessions with me."

"No, thank you."

"Your mother's going to die, Mr. Rockenberger. Let me help—"

"Get out of this room," Jackson said, flatly. I left.

I should've been more professional, but I couldn't leave my bias out of the equation. I didn't like Mr. Rockenberger. In '97, Ms. Rockenberger had a small stroke in the left lobe of her cerebellum. After, her doctor had me address her depression. After several sessions, she confessed some intimate dysfunctional sexual behaviors between her and her son, Jackson, when he was a boy. Later, I tried to discuss these things with Jackson. He didn't take to it well, and physically assaulted me. I didn't report the incident, but I never forgot it. In some dark way, I felt he and I were bound by similar crimes against our youth; I felt connected to him. His rejection of me made me resent him like I'd never resented any patient.

Today, when asked to address Jackson, I was already in a bad mood because I could sense that Flora was about to dump me. I didn't want to even talk to Jackson, and I knew he'd reject my help anyway. In mother-son relationships such as his, the boy usually matures into one of two types of me:

1- the man who hates his mother and takes it out on all the other women in his life or

2- the man who distorts his childhood memories into something that is more normal and pleasant. This man spends his life seeking his mother's love to validate his existence.

Jackson became both of these kinds of men.

Jackson

I knew Mother was going to die. I didn't need some shrink-asshole to tell me. Mother was leaving, and I'd be left alone. I had a son, we were strangers to each other. I wanted to meet him; I wanted to know him. Why had I not?

How much time is left with Mother? What am I supposed to do with these last moments together? There will be no final speech from her, no exchange of love, no parting words of wisdom, nothing.

A fat old bath nurse entered.

"Time for your mother's bath," she said.

"Don't bother. She's dying."

"Sir, your mother deserves the dignity of being clean."

"Get out!" I yelled.

Mom is dying, and there isn't a damned thing I can do about it.

I stared at the EKG as it drew long, red lines. Soon, it would stop. I counted all the tubes and lines. There were nine in all. One was a morphine drip. I wanted it.

Mom's breathing became different. She usually took heavy breaths, almost like a snore. But now it sounded like a wet gurgle. Moisture was audible with each inhale; her lungs were filling. It sounded like she was at the bottom of a lake trying to suck in air.

Will she be with Dad in her next life? Will she want to be? Has Dad been watching me all these years since he passed? I wonder whom she loved more, me or him?

I was lonely and sad, and I needed something to kill the loneliness.

An Asian nurse entered. Thin, young, pretty. Her nametag read Flora. She began checking my mother.

I should talk to her. She'd fuck me; I need to fuck. But why bother? She wouldn't love me, and I wouldn't love her; it'd be just a fuck, like all the others. It wouldn't kill the loneliness.

"You okay?" Flora asked me.

"Yeah."

"Ring por me if you need," Flora said. Flora had seen a thousand people die. She was numb to it and didn't care about my mother. I hated her calloused and impartial attitude.

I was driving myself crazy and needed to slow my thoughts. *Can I turn on the television? Would that be tacky?* Yes, it would. I need to spend these last few hours bonding with Mom. But how do I bond with her when she doesn't know I'm here?

I lay in bed beside Mom and turned on her favorite soap, *The Bold and Beautiful*, to watch with her.

Then Mom died.

Dr. Juan Salazar

"Come with me, Ella May. Let's leave this place forever."

"I can't do that," Ella May said, then walked away.

The name, Ella May, it's musical. It's practically a song. Ella May moves with graceful, calculated movements that would appear improvised to the untrained eye. I love everything about her. I hate Dr. Rackferd. I know he wants to hurt her, and she's too young and naive to protect herself.

I wished I could walk through the television screen and save Ella May. I wished I could walk around falling in love easily, like in these soaps.

I hadn't left home in days and was living vicariously through television characters. I wanted an easy life, one that always works out, like on TV. I wanted to live in a TV drama. But one without commercials; they depressed me even more. All the advertisements were geared to the lazy daytime demographic I'd pushed my way into. Law firms advertising to settle viewers' work-injury suits; mail-order tech schools offering degrees for jobs that a chimpanzee could do; pharmaceutical companies advertising products for depression and arthritis.

My *stupid box*, as my mother referred to it, my television, was my pacifier. I couldn't take my eyes off of it because Flora's absence was everywhere else I looked.

Since Flora left me, everything about my apartment reminded me of her. I couldn't stand to remove anything of hers: the black hairpin that rested on the lip of the porcelain sink, Flora's eyelash sleeping on the pillow that smelled like her, or her white panties with a single pubic hair sitting at the foot of the bed we once shared. At night, when I close my eyes, I see Flora's face painted on the inside of my eyelids. The only way I could fall asleep was to lay on Flora's side of the bed. That way, the empty side was my own. And when I did finally sleep, I dreamed only of Flora.

When Flora broke up with me, she took away all the good parts of me. I was left with a crater-sized hole, which allowed my inner ugliness to spread out and reclaim me. The silent darkness within me had been in charge since the day my best friend Tamara was ruined under the Santa Monica pier. Flora had been a nice diversion, but I knew it would never last; the darkness would always control me. The neurosis and compulsive behaviors, perverse thoughts, and the desire to kill myself, all of it came back the second Flora walked out.

I love Flora to the point of pain. Unfortunately, loving someone doesn't obligate them to love you back.

Jackson

I had no desire to leave the house after Mother died.

But I should have gone to her funeral.

I'd gotten progressively more intoxicated every day. I was up to five hundred milligrams of OxyContin mixed with a random smorgasbord of Soma, Vicoden, Valium, Norco; whatever was handy. I wasn't far from crushing and shooting the pills.

Most days I fucked Reece or Joanna. I said I'd never fuck Joanna again, but sometimes she was the only person around, and fucking was like a band-aide to my wound. But it always ripped off before I healed.

So I'd just take more pills.

I'm not addicted. I can quit whenever I like.

But I didn't want to quit. I wanted to stay high, to numb the pain of not being loved.

My son, Jonathon, would love me if he knew me.

I was a professional football player and a cool guy, a stud with the ladies. Any young boy would love to have me as a dad. Jonathon could be the cure to all my woes. I had to get the courage to meet my son and get involved in his life. My life was about to spin out of control; the only thing could save me was purpose. Jonathon, my son, could be my purpose.

Somehow, I was able to motivate myself to get out of the house, which was no small feat. I was going to Beth's, to demand her to introduce me to my son. I wanted this whole experience to be about him, but it wasn't, and I didn't even try to lie to myself about that. This was about me needing him.

I knocked. Beth opened the door and looked up from a magazine.

"Hi, Beth," I said. Beth didn't respond. She stared into my eyes, searching for my motive. "Can I come in?" I asked.

"Why?"

"To talk."

"What's wrong with your eyes?" Beth asked.

"Nothing."

"Your pupils are huge... You're high, aren't you?"

"No. Can I come in?"

"Why?" she asked again.

"I want to talk about Jonathon."

"You're ahead of schedule with child support, so there's nothing to talk about."

"I want to be involved."

"Get out!"

"What?"

"Get out! Get out of here right now! Get out of here right now or I'm calling the cops!"

"Beth, wait, I—" Beth started hitting me over the head with her magazine.

"Get the fuck out of here!" I restrained her. "Beth, just settle down for a minute!"

"I will not settle down!" she said. "Who the hell do you think you are? You got me pregnant and disappeared. And now, at your convenience, you want to be Daddy?"

"Beth, I've been sending money weekly."

"Money doesn't make you his Daddy!" She yelled, wiping sweat from her forehead.

"I have the right to see him."

"You have no rights. You signed away the right to see him a long time ago. You actually had it written into the contract that he could never even be told who his father was. You wanted that, not me!"

"Beth, I've changed."

"I doubt it."

"Look, you know damn well I can hire the best lawyer money can buy. I'll paint you as the incompetent mother with the fucked-up gay daddies and lesbian roommate. I'd end up with full custody. Do you want that?"

Beth poked me in the chest. "Fuck you, you asshole! No judge in this world would give a strung-out junkie custody of a child. None."

"I don't want custody. I just want you to let me see my son and get to know him."

"And why should I let you?" Beth asked.

"Because Jonathon needs a father to look up to. I mean, his father figures are a dyke and two gay men."

"Leave my family out of this. They're good to my son."

166

"Our son."

"You do not have the right to say that!" Beth balled up her fist like she was going to punch me, but she shoved me instead. "You tried to force me abort him! You're a sperm donor and a checkbook, you are not a dad."

"But I want to be. I want to teach him to throw a ball, teach him about girls. Can't you see he needs that?"

"He may need a father, but he doesn't need a self-absorbed junkie for a father."

"I'm self-absorbed, that's fair. But I'm not a junkie. I take pain pills because of football injuries."

"Bull," Beth said, but she still hadn't asked me to leave, which was encouraging.

"Beth, you are obviously in charge here. You tell me what can I do, at this point, to earn a chance to meet my son."

"I don't know, Jackson," she said, taking a breath from her anger. "Listen, get yourself into rehab and get sober. If you do, I'll let you meet Jonathon, but only under the premise that you are a family friend or something. That's the best I can do. But don't mess up. You only get one chance."

"Thank you, Beth. I don't need rehab, but I'll do it for Jonathon. You won't regret this."

"I hope not."

"And Beth, I want to say that I'm— Well, you know."

"What?"

"I'm sorry."

"Don't give me that crap. You're not sorry."

Beth

Was Jackson sincere? I wanted him to be sincere, and I searched his eyes for the truth, but they were deep chasms of nothingness.

In the angle of his chin, his protruding cheekbones, and his deep-set eyes, and his competitive nature, I saw a lot of my son in Jackson. I didn't want to, but I did.

I was amazed at how mean I was to him. I'd never acted that way toward anyone. Jackson flinched when I raised my hand in a fist, and because of this flinch, he became smaller and weaker than me for the very first time. Defeated, he climbed on his Harley and drove off, a tornado of white smoke from the tailpipe signifying his surrender.

Amber came back from a lunch shift at Starr, and I told her the story.

"I'm proud of you for standing up to him," Amber said. "Jonathon doesn't need him. He's got us, and that's all he needs."

"Amber, you're great, the greatest. But if Jackson can get clean, I think I'd like Jonathon to know him. My son deserves a father. All kids deserve two parents. I know I'll always wish I'd met my mother."

"Well, I'd like to have known my father, too, but it didn't work out that way, and you know what? I'm fine without him," Amber said. She sounded defensive. "What if Jackson develops a relationship with Jonathon, then disappears again some day when he grows bored of the whole thing? That's how men like him are, and that would be worse for Jonathon than never meeting him at all."

"Do you really think that would be the worst thing? I mean, if you had the option of getting to know your dad for just a short while, would you choose that over never meeting him at all?"

Amber hesitated before answering. "I don't know, Beth."

"Me neither."

"Well, for you and Jonathon, I hope Jackson gets straight, and I hope he's sincere with his intentions."

December 1999
Jackson

After leaving Beth's, I immediately went home and flushed my drugs. Then, I went straight to Promises rehabilitation center. I felt motivated for the first time in a long time, and I knew it was now or never.

After a week, I couldn't take it anymore. I called Joanna and asked her for a favor. She went to Mexico, purchased some OxyContin, stashed the pills in her vagina when crossing back into America, and then did the same when she came to Promises.

My rehab counselor would call Joanna an enabler.

Joanna wasn't an enabler; she was just desperate to keep me as her own. If I felt Joanna loved me, then I may have been able to love her too, but Joanna's need to have me in her life had very little to do with anything resembling love.

Joanna came in my room and smiled big. She dropped her pants and pulled out the pills. Then she dropped my pants and wrapped her body around mine.

I was so tired of her vagina, but this time I owed it to her.

I survived exactly three more days in Promises, and was three days closer to meeting Jonathon. However, this morning, my case manager walked in my room at the exact moment I was tossing a handful of pills down my throat.

I was asked to leave the facility.

I was crushed, I knew I blew it. And not thinking clearly, I went straight to Beth's to see my son.

"Who's that, Mommy?" Jonathon asked, appearing at Beth's side. He was beautiful. He looked like me. I loved him instantly.

"Nobody, honey. Go inside."

"I'm your Da—" I tried to say, but Beth slammed the door in my face.

Beth shouted through the door, "You're stoned, Jackson. Go home!"

"I want to see my son!" I knew there was no hope. I was desperate and out of control. I banged on Beth's door until my fists bled, screaming and yelling and begging. I continued banging until the cops came and took me away.

Beth got a restraining order.

This final rejection from Beth made everything crystal clear to me. All of this happened because when I got Beth pregnant, I'd been too proud to be with her, or even acknowledge that we had a child together. When my mother died, and left me all alone, I began to realize that some things, like being loved, were more important than one's image, money, and accomplishments.

I'd acquired enough money to live five lifetimes, more houses than I could keep track of, and countless trophies to decorate them. And for what? Love is the only trophy that makes a man worth his own salt. I'd become a failure. I became the one thing I never wanted to be. My father.

My son would never love me.

My mother never loved me. I wasted my life begging for her love.

How could anyone love me?

I don't even love me.

I need warm purple light to rush over me and take away the hurt.

Defeated, I went home. I knew my life would never be what I wanted. I turned on the television, grabbed 600 milligrams of OxyContin, and made the conscious decision to take the final step into the life of the upper-class junkie. In this condition I would live out my life. I crushed the pills, added a splash of water, cooked it up in a bent spoon, filled my syringe, and shot the velvety smooth drugs into the thick vein in my left forearm.

The images on the television blurred and sound disappeared. There was nothing but a symphony of flickering lights and warm purple light.

Kimberly Johnson, 7

"You ain't got no daddy! You ain't got no daddy! You're ugly and a fatty!" chanted the mean boys who were dancing around me.

And boy was I cryin'. I wanted to say stuff about sticks and stones breakin' bones and words not hurting, but that isn't true. So I closed my eyes as tight as I could, and put my hands over my ears to block out all their stupid noise.

I was always closin' my eyes. I'd close 'em and 'scape to someplace else, usually Hawaii. I never been to Hawaii, but I seen pictures. It's pretty. Some day, I'm going to take Mommy there with me and buy her a horse. She had a horse when she was little, and it was her best friend.

I guess I wasn't pluggin' my ears tight enough because I could still hear all them mean boys. One boy, Matt-chew, kicked dirt at me. I took my hands off my ears and charged him. Matt-chew and his friends was bigger than me, but I didn't even care. Mommy spent a ton of money to get my new shoes, and money 'does not grow on trees,' she says; so, I'll be a dog's butt if I was gonna let some mean white boy ruin 'em. I charged Matt-chew then kicked and punched and hollered as loud as I could. Susie pulled me off him or I mighta kilt him. I'm pretty sure Matt-chew was 'barrassed 'bout gettin' beat up by a girl. His friends just stood there with their stupid, ugly mouths wide open like they were tryin' to catch flies. Then all Matt-chew's friends left because I think they was 'barrased of him even more than he was 'barrased of his-self. I hate Matt-chew and all them other white kids who walked around school in their fancy clothes like they be so much better than everyone else.

"I done messing with you anyway, you stupid ugly nigger!" Matt-chew said, and then he spit on me. I woulda chased him all the way home if Susie didn't have hold a me.

"I ain't ugly, and I ain't no stupid N-word!" I yelled at Matt-chew.

Nobody shouldn't never be callin' nobody a N-word. Mommy said it's a horrible thing to call a person. Once, I heard two of Mommy's grown up friends, or act-qua-tan-ces as she calls them—because she says they're not really friends, and she don't really like them, so they just act-qua-tan-ces—anyway, them act-qua-tan-ces, Fat Pete and Lazy Sam—that's what Mommy calls them—was outside talkin', and Fat Pete called Lazy Sam the N-word and then high-fived him. I went out and yelled and hollered at them. I said, "That's the worst thing you can say. That's worst than F-word! Don't you know nuthin'?" And them men just laughed at me. Mommy told me sometimes friends call each other N-word, but that don't make it right; it's still a nasty word. So, to be honest, I'm sorta all confused on that N-word. All I know for sure is when Matt-chew called me it, I ain't never got that mad before. I wouldn't never call nobody no N-word; not my friends, and not even Matt-chew, and he's the worst person I know. Maybe if he kilt someone, which he prolly will one day, then I'd call him an N. But right now, I keep nasty word out of my mouth.

Matt-chew was walkin' away, lookin' back and smilin' at me. Susie still wouldn't let me go. Matt-chew musta seen else he wouldn't had the guts to say what he said next. He looked back over his shoulder, smiled, and yelt, "You ain't got no daddy!"

I was so mad! I almost threw Susie off me and went after Matt-chew, but right then Mommy's friend Ron drove up.

"There's my daddy," I said and pointed.

"You got a white dad?" Matt-chew yelled back.

"Duh."

"Half-breed!"

I shrugged off Susie, ran at Matt-chew, and kicked him in the shin.

I didn't know what half-breed meant, but comin' outta Matt-chew's mouth, I could tell it was nasty. Anyway, Ron is the nicest, but he ain't my daddy. My daddy was a hero. He flied fighter jets for the army and got two metals for bravery. I keep 'em above my bed. I wish I coulda met my dad. He died in a car crash before I was born.

When I was almost all the way to Ron's car, Matt-chew got all brave and started yelling again. "Go run to Daddy, half-breed!" I ignored him this time because Ron was lookin', and I didn't want him tellin'

Mommy I was fightin' boys.

My mommy says my daddy was white. She say I'm half-white and half-black but that don't make no sense to me—I don't feel like I'm half nuthin'. First time Mom told me I was half, when I was like five, I ran to the mirror lookin' for black and white stripes on my body or somethin'. Wasn't no black in me, and the only white I found was in my teeth. Now I'm growed up and know better what she means, when I think about me runnin' to the mirror lookin' for zebra stripes, it's funny.

Susie's mom told Susie she's half-black and half-white, too, but she weren't either. Me and Susie decided them white kids like Matt-chew wasn't even white either. They was like orangy-yellow. And the kids who say they's black, they ain't. They're brown. Except Darrell, that boy's black as night. Anyways, I don't care 'bout being black or white or nuthin'. I just don't like being called no names, and I don't let nobody be talkin' 'bout my Daddy.

Ron

This morning, I returned from San Francisco and a three day weekend with my mother. She was shocked to see me, and at times it was rough; things were said; there was a lot of crying and yelling. We didn't heal all the wounds, but our relationship took definitive steps, and we made plans to get together yet again.

After I got home from the airport, Amber asked me to pick up Kimberly from school. I did, and though I have no explanation for it, I almost always do what Amber asks me to. At Kimberly's school, she got in my car without greeting me; her dark, straight hair lying over her eyes and mouth, muting her typically animated face.

"Is everything okay, Kimberly?"

When Kimberly told me what happened, I was disgusted. I used to be that mean white kid like Matthew.

"Kimberly, don't let those jerks bother you. You're better than them."

I took Kimberly to McDonald's to cheer her up. We had fries and chocolate shakes, and a lot of fun eating them, too. Kimberly dipped her fries into the shake. "They taste better all mixed together," she said, stuffing the soggy fries in her mouth.

"Really?" I asked. Then, I tried it. "Hmm, kinda good." I grabbed as many fries as I could hold, dunked them in my shake, and stuffed them in my mouth. "Dhis if bery good," I said with fries falling out the corners of my mouth.

Kimberly's face yielded from a hard pout to something softer. "You're funny," she said.

Kimberly's a beautiful child. She's thin and wiry and all triangles: sharp cheekbones, an angular chin, pointy, ashy knees, and jutting elbows. In addition she, has a warm personality that matches the roasted walnut color of her face. She's a few shades lighter than Amber, but other than that, she's a spitting image of her Mom.

Kimberly wears her emotions on her sleeve. There's no filter between what she's thinking and what she says, and she get's away with it because she's a kid. Adults can't do that. Last week, at a restaurant, our balding waiter had a really bad comb-over in which he combed the back hairs forward over the front of his head. It looked ridiculous. Kimberly pointed at his head, laughed and said, "that looks like a skunk's tale!" I tried not to laugh, but I couldn't help myself. Amber and the waiter looked incredibly embarrassed. Kimberly wasn't trying to be mean, she was just pointing out the truth, and I love that.

Amber and Kimberly saved my life; they changed me. I hated myself for not having the guts to come clean with Amber about stealing from her on our first encounter, but if I lost Amber's friendship, I knew my life would spiral out of control the way it always had. For different reasons, I'd have to lie to Amber about Kimberly's day at school. The truth might cause her to run off and kill the little morons.

Amber

During a lap dance, a customer put his hand where it didn't belong. I told him to stop, but he he didn't. When I tried physically to remove his hand, he forced under a digit under my panties and inside me. I went off. All the anger I've ever felt towards men and their abuse came out in that one split second. Without thinking, I punched the jerk and then kneed him in the balls. I reported the incident to the manager, he kicked the guy out, but his response to me was, "You never hit a customer."

Fuck men.

When I got home, Ron was there, spinning around in circles with Kimberly. "Stop that, Kimberly. You're going to get dizzy and ruin your appetite."

"I like getting dizzy, Mom."

"Me, too," Ron said. Kimberly laughed.

"Ron!" I said, firmly. He stopped and tucked his tail between his legs like a scolded puppy. If I wasn't pent up with anger from my day, I might have found it cute. Kimberly was still spinning, and i didn't have the energy to deal with her.

"Amber, something happened to Kimberly at school today," Ron said. There was hesitation in his voice, so I knew it was something bad.

"What?"

I was outraged at what Ron told me. I wanted to march down to Kimberly's school, find the boy who hurt my baby, and beat him until he coughed out the breath that fueled his filthy mouth. I'd grab him by his tiny red neck and choke him until his mom felt the pain in her uterus, the way I feel it in mine whenever someone hurts my Kimberly.

"I'm going to school with you tomorrow to have a talk with your teacher."

"Mom, don't. It's okay. Ron made it better."

"Is that so?" I looked at Ron. He shrugged his shoulders. "Well, Ron, thanks for looking out for Kimberly." I was mad at myself for not being there to defend her and a little bit jealous of Ron for being the one to comfort her. Mostly, though, I was angry at the truth. The boy said Kimberly had no dad; that was the truth.

"Kimberly run upstairs to play," I said.

When she left, I addressed Ron. "I'm happy to have found another person besides Beth who I can trust with Kimberly," I said, begrudgingly.

"Kimberly's a wonderful girl, and I feel blessed to be a part of her life," he said.

"I appreciate the way you care for Kimberly, but please don't try to parent her again."

"Sorry, I was just trying to make her feel better."

Beth came in. "Hey guys," she said.

"Hey, Beth," I said, obviously agitated. Beth always picks up on my modds and I knew she was about to ask, so I just told her instead. "Kimberly was harassed by some little pricks after school."

"Oh, no."

"You should have yelled at that little fucker, Ron," I said.

"What? You just told me not to parent her, and now you want me screaming at some little kid? I didn't see the incident happen, and even if I did, I'm not going to run around screaming at kids."

"Why? Because he's a kid or because he's a little white kid?"

"Amber, that's not right," Beth said.

"Look, Amber, I did the right thing. Cut me a little slack."

"You did nothing, and by doing nothing you enabled that little bigot."

"Why don't you tell me what you really want to say."

"You saw a piece of yourself in that little jerk, and that's why you didn't do anything about it."

"Screw you, Amber," Ron said. "I'm leaving."

"Good!" I said. Ron slammed the door behind him. "Don't come back!"

"I won't!" he yelled through the closed door. I turned around to find Beth giving me a nasty glare.

"Amber, Ron loves Kimberly, and unless you're blind, you see he loves you, too. You've got nobody but yourself to blame if you lose him."

"Screw Ron."

"You're a real mean dyke sometimes, Amber."

"Screw off."

"Maybe I should."

"Good. Go run to your gay white daddies."

"Why do you always point out a white man's color? *You're* the bigot."

"Just leave already!"

"Fine. Maybe I'll go find Ron."

"Good."

Beth ran upstairs, grabbed Jonathon, and they left. "Bye!" she yelled on her way out. But the only thing Beth took was a jacket for Jonathon, so I knew they'd be back.

Regardless, I knew Beth was right, which was even more infuriating. I was a bigot. I didn't want to be, but I was, and that disgusted me. I'd been a bigot since the day a white man violated me, and now it may have cost me my two best friends.

Beth

Jonathon and I left. I had no plan other than to get away from Amber. Sometimes, she could be really hurtful. I found Ron outside seated on the curb—pouting. It broke my heart.

"Hey, Ron," I said.

"Hey, Beth. Hey, Jonathon."

"Hey, Ron," Jonathon said. He gave Ron a high-five. So cute.

"Ron, forget what Amber said. She's just in one of her moods."

"She's always in one of her moods."

A warm ocean breeze blew through, we don't typically get those that far inland. The smell of the ocean was comforting.

"Ron, maybe it's time you tell Amber how you feel."

"What do you mean?"

"Come on, Ron" I hoped he'd respond without me having to say it out loud. He didn't. "Ron, tell her you love her."

"What? That's crazy. She's a lesbo."

"That doesn't mean you don't love her."

"Whatever," Ron said, shifting away from me.

"Ron, can I ask you something about me?"

"Go ahead."

"Do you think I'm weird?"

"Very," he said, then laughed. It lessened the tension. "Why are you asking me this?"

"I was raised by two gay men. That's weird. Am I weird?"

"I don't know. It's none of my business, really."

"Mommy, let's go please," Jonathon said, tugging at my sleeve.

"One second, darling… Ron, I need to know. Please tell me what you think."

"You don't want to hear what I think. I'm a bigot, remember."

"We both know, as well as Amber, that you're not a bigot. Now tell me what you think."

Ron laughed. I'm not sure why. "Well, actually, I am— er— was a bigot. That's why Amber said that. She knew it'd hurt. I thought I've evolved, but maybe I haven't."

"You're not a bigot, Ron. Now tell me, am I weird?"

"Okay, fine, but you can't get mad at what I say."

"Have you ever seen me mad?" I felt myself getting defensive already.

"Here it is—if someone wants to be gay, then fine, go be gay. But I don't think it's right for gay men to adopt children. It's not natural."

"So, you *do* think I'm weird and screwed up."

"We're all screwed up; you're no more screwed up than the rest of us. And you didn't turn out gay so I guess your dads didn't screw you up."

"Jeez, Ron. People don't choose their sexuality. I mean, why would anyone choose to be gay. It's a guaranteed lifetime of persecution."

"You said you weren't going to get mad."

"I'm not getting mad!"

"I think some people go gay because it's hip. Besides that, I think some people enjoy being persecuted."

"Really? Come on, Ron; you're smarter than that."

Ron didn't answer. He looked like he wanted to get up and run away from our conversation. It wasn't fair of me to be snapping at Ron, especially after what he had just gone through with Amber. A cloud covered our warm sun, and I felt a chill run through me.

"Ron, consider this. What if you thought being gay was cool and you wanted to be gay?" Could you make yourself be gay?"

"No."

"What if I paid you a hundred thousand dollars to make love to a man. Could you?"

"I don't think I could physically get it up."

"Then what makes you think anyone else could make themselves be gay? Being gay isn't a decision, nor is it something you catch like a virus. It's just something you are," I said. I'd made my point.

"Okay, fine. I guess you're right. Sometimes I still think in archaic ways. It's because of how I was raised, and unless I really sit down and think about an issue, then those beliefs from my childhood remain."

"Maybe being raised by two gay men isn't natural, but my dads raised me well."

"Sounds like you have it figured out. So why are you asking me?"

"I guess I needed reassuring. Amber gets me second guessing

myself sometimes."

"Yeah, me too."

"Ron, tell Amber you love her."

Jonathon tugged on my sleeve. "Mommy, can we go?"

"Okay, baby. We'll go... Ron, tell her."

"Why?"

"Because you love her."

"She's gay, and you just said being gay isn't a choice."

"But you love her."

"Are you saying she's not gay?"

"I'm just saying you need to tell her you love her, for your own peace of mind."

"Mommy, now," Jonathon insisted. I knew he'd be crying in about two seconds if we didn't leave right away.

"You better go, Beth."

"Yeah, okay. I'll see you later, I hope."

I hugged Ron and left. Knowing how stubborn both Amber and Ron are, I had a feeling I wouldn't see him again for a while.

December 2000
T.J.

I'd decided I was going to move back to Oregon. Again. Back and forth yet again. If I couldn't make it as an actor, at least I was getting to see the country between moves. I swore to myself that this move home would be my last move. There, I'd embrace my destiny as a nobody in a nobody's town.

I went rollerblading one last time down Venice's Ocean Front Walk on another mild winter day in L.A. The cool breeze parted my hair. Huey Lewis and The News' *Sports* was my album of choice. Though everyone else in the world had graduated to CDs, I was still playing cassettes on my old five-pound Walkman.

My shadow dragged along the concrete wall. Even my shadow looked ridiculous. I wore protective knee and elbow pads, wrist guards, and a helmet, all of which were necessary to minimize injuries from my frequent falls. Luckily, today I made it all the way from Santa Monica to the end of Venice without a single fall. It was a first for me, but of little consolation.

Yesterday, my worthless roommate told me he was moving to Vegas to pursue his passion — sports gambling. I couldn't make rent alone, and though I could have found another roommate, I decided it wasn't worth the effort. Why stay in the City of Angels? I've never seen any angels. I don't even know why they call it that? There's a lot of beautiful women, but they sure as hell aren't angels. Los Angeles is a city constructed from tinsel, silicone, and recycled screenplays. I'd had enough of its polluted ocean, droughts, wildfires, mudslides, earthquakes, and attitude, and was glad to be moving on once and for all.

Wow! I about broke my neck attempting to check out a hottie who blew past me in the opposite direction, on a skateboard. There are a thousand hotties on the beach everyday in Los Angeles; however, they were all out of my league. I wanted to blend in here in this town and be one of the cool guys who got the girls, but it wasn't happening.

I'd spent years in Los Angeles and had nothing to show for it. Over the years, I'd spent approximately $7,500 on headshots and acting classes and booked only four jobs that paid a pathetic grand total $997, before taxes. Three of the jobs were small speaking roles in quirky, low-budget, straight-to-video films that fell into the category of *cult.* Cult meaning nobody actually watched the crap.

My fourth job, and sadly, my best job, was a commercial for Rockenberger Rum. I played the part of the loser guy who drinks the loser-guy beer and loses the babe to the smooth-talking stud who's drinking Rockenberger Rum, *The drink of the successful, adventurous man.*

"Hey, darling, can I buy you a drink?" I ask the girl in the commercial. She takes one look at my generic beer and says, *No, thank you.* I walk away, trip on my untied shoelace, fall flat on my face, and spill beer all over myself. Then, the hero picks me up, gives me a sympathetic pat on the shoulder, and smiles. Obviously, he gets the girl because of his good looks and his choice of beverage. The two of them leave the bar hand-in-hand, and the commercial ends with me sitting alone at the end of the bar marinating in my-beer soaked shirt.

That commercial, in a nutshell, is my life.

At twenty-seven-years-old, still chasing a pipe dream, I decided it was time to go home and admit to my father that, once again, he was right and I was wrong.

But then, almost at the end of Ocean Front Walk, I saw new promise, an old house in such bad shape that it appeared to have been eaten alive by an ancient plague. The gray paint was peeling in long strips that flapped against the house in the ocean breeze. One window was boarded up, and the two others were opaque with dirt. It was an ugly, open sore among beautiful homes owned by millionaires. It was exactly what I needed to turn my life around.

Room for rent, $700/month.

That was less than half the rent of the two-bedroom shithole I had been living in, two miles inland. Here, in this affordable beach pad, I'd become a beach guy. I'd learn to surf and become one of those dudes who doesn't even need to talk to a woman to score. Women would come to me because I lived in a beach pad. I'd sit outside and watch the beautiful women walk by, women who'd stop and strike up conversations, asking about my pad. I'd nod my head, all cool-like, because I was the guy with the beach pad and they were just pedestrians with inland apartments. I'd be the envy of all my friends, or all the friends I'd end up making. Some people would use me for my beach pad, but I'd be okay with the arrangement because I'd be using them as a means to more popularity and more casual sex with more random women who wore thongs while roller-skating with their long tanned legs, knee high socks, and large breasts. I'd be King of the Beach, the guy everyone knew. I'd have a golden retriever named Jake; everyone would know him as Party Dog Jake, and he'd be infamous for his Frisbee skills and keg stands.

I had to get the room!

Just as I was about to burst in and ask if dogs were allowed, another man, a very large man, beat me to it and knocked on the door.

Dylan

His smile was the biggest I'd ever seen, ten times as huge as Joan Rivers. His teeth were all mangled and jagged and long. It was as though some kind of antlered creature was trying to fight its way out of his mouth, antlers first.

"I want this place," he said.

"Wooh boy, slow down. I'm Dylan, nice to meet you," I said and extended my hand.

"Hi Dylan. I'm Dirk," he said, digging a finger in his ear.

"Umm, yeah. So, you want to come in and see the place?"

"Umm, not really."

This Neanderthal had such bad halitosis that I doubted he'd brushed his teeth since his ancestors first roamed the earth.

180

"Do you have any lifestyle issues?" I asked.

"No," Dirk said, inching closer. He towered above me, his chest now only six inches from my nose. The foul odor emanating from his mouth and body descended upon me in a cloud of deadness. I took two steps back.

"Questions?"

"I got a pet, named Dog." Dirk said, looking at me. His huge eyeballs gave me goose bumps— and not in a good way. Dirk's midnight eyes were like two black holes whose gravitational pull was sucking anything resembling an intelligent thought right out of my head. I was getting dumber just by looking at this lug, yet I couldn't stop looking.

"Was that a question?" I asked.

"I have a pet named Dog."

"I'm sorry. No dogs," I said. I felt myself slipping into the void behind his eyes. I had to end this encounter before too late.

"He's not a dog. He's sort of a big snake named Dog."

Huh?

"He's *sort of* a big snake or he *is* a big snake?" I asked.

"Well, Roy, he's—"

"My name's Dylan."

"Yeah. Well, he *is* a big snake. The problem is I think Dog's allergic to salt. It makes his skin all weird. Is the air really salty around here?"

"Dirk."

"Roy."

"You see that thing out there." I pointed.

"Yeah?"

"That's the ocean."

"Duh." Spittle flew from his mouth and landed on my shoulder. I felt peeked, and must have looked it too. "You okay, Roy?"

"Dylan," I said.

"Huh?"

"Never mind."

"So what about it?" he asked.

"About what?"

"The air?"

"I'll tell you what, Dirk. I'll call the local air commission and find out what the latest readings have been on the saturation level of the salt in the air. Leave me your number, and I'll give you a call once I know."

"Okay, Roy. Thanks a lot."

"Okay, I'll be talking to you soon." I shut the door, but Dirk's stink remained in my house. I began to fire up a fat bowl of weed to kill the scent. I pictured Dirk climbing into his Ford F-150 with the Calvin-pissing-on-a-Chevy bumper sticker and driving to the pet store to pick up a dozen rats to feed his snake. I'd rather have given up my beach paradise than live with that prehistoric anomaly.

Dirk, my third applicant, was as big a bust as the first two, and I didn't expect future prospects to get much better. Though I was renting a room on the beach, it was such a disastrous shithole it depreciated the property value of every millionaire's home within a four-house radius. My next-door neighbor tried to buy the house so he could knock it down, but luckily for me, my landlord was a stubborn, ambitionless drunk who'd inherited the property and lived off its rent. He never fixed anything, the house was infested with black mold, the plumbing was unreliable, and rats came and left more often than visitors.

It was exactly what I'd always wanted.

I lived in filth, but to me the benefits of living oceanfront outweighed the negatives of this particular home. I spent a lot of time sitting in the surf, letting the tide run over my feet and watching waves folding over themselves before slamming into the ocean floor. This dump of a house was my only treasure in life, and I couldn't bear the thought of losing it.

My third roommate had just moved out in just as many years. I was beginning to think that the reason they moved out was me. *Am I really that hard to like?* I peered out the window, and saw an old man, at least sixty, biking on a homemade wooden beach cruiser with a wicker basket. He had long hair pulled into a ponytail with a black bandana holding it in place. In the basket was an old school boom box, circa 1986, blaring Warrant's *Cherry Pie.* To me, musical taste is a window into a person's soul; it's personal. This guy's music was offensive, but I think it was just part of his *fuck you* to society. I understood and admired that. I wanted to chase him down Ocean Front Walk and ask him to show me how to genuinely not care what others thought of me, because so far, I'd just been pretending not to care.

Regardless of what anyone thought of me, my writing, my home, the way I dressed, or anything else, if I couldn't find someone suitable to rent this house with me, I'd have to move inland or back to my hometown. Neither of those options sounded very good.

T.J.

I was daydreaming about Jake The Party Dog when the huge guy finally left my future house. After he left, I practiced what I'd say. I had to sound confident and cool.

After rehearsing, I went to the door and knocked. The door opened, and a guy appeared behind a cloud of smoke. "Hello," he said.

"Hello, I'm T.J. and I'd really like to live here."

"Hey, T.J." He blew out a thick breath of smoke in a ring of pollution, strong enough to kill all plant life within a five-foot radius. He dropped his cigarette outside the door and stepped on it. His face was leathery, his eyes red-rimmed, and his jet-black hair jumped off his scalp in sharp spikes. He had unusually long fingernails, and I think he may have been wearing eyeliner.

"Is the room still available?" I asked, feeling a little intimidated by his odd appearance.

"Yeah."

"Good," I said. After the smoke smell cleared, I noticed the sharp smelling mixture of rat urine and decaying vegetables. And maybe marijuana. "Can I come in and check it out?"

"Come on in," he said.

I forgot to take off my rollerblades and a wheel caught the metal threshold of the doorway. I fell flat on my face. So much for being cool.

"Good thing you're wearing helmet."

"Yeah, good thing," I said with my face buried in a carpet that smelled like stale baby vomit.

April 2001
Ron

After Amber threw me out, I disappeared from her life. Months passed without speaking to her, but I don't think more than a couple days passed when I hadn't thought about her. I wrote about her every single day in my journal. I felt a heavy burden for the lies I'd told her and for never confessing I'd robbed her in that parking garage. That was a constant struggle for me— I was no longer that guy, and part of me felt I didn't need to acknowledge the existence of that man in Amber's life before our friendship began. Another part of me felt our relationship could never be real until I told her everything. I wanted to call her, but Amber shouldn't have called me a bigot, even if it had been true; she said it to hurt me, and all I'd been trying to do was help her daughter.

I wouldn't call her unless she called me first. No matter how sexy she looked on a pole—

And she does look sexy.

I was at Starr, seated in a dark corner of the room, wearing a hooded sweatshirt, hanging out to get a glimpse of Amber. Regardless of how creepy it was, I had to see her.

Amber's dance finished, she picked up her dollars, and went back to V.I.P. for a private dance with some dickwad who looked like a walrus, mustache and all. I wanted to tell the dickwad that Amber was a lesbian; I wanted to grab Amber by the hand and take her out of this shithole. I did neither. I ordered another gin and tonic, got a lap dance from a stripper named Brooklyn, and lifted the dickwad's wallet after he returned from V.I.P. I left Starr having accomplished nothing with Amber, but at least I had a few extra dollars.

September 2001
Amber

He was the size of a flea on my television monitor. He stood in the frame of a shattered window high above the earth, faced with the option of burning to death or jumping.

He chose the latter.

So did many others.

Suddenly, New York looked like a Third World country.

There were thousands of nameless, terrified people. I searched their faces to find one who matched mine. Every black man they put on the television caused me to wonder.

I knew my mother met my father in New York, and I knew that he lived there for as long as she knew him. I knew his first name was Antoine. But that's all I knew. I never met him, had no idea what he looked like, what his voice sounded like, what his life was like, or why he disappeared from my mother's life before I was born. I'd created a flattering image of him in my head, the same way I created the sketch of a father that Kimberly clung to.

Kimberly came down for breakfast. "Mommy, are you ready to take me to school?"

"School's canceled today, baby. Go to your room and read that book I got you." I couldn't deal with being a mother while all my thoughts were focused on being some stranger's daughter.

I needed a hug from my father today. I felt like I needed to find him and tell him I loved him in spite of his leaving. I wanted to beat his chest, slap his face, and make him bleed as I bled when I was raped. He should have been there to protect me.

Despite my father's absence, I believe there's some kind of magical, invisible rope connecting our souls. Nothing, not even death, can cut this rope.

I wish I could follow my end of the rope all the way back to him.

The second tower fell. Smoke and dust rolled and wound through the streets of New York. More death. More faces. More fear. More questions. And the aftermath would be worse. Grief. Mourning. Funerals over mass graves.

Along with millions of other people in America, I felt lonely and sad.

I could've asked Beth to hold me, but I didn't. I called someone I should have called months ago. "Hello, Ron?"

"Amber? Hi. Are you okay?"

"No."

"It's good to hear your voice, Amber."

"Can you come over?"

"I'll be right there," Ron said. He didn't question why I called, and he didn't bring up the past. I was surprised how willing he was to forget and move on. That's a good friend.

Ron arrived in less than fifteen minutes. Before I could say hi, he wrapped his arms around me and gave me the hug of my life, the hug my father had never given me.

"Everything will be okay," Ron said, but I didn't feel it would. "I've missed you, Amber."

"I have something I need to tell you, Ron."

"You don't need to apologize."

"Huh? I wasn't going to."

"You weren't?"

"No. Well, yes. I mean, I owe you an apology, big time—"

"Forget about it," Ron said.

"Thank you, but I do owe you one, and I'll give it when I can do it properly."

"Well, Amber, I owe you an apology, too."

"No, you don't."

"Just trust me, I do."

"For what?"

Ron sighed. He looked at his feet, and he took my hand. "I just need to know you forgive me," he said.

"I don't know what I'm forgiving you for," I said.

"Just tell me you forgive me, and then I can tell you."

"Fine. I forgive you, Ron. But I called you because I need to talk about something before I lose my nerve. Can we do yours later?"

"Yeah." Ron sounded relieved. "What is it?"

"I'm scared. I've never shared this with anyone before, not even Beth. It shames me."

I wanted another hug. I wanted to ask for one, but Ron hugged me again before I needed to ask. It was like he knew what I needed as I felt the need. I was shaking in his arms; I knew he could feel me shaking. Strength flowed from his arms.

"Close your eyes, Ron. Now take a deep breath and hold it as long as you can."

"What?"

"Please do it." I wanted Ron to feel my struggle, my desperation for air.

Ron took in a deep breath, and I let mine out. And for the first time ever, I talked out loud about being raped, about the pain, the humiliation, the feeling of suffocating in that awful green shirt. Ron held his breath until his face started turning purple. I believe if I hadn't told him to breathe, he'd have held his breath until he passed out. I don't know much, but I know that's love, at least in some form.

Ron caught his breath, and I continued, sparing no detail. Ron held me when I needed to be held and pressed tissue to my nose when I needed to blow. I knew Ron was feeling the same things I felt the day he told me about his mother's rape. We were bonded in our ugly histories.

After I finished, Ron hugged me again and allowed me to let loose the emotional pain that had been building for years; tears ran down my face and all over both of us. I cried for the dead in New York. I cried for my father, my mother, and my rape. I pulled away from Ron and blinked away a watery haze so I could see his beautiful deep green eyes. Those eyes— green like the rolling hills of safe places I'd never been. And for the first time, I felt safe.

Ron

I wanted to hold Amber forever and protect her from pain, but inside, I was burning.

I wanted to find the rapist and destroy him. Sodomize him with a serrated steak knife. Maim him for life and haunt his dreams with the gory memories. I wanted to drive a rusty railroad spike in and out of his flesh until he was nothing more than a soupy mess of blood, fat, and muscle.

I wanted revenge for Amber.

And for my mother.

Dylan

"I got an email from your sister today. She was with your mother in Central Park when it happened. They're both okay," my dad said over the phone.

"Thank God. I can't believe all this. What's next?"

"Another world war."

"I hope not," I replied.

"This is a pattern. Money and religious fanaticism have, and will forever, cause us to go to war with one another. I'm sure that's why those bastards attacked today," he said.

"Killing for religion. Seems hypocritical," I said.

But Dad was right. The world's history is made of an endless string of religious wars. The Revolutionary War, the world wars, the crusades, the Rwanda genocide, the Armenian genocide, the never-ending fighting in the Middle East. And the wars that weren't about religion, were about money. So many wars, so much death. And for what?

"I hope this doesn't end in war," I said. I put the phone between my ear and shoulder and started doing dishes. I never wash dishes, but it was a good distraction from the thoughts blowing through my head.

"Our world's obsessed with war. For a while, war quenches our taste for death, but eventually a crazy dictator or religious terrorist or power-hungry president finds reason to start another."

"We need to fight to protect ourselves," I said, scrubbing harder. "But this won't lead to a world war," I said, hoping more than believing. My Dad was about the smartest guy I'd ever known and also the most nakedly honest, and though I wanted to hear him comfort me with his opinions, I was expecting the brutal truth. "I mean, with today's weapons, a world war could end civilization. I hope we've learned enough from our history to avoid that."

"People talk about history and things like slavery, genocide, and religious persecution as horrors that happened because we were ignorant. But nothing's changed. We still hate what we don't understand; homosexuality comes to mind. History repeated itself today because some low-life religious fanatics tried to destroy something they don't understand."

"It sucks," I said.

"Let's just be grateful our family is okay," Dad said.

My hands were shaking so badly I had to stop washing the dishes. I couldn't put my finger on exactly why I was so shaken, but I was, and tears started flowing. I could do nothing to stop them.

"People died today for no reason. Why them instead of me?"

"What happened isn't about you. Internalizing the catastrophe is selfish," my Dad said. Maybe he was right, but it didn't help.

We talked a few more minutes and said our goodbyes. By the time I got off the phone, tears were streaming down my cheeks— it was the first time I'd cried in years. I wiped my eyes, forgetting my hands had soap on them. Now I was weeping and burning. I put a cloth to my face, went to the couch, and clicked on the television. I needed some good white noise to chill me out. But there was nothing on the television except for the attack. Through my watery eyes, I saw it, over and over, on every station. I turned it off and stepped outside.

Part of me wished I'd been in those towers. If I'd died, then the agony of life would be over. The human struggle and need to matter and be import would be gone, and maybe, in death, I'd accomplish what I could not in life. Maybe dying in a tragedy would be cause for some publisher to print and immortalize the words that I scribble every night in a haze of marijuana. Tragic death validates an artist.

But that's just me being narcissistic and selfish, just like Dad had said.

Skye

Watching those towers fall, over and over and over, every single day on television for the last month, was a horrific reminder of how fragile and vulnerable we all really are. Soon, our Nation would be involved in a full blown war.

A month removed from the attacks of 9/11, and we are still reminded everyday of the events. They play those images of the towers falling as if to make sure we stay afraid and angry enough so that we will support America's counter-attack, which is surely coming.

I see no point to it. Fight violence with more violence? What does that solve? Why do we, as humans, hurt one another? Human nature is to take and take. No matter how much we have, we always want more. And for one country or one person to have more, someone else must have less. This makes it impossible for a billionaire to be an ethical person. How can one person feel good about going to bed with billions of dollars that he will never use, while so many homeless children go to sleep on America's streets each night?

It wasn't too long ago that I was one of those homeless children.

New York used to be a place of happiness and dreams, now it's a place of chaos. I remember taking our one and only family vacation to New York when I was a kid. It was mid-October, and the trees had traded their thick green foliage for beautiful shades of gold, red, and tan, which occurred because the leaves were dying. After being sexually molested as a child, I felt like those dying leaves.

Because of my father selling my body for drug money, sex has been ruined for me; I've never found pleasure in intercourse. The only times I've ever climaxed had been when I did it to myself. There's a loud silence to a self-induced orgasm, and the solitude of it is nice.

I get no pleasure from sex, but sometimes I find comfort in the dirty, degrading, and disgusting aspects of it. Sex sometimes allows me to express the raunchy feelings inside me. Sex is two people exchanging bodily fluids, exposing themselves, and being mutually humiliated. And sometimes I need that.

All this talk from women about sex and *the magical connection when he looked into my eyes and entered me* is all fairytale bullshit girls are conditioned to believe they should feel. When a man puts his hand in my underwear, love is the last thing on my mind.

Last month, Jackson, my label owner, tried for about the billionth time to get with me. As usual, I rejected him. I wanted to believe he signed me because of talent, not because he wanted in my pants. But in reality, he'd signed me so he could sleep with me, and once he did, he'd likely dump me from the label.

I haven't heard from him in quite a while. Thanks to my irresponsibility and growing dope habit, I was completely out of money, and my check from the label hadn't come this month, which was odd because my money was never late. So, I went to Jackson's office looking for him. Instead of Jackson, I found Joanna.

"We're letting you go from the label," Joanna announced, all too happy.

"You're not dumping me. Jackson wouldn't let you."

"Jackson signed over the rights to the company to me last week."

"Jackson gave you the company?"

"Yeah."

"Why?"

"That's none of your business."

"You never liked me. You're just getting rid of me because Jackson wanted me more than he ever wanted you."

"You're right. I don't like you. But that's not why I'm firing you. I'm firing you because you're a talentless hack. Goodbye," she said. Then she asked me to leave.

The album I put out on the Rockenberger label failed because it wasn't radio-friendly. Jackson tried his best to turn me into a pop queen, but pop and I were more water and oil than sugar and spice. If he'd just let me be myself, do my own blood and grit thing, then I know I could've made it.

But I didn't.

And now I was in a bind. I was no longer a functional dope user. My smack habit had become a hundred-dollar-a-day monster that I couldn't manage without the label's money. After I ran out of money, I'd be forced into a miserable, dope-sick sobriety. Ironically, I'd used my talent to get money to feed my dope habit, which ended up costing me my contract with the label. I'd fucked up and lost the only thing that ever truly loved me, my music.

Music eliminates my gravity. When I'm performing, I'm a bird; no, I'm a ravenous pterodactyl. I'm alive and free and hungry, and I know who I am. But now, the flood is coming; it's weighing me down, making

190

me prisoner to my loneliness and pain.

And the emptiness swells within me.

And I need to fill it.

I hadn't gotten stoned in a day, and dope-sickness was already creeping in. It begins with my feet feeling freezing cold while the rest of my body sweats. Then, I begin to get nauseated. At that point, I've got maybe 12 hours to get some dope in me to avoid a full fledged attack. As soon as I felt the chills coming on, I pawned my guitars, I had no choice. I tried to fill the emptiness with dope. I tried to forget about my father whoring me out. I tried to kill the sadness of losing my baby.

I began a binge that lasted for five or six days. I'm not really sure. I'd only leave the apartment to get more dope. Eventually, after bombarding my system heavily enough, my brain finally stopped thinking, and there was a wonderful absence of discomfort. But I ran out of money, and then came the strikingly terrifying reality of my life, like a slap to the face. I had no guitar, no job, no money, and no future.

October 2001
Kelly

I quit working for King Jackson right after he molested my wife's mouth with his penis. I'd like to say I was shocked Reece would do that to me, but that wouldn't be honest.

After quitting, I went back to Brotman and begged for my old job. Begging worked.

Yesterday, after months of putting in solid work there, Reece called me and started giving me crap about 'being a lazy loser who's always late with the alimony.' I lost my temper and screamed into the phone, "Screw you, you old wrinkly tramp! You think you're too good for me? You've got lopsided boobs and you need Botox injections in your wrinkly old ass that sits on the couch all day watching soaps! So who's lazy?" I was in the treatment room not five feet away from a patient while I was yelling this. I was fired later that day.

Because of my verbal indiscretion, the only work I had left was part-time work at the nursing home. The only good thing to come from this awful day was that my penis-sucking ex-wife would now get less money from me because alimony is based on percentage of income.

Reece was rewarded custody of Teddy and enough alimony so she could stay home and suck penis every day. Reece got everything; the bitch even got my old vinyl record collection just to spite me; she doesn't even like my music.

Today, I was at Reece's to pick up Teddy. "Ya ready, Teddy?" I yelled over Reece's head after she opened the door. She hates when I call him Teddy.

"I'm ready, Dad!" I heard his little feet pitter-pattering down the stairs, which gets me excited every time.

Since the divorce, I'd become less of a disciplinarian and more of a cool dad. Teddy and I are more like best friends than father and son. He was only three and a half, and I was nearly thirty years older, but we're great buddies.

"Hey, Teddy," I said as he flew around the corner. "Give your best bud a hug." Teddy gave me a delicious hug, and we turned to leave.

"Wait, Theodore. Go upstairs and get a jacket. It's cold."

"K, Mom." He tried to turn and go back in the house, but I wouldn't let him. "Oh, no! Not again!" Teddy said. Teddy and I play this game where I hug him and pretend my arms are mechanical clamps that have malfunctioned and are stuck around him. The mechanical arms can't release unless Teddy pushes the emergency release button (my chin). Teddy twisted, wiggled, and kicked. "I got it!" Teddy laughed, touching my chin. The sound of his laugh is my favorite noise in the world. With Teddy's hand on the button, I released him. He let go of my chin and darted away before the mechanical clamps could collapse back upon him.

"Grow up, Kelly," Reece said.

"Never!" I said with a defiant fist in the air. Reece shook her head in disgust.

After Teddy returned with his jacket, I put him in the car and went back inside to break the news to Reece.

"You what?" she yelled.

I tried my best not to smile. "I got fired because you were yelling at me on the phone. Now I'm only working at the nursing home a few days a week."

"Where the hell does that leave me?"

"Aren't you making tons of money acting?"

"You know goddamn well I haven't gotten work in over a year. And wipe that obnoxious smile off your face! This is fucked, Kelly! How am I supposed to pay all my bills? And what about Theodore?"

"If you're having problems making ends meet between your

shopping and your… shopping, then I'd be more than happy to take Teddy for a while."

"You aren't getting my kid. I'll get a job if I have to. I'll do whatever it takes for that boy."

"Yeah, you're a really great mother. I know you'll do whatever it takes." Reece was a decent mother when it was convenient to her lifestyle. She'd shower Teddy with love and affection when she needed attention back from him. But when Teddy needed her affection first, she was an emotional vacuum. Reece was always buried in the next audition she'd butcher or the next penis she'd— butcher.

"I'm a great mother, and I was a great wife. You never appreciated me." Then she began fake crying. She truly was a horrific actress. "How can you do this to me?"

While we were married, I really believed I loved Reece. It wasn't until long after our divorce that I realized what I really loved was the way other guys looked at me with envy when she was on my arm. My marriage was validated by others' approving stares.

"Hey, maybe you could get a job as a cleaning lady or something. I know how much you love spending time on your knees!" Reece slammed the door in my face. Had it not clipped my nose I would've enjoyed her angry reaction; however, it had, and I was in pain. I wanted to swear, but I don't swear around Teddy. Rubbing my nose, walking to the car, I saw Teddy's window was rolled down. I was embarrassed he'd heard us fighting. Reece and I had a rule not to fight in front of Teddy.

"Daddy, can we get ice cweam?"

"Duh!"

"Goodie! Daddy, why Mommy yelling?"

"Mommy was mad because I lost my job."

"Where?"

"Where what?"

"Where you lose it?"

I gave the easy explanation. "I don't know where I lost it. That's why it's lost."

"I hope you find it."

"Thank you, Teddy."

"Why Mommy love being on knees?"

"Umm… Hey, let's sing a song." I turned on the radio, and *Black* was playing. The outro of *Black* used to make me think of my mom; she was the *star in the sky* I could never have. But since Reece and I met and sang the song together while driving next to each other on the 405, *Black* has reminded me of that day, which is one of the only happy memories I have of Reece. Teddy sang along with Eddie into the unplugged microphone that I keep in my car, just for this reason. Teddy makes up his own lyrics and lays into the microphone

I love that Teddy likes the same music as I, the same sports teams, the same food, the same everything. Teddy is my boy; his brain is my safety deposit box, and in it I can deposit my opinions on music, movies, sports, politics, art, history, the future. Teddy is smart; he soaks up every tidbit of information around him, and someday he will form his own opinions, but for now, it's cool to have a buddy who agrees with everything I say. Teddy isn't even four yet, but he's the smartest kid I know; I'm sure he's some kind of child savant.

When Teddy and I are together, the world around us shrinks. It's us against the universe, and the universe is no match for our brilliance.

Teddy pressed his face against the passenger window, stuck his thumbs in his ears, made moose ears with his fingers, and yelled *neener neener* as we passed an elderly couple. "Nice one, bud!" I said. I taught him that.

"Will you play guitar tonight? I be wrock star!"

"Absolutely. But only if you rock hard!"

"I always wrock hard, Daddy!" Teddy ripped out a chord on his air guitar.

Seeing Teddy laughing and playing the air guitar, suddenly it all made sense. Being fired, having much more free time, I decided to do something I'd already done; only this time I'd do it better.

"Teddy."

"Daddy?"

"I'm going to get my college band, Christmas Party Junkie, back together."

"Yeah! Rock out!" He said. Then he broke his air guitar in two over his knee.

"Hey, buddy—"

"Yeah, buddy?" Teddy answered.

"I've got a big surprise for you at the house."

"A puppy?"

It was a puppy. How the heck did he know? He's a child savant, that's how.

Teddy named our new brown lab Brady. We played with Brady all day.

At the end of the weekend, I had to explain that Brady had to stay with me instead of living with him and Reece (Reece says she's allergic to dogs. And cats. And turtles. And anything else that might require more responsibility from her). Teddy cried for an hour.

"I'm sorry, Teddy, but Mommy hates puppies, so Brady has to stay here with me. But it'll be okay. Daddy will take good care of Brady, and Brady will be here next weekend when you come back."

"I can't wait!"

I'm sure at least fifty percent of his enthusiasm to return was because he wanted to see me.

November 2001
Kimberly

I thought I was dying.

Susie and I was playing hop scotch. "You're bleedin', Kimberly," Susie said. And then I saw a couple drops of blood on the chalk. "Are you okay?"

"I don't know." It didn't hurt none, but I was scared.

"There's a spot of blood on your dress, too. I'm gonna get your mom."

"No! You can't get her," I said. I'd begged Mom for the expensive dress for months, and she bought it for my birthday. It was my best dress, and I couldn't let her know I ruined it.

"So, you just gonna stand there and bleed?"

"No. Let's go in the bathroom and fix it," I said.

"You got some band-aids?" Susie asked.

"Yeah."

I went to the bathroom, got the bandages and gave them to Susie. She took them, but then looked at me like she was scared. "I don't want to have to touch it. It might be catagious," Susie said. She meant contagious, but she's one year younger than me, and only a second grader, so she doesn't know words like that. I took off my dress in the bathroom.

"Where you cut at?"

"The bloods comin' from my kiki!" I said, once I realized it.

I squatted in the corner, and Susie soaked my dress in the tub. I knew I was okay, but I was still crying.

"You gonna have to tell your mom so she can take you to the hospital."

"I ain't tellin' Mom, and I ain't goin' to no stupid hospital, so just shut up, Susie!"

"Miss Johnson! Miss Johnson! Miss Johnson!" Susie said, running out of the bathroom.

"What's wrong, Susie?" my mom asked from the kitchen.

"Kimberly's hurt. She's bleedin' all over the bathroom."

Mom ran in, looking scared at first. But then when she saw me she smiled for some reason.

"Susie, you run on home now, okay? I'll take care of Kimberly."

"She gonna be okay?"

"She'll be fine."

"You gonna beat her?"

"What? No. Why'd you ask a thing like that?"

"Cuz she be bleedin' on her best dress."

"Susie, go home to your mother. We'll see you tomorrow."

"K. Bye, Miss Johnson. Bye, Kimberly."

"Bye Susie," I said. I felt a little more calm after Susie left. But for some reason, I started cryin' again. "Mom, I'm sorry I ruined the dress. I promise I didn't mean it."

"Oh, love. It's okay. You're going to be fine. And don't worry about the darn dress. Just calm down. You're okay."

"How's it okay when I'm bleeding out my kiki?" I asked. Mom smiled big. "What's so funny?"

"Oh, baby. I'm sorry," she said, but she was still smiling. Then her eyes got all wet, too. "This is normal, love. I wasn't expecting to have this conversation for a couple years, but it's time."

"What time?" I was still kinda cryin', except now I felt like my tears was fake crocodile tears.

"You're menstruating."

"What's menstraighten?"

196

"It's your body going through its womanly cycle."

"Huh? I thought maybe I got my first period."

"Oh, baby," Mom said then wrapped her arms around me. "You did have your first period. That's what menstruation is. You're changing into a woman. This is going to happen once a month for you now."

"It doesn't hurt none. So, why am I bleeding?"

"Well, your body's using blood to flush an egg out of you."

"I don't see no egg, just blood. And why would there be eggs in me?"

Mom explained the egg is for baby makin'. She said the egg's so small it can't be seen by my naked eye.

"I can have a baby now?"

"No, love, you're only nine and a half. You're too young."

"I thought you said the egg is for baby makin'?"

"Yes, the egg is for making a baby. But you need to wait until you're mature enough to care for a baby before you have one."

"So, Mom, when I'm ready to have a baby how do I get the egg to hatch?"

Mom laughed, but I didn't see nuthin' funny about it.

"You get married, and your husband helps you hatch it," Mom said.

"You didn't get married. How did you hatch me?"

"Hmm. Good point. Well, you don't exactly hatch the egg. You need to fertilize the egg—"

"Fertilize? Like with manure?"

"I don't know if you're ready to hear all this," she said.

"Mom! Tell me. I wanna know. If you don't tell me then how I'm gonna learn? Marlisha, in the fifth grade, she knows how to hatch em'; she's gonna have a baby."

Mom looked worried when I said that. "Okay, love. If you really want to know, then I'll tell you."

"I really wanna know."

Mom started to tell me about how you fall in love with a man and then he puts his thingy into the girl's kiki and then fertilizes the egg so it can grow into a baby. Mom was blushin' the whole time she was talkin'. I thought I was gonna puke. I couldn't imagine lettin' no boy even see my kiki let alone put his thingy in it.

"This is gross, Mom. I don't want to hear any more."

"Okay, love. But now do you understand why you're too young to make a baby?"

"Yeah, I understand. I don't think I'll ever be old enough to make one. Mom, you were fifteen when you had me. Were you ready?"

Mom didn't answer for a minute and her head turned all sideways like she was tryin' really hard to think.

"Baby, you're the best thing ever happened to me. I wasn't mature enough to be a mom, but you helped me to grow up."

"Maybe someday I'll be a mom and my baby will help me become more grown up."

Mom sighed, and then brushed my hair out of my face. I love it when she does that. "No, Kimberly, you're going to wait until you fall in love and get married. That's the right way to do it."

"So you did it the wrong way?"

"Nobody ever taught me the right way. That's why I'm teaching you."

"Yeah, your mommy wasn't around to teach you because she died, huh?"

"Yes, love."

"I'm sorry your mommy died. I wish her and Daddy didn't die."

"Me, too."

"Mom?"

"Yes, love?"

"I'm sorry I got blood on the dress."

"Don't worry about it, love. I'll get you another one for Christmas."

"Really?"

"Really."

"Thanks, Mom."

Mom helped me get cleaned up and then she gave me somethin' that looked like a diaper; she called it a maxi-pad. She taught me about how this was gonna happen for the rest of my life and how to clean myself so that I could be santa-tery and fresh. Then she gave me a big hug. "I love you more than anything in this world, Kimberly."

"I love you more than anything in this world, Mom."

"More than all the cotton candy in all the clouds in the sky?" Mom asked.

"Mom, I'm almost ten. I got baby-makin' eggs in me. I'm old enough to know there ain't no cotton candy in the sky."

Mom laughed, gave me another big hug, and went back to the kitchen.

As soon as she left, I ran to the living room and called Susie.

"Guess what?"

"What?"

"I was just menstraighten. I'm a woman now. I got eggs in me that my husband is going to fertilize to make babies!"

Amber

When I first became pregnant with Kimberly, it was very hard to convince myself I would love the baby of the man who raped me. Then, one day, I felt the life inside me, the baby tugging at my insides. It was at that moment I realized the life developing inside me wasn't him; it was a brand new human taking form in my womb. From that point on, loving my baby was about the only thing in life that came easy.

Now, Kimberly was becoming a woman. I was proud of her, scared for her, and scared for me. I'd like to arrest time and keep her at a young age, before the time when she notices boys, falls in love, and then leaves me forever.

Please don't ever leave me, Kimberly.

But for all the lies I've told Kimberly and the awful parenting mistakes I've made, I probably deserve to be left by her, and eventually Karma will restore balance to our universe. I hate myself for lying. Some day, I'll tell Kimberly the truth and hope she can accept it.

Kimberly, I'm a liar. Somewhere, my mother and your father are alive.

I ran away from my mother.

Because your father raped me.

December 2001
Skye

Long ago, when I was introduced to heroin, the drug and I

quickly developed a romantic, beautiful relationship. It felt healthy. Heroin helped me express my feelings through music. However, this relationship, like all others in my life, went sour, and my romance with heroin turned abusive.

After I ran out of the money I'd gotten from pawning my guitars, I started begging for drug money. I'd come full circle. I went from living on the streets to rocker chick with a record deal, and back to begging others for money so I could survive and get high.

However, this time around my habit was bigger, and I couldn't get anywhere near enough cash to keep up with it. I spent every waking moment figuring out how to get my next fix and fight off dope sickness; withdrawal is the most painful thing I've ever experienced. Last month, I was sick more often than not because I couldn't get enough dope money to stay well; so, out of options, I decided to check into a free rehab clinic. This wasn't the type of clinic that helps addicts get well with therapy and meds; those clinics cost money. This was the type that locked you in a room and kept you in there until the horrible sickness passed.

I'd tried to get clean before, but I always gave up when the going got tough. Getting clean was almost exactly like I'd seen in the movies, only worse: cold chills, night sweats, puking and diarrhea at the same time, vertigo, hallucinations, total insanity, and pure physical pain.

Today, thirty days later, at least 15 of which were worse than any hell I could ever imagine, I was back in the real world, sober, but not cured. In the cab ride home, I thought about how I'd grown to become my drug-addicted mother.

I caught a glimpse of myself in the rear view mirror. I had the same worn look my mother had, the look of a domestic abuse victim and drug addict. And even though the grayish-green bags under my eyes were fading, despite the fact I'd gained enough weight to start looking like a person again, and regardless of the fact that I'd again started practicing simple hygiene such as shaving my legs and washing my hair, I still had that look of desperation on my face and felt that intense burning in my belly. After a month in rehab, I knew I had a lot to sort out—but first I had to get high. After all that torture, I needed and deserved just one taste to ease my stress.

But just a taste.

The cab dropped me off in the Mecca of cheap heroin, Venice Beach. I went looking for my friend, Berthina, who I'd met at a twelve-step group meeting years ago. By the time I found Berthina's studio apartment, I'd allowed myself to forget the hell of rehab that I'd just been through and convinced myself I could get high just this one more time.

Step one— admitting you have a problem.

"You want the good news or the bad?" Berthina asked. She was bombed. Her speech was slurred, and her eyes were nearly closed.

"I'll take the good news."

"I've got a quarter of the best mother-fucking Thai shit ever."

"Great. What's the bad news?" Berthina didn't respond. Her eyes were too heavy to keep them both open, and the right one fell shut as she let her head fall back. Then she put her dirty hand between her legs and started scratching at her crotch. "Berthina!"

She snapped her head upright. "What, dude?"

"What's the bad news?"

"What bad news?" Berthina asked.

"You said there's bad news. What is it?"

"Fuck, dude. Just chill."

"Whatever," I replied.

"Hey, I'm gonna hit this then you can have a hit, but just one."

"Thanks," I said.

"Oh, hey, there's a problem," she said.

"What's that?"

"I only have one pick."

"Was the bad news?"

"Duh," Berthina said. She was scratching her crotch violently. She pulled her hand away and her fingertips were bloody. She didn't even notice. Watching the ugly horror of a heroin addict, from a sober point of view, was terrifying, and nearly scared me away from getting my hit.

Nearly.

Because as scary as it is, and as awful as that bumpy road will be in a few days, that high seems a thousand times worth it.

"But, hey, today's Friday," Berthina said. The junkies are everywhere on the weekend. You should be able to find a pick somewhere."

"No, today's Tuesday."

"Dude, how can today be Tuesday when tomorrow is Saturday?" she said. I ignored her. I didn't care what day it was; I just wanted to get high.

Berthina cooked up, added the cotton, put the needle to it, and then pulled the plunger. Her syringe filled with a huge shot, and with trembling hands, she stabbed her forearm. She pulled the needled out then stabbed her ankle then her foot and then the back of her hand as she treated her body like a pin cushion while looking for a useable vein. Berthina had so many track marks that her arms and legs resembled a roadmap. Watching as she burrowed through her flesh trying to excavate a healthy vein, I wondered how long it would take my body to deteriorate as badly as hers.

After about fifteen minutes, Berthina finally found a usable vein in the back of her ankle. She shot it and kicked back, and her entire body glazed over with a moist comfort.

"Berthina. Berthina. Berthina!" I yelled, finally getting her attention.

"What, dude?"

"Here's twenty-five dollars. Can I get five dimes for that?" I asked.

"I said one small hit, dude," she said. "Why would I want your money? I'd just buy more dope."

She closed her eyes and started talking. She wasn't talking to me or to herself; she was just kind of thinking aloud in words, so mumbled I couldn't tell where one word ended and the next began. Then, she fell asleep. Classic junkie mistake. I could've taken her entire stash…

But all I wanted was a taste.

Just one big taste.

I put the money on her lap and took five balloons from her stash. She had more than enough to sell me. I spread the contents of all five bags on the glass table. I could have washed Berthina's pick out with ammonia and taken my chances with it, but because of the thousand horror stories I'd heard about AIDS while in rehab, I decided not to. I blew my nose, cleared my nostrils, and snorted one ganking line of Thai White after another. By the time I finished, I'd inhaled about ten times more junk than Uma Thurman did when she overdosed in *Pulp Fiction*. Then, I lay back and waited for my heart to pump my dirty blood to my brain.

Snorting is a decent high, but it's not the same. I wanted to slam it.

I wanted a syringe—

To stab into my arm and melt away the memories of what my

father did to me...

New Year's Eve, 2001
Skye

It was New Year's Eve; I hadn't yet gotten high and I was in a bad mood.

I could've been in Los Angeles, New York, Philadelphia, Bangkok, Rio, Jupiter, another galaxy, anywhere, and there would've been the same bunch of idiot drunks dancing around to the same stupid song. Oh well, I'd be wasted soon enough.

"I hate New Year's Eve!" I yelled over the loud fake Reggae the band *We Girls* was playing at Harry O's in Manhattan Beach. The lead singer mumbled more than sang, and his mumbles blended the lyrics into some kind of word soup. The guitarist abused her instrument, and watching made me sick that I'd sold mine for drug money. "Let's go home."

"Come on, Skye, just be happy tonight," Flora yelled. "It's New Year's Eve. Party! Woo!" She hoisted her Piña Colada overhead and executed a cute, silly hip-wiggle dance only she could make sexy.

When I met Flora years ago at one of my gigs, she was FOB, *fresh off the boat*. She was obsessed with American pop culture, and her English was horrible.

We became good friends because of our mutual love of music. I helped Flora with her English, which helped her in her nursing classes. She taught me about Filipino music, and I incorporated some of the Filipino uber-pop flavor into my gritty sound to give me something truly unique.

After only a few years of studying, Flora's English and even her diction became better than mine. The crowning moment of her mastery of English was a while back when I asked her, *Can you get me a soda when you're across the street?* Flora said, *Of course I can. But what you mean is, will I? Will you get me a soda when you're across the street?* I laughed my ass off at that.

Flora's my only real friend; I respect her for the way she's taken care of herself and defeated the ghosts of her past. She doesn't speak of them, but it's clear that she ran to America more-so to get away from something than anything else. Flora's stronger than I, but she's a little naïve. And though I've given her snippets of my life history, she's never really fully understood the scope of my abuse. I was ashamed of having to go back to rehab. So, instead of telling her that I was going, I lied, and told her I was headed out east on tour. She bought it. When I got out of rehab, she wanted to go out for lunch and catch up. I couldn't afford lunch. I had to make up some story about the label being behind on payments to me; I was too ashamed to tell her they'd dumped me. And of course, once I told her this, just last week, it was Flora to the rescue as usual. She got me a job at her hospital, as an orderly. It was shit work, but it was work, and I was eternally indebted to her for it. I knew I'd eventually get fired, so in the meantime, I was trying my hand at acting. Being a former recording artist, landing an agent was easy. Though making it as an actor was a long-shot, I had to take the chance. I'm an artist, and artists like me have a hard time keeping nine to five jobs. Some people think that is just an excuse for failure, but I don't know. When I work a nine to five I seriously feel exactly like I imagine I would feel were I in prison. Sometimes I consider working versus being homeless again, and wonder which was worse. It's a tough call.

Flora, like me, has been through a lot. However, somehow, she always manages to have fun and always looks beautiful while doing it. I watched her on the dance floor; she was dancing alone, but surely some guy would approach her. She's beautiful, but very approachable for some reason. When Flora dances alone, she's as carefree as a child; her steps are light and playful, and all eyes are on her.

I envy Flora—

She's a human being, and I wish I were, too.

I approached her on the dance floor, "Oh, hey Flora. I didn't ask how your date went with the actor guy the other night," I said.

"Well, he was a super nice guy, not the best looking, but a real sweetheart."

"Fireworks?" I asked.

"Umm, not really, more like sparklers. I wanted him to kiss me at the end of the night," Flora said, loudly over the band.

"And?"

"Well, he walked me to my door, and I was trying to decide whether or not to ask him to come in when all of the sudden I heard a thud behind me. He'd caught his foot on the step and fell on his face. He bashed his nose pretty badly."

"What?" I yelled. The band finished their song.

"I said he fell and bashed his nose."

"Good thing he was on a date with a nurse," I said, laughing.

"I'm a nurse assistant, soon to be R.N., maybe, if I don't fail this semester," Flora said. "Anyway, I took him inside to clean up his nose. I still kinda wanted him to kiss me, but the moment was gone."

The music started again, and Flora reflexively began moving to its awkward beat. "I was sort of hoping he'd ask me to go out tonight for New Years, but he didn't. No biggie. You and I are having fun, right? So hey, when are you going to go on a date, Skye? I can't remember the last time you had one."

"Why bother? I can get laid without wasting my time dating."

"We can all get laid without dating. That's not the point."

"What is the point?" I asked, but I didn't feel like having that conversation.

Flora leaned in toward me. "The point is we all need someone."

"I don't."

"Don't you want to find someone to settle down and grow old with?" Flora's tone was serious and motherly, but her body was still gyrating playfully.

"No, not really."

I'm lonely, sure, but it's of my own will. Most people are lonely because someone left them. Nobody left me. I own my loneliness, cherish it. It's mine, and nobody can take it from me.

"So you see no purpose for men other than for sex?"

"And they aren't even good at that!" I said. Flora gave me a high five.

"Hey, I'm gonna take a spin and see who's here. You want to come?"

"No, I'll stay back," I said. Flora moved off, dancing her way through the crowd.

Looking around, it seemed most people were pretending to have a good time. Everyone was talking to the people they came with, listening to the same boring stories they'd heard from the same boring people a billion times before. They'll pretend to care what the other person says, but they don't; they're out this evening because they're lonely and hoping that this will be the night they fall in love.

You feel like dancing? One friend will ask another. *Not just yet. I need a couple more drinks,* the friend will reply. They'll pound their drinks and order more, and the color of their drinks will get progressively lighter as the night wears on. They try to summon the nerve to talk to someone of the opposite sex, but they'll fail and go home alone, waking up hung-over, irritable, and alone.

We're all wasting time, wasting space, wasting each other's time and space. We should unite, mobilize, lose inhibition, and become a force. We should be doing something important like figuring out how to feed starving babies in Africa. Or we should all get naked, take off our brand name clothes, march to the White House, and start a giant protest against corporate America.

Nah. Maybe not. I don't want to do anything that involves groups of people.

I'm different than everyone else. I'm an old, bitter lady trapped in the body of a twenty-two-year-old. I'm a freak, and everyone knows it.

I needed to level off, so I went to the bar.

"Hey, beautiful. Can I buy you a drink?" Some guy asked.

"Yeah."

"What do you want?"

"How about a shot of 151?"

He smiled and ordered, and when the shots came, we toasted to some bullshit about next year and downed them. The liquor burned, sliding down my throat.

"That's harsh stuff," he said.

"Let's do another," I said.

"Really?"

"Yeah."

He ordered two more. We shot them. Burning. I had to run.

I walked briskly to the bathroom, opened the stall, and in the moment before I vomited, I thought about how many different toilets I'd been intimate with in my lifetime.

The rum burned as much on the way up as it did on the way down. It felt familiar and comforting. I lay my head on the toilet, my porcelain confidant, the only thing in the world that knows how truly abusive I am to my body, and let it all out. Then, after resting for a moment and catching my breath, and without the appropriate cooking tools, I got down on my knees, laid out my goods, and snorted some junk off the plastic seat. I'd decided if I was snorting heroin, instead of shooting it, then I was no longer addicted to it.

Addicts tell themselves all kinds of lies to justify their use.

The dope moved through me and moved my depression and emptiness to the backburner of my mind. At least for a short while.

Though Flora set me up with a new working gig, I knew I'd blow that money on drugs, too, and eventually I'd get fired. It was inevitable; I was destined to be strung out and living on the streets.

I did three more rails off the toilet seat to lift my spirits enough to be pleasantly social. Tomorrow, I'd go to the gym, sit in the dry sauna, and sweat out the toxins, to make room in my body for new toxins.

Coming out of the bathroom, I noticed some girls in grass skirts and coconut bras pouring shots down the throats of frat guys and old, lonely men. Some poor bastard was walking around with the girls, pimping product, in the same grass skirt. Ironically, the product was Rockenberger Rum, which was owned by Jackson, the ex-owner of my ex-label.

When I found Flora, she was dancing with some bald loser who stood three inches shorter than she, and she's only 5'4". His proud smile stretched as long as the Santa Monica Pier that I buried my dead baby under.

I miss my baby.

Flora Perez, 21

I love to dance to a thick baseline. It grabs me by the spine and rattles my teeth. My heart beats faster to keep up as I shake, bend, and twist. Sweat beads under my arms, at the back of my knees, and on my scalp. A deep, radioactive heat cooks inside me. I feel it in my gut, my toes, and in the walls of my labia. Endorphins pop, and I catch a natural high that's as real as any alcohol buzz.

The song ended, but the music echoed inside me. The short guy thanked me for the dance and waddled away. He seemed lonely.

I felt my hip vibrating. The infamous Dr. Juan Salazar was calling, again. He's infamous because he's odd. In fact, he's the oddest person I've ever known. He keeps to himself, but everyone at the hospital knew him by his neurotic behavior. Letting myself get mixed up with him was a mistake. It'd been a long time since our break-up, and he still called weekly. I refused to engage in conversation with him, because there was never any conversation, just him talking. He was the worst listener I'd ever known.

Shouldn't listening skills be a job requirement for psychiatrists?

I should've broken up with Juan the first time he forbade me to go to the grocery store alone. He was so scared that I'd leave him, and so possessive, but I stayed with him because I was alone and scared and needed someone in this big new country. Though Juan was obviously damaged, he had the unique talent of making me think his flaws were my fault. I was young, I was in a brand new country, and I was trying to escape my own demons. Juan used all that to his advantage, hoping to have me there, to love, forever.

But Juan didn't know how to love me.

I need to be loved the way the moon loves the sky. It comes out at night to keep the sky company and they are beautiful together. When daytime comes, the moon disappears, or sometimes it stays but in the distant background. I need to be loved like that; I needed a little space. I don't understand these couples who need to be together every second of every day.

I was happy to be out dancing on New Year's Eve, but I would've been just as content at home. Sometimes I think I'm manic-depressive. No, that's the wrong term. Juan would know the right term. I can be the biggest social butterfly in the world, but other times all I want is to be alone. Not because I'm sad, but because I like my own time. I like to hang out and read or dance alone. I don't get lonely when I'm alone. I get lonely when my thoughts drift to my family in the Philippines and my brother Deang's death. That's when I need company to distract me.

Skye came back from the bar with drinks for us. I met Skye when she came in off the streets, overdosed on heroin. We bonded but she was constantly in and out of consciousness and I don't think she really processed meeting me. We didn't keep in touch after. I ran into her again at one of her local performances, and though she didn't remember me, we quickly became best friends. I was drawn to her musical talent and the dark mystique surrounding her. Filipinos, as a people, are drawn to dark souls, souls in need; we have this innate need to nurture; I'm not sure why. And although Skye never talked about her drug abuse, I knew it was still an issue, and I wanted to help her.

Helping others is my passive way of dealing with my own pain… Dr. Juan Salazar taught me that.

"Hey," Skye said. Her left nostril was crusted with a ring of dark dried blood; she must have snorted something.

"Dance with me, Skye."

"I don't feel like it."

"Why?"

"Because I don't want people to laugh at my *Teutonic flair*," she said, accenting the words I'd once used to describe her dancing.

"Come on," I pleaded. But Skye wouldn't. The only time we'd gone out dancing together, Skye was rigid, almost militaristic. I told her she danced with a Teutonic flair, and then I mimicked her. *I don't dance like that*, she said. Then she started bouncing around and smiling and laughing and jiggling and wiggling. *Look at me, I'm Flora! Yeah! I'm so cute and bubbly and perfect! Yeah!*

"Look at that guy," Skye said, changing the subject. "He looks familiar in some weird former-life kinda way."

"What guy?" I asked.

"That guy. How much do you think they pay a poor bastard to dress up in a grass skirt?" Skye asked, pointing directly at T.J.

"Oh crap."

"Oh crap, what?" Skye asked.

"Nothing, never mind."

"Oh no you don't. Oh crap, what?" Skye persisted.

"That's T.J., the actor guy you were asking about. The one I just went on a date with," I mumbled as T.J. gyrated his coconuts and his little round belly while pouring a shot of something down some skank's throat.

"That's him? The guy who fell down before kissing you goodnight?"

"Yes."

"Well, explains why he has a bandage across his nose… Wait a minute. I know that guy. That's the cute, goofy, klutz I met on my flight from Oakland after my mini-tour!"

"Are you serious?"

Run, Flora, run.

I knew this would get worse before it got better. Skye has a knack for exploiting other people's humiliation.

"Let's go say hello," Skye said.

"Let's not. He's busy."

"I'm going to say hello."

Run!

T.J.

Single for another New Year's Eve, but it could be worse, I thought as I poured a shot of Rockenberger Rum down the throat of another out-of-my-league sex pot.

"Hooolyyyy crap," I said. I'd just caught a glimpse of Skye, the sexiest girl I'd ever shared time and space with.

Lost somewhere on memory lane, I'd forgotten I was pouring Rockenberger down the sexpot's throat.

"Asshole!" she said as the rum poured all over her face, running into her eyes. "Shit!" she screamed, grabbing her burning eyes with one hand, and trying to scratch mine out with the other.

When her nails met my face, I dropped the bottle, which shattered on the floor. I bent down to pick up the glass, and when I stood up, I smashed the back of my head into the bottom of the bar; it dizzied me, and I tumbled to the floor.

Kill me now.

Everyone was looking and laughing. Mercifully, the band began playing, and the laughter was muffled.

"Are you okay? Do you need a hand up, T.J.?" she asked. It was déjà vu of the humiliating incident in the airport terminal two years earlier. At least she remembered my name.

"Hi, Skye." I took her hand. It was as soft as I remembered.

"Good to see you again. I'd give you a hug, but your coconuts are drenched with whatever you were pouring down that little girl's mouth."

"It's Rockenberger Rum."

"I didn't expect to ever see you again," she said.

"I figured as much when you didn't give me your phone number after we landed," I said. Skye's eyes were no longer blue like when we met. Now, they were brown. Maybe she was wearing those brown-colored contacts or something.

"So, T.J. You'll never guess who I came with tonight."

"Brad Pitt?"

"Nope."

"Then I dunno. Some other rich, good-looking dude with charisma and coordination."

"Nope. I'm here with a girlfriend who would like to say hi to you. She's over there."

Un-be-lievable. Skye pointed toward the only girl I'd been on a date with in the past year. Flora. My breathing quickened; I felt like an invisible midget was standing on my heart. The circumstances couldn't have been worse.

"Oh, you and Flora are friends? What are the odds? I guess I should go get this humiliation over with," I said.

"I'll walk you over." Skye said, grinning like Satan. She was loving it. Bitch! Sexy bitch!

The band finished a song, and during the silence the jingling bells in my grass skirt could be heard with my every step towards Flora.

"Hey, Flora. Look who came to say hello," Skye said.

"Hi, Flora."

"How's your nose?" Flora asked.

Like a dipshit, I put my finger to my nose, forgetting that I fell on our date. "It hurts some, but not as much as the back of my head."

"Yeah, I saw you bang it on the bar. Ouch. Anyway, you look, umm, cute in your outfit," Flora said. Skye choked back a laugh, which caused her drink to shoot out her nose.

"Sorry," Skye said, her body convulsing in laughter.

"Well, it's great to see you again, Flora. Please excuse me, I'm going to go outside and, um, have a cigarette, and then maybe kill myself. I'll see you both later." I'd never smoked a cigarette in my life.

"It's good to see you again, too, T.J.," Flora replied.

I slogged my way out the door, fake grass skirt bells jingling.

"Why'd you embarrass him like that?" I heard Flora yell at Skye.

I went to the corner mart. I had no plan other than *not* to be in the bar. The only problem with plan was that my supervisor wouldn't be cool with it. Though my job sucked, I couldn't afford to lose it.

I grabbed a bottle of water and walked back. I tried to think of a way to avoid the girls without being rude and without getting fired.

When I tried to cross the red velvet rope to get back inside, the larger of the two bouncers asked, "You got a wrist stamp?" He spit when he spoke, and I could see his saliva whizzing past my head.

"Uhh, no."

"Then you need to wait in line and pay cover." Speckles of his spit landed on my face and lips. He looked familiar, but I couldn't place his big ugly head.

I wiped his spittle with my naked arm. I'd have used my shirt were I wearing one. "You're joking, right? I'm working a promo."

"How are we supposed to know that?" asked the lesser of the two bouncers.

"Because I'm wearing a friggen' grass skirt!"

"And?"

"And? And, how many friggen' losers have you seen dressed in friggen' grass skirts with little friggen' jingle bells tonight?"

"Tonight? Just you. Slow night," said the larger to the lesser.

"Yeah, slow night, huh, Dirk? Now, sir, get in line before I toss you in the street."

I tried to stare them down, but that didn't seem to work.

"Get in line!" the bouncer, Dirk, commanded. His saliva flew into my open mouth.

It tasted disgusting and I could smell it. I wiped my tongue on my sleeve and hacked up as much saliva as I could. As soon as I got inside I would rinse my mouth out with boiling water. Who knows what kind of monkey pox or bird flu that orally diseased monster had in his saliva. After riding myself of all the saliva I could, I retorted, "Don't take it out on me because you're fat and your life sucks."

"Listen, hula-bitch. I'll beat your ass, AND get you fired."

"Please do. I'm wearing a grass skirt and working a humiliating job on New Year's Eve. How much worse do you think my night can get?"

I retreated to the back of the line to wait with the rest of the loners in dance club purgatory.

This is my life in L.A. I spend fifty percent of my weekends standing in line outside clubs I don't really want to go to, with friends I don't really like, watching as saline-enhanced women, ridiculously wealthy dickheads, an occasional celebrity, and friends of the bouncer skip the line and go inside, laughing at all us pathetic line standers.

I stood there, angry and freezing. *It's surprising how little warmth a fake grass skirt provides.* My red-hot anger was the only thing keeping me from freezing to death. However, I wasn't about to give the bouncers the satisfaction of seeing me shiver.

Two minutes later, I was at the front of the line. "ID?" Dirk asked.

"Seriously? This outfit has no pockets," I said, my eyes almost begging.

"Just messing with you. Go in."

212

"Thank you," I said, like a coward.

I slinked back inside, frozen and shrunken beneath my grass skirt. It took a solid ten minutes for my body to thaw. I tried to be as inconspicuous as a guy in a skirt can be; I watched Flora from a distance, and tried to keep myself on the opposite side of the bar from her at all times. I managed to avoid her the rest of the night. When the clock finally hit twelve, Flora jumped in the air and pinched her nose. I don't know why, but it was cute. I wanted to kiss her. I hated myself for screwing up our date.

Out of nowhere, Skye came up from behind me; staggering drunk. She grabbed me and kissed me, and like any red-blooded American man who hasn't tasted a woman's lipstick in too long, I kissed back. Our kiss lasted much longer than the average Happy New Year's kiss. It was intoxicating. Or maybe that was her breath. Oddly, once our lips parted, instead of saying something to commemorate our kiss, I looked to make sure Flora hadn't seen us. By the time I turned back around, Skye was gone.

January 2002
Skye

"Watch your tone, buddy. You don't want to mess with a girl like me!"

Libby turns her back on the criminals then pivots with guns blazing.

"I can do this. I can do this. I can do this. They're going to love me. I'll become Libby Tonerelli!" I repeated, standing in front of the bathroom mirror, nervously messing with my uncooperative hair, and rehearsing lines.

The unwritten rule of the industry is to show up no more than ten minutes early or ten minutes late for an audition. However, in L.A., the unpredictable traffic makes it impossible to get anywhere at any exact time. I was thirty minutes early, so I had twenty minutes to waste in the ladies room, which was exactly nineteen minutes longer than I needed to psyche myself out.

My music career was dead as dead can be, and I knew I'd eventually lose my orderly job at Flora's hospital, and if I didn't, then I'd probably kill myself. So, acting was a way out for me. It was a long-shot, but so was my entire life. I had a bit of a talent for the dramatic. This was my first job audition, and I'd gotten a call-back, and now a screen test. It was down to three of us to land the gig.

Still waiting for my turn to audition, I got down on my knees in front of the toilet, my confidant, and did a big ganking line of coke. Since today's audition was so huge, I decided to stay alert and opiate free. Two minutes later, my brain was feeling speedy, so I chewed a Valium to mellow out. Finally, at 2:50, I went to the waiting room.

I was running my lines in the waiting room when another candidate came out of casting. She had perfect fake boobs and a flawless little anorexic body. She wore an expensive pair of pumps with three-inch heels that, I'm sure, were the best that money could buy, and her gait was straight out of the *Miss America* beauty pageant.

"Hi." She squared her shoulders to me as she spoke, but kept her hips turned sideways to give a slimming effect to her midsection and put even more emphasis on her chest. She had the kind of boobs that make life much easier for a woman. My boobs would need a wire push-up, duct tape, and some kind of anti-gravity device to hang so perfectly, like hers.

"Hi. How was the audition?" I asked.

"I think they liked me."

'I think they liked me.' Duh. They're men, and you're not wearing a bra. How could they not like you?

"Well, good luck—"

"They're only testing three of us, so we each have a thirty-three percent chance," she said.

Wow, you did the math so quickly.

"I'm Maria. Maria Orlando," she said, extending a hand.

"Skye Garucci," I said, taking her hand in mine.

"Well, break a leg, Skye."

You break an effin' leg.

"Thanks," I replied. Then Big Boobs Maria left.

Hollywood is full of spoiled phonies like Maria. Girls like her sleep until noon and spend their whole day primping so they can look good while they dance their night away under the disco ball of whatever L.A. club is the current flavor of the month. Girls like Maria contribute nothing to society and waste our dwindling natural resources by spending hours in the bathroom trying to get pretty.

"Ms. Garucci, you're up," said a cold voice from the casting room.

I walked in, slated for the camera, gave my profiles, and tried to dive into the role, but I was having a hard time giving myself to the character. The sound of my voice was irritating me, and the bright lights were making me sweat, and for some reason atypical of me. I made it through the audition fully aware of the fact that I was bombing.

"Very nice, Ms. Garucci. Thank you for coming."

"I can do it differently if you'd like. I worked on a more conflicted Libby, like Wynona Rider in *Girl, Interrupted*. Want to see it?"

"No, that will be all. Thank you."

"Shall I do the monologue I prepared?"

"Not necessary. We'll be in touch."

Liars.

February 2002
Ron

They say the life of a criminal is a dangerous one, but I don't recall ever getting a hernia while lifting someone's wallet. But now, working as a grip for Uptown Productions, I was lifting ridiculously heavy cameras every day, and I'd acquired an inguinal hernia, sciatica, and something called thoracic outlet syndrome.

Today was the first day of filming for a cheesy action flick called *Libby and Her Guns*. The film was about a sexy chick running around New York City shooting criminals to avenge her sister's death.

Why, in film, does America glorify violence?

I'd never killed anyone. I'd never even held a real gun. Libby Tonerelli would kill eighteen people in this movie, and the crowds would cheer her, but I steal from a rich old lady, and they want to crucify me.

"Maria, you're on," the director said.

Maria walked on set wearing a camouflage tube top, no bra, green army fatigues, and combat boots. She had an M-16 at her side. Being that her character was about to commit murder, I thought her attire was a little flamboyant. In real life, were she logical, she'd have tried to camouflage herself into her surroundings, but I guess logic doesn't sell movie tickets as well as tube tops do.

During break, I was leafing through the *L.A. Weekly*. Maria was all over the thing. She was in a full-page advertisement for Diesel on page 97. On page 112 the blossoming starlet's likeness was in a small advertisement for her last film, *Father's Daughter*. Then, on page 227, I found her in a picture with her real father at a charity event at his restaurant. I recognized him immediately, mobster Antonio Orlando; I don't know how I hadn't made the connection before. My criminal mind started scheming.

Maria

It was eight o'clock on our first day of the shoot, and we'd just worked a twelve-hour day. I was terrible. I flubbed a ton of lines, I was missing my marks, and my fat, bloated belly was practically pouring out over my army fatigues.

"That's it for today," the director said.

Instead of going home, I went to Daddy's restaurant. Later, Paul and I were having dinner with Dad at his place, and I wanted to visit Dad ahead of time to make sure he wouldn't start another religious argument with Paul.

When I got to the restaurant the hostess, stopped me, "Nobody's allowed upstairs right now, Maria."

I knew something was up. "I'm going up."

She picked up the phone as I headed up the stairs. I found Dad in his office with Fat Tony, a boss of the Scalesci family. A meeting with him couldn't have been about anything on the straight and narrow.

"Dad, what's going on?" I asked.

"Tony, can you give us a minute?"

"Sure," Tony said. He stepped out, escorted by Double Gut, Jimmy Branzo.

I was pissed. Really pissed. I'd had it with Daddy's lies. Every time I allow myself to trust him, he turns out to be just like every other man out there. "You lied to me, Dad!"

He stood and reached for me, "Baby doll—"

"Don't baby doll me right now. One of these days you're going to get yourself killed!"

"Sugar Plum, I—"

"Dad! Just stop! My God, you just bought your way out a prison sentence, and now you're right back at it. When will this stop?" I knew my father was a bad man; I knew many men feared him, but he was my dad, and I loved him. "Daddy, you promised me you would give up this thug life!"

"I'm not a thug. Thugs live in Compton. I'm a businessman."

"I'm making plenty of Hollywood money now. We don't need your blood money. I can support both of us."

"Baby, how do you think you got the—never mind."

"What, Dad?"

"Forget it."

"What were you going to say? How do I think I got the what, Dad?"

"Just forget it," he said.

I knew what Dad was going to say. He was going to tell me I got the part in the shitty movie because of him. It was the same way I got my starring role in our second-grade play and probably the same way I've gotten everything in my life. I was the talentless daughter of a powerful mobster who put the fear of God in people.

"Look, sweetie, I'll quit the business. I promise. I just have to finish one last job. There's no way out of it."

"Dad, you're a liar. Screw you." I said. It was the first time I'd ever back talked him. I half expected he'd throw me across the room.

He didn't. "Baby, don't talk that way. It reminds me of your mother. You're better than her. I love you, and I'm sorry, and I promise you I will make this better."

"How?" I asked.

"I'll start tonight. I'll be extra nice to that boyfriend of yours. And tomorrow, we'll talk about our future. Okay?" he asked. I didn't respond. But then he got up and put his arms around me. I've never been able to resist Daddy when he gets like that. "Okay, pumpkin?"

"Okay Daddy, but you have to promise."

He put his hand behind my head, put my head on his shoulder, and said, "I promise. Now, get outta here. I got business to conduct, and you're making me look like a softie."

He broke away and smiled. I knew he saw the tears in my eyes. That's why men rule this world—they are heartless, they know we aren't, and they know how to pull at our heart-strings. Caring is women's biggest strength and our biggest weakness.

Paul

The first thing I noticed was the sound of veggies hissing on a frying pan; the second thing I noticed was Sinatra. The entire house was a shrine to him… except for the shrines to the Virgin Mary.

Maria tilted her head to receive her father's kiss on her cheek, and then she whisked away up the stairs and left me alone with him. Maria never talked about her father's *occupation*. I brought it up once, and she killed the subject quickly. But I knew what he did, and it scared me. Mr. Orlando didn't like me, and though he never threatened me directly, sometimes I felt threatened.

"So, what's been going on, Paulie boy?" Orlando asked. Some days Mr. Orlando thinks he's Joe Pesci in *Goodfellas*, other days he thinks he's Brando in *The Godfather* or Pacino in *Casino*. Today he was doing his Pesci. His jokes are usually at my expense, but the real comedy is in the unintentional humor. For example, over half the women in his extended family are named Mary or Maria, including my girlfriend. It's completely hysterical, but I seem to be the only one who gets it. Some unintentional ironic comedy would be the fact that Mr. Orlando, a murderous gangster, lectures me on religion.

"How are all the *protesters* at your *protest*-ant church these days, Paulie boy?" Mr. Orlando always makes a point of putting the emphasis on the first two syllables, *pro-test*.

"Great, thank you."

"You got your sermon down under ten minutes yet?"

"Eight minutes is my record."

"You protestors treat church like it's a fast food joint."

"Yeah, we're considering omitting prayer completely so everyone can get home before kickoff on Sundays."

"Is that so? Wouldn't surprise me. People don't have the discipline to sit through a real Catholic mass anymore. They'd rather get their ten-minute fast-food serving of God from you protest-ants. Some day you guys will have a church drive-through."

Some wars, like Vietnam, are fought for generations. The war between Orlando and me, on a smaller scale, was becoming like that.

"How many people are coming to your church these days?" he asked, intentionally fiddling with the Virgin Mary medallion he wore around his neck. If Catholics spent half the money on goodwill they spend on statues to all their beloved Saints, world hunger would be solved.

I was staring at a painting of the Virgin. He has four large paintings of the half-naked subject—and that's only counting the ones I've seen. There's a weeping Madonna in the living room, a Madonna holding baby Jesus in the kitchen, Madonna with Mary Magdalene in the downstairs bathroom, and Madonna wiping Jesus' tears when he falls with the cross; Madonna's everywhere. Orlando's interior decorator was probably the Pope himself.

"Yo, Paulie boy!"

"What?"

"I asked you a question."

"Oh. I'm sorry. I was just admiring that painting of Mary," I said, pointing.

"Yeah, I love that painting. Why won't you protestors give Mary her due respect? You guys take Mary out of church, get rid of all the ritual and the stuff about Judgment Day, and that's how you end up with a ten-minute sermon. People go to your church because it's easy."

"Yeah, maybe. Or maybe they realize a good preacher can deliver a better message with a short, interesting sermon than a boring half-hour homily," I said.

"Paul!" Maria scolded me on her way down the stairs. It's a good thing I didn't have the guts to say what I was really thinking, which would have been, *People come to my church because they know we don't molest little boys.*

"Paulie, you should repent for rejecting His church all these years. God will forgive you if you repent."

"Is it that easy?"

"Well, you might get a few thousand years of purgatory," Orlando laughed. I think Mr. Orlando actually believes he can go out and whack somebody tonight, confess to his priest tomorrow, and everything will be forgiven. "We're having pasta tonight, Paulie boy. Maria's mother's old recipe." Maria's mother, also named Maria, divorced Orlando when my Maria was a young girl. Mother and daughter have had practically no contact since. Maria's grandmother, Maria, died when my Maria was a young girl. She's had no female role models growing up. "You okay with spaghetti, Paulie boy?"

"Spaghetti's my favorite, Pops. For-get a-bout it." I hated spaghetti as much as he hated when I called him Pops, and he knew it. And I hated when he called me Paulie boy almost as much as he hated when I said *forget about it*—I made sure to say it as pedestrian as possible.

"Will you two please try to get along for my sake?" Maria asked.

"Okay, honey. *Fughetaboutit,* Paulie boy," he said, shaking a finger at me.

"I already for-got a-bout it, Pops."

"Listen, I don't want to hear you call me Pops until you're married to my daughter, and I don't see no ring on my Maria's finger. Thank Jesus for that," he said, kissing the gaudy diamond studded crucifix around his neck and then the Virgin Mary medallion—then loaded his plate five inches high with piping hot spaghetti.

Orlando is a stereotype wrapped in a caricature, stuffed inside a cliché.

"Funny you mention that, Mr. Orlando," I said. Maria was waving me off, but I ignored her.

"Huh?" Orlando's voice was muffled by a fist-sized meatball he'd shoveled into his fat head.

"Mr. Orlando, I came tonight to—" I began, but Maria stepped on my foot, under the table. "Ouch!" I looked at Maria; her big eyes were locked on mine as if to say, *Don't you dare tell him.* "Mr. Orlando, I'm here tonight to announce that Maria and I—"

"We're going to Italy—after I finish the film," Maria lied through her crooked smile.

"*Fughetaboutit!* Oh, that's great! Paulie boy, you're going to love Italia!" He slapped both my cheeks, a little harder than necessary. I'm not sure I'll ever understand the need to give someone a good hard slap on the cheek.

After Maria announced our *vacation plans,* Mr. Orlando said grace, all the while keeping an eye on me. The last time I was invited to Orlando's for dinner was Thanksgiving in 2001. I didn't cross myself during grace, and Orlando didn't invite me back until recently when Maria threatened to sever contact with him.

Today, I crossed myself, but I intentionally went up-down-left-right, instead of up-down-right-left. I knew Orlando saw and knew he was pissed, but he didn't say anything.

We ate and drank for an hour. I can't think of many things more disgusting than watching Orlando eat. He'd cut a meatball in half, wrap his mouth around it, and chew without taking a break from talking. Meatball particles flew from his mouth like grenade shrapnel. One saliva covered meatball chunk flew into Maria's wine glass as she was putting the glass to her lips. Before I could warn her, she drank it. My gag reflex kicked in, and I puked in my mouth, choosing then to swallow it rather than spit it out at the table.

After dinner, we retired to Orlando's ridiculously gargantuan living quarters for the purpose of smoking some ridiculously expensive cigars and conversing about ridiculous topics, making sure to say *fughetaboutit* as many times as possible. Halfway through my cigar that I hated even more than the dinner I'd forced myself to eat, Maria got up and left without excusing herself. That was unlike her. Ten minutes later, when she'd failed to come back, I put my cigar out in Orlando's tacky ashtray shaped like Italy, and excused myself.

"Don't be long. And no fooling around! Or—"

"For-get a-bout it." I said, finishing his thought.

I walked up the spiraling staircase which leads to Maria's old bedroom, but she wasn't in there. I found her in the bathroom, on her knees, with her finger down her throat. Again.

"I'm sorry," Maria cried, hacking on a piece of food caught halfway down her throat.

I hadn't seen Maria force herself to vomit in a very long time, and I surprised myself with the intense anger I felt. For the first time since I was a young man, I felt a familiar, uncontrollable violence, bubbling to the surface.

"I'm leaving," I said. And so I left.

I left to keep her safe from my anger.

March 2003
Dylan

I was alone at the Viper Room, waiting to see one of my favorite bands, Crooked Fingers. The air in the legendary venue was thick with greatness. The walls were saturated by the breath of icons like Johnny Cash, Iggy Pop, and Springsteen. And the lingering soul of River Phoenix, who died there, wrapped the bar in a cool darkness.

I was sipping a Seven and Seven and thinking about the irony of fermentation.

Dead decaying plants birthing edible poison.

About then, the emcee announced the opening act. "Presenting, Skye Garucci!"

The curtains parted, and there stood Skye, alone with her guitar.

And then the world stopped.

It was just she and I.

Waves were moving through me.

And I wasn't comfortable with how I felt.

Skye was sickly beautiful, like an injured fawn lying on the side of a freeway. Her face was poetic, wonderful, and disturbing. She was the final image from a terrifying movie that would fuck with my dreams for weeks.

She started strumming her guitar. It was soft, but obsessive. She sang the first verse:

"Pink pills in a purple bottle;
Can't stop lead foot on the throttle.
You lied when you said you loved me;
me believing you hopelessly.
I felt emotionally raped;
a victim floating in your wake.
Don't fucking ask for my charity;
I hate you and I hate me."

Her voice was passionate, haunting, and disturbing; it made me think of cancerous tumors, dead roses, and decapitated puppies, but even more disconcerting. I wanted to pluck a handful of sound out of the air and keep it in my pocket for later when I needed to hear something moving.

Then, after her first verse, the tempo changed, and Skye spit out the chorus like venom.

"My empty dead body, I've forgotten how to long.
Music is my weapon, I'll kill you with my song."

It felt like Skye gave an honest depiction of her world rather than prettying it up. The beauty in her song counterbalanced her pain. Her pain was an obvious inspiration for the song, and the suffering she endured begat beautiful art, giving a positive element to her pain.

At least that was my take on it.

After just this one song, I felt like I knew Skye. But then she sang a love song, which completely threw me off. Her third number was pop-punk, and her fourth number couldn't be labeled—it was pure energy, hatred soaked in gasoline.

Skye played out like an odd fusion of The Ramones, Blondie, with a dash of Motorhead and a pinch of Alanis Morissette. She didn't fit any genre, and her music is hard to label, but if I were forced to somehow categorize it, I would describe it like this: Skye's music is her response to the impossible question we all have balled deep inside ourselves—why the fuck are we here? And when we've exhausted all possible answers, we give up and scream, *Fuck you,* as loud as we can to the tune of three miserable chords.

After Skye finished her only set, Crooked Fingers took the stage. They would rock like they always do, but I couldn't stop thinking about Skye.

I rushed to the bar between sets. "Sorry," I said after accidentally plowing into someone's back. When I saw her face, I got a lump in my throat.

"Skye?"

"Yeah?"

"Hi. Wow. You put on an amazing show."

Skye was as beautiful up close as she was on stage. I wanted her to like me; it was the first time I cared what someone thought of me in quite a while.

I should've showered.

"Are you touring with Crooked?" I asked.

"No. Just opening for them tonight. I wish I was touring."

"You should be. You're as good as anyone I've heard recently."

"Yeah, right," she scoffed. "That's why there were only twenty people here to see me."

"People don't know shit. You're amazing," I said.

"Thank you. Who are you?"

"I'm Dylan. What are you drinking?"

"Rum 151. And beer."

"This round's on me," I said, signaling the bartender.

"I've got to run to the bathroom. I'll be back," Skye said.

Skye

As I snorted my antidepressant off the toilet seat, I thought about the fact I hadn't been drug-free for a single day in months. Though my drug diet was 90 percent heroin, I did coke when I performed because it gave me more confidence.

Unfortunately, all the confidence in the world wasn't going to get me back with a label, but at least I was playing small clubs again.

I met a guy named Dylan at the bar. After visiting the bathroom, I went back to the bar to have a drink with him. We toasted to my music, slammed Rum 151 shots, and then I took a long pull of beer to cool the burning in my throat.

"Wow. That's strong stuff," Dylan said.

"Yep."

Black lipstick framed Dylan's yellowish teeth. His face had a heavy white foundation, and he wore black eye shadow. His outfit was all black to match his make-up and his black spiked hair. Dylan's look had been done before. It was a boring combination of wanna-be punk rocker and part gothic-suicidal loner. Regardless, I found him attractive.

"Your first song tore me up," Dylan said. "There was something sickly beautiful about it."

"Thanks," I said.

He was half right. The song was mired in sickness. It was about my father prostituting me as a child; there's no beauty in that.

"Your music is passionate and honest, and those are the two most important things in any art. I mean, take the passion out of the Beatles, and you're left with a boy band like *NSYNC," Dylan said.

"Are you some kind of music critic or something?"

"No, just a music lover. Actually, I'm a writer, but I'm not working now."

An unemployed writer in Hollywood. As cliché as starving musician. We're perfect for one another.

"You want to step out for a smoke?" Dylan asked.

"Sure."

Outside on Sunset Boulevard, Dylan stepped in close to light my stick, and I smelled B.O. I found it more humorous than foul, and I wondered if he was aware of his own scent.

"Skye, can I ask you something?"

"Ask."

"Why do you wear those fake blue contacts? Your eyes are brown, right?"

"How did you know that?" I said. I took out one contact.

"Yep. Brown," he said. "They're beautiful and sad. They suit your music more than the blue."

"Thank you," I said, impressed and a little creeped out.

Dylan scratched his head as he looked me up and down. "Yeah, the natural brown definitely suits you more. Why hide all power behind those fake contacts?" he asked.

His comment was off-putting, honest, and comforting all at the same time. "Isn't it hypocritical to comment on my fake contacts when your entire appearance is fake?"

Dylan paused and genuinely considered what I said before responding. "You're right. That's completely hypocritical," he said. He pulled out and lit a second cigarette.

"You a big smoker?" I asked.

"Kinda."

"Keep it up and your yellow teeth are going to be the same shade as my brown eyes," I said.

"Hey, Crooked's getting ready to start their next set," he said, either ignoring my little insult or not caring about it. "Let's get back inside and get a spot by the stage."

"I prefer the back row over being mashed against sweaty bodies up front."

"Okay. Mind if I hang back with you?" Dylan asked.

"Hang away."

We stood together in the back until Crooked Fingers finished, and then we hung out backstage with the band. Dylan was a little intimidated. He was an obvious backstage virgin. Eventually, he loosened up, and we had a good time. However, no matter how much blow went up my nose, the depression was coming on strong, and I knew to feel better I needed to get somewhere where I could get some heroin in my blood. But I also felt the need to take Dylan with me wherever I decided to go. I never feel the need to have people around, especially men, unless it's one of those rare occasions when I need to be fucked, physically hurt, to mute the pain in my head. But this didn't feel like that. Dylan didn't seem like the aggressive type, and there was at least a 50% chance he was gay.

When closing time came, Dylan suggested we *just go for coffee*. I hate that phrase. By suggesting *just coffee*, is a coward's way of suggesting a date without actually having to ask.

I trashed his coffee idea and asked him to go with me for another drink at an after-hours club. We went to a seedy place where I knew I could get some smack. We talked about many subjects, and we discovered a mutual love for the word of Kerouac and Vonnegut, and a good alcohol buzz. Drinking mellowed me out, and I felt a little more serene, and by the end of the night I felt I'd just acquired my second real friend.

Kelly

"That's life, that's what all the people say.
You're ridin' high in April, shot down in May."

I was singing Sinatra's *That's Life,* a really great song that I really butchered. Thankfully, most of my audience was hearing impaired.

I followed up on my promise to my son, Teddy, and attempted to reassemble my old college band, Christmas Party Junkie, but it didn't happen. None of my old band mates were willing to drop their jobs and divorce their families, move to Los Angeles and take on the Sunset Strip.

Cowards.

So, I put together a new band; we call ourselves Dandelion Soup. We play small gigs in dirty, cramped bars in crappy sections of L.A. like Palms, Culver City, and Mar Vista. Every gig is a blast. During a Dandelion Soup original, *Hey Bartender,* Tommy rocks a drum solo while the rest of us go to the bar and do a shot. Then we return to stage and finish the song. That was my idea. Maybe corny, but definitely fun.

Dandelion Soup is quite the motley crew. Like the original Motley Crüe, we have an alcoholic drummer named Tommy. During one gig, he passed out in the middle of our favorite song, *Sushi Whore.*

Our lead singer, Barry, is a good-looking, twenty-three-year-old blond kid with an amazing voice. Barry is too talented for our band, and it's only a matter of time before he ditches us. Our bassist is a fat, black dude named Joe. I know it's stereotypical to have a fat black bassist, but that's what we have. As lead guitarist, I'm the oldest member of the band by eight years. I love the band, but I rarely get to rip out any ear-melting solos; the skilled art of the guitar solo seems to have died with the new generation of emo wimp rockers, which seemed to be the direction our band was trying to take. As the founder of the band I thought I should get to choose the songs we perform, and emo was not my style.

Our band has a modest following… Actually, to be honest, we have four fans. There's Dave, who is drummer Tommy's brother; there's Toni, bassist Joe's girlfriend; and there's Clarissa, Toni's slutty friend and our only band groupie. Lastly, there's Dirk, he's our number-one fan; he never misses a show. Unfortunately, Dirk's breath could wilt a geranium with a plutonium stem. To make matters worse, he's a close talker, one of those people who stands two inches away when talking.

Today I was in the activities room of the nursing home I work at, doing a solo gig.

I finished my Sinatra cover and received light applause until the leviathan Dirk screamed, "You rock, Kelly!"

"Thank you, Dirk." I figured Dirk was at the nursing home visiting his grandmother or something.

Armed with only a karaoke machine, I play gigs at the nursing home because it provides me the chance to give something honest to the elderly. I feel I owe them that since my physical therapy sessions with them lack conviction.

I played, *Brown Eyed Girl,* and Dirk applauded wildly. The rest of the crowd, or those with two functional arms, applauded as well. Mrs. Taglebomb stood from her wheelchair and lifted her gown about waist-high to flash her drooping breasts. She flashed me after every song, but that doesn't make me special. She flashes the nurses when they bring her medications, and she flashes the entire cafeteria just about every meal.

"Mom, put your gown down," demanded her son.

"And thank you, Mrs. Taglebomb," I said. I can still titillate the girlies when I rock the microphone.

I put my equipment down and made my way around the room.

"Kelly, you are a wonderful talent!" a patient said.

"Thank you so much."

"Kelly, did I ever tell you about how Henry, my husband, used to bring a flower home to me every day of the week?"

"You have," I said, and she had, every single time I'd ever seen her.

"Have I ever told you Henry, my husband, worked a second job to save enough money to take me back to Vietnam to visit my family? Then when we got there, he surprised me with a second wedding ceremony my family could be part of. Did I ever tell you about that?"

"Yes, you have, dear, but you can tell me again," I said.

These old folks have been cast off by their families, to die here; they're lonely and bored and just want someone to listen. In listening, I allow them to relive the moments of their lives they wish they could go back to. And when they tell these stories, their eyes light up, and for a minute, they disappear from this institutionalized hell called a nursing home.

After the patient finished her story, I turned to walk away, but Dirk appeared in my face. "Kelly, dude, you totally rocked the Sammy

Davis number."

"Thanks, Dirk." I said, shook his hand, and took three steps backward to get out of his rancid air.

"Dude, I'm having a party at my pad next weekend for the Southern California Snake Lovers' Society. I'd be honored if Dandelion Soup would play."

There's no way I'm stepping foot in Dirk's house.

"We'll pay you of course."

"We'll do it." Our band never had a paying gig.

"Thanks, dude." Dirk smiled, exposing the roots of his long, mangled teeth. His diseased gums have been running away from his teeth for years. "Hey, I gotta run. It's Martha's feeding day. I'll catch you later."

I knew about Dirk's iguana, Aisha; his boa constrictor, Bo; his python, Lord Hercules; and his black snake, Dog. Martha was news to me. I couldn't wait to find out what kind of exotic animal it was.

"Okay. I'll see you at the party," Dirk said.

"All right. We'll see you then. Give my love to your—who are you visiting here?" I asked.

"Oh, no man. It's not like that."

Huh?

Dirk waddled off, leaving me wondering what exactly he fed Martha. Guitar players maybe.

"Kelly, can I speak to you for a minute?" Mrs. Taglebomb's son asked.

"I swear I didn't look at your mom's breasts when she flashed me."

"Everyone in L.A. county has seen my mom's breasts," Mr. Taglebomb said.

"Oh, and here I thought I was special. You really know how to take the wind out of a man's sails," I said. He laughed.

"That's exactly the kind of sense of humor I'm looking for. I wasn't joking earlier when I told you you'd be perfect for our show, *Single Parents.*"

"Seriously?"

"Seriously. Here's the concept: an attractive, single mom blindly asks questions of our three single dads. Then, without ever seeing them, she picks the one she likes best."

A regurgitated version of *The Dating Game*.

"I'm a musician. My band mates would call me a sellout if I did your show."

"It's tasteful. We're not out to make anyone look bad," he said, not even trying to cover his smirk.

"Yeah, right."

"And the winner gets one thousand dollars to spend in Hawaii with the woman who picked him."

"Sign me up," I said. That makes twice in the last ten minutes I'd sold my integrity for a few dollars.

Why not? I hadn't even kissed a woman since my divorce, unless groupie Clarissa counts. She doesn't.

April 2003
Kelly

"So, this might be kind of fun, huh?" I asked Beth backstage on the *Single Parents* set.

So much for her *blindly* picking a guy.

There's nothing real in reality television.

"I just hope I don't fall down in these heels. I haven't worn heels in a couple years."

"Well, you look great."

Beth looked like a blond version of Janeane Garofalo from *Reality Bites*. Her skin tone was pale, and other than her green eyes and the birthmark over her right eye, her features were indistinct. She had thin lips which blended into the rest of her face, her light eyebrows were barely visible, and her nose was neither big nor small. She was very average.

The P.A. motioned to Beth. "Okay, Beth, big smile when you wave to the audience. You're on in three, two, one. Go!"

I hope she picks me. I wasn't attracted to her, but, hey, this was national TV.

"People! Get on your feet to give a warm *Single Parents* welcome to single parent, Beth! Beth's been single since she got pregnant. Today we're going to find her a mate! Let's hear it for Beth!"

"Okay, Kelly. You're on in three, two, one. Go!"

"And here comes our first bachelor. Give a warm *Single Parents* welcome to bachelor number one. He's a physical therapist and a single father whose wife cheated on him with an ex-NFL superstar."

Oh, God. This is gonna suck.

Ron

I'm a big fan of breasts. I enjoy them in all shapes and sizes, lopsided or even. But this woman's droopy breasts made me uncomfortable. They were stretched out and stringy all the way down to the baseball-sized lumps of fat that sat on top of her belly. I doubted her breasts had ever touched a bra. Charice was in her twenties, but her breasts looked eligible for social security.

Is it normal for a woman to parade around topless inside another woman's apartment?

When Charice folded her arms on top of her head, I tried to pretend I didn't noticed the tangled mass of hair in her armpits in the same way I tried to pretend not to notice the giant herpes welt on her lip, but her B.O. was unavoidable. No actor in the world could pretend not to notice.

"Jesus," I said, out loud, before my brain filter told me to stop.

"Jesus what?" the man hater asked. She was frothing at the mouth for a chance to mix it up with the enemy. "Are you uncomfortable with my femininity? Should only men be aloud to walk around with their shirts off, scratching at their crotches?"

I was ready to go toe to toe with this man-hater. "No, your breasts don't bother me in the slightest."

"Really?"

"Yeah, really. But your B.O. made me vomit in my mouth," I said.

I heard Amber chuckle from the kitchen.

Charice flipped me off. The she casually picked her nose, rolled the booger along the length of her jeans until it formed a bluish lump. She stared at me.

You better not.

She did. She flicked it right at my head. Had Amber not walked into the room at that second, I may have thrown one back her way.

"Well, kids, I have to go pick up my niece. It was nice meeting you, Ron," Charice said, then blew me a kiss.

I jumped to the side to avoid her herpes infected air kiss.

Charice threw on her top, no bra. Her woman lumps bulged through her baggy T-shirt just above her navel. "Bye, Amber," she said and left.

I noticed Amber smiling at me. "What's so funny?" I asked.

"Please, Ron. Don't act so cool."

"Well, okay then. I'll ask. Is that normal? Is that what you girls do?"

"Us girls, as in lesbians?"

"Yeah."

"No. It's not what we do. Well, I don't. And Charice wouldn't typically do that. She was being territorial, protecting me, a lesbian, from you, the enemy; she was trying to make you uncomfortable."

"Mission accomplished. I was definitely uncomfortable. Is she your girlfriend?"

"No. Just an old friend. We haven't talked in a long time. She's been mad at me since I started hanging out with you. She thinks I'm a traitor to the lesbian community."

"That's stupid," I said.

"Why?"

"My friends wouldn't think I was a traitor to straight men if they knew I was hanging out with lesbians. And my friends definitely wouldn't be walking around with their cocks out in front of you."

"Ron, you don't have any friends besides me. And if you did, they'd think it was hot that you were hanging out with lesbians. *Did you get a threesome?* They'd ask."

"Yeah, you're probably right."

Amber disappeared to the kitchen and returned with some potato chips just as the commercials ended and *Single Parents* came back on the tube. "Beth looks great on TV," Amber said. She leaned on the couch behind me. Her warm breath rested on my neck and gave me goose bumps. "It took me all week to convince her to wear that top," Amber said.

"She does look a bit sexy. I never noticed before," I said.

"That's because perverts like you only notice a woman if she shows cleavage." She sat next to me. My nose was still traumatized by the scent of the lesbian herpes kiss blower, but I knew Amber smelled great. She always does.

"I think she's into bachelor number one," I said.

"She's not into any of those guys."

"You sound jealous."

"Actually, no. I'm not," Amber said.

"You're jealous."

"I'm not jealous."

"You reek of jealousy," I said.

"Do not."

"Then what's that smell?" I said, sniffing around her nape, playfully.

"That's the urine/beer/sweat/man-stench that follows you everywhere you go."

"Please. You have as much a man-stench as I do, you big lesbo."

"That's Ms. Lesbo to you. And I don't have a stench. I have an aroma."

"You're hilarious," I said.

"I have an aroma, and I'm hilarious. I'm the total package."

Amber was hilarious, and whatever she smelled like, it was sensual.
And today I was more horny than usual. Instinctively, I decided at that moment that our friendship needed to step up to the next level.

Amber and I should get naked.

We should do it, right this minute, on her pink sofa. We'd known each other for years. We'd been casual best buddies, and it was bound to happen sooner or later, regardless of whether Amber liked women or not.

I did my very best to convince myself that Amber was desiring me in the same way that I desired her.

Amber picked up the bag of chips, ate one, and then set the bag down on the coffee table. "I'm craving something else," she said. Maybe she was being metaphoric about her burning sexual desire for me. She went back to the kitchen.

I should follow her in there. We'll get naked, and we will have sex. We will become best friends *with benefits.* It doesn't matter she's a lesbian. It'll just be a thing on the side for both of us.

She came out sucking on an icy purple Otterpop.

"How's your popsicle?" I asked, thinking about sex.

232

"Delicious. Want one?" she asked, running her tongue along the length of the icy stick. She was teasing and taunting. Her message was clear.

I put my arm around her shoulder. "No, thanks," I said.

"You sure? They're really good." Amber circled her tongue around the tip.

We should go into the bathroom for a quickie. No, that wouldn't be romantic. *The bedroom?* We can turn the television volume up loud so Kimberly doesn't hear us. We must have sex! There's sex in the air; that's what I'm smelling. It's sex! We need to have sex! Gotta do it while I have the nerve—

"Now!" I said.

"Huh?" Amber asked.

"I'm horny," I blurted.

"I see."

I see? What the hell does *I see* mean? Is she thinking about it? *I see?* Do I have an erection? Does she see it? No, I don't have an erection. A little chubby; no erection.

There was no more conversation after that. It was awkward. At the commercial break, Amber got up and went into her bedroom.

Is that a signal? Why is she making this so difficult? It must've been a sign. I'm going in.

When I stood up, Amber came out of her room with a Victoria's Secret catalog. "Here," she said, handing it to me.

"What's this?"

"A remedy for horniness. We don't have *Playboy.* Use the bathroom." Amber laughed. Then Amber stuck out her tongue; it was purple from the Otterpop.

"Your tongue's all purple," I said. I laughed; I put my hand on her back and rubbed it gently. "You're such a great friend," I said, then hugged her. Amber hugged me back. After a second or two, I felt Amber's grasp loosening. I squeezed her a little tighter. She felt good in my arms, natural even. As natural as a lesbian can feel in a straight man's embrace. Then a brilliant idea overcame me.

We should have sex.

Before I could share my idea, Amber pulled away. I looked at her, hoping we'd share one of those earth-shattering, narcotic mutual stares two people exchange moments before tearing off each other's clothes.

But then the show came back on. Amber's attention turned to it. I sat and pouted.

"I like hanging with you like this. It's nice," I said, thinking about sex.

"It is," she said, smiling and maybe thinking about sex as well. "You know, I still can't believe Beth had the guts to go on this freaky show. It's so unlike her."

And our moment, which had never been a moment anyway, was gone.

Amber

"Can I get an Otterpop too?" Ron asked, defeated. I choked back my laughter. I admired the fact he had enough confidence to hit on a lesbian.

"Sure, Ron. Go crazy."

"Thanks." Ron went to the kitchen and came back with a handful of Otterpops. He bit the end off one and let out his frustration on the icy, pink meat of the popsicle.

"Ron, do you have to be so grossly loud when you eat? You know the noise disgusts me."

He replied with a flippant, "Sorry," and continued sucking and slurping. I regretted giving him carte blanche to my Otterpops.

Ron had somehow become family to me, as much as Beth was. But we weren't exactly the All-American family. I was a twenty-six-year-old single mother and lesbian stripper raising children with my conservative, straight best friend, who at the moment, was totally hamming it up on a televised dating game show. I'd never known her to flirt. I thought I'd get jealous watching the show, but I didn't. In fact, I found the whole thing entertaining and funny.

This was the first time I could recall watching television in years. Long ago, I grew to hate how TV sitcoms portray women, and decided to stop watching all together. One day I'd like to crawl through the set and go on a woman hunt for Marian Cunningham, June Cleaver, and Edith Bunker. I'd take Weezie Jefferson with me, and we'd slap those bitches around until they understood the hole between a woman's legs is more than just the place where they don't have a penis. The women's movement gets set back fifty years every time an impressionable young girl sees a rerun of those stupid shows.

"Oh no!" I yelled.

"What?" Ron said.

"Beth has a nose bleed! This is going to be just like Mike Coppermen, in the seventh grade, all over again! She's going to be humiliated!"

"Who's Mike Coppermen?"

The producers apparently saw the nose bleed too and they quickly cut to commercial. I felt humiliated for Beth. I didn't expect her to find love on this stupid show, but she hadn't been on a single date since Jonathon was born, and she really needed this for her self-esteem and to get her back in the game.

Dylan

All I wanted to do when I got home from work was sit in my old, worn beach chair, smoke a bowl, and watch the sun fall out of the sky and disappear behind the ocean's horizon.

A Venice Beach sunset is one of nature's most perfect pieces of art. The setting sun casts pinkish-red flames that slash through the dull purple hue lying atop the horizon like an electric blanket. I watch nightly and wonder how anyone could be content without having the beauty of a Venice sunset in their lives.

Tonight was going to be extra-special because T.J. was out, and I was expecting company. As I pulled into my driveway, the tension from working with a bunch of morons began to ease. But after I opened the door, everything knotted back up.

"T.J.! What are you doing here? I thought you had a date with what's-her-name."

"What's-her-name canceled." This was the third time in a row an Internet date cancelled on T.J.. "So, I'm spending some quality time with the remote control. Reality TV followed by late night Cinemax programming. I might get lucky."

T.J. spent so much time on the couch his hairy ass was starting to grow roots into the cushions.

"That sucks," I said. T.J. was watching another mindless reality dating show. "Why do you watch that garbage?"

"It's not garbage. It's about love. You may not believe in the concept, but I do," T.J. replied.

"That crap isn't about love. It's all contrived lies that dumbs down viewers so advertisers can sell them more shit they don't need."

"Whatever."

At one point in my life, I think I enjoyed mainstream television. It was sometime after I first read Dickens' *A Tale of Two Cities* that I fell in love with literature and became bored with TV.

"Let me ask you something, T.J. You go to work day after day doing crappy jobs to make cash to improve your quality of life, correct?"

"Correct," T.J. replied.

"Then why don't you go out tonight? Go spend some of your hard-earned money on something that will actually improve your quality of life," I said. I was desperate to get him out of the house.

"What the hell do you think I bought this television with last month?"

"Watching television isn't exploring."

"Have you ever watched the Discovery Channel? Or the news?"

"You should be out there making your own discoveries instead of watching the Discovery Channel. Besides, you aren't watching the Discovery Channel. You're watching a game show. And don't give me that shit about the news. The news is nothing but a voyeuristic exploitation of other people's drama."

"Listen, Mr. Fancy pants with the fancy vocabulary, and listen good. You are a hypocrite. You tell me I'm wasting time watching television when you spend most of your free time smoking pot and listening to old records?"

"Music is art, and art is never a waste of time."

"And pot?"

"Pot helps me appreciate art."

"That's a crock. You're a pothead."

"At least I'm not so lonely and bored I need to live vicariously through losers on dating shows."

"Thanks. I thought I was already depressed enough, but I guess I wasn't. Thank you for throwing salt in my wounds," T.J. said.

"That wasn't salt in your wounds."

"Huh?"

"That wasn't salt in your wounds," I repeated.

"That was salt in my wounds," T.J. said as he turned up the

volume on the television.

I grabbed the remote out of his hands and hit the mute. "No, it wasn't. The expression *salt in the wound* comes from old medicine when salt was used to cauterize cuts so they would stop bleeding and could heal. My comment did nothing to heal your wounds. As you said, it depressed you even more. I'd consider it more 'insult to injury' than 'salt in the wound.' You'd learn things like this if you'd pick up a book once in a while."

"Like you? Should I be more like you, Dylan. You seem like a really happy guy. So what should I read? Fiction? Or one of those religious texts you're always disappearing into. Which one should I read? The Koran? The Bible? The Torah? The Pali Canon? A book on demonology? Have you found a god yet?"

"I found God a long time ago," I said.

"So what religion are you?"

"I have no name for what I believe. I believe all religions have merits and problems. I believe God lives in each of us. We're God. If we acted accordingly, maybe we'd stand a chance of improving this fucked up world."

"So you read the books from all religions so you can mix and match and form your own?" T.J. asked.

"Sort of. But mostly I just read them because they're great literature."

"You're weird."

"Yeah, I am weird. I'm a seeker. Reading helps me find answers to the questions."

"What questions? I'm not here to find a deeper meaning to life. People like you believe knowledge is power. It's not. The more you know, the more you have to worry about. I'm just trying to enjoy my life," T.J. said. He stood from the couch, snatched the remote back from me, and turned on the sound as if he had made his final point and the conversation was over.

T.J. being home was going to spoil my plans with Skye. I was either going to talk him out of the house or ruin his night as well. A fight had been building up between us for quite a while, and this seemed as good a time as any for us to let recriminations fly. So, rather than let him have the final word, I spoke over the annoying dating show. "Well, T.J., obviously your philosophy isn't working because you're every bit as miserable as I am."

"Maybe, but at least I can smile at the simple things. I don't need to complicate everything. I can be entertained by things like reality television without worrying if I'm wasting my life."

"I'm just saying it wouldn't kill you to get off the couch once in a while," I said.

"And do what? What makes your life so much better than mine? You're always talking about books and art. You claim to be a writer, but you never write. You work a stupid job you hate, just like I do, and then you come home and get stoned."

"You're a dick sometimes," I said. But T.J. was right. I smoked too much pot, and I hadn't written anything in forever. Art needs inspiration to be birthed. It needs tragedy, death, angst, or the greatest inspiration, love. I had no inspiration; my life had become bland and gray.

I really had no comeback for T.J. So, I retreated to my room, grabbed a book from the towering pile outside my room, sat on my bed, and lit up a joint. My room was the size of a walk-in closet, which choked out any creativity that may have stirred inside me were I inspired at any given time. So, typically, I'd just lie on the covers and read until I fell asleep. There isn't a much more pathetic existence than mine; a twenty-eight-year-old talentless hack doomed to read other people's genius for the rest of his life.

The only time I ever do truly create is in my sleep. There, I become an artist, dreaming in beautiful poetic words. Literally. Sometimes, I dream of myself lying on the beach, and a wave of words washes over me. Sometimes, fascinating stories come to me in my sleep. Sometimes, I realize I'm dreaming, and I plan to write the ideas down when I wake, but I never do.

I'd been withdrawing from society more and more every day, becoming the guy who lived in a world created by others, a recluse who disappeared into books, lived in them, but stopped actually living. Skye was the first glimmer of hope that I'd break out of that. But T.J. was screwing that up for me. I put down my book, hit my joint again, and returned to the common area.

"Please change the channel, T.J. This stuff is for teenage girls."

"Yeah, and so is your eye-liner."

I took a flying leap and dropped an elbow squarely into T.J.'s back, WWF style. T.J. knuckled me in my ribs, and it was on. I got winded quickly and needed to pin him before my lungs ruptured. I got on top of T.J. and put all my weight on his chest. I made the scrawny, pot-bellied bastard cry uncle then I got off him.

"I thought you were trying to fuck me," T.J. said, laughing.

"Nah, you're too ugly," I said and retreated to my room.

T.J.

"If you were a bird and you could fly anywhere in the world for one day, where would you fly?" Bachelorette Beth asked bachelor number two.

"I'd fly to the top of Mount Everest and sing a beautiful song for you. Then I'd take a flower from the top and bring it to you."

"I don't think there're flowers on top of Mount Everest; it's too high," bachelorette Beth said.

The audience laughed at the contestant, and the host took the program to commercial. I changed the channel to ESPN.

I'm a clumsy, clumsy man, but with a remote control, I'm a world class athlete. I'm as graceful with a remote control as Fred Astaire is with Gene Kelly in his arms. I have the innate ability to anticipate the exact moment when I should change channels to catch my programs returning from commercial. My show goes to commercial and I click to ESPN, then after exactly 122 seconds, and without the use of a clock, I hit the clicker again and returned to the dating show just at the exact moment the host welcomed back the TV audience.

This talent is my one gift.

Dylan was right about me: my life was pathetic.

A knock at our door interrupted my program. I wasn't expecting company, and Dylan doesn't like people, so I figured it was a steak knife salesman or something. Last week, a sexy saleswoman hawking magazines came to our place and I ended up buying subscriptions to *Sports Illustrated*, *The Sporting News*, and *People*. I asked for her number, and she gave it to me. But two days later, when I called, it was out-of-service.

I considered the exciting possibility that maybe the saleswoman had returned to see me, and I peeled myself out of my warm groove in the couch.

"Who is it?" I asked.

"It's me," replied a familiar female voice.

I anxiously opened the door.

Skye

"Skye? What are you doing here?" T.J. asked.

This is weird.

It was my third random encounter with T.J. in this life. First, the airport, then New Years Eve, and now this. Maybe the universe was trying to give me a clue.

"Hi, T.J.? Wow, um is this 20 Ocean Front Walk?"

"Yeah. How'd you know where I lived?"

"I didn't."

"Are you selling something?"

"What? No... Does a guy named Dylan live here?"

T.J.'s confused smile disappeared. The light in his eyes went dark. "You're here to see Dylan?. Dylan, my roommate Dylan? Dylan, as in the guy I live with, Dylan?"

"Umm, I didn't know he was your roommate, but yeah. We met a couple weeks ago."

His pale face began turning peeked. I thought he might vomit.

"This is pretty awkward, huh?"

"This is the Super Bowl of awkward," T.J. said.

"Yeah... well, is he here?" I asked.

"Who?"

"Dylan."

"No."

"May I come in and wait for him?"

"The thing is—whatever. Yeah, come in. Make yourself at home," T.J. said, but he didn't move an inch. I squeezed past him and into the apartment. I've been in some pretty decapitated bachelor pads in my day, but this one took the cake. Their rugs were an undeterminable shade of grayish-brown, and once inside, you couldn't see the outside world through their dirt covered windows. I walked to the couch and sat. I felt something crunch beneath me and stood, reflexively. I brushed off my butt, moved to the love seat, and plopped down, which caused cloud of dust to blow out from the cushion. The whole place smelled. It reminded me of a pair of old sneakers I wore, without socks, throughout an entire Oakland summer. I expected Dylan's place might be messy, but I wasn't expecting this biohazard.

T.J. was still standing in the doorway, still staring outside. "You want something to drink?" T.J. asked, flatly.

"No thanks," I said. "I'm not thirsty." There was no way I'd drink out of a glass in their house. There were soiled dishes covered with flies spilling out of the sink. It was as bad as any dope fiend's apartment I'd ever been in. "T.J., are you okay?" I asked.

Then, without answering, T.J. walked outside and screamed. "Argghh!" A minute later, he came back in. "Dylan! There's someone here to see YOU!"

"I thought you said he wasn't here."

"Yep. That's what I said."

Dylan emerged from a small, hidden room behind a pile of books.

"Hi, Skye," he said. "I guess you've met my roommate, T.J.?"

T.J. ran outside again, leaving profanities in his wake.

May 2003
Kelly

Beth chose me on *Single Parents...* Well, actually, she chose another guy, but after her nosebleed incident, he didn't seem interested. I was, and so after the show, I asked her out. She said yes. So, I guess I chose her. Beth wasn't the best looking girl in the world, but I'm not exactly Brad Pitt. She was nice, and after being married to Reece, nice was a quality that I cherished.

Tonight we were going out again, date number five. There hadn't been any sex in our four previous dates, and I'm not sure why, but there hadn't even been a kiss. We seemed to have chemistry, but something was keeping me from pulling the trigger. I hadn't had sex in nearly a year, and I was as nervous about it as I was impatient for it.

I rang the doorbell outside Beth's. I was early, but I was meeting the parents, so I wanted to make a good impression. It's not typical to meet the parents before you kiss the girl, but this relationship, which started on a television game show, was anything but typical, so this was par for course.

Nobody answered the door. A loud Barbara Streisand tune was spilling out from the house, and I worried. Music is important to me, and though I hate to admit it, I judge people by the music they listen to. Beth listened to cool music, but apparently her parents didn't. I banged louder on the door, and finally it opened. Two men, one effeminate looking, greeted me. "You must be Kelly. You're early. I'm David, and this is Gerry, We're Beth's dads. Welcome."

"Umm, yeah. Umm, hi. Dads? Beth didn't tell me. I mean, both her parents were gays—I mean guys," I said, completely embarrassed.

"Yes, we are gays, and yes, we are guys. I'd think Beth would've told you that," David said, laughing.

"Yeah, you'd think," I replied.

"I hope it's not uncomfortable for you," Gerry said.

"No, not at all. I didn't mean to be rude. I'm sorry."

"No apology necessary. Please come in," he said.

I entered. The house smelled of roasting meat. I was hungry. I looked around for Beth; there was no sign of her. I was agitated she hadn't informed me of this situation. How do you invite a guy over to meet the parents without informing him that the parents are both dudes? I believe it's somewhat relevant. I could've saved the twenty dollars I wasted on flowers for her mom.

My phone rang. Beth was calling. I answered. "Kelly, before you come over here, I need to tell you something."

A cute woman stepped out of the other room and shouted upstairs to Beth, "Beth, Kelly's here!"

"Ohmagod, he's early!" Beth shouted back. I heard her voice from upstairs and through the phone. I'll be down in a minute or two, Kelly!"

"Okay. Take your time. I'm just hanging out with your DADS!"

"Can I get you something to drink?" asked Gerry, the more feminine dad.

"Whiskey?" I asked.

He went to the kitchen and came back with a beer, "Sorry, we don't have any liquor."

"Hi, Kelly. I'm Amber, Beth's roommate." Amber was black. For some reason, I pictured her being white when Beth spoke about her. I'm not sure what that means about me.

Does it mean anything? Why do we ever even consider these things?

"Hi, Amber," I said, shaking her hand.

"You look exactly like you did on the show."

"I'm so embarrassed about that show."

242

"Well, you met Beth, and she's the best woman I've ever known, so don't be too embarrassed."

"She's the best girl we know, too," said Gerry.

"I'm coming down," Beth yelled from the top of the stairs. She wore a long, light-green gown that pulled multiple shades of green off the surrounding walls and made her green eyes twinkle. The plummeting neckline showed a lot of cleavage and clung to her curvy body all the way down to her knees where it blossomed into an upside-down flower. With every step, her dress swept from side to side in cadence with the *click, click, click* of her high heels.

Downstairs, Beth kissed her dads and then hugged me. Her ample cleavage pressed into my chest and irritated my sex drive like an unreachable itch.

"You look amazing," I said, and I meant it.

"Thank you." Beth took the flowers from my hand, thus relieving me of the impossible task of deciding which dad to give them to. "Thank you for the flowers. They're beautiful."

For the record, I was leaning toward giving them to the more effeminate Gerry.

"Let's eat," Gerry suggested. "I made lamb chops and asparagus topped with caramel-coated almond slivers."

We took our seats around the mahogany table that was elaborately decorated with perfumed candles in crystal bowls, expensive-looking white chinaware with blue floral patterns, fine silver utensils, and a bouquet of orchids as the centerpiece. Above the table hung a large chandelier that caught and reflected the flickering light the candles emitted.

I sat between Amber and Beth's son, Jonathon, about whom I had very difficult and mixed feelings. By the workings of our mysterious Universe, I had somehow managed to hook up with the only woman, in a town of four million women, who bore a child from King Jackson Rockenberger, the man who turned my wife into an adulteress. The odds my next girlfriend would have a child from a man whose penis had been in my wife's mouth had to be as unlikely as us putting a man on Mars before the end of the decade.

I found out Beth had a child on our first date. During dinner conversation on date two, I confessed to her about catching my wife cheating on me. After, she confessed to me about her nose bleeding history and the Mike Coppermen incident. During date number three, we made the discovery that Jonathon's biological father was the same guy that Reece tried to turn into a human pacifier. This was a hard pill to swallow. I reacted inappropriately and didn't see Beth again for two weeks. Time passed, and I became lonely; so, I picked up the phone and called. Surprisingly, she had missed me also. Date four was probably the best non-sexual date of my life. We saw a great concert and then spent the night at a cool Hollywood coffee shop talking about our kids. Though I wanted to hate the bastard son of my ex's adulterer, the way Beth spoke about her son dampened my ugly dissonance. Her love for her Jonathon reminded me of my love for Teddy. I met Jonathon, when I dropped Beth off after date four. Jonathon's complexion was fair. Beth's pasty whiteness had drowned out most of Jackson's light brown. That made it marginally easier to keep Jackson out of my mind when I was around Jonathon.

Staring at Jonathon and contemplating all this, I felt someone's foot tickle my leg under the dinner table.

Please, God, I hope that's Beth.

Gerry smiled at me. *Was it him? Is he flirting?*

I hope he thinks I'm at least a little bit attractive.

Why does my brain do that?

After dinner, we had chocolate cake and coffee. After Beth's second cup, she asked Amber to watch Jonathon and suggested she and I head out for a drink. I was ready for the alone time. Our non-kiss was the elephant in the room, and we needed to kiss tonight or we'd both likely explode.

We had a nice time at a small Hollywood bar, off Vine. A band called Diary Thieves played a couple good sets, and Beth and I shared good conversation.

But still no kiss. I tried once. I closed my eyes and leaned in. Beth apparently hadn't noticed. She was trying to scratch an itch on her back. My move and her scratching happened with perfect synchronicity—I kissed her armpit. I was horrified. It was humiliating. Beth made a cute joke about it to let me off the hook, but still, no kiss.

Later back at Beth's apartment, sitting on her bed, sharing a drink, the mood was set for the big kiss. I was about to move in as Beth started talking. She apologized for not telling me about her parents. "After we'd discovered my son's father was your wife's friend, I didn't have the guts to tell you about my dads. I didn't want to give you one more reason to stop seeing me," she said. She apparently felt she needed to clear the air. Maybe she thought her lack of disclosure was what was holding up the big kiss. It wasn't; it was my awkwardness. After Beth's apology, she relaxed. She looked up at me with sinful green eyes, almost begging me to move in closer.

I slid a little closer, our thighs now touching as we sat there on the bed. "Don't worry about it. I like your dads," I said.

"That's sweet," Beth smiled. Her eyes flittered and her mouth was softening.

"And, Beth, there's something I want to tell you," I said. I was leaning in closer so I could make my move to kiss her. Then, I realized that what I was going to tell her would completely ruin the mood. Mood killing is something that I'm a borderline Olympian at doing. This time, I caught myself and stopped.

"What is it?" she asked.

"Um, never mind," I said, resting my hand on her leg. "I shouldn't have mentioned it."

She took my hand off her leg. "Now you're killing me with curiosity. I have to know."

Realizing I'd already ruined the mood, I gave in. "Fine. Well, what I wanted to say is we have more in common than you think. You're not the only one who was raised without a mother. I rarely talk about it, and it's probably because I still feel somewhat responsible for it... My mother died giving birth to me."

"Oh my God. I'm so sorry. I understand how you feel. Ya know, sometimes I think it's my fault that my mother gave me up for adoption. And, Kelly, there's probably something else I should tell you."

"Wow, we're breaking the world record for secret sharing. What is it? Wait, let me guess," I said, holding a finger to her mouth in silence. I was desperate to lighten the mood and get us closer to that kiss. "You've decided to become a nun."

"No, but close. I haven't had sex since I slept with Jackson years ago. I've been holding out until I knew I could trust my next partner."

I looked in Beth's eyes, and I knew she meant it. Beth wasn't going to be a casual sex kind of girl. This was a dilemma because, despite the fact I hardly ever got laid, I was aspiring to become a casual sex kind of guy. But the reality was that I was a no-sex kind of guy.

As I contemplated this juxtaposition, Beth decided to take charge. She threw me back on the bed, pinned my arms and legs down and said, "If I get a nosebleed while we're kissing, it just means that I really like you. So, please don't call me Period Face."

"As long as you never call me chicken legs."

She looked at me awkwardly.

"That's what the kids called me in junior high."

"Oh."

"Can we kiss now?" I asked.

Beth smiled, tightened her grip on my wrists, and kissed me. It was a decently good kiss, but during it I was mostly thinking, "thank God we've gotten that out of the way. Then, she came back in for the second kiss. It was wonderful.

Ten minutes later, we were naked, making sweaty, great love. Shy, reserved, quiet little Beth, was an absolute tiger in the bedroom. I couldn't believe it.

We slept, woke hours later, and did it again. It was nice. I was reeling in the pleasure of it as Beth leaned in.

"I've been waiting a long time for you," she said.

And I knew I'd just done something big, something I couldn't undo.

Ron

Once I learned that Maria Orlando was the daughter of a big time mafia boss, my internal criminal alarm went bonkers. I decided to investigate and find out if there was any way for me to exploit the situation. Digging into her life would be risky, and I wasn't living that kind of life anymore; however, life has a mysterious way of unfolding and bringing us all back to our roots, and I couldn't let an opportunity like this pass me by without at least looking into it.

I spent the next couple months researching the Orlando crime family, their crime of choice, and how I could seamlessly appear into Orlando's life. I went to his restaurant and talked to the maître d'. I told him I wanted to see the "big boss." He told me the owner wasn't in. I told him I had, "a big opportunity" that Orlando would be interested in, and I asked him to have Orlando contact me.

I didn't hear anything for a month. Then yesterday, out of nowhere, I got a call from one of Orlando's men. I'm sure Orlando didn't wait a month to call me by accident. He must've been looking into my background, and testing my patience. I mean, from what I know about the mob, it's pretty much like any criminal pyramid scheme. If they stood to make money, they'd entertain a proposal.

Today, sitting in my beat-up '71 Pinto I'd ironically purchased at a police auction, I tried to summon the courage to enter Orlando's restaurant.

What the hell am I doing? Maybe Dr. Salazar was right. Maybe I am totally nuts.

By the time I went in, I was completely off my game. I'd tried to get into a gangster mentality, but I felt more like Billy Crystal in *Analyze This* than Brando in *The Godfather.*

"Hello," the leggy hostess said. Her thick perfume made my eyes tear.

"I'm here for Mr. Zantini," I said. Zantini was Orlando's man.

The hostess led me through the kitchen, holding me by the hand, which was odd and nice all at the same time. Her body was built for the cover of Vogue or another chick magazine that guys use in prison as temporary girlfriends.

We went through a back door in the kitchen, up a flight of stairs, and to Mr. Joseph Zantini's door. The hostess knocked.

"Mr. Zantini, Mr. Ron Griffin is here to see you." The hostess left. I'd have felt safer had she stayed. Mr. Zantini was Orlando's number one soldier and a very intimidating man.

"Come in, Mr. Griffin."

"Thank you, Mr. Zantini."

"Shut the door," he said. I did.

"Lock it." I did.

Before I could turn around, two obese Italian men with the strength and stench of a couple of Redondo Beach sea lions put my face into the wall and patted me down. These guys were so stereotypical that my mind immediately wandered into mob movieland. I started wondering what their mob names were. *Baby-Face Bernie? Frankie the Fist?* Everything I knew about the mob I'd learned from either prison, or the movies, *The Godfather, Goodfellas, Casino.* And from what I knew, everyone had a nickname.

"He's not holding," one goon said. *Johnny Nine Toes?*

"You a cop?" Mr. Zantini asked as he rolled his wedding band in circles around his hairy knuckle.

"No, sir."

"Wearing a wire?"

"No."

Take off your shirt."

"What? Why?"

"I'll ask the questions!" Zantini slammed his meaty fist into the table. Vibrations traveled through the desk, to the floor, and up my legs, which were quivering so fast that they looked like reflections of knees in a pool of rippling water. I was scared, and Zantini knew it. I took off my shirt.

"Oh man, gross," said one of the goons. "Put it back on."

Like you're Mr. Olympia, I would've said if I was one of those cool and brave kick-ass characters in a mob movie. But I wasn't, and I didn't. One of the goons slapped me on the back. *Vinnie the Hammer?*

"No wire. Good for you." Zantini pulled a revolver from his desk drawer and sat it on the table. And even though it was one hundred degrees in the room and I was marinating in my own sweat, I broke into chills and struggled to keep my teeth from rattling.

A fine crook you are, Ron.

"Mr. Orlando will be in to see you in a minute," Zantini said. "Sit down and wait."

I did.

Zantini placed a call. I couldn't interpret the code he spoke in. "Go to the butcher. Get the salami. He'll know. Make the exchange and take it to the zoo. Call me."

He's ordering somebody's whacking.

Or dinner plans with his mistress.

Or he's placing a bet.

I flipped through all the scenarios in my mobster-movie Rolodex.

Then, the man appeared. Mr. Orlando. He was a pretty rotund guy. The diamond studded cross he wore around his neck was nearly as big as the original crucifix.

"Mr. Griffin, thank you for coming."

"Thank you for having me, sir." The words were sticking in my throat because I knew Orlando wouldn't hesitate to kill me if he was suspicious of my intentions.

"Are you okay?" he asked.

"Yes, sir. Never better."

"Bomber, Stink, you monkeys can beat it," Orlando said to his soldiers.

Bomber and Stink. Too obvious. Bomber and Stink headed

downstairs for their next feeding.

"So, tell me about your little proposition, Mr. Griffin?"

I calmed myself enough to tell Orlando my plan—or at least the version of the plan I wanted him to know about. I told him everything about the cameras at Uptown Productions' studios, my idea for camping out in the storage room at the end of the work day after I put the last of the equipment away. I told him about the simple alarm system and how easily I could disarm it, the trucks that came in nightly to deliver props, and the backdoor to the props room the delivery guys use. I told him I could get him the necessary papers for him to get a truck on campus.

"It'd be an easy score," I said.

"If it's so easy, why hasn't it been done before?"

"Probably because nobody's thought of it or had the connections to make it happen. I had the idea my first day on set, but I didn't have the means to make it happen. That's why I've come to you."

"So you think you're a smart guy?"

"No. I'm just a small-time ex-con in the right place at the right time. Look, the cameras are worth about a hundred grand each. We could get 20 to 25 of them, and you could sell them overseas for twenty-five to fifty thousand, each. We'd make a killing. We need each other. I need your trucks to do the job, and your international business connections to make the sales. You need me to get you inside."

Orlando listened, and when I finished, without saying a word, he left. Another goon entered and watched me. This goon had an unnerving emptiness in his eyes. We stood there, ten feet apart from each other, for about twenty silent minutes. The entire time I felt my life was in danger. I was about to leave when Mr. Zantini entered the room; Orlando was nowhere to be seen. I didn't know if they were doing good cop bad cop, or what.

"What happens when the authorities connect you to the crime?" he asked.

I was nervous and dizzy from the wait, and it took a second to regain my composure. "They won't. The surveillance tapes will show me leaving the building at the end of the day. I'll get back inside through a backdoor I'll have left unlocked. Nobody would ever think to check that door, and this studio has never had a burglary, so it's not even on their radar. Once I'm inside, I'll disguise my appearance so the indoor surveillance camera won't be able to identify me. As long as the night guard doesn't see me in the two seconds it'll take to cross the stage and get into the storage room, I'll be fine."

"What happens if someone does check the lock or if the security guard does see you?"

"He won't see me. I know the guy, and I know he sleeps through most of his shift. And nobody's gonna check the lock. It's just not big a deal."

"If they do?" he asked as she scratched his belly.

"Abort mission I guess. But they won't. Nobody ever checks. The grips are the last to leave. Or the janitors. Either way, you're talking about minimum wage workers who don't give a shit."

"You didn't answer my first question. What happens when they connect you to the crime?" he asked. He wasn't going to let me slide on this.

"In the unlikely event that they pin it on me, I'll confess that I'm working for a crime boss I was in prison with. His name is Anthony Banilli and he's out now. They'll buy it because it will make perfect sense."

He took a long pause, pulled a cigar out of his pocket, casually cut the end, put it in his mouth, and then one of his goons lit it without Zantini having to ask. He took a few puffs, stuffed it out, then spoke, "So we're talking about close to a million dollars. A seventy-thirty split," Zantini said.

"Fifty-fifty. I appreciate your help, and I'm willing to give you fifty percent," I said, feeling gracious.

"I meant seventy percent for us."

"Seventy-thirty sounds fair to me," I replied.

"We'll consider it, but there are going to be conditions."

"Conditions?"

"One, Orlando's daughter hears nothing of this. She learns about it, *fughetaboutit.* Two, we never speak to you again after the job is done. We'll wire your money into a Swiss bank account and leave you the account information in a locker at the bus station on Alameda. The key to the locker will come to you by mail. Three, if any of this ever comes back on us, then I'll kill you and everyone you know," he said the last part as casually as someone might say, *I'd like fries with that.* "We'll make all the arrangements Wednesday night in my associate's luxury suite at the Dodger game."

I was scared out of my mind. Not only was I risking death or imprisonment, but there was also the possibility of doing the job and them screwing me out of my take. I mean, really, what could I do about it?

Still, despite all this, if they agreed to do it, it was on. I saw no other way to accomplish what I needed to accomplish. I saw no other way to help Amber.

Dylan

My reclusive behavior was getting worse and worse. Thankfully, I had Skye. My relationship with her was my only attachment, outside work, to anything real.

"This stuff is pretty alkaline," Skye said. Then she added a dash of lemon to the heroin concoction before cooking up.

It was the third time I'd done heroin with Skye. I loved it, and that wasn't a good thing. Skye put the needle to the spoon, pulled the plunger, took my arm, and delivered the shot of liquid heaven straight into a pulsating red vein in my arm.

The heroin slowed down life and let me hover in half-time. It whittled away at the world and all its problems until there was nothing left but Skye and me.

Skye self-administered her shot. I popped a Viagra, and thirty minutes later my cock was steel. My sex drive is pretty average. But Skye does something to me, something chemically, that turns me into a fuck machine. I kissed Skye and put my hand between her legs; she was thick with wetness.

We started making love. It felt incredibly good, almost too good. I had to think of dead rats, rotting bleu cheese, maggots, wet garbage, and public restrooms to delay the inevitable just long enough for Skye to be able to reach ecstasy at the same time as me. We shared a simultaneous, cataclysmic orgasm. It started in our loins, radiated through our torsos, up and down our legs and arms and to our brains and fingers and toes, and then hot lightning shot out of the tips of our hair.

I lay back and relaxed, fully exhausted and levitating on an airy blanket of wet heat. In the six weeks I'd known Skye, I'd developed feelings that were stronger than they'd been for Allison and Melinda and every other girlfriend I'd ever had combined and multiplied by ten. I opened up my heart, secrets, and feelings to Skye in ways I never dreamed I would with anyone. Loving Allison scarred me for life. Loving Melinda led to an aborted baby I'd never know. If this relationship with Skye went sour, it would be the death of me.

Skye

When I was a kid, I heard my mom's sister talking with my mom about her cheating husband. My aunt said, "Never trust a man's stated intentions. Because women, in the eyes of men, are either virgins or whores. And ultimately, they will always treat us this way."

I never forgot the advice. When my father sold my young body for drugs, he proved merit in my aunt's beliefs. I'll never forgive my father, and because of him I've never had a healthy relationship with a man.

Dylan was the first man I'd ever slept with who made me feel loved instead of used. My orgasms with Dylan were unlike anything I'd ever experienced. They were the first and only real pleasure I have ever known from intercourse. He gave me orgasms that would start soft and slow, and then, as the insides of my eyelids turned from black to screaming red, my heartbeat would fall from my chest to between my legs where it thumped almost audibly, bordering between pleasure and pain. These orgasms were smooth blue velvet soaked in alcohol and lit on fire. I'd never fall right asleep after coming, but instead, I'd drift off slowly and comfortably. Six hours later, I'd wake; my orgasm would be lingering inside me, reminding me of how incredible it was. Hoping to recapture its intensity, I'd roll to my side, prepare a shot, and slam it down the first vein I could find. Then I'd lay back and let it creep through me like a gentle thunderstorm.

Dylan and I were in the throws of passion, making intensely passionate love. We came together in a barrage of pyrotechnics, and then, exhausted, Dylan rolled off of me. I looked in his eyes. I was already in love with Dylan, and I knew it. The love was so grand I couldn't contain it and there was no use in fighting it.

I didn't want to tell Dylan how I felt about him, but the love was too much for me to keep it secret. I had to share it, let a little out, less my heart would explode. The love I felt for Dylan was dangerous. Dylan was a vine rooted in my heart and growing throughout my body. I loved him, but like any vine, I feared he may spread through my body, choking out everything else. I had to remain an individual; I couldn't give myself entirely to a man again like I did with my father. He destroyed me.

Dylan was sleeping. I closed my eyes and ran my fingers over Dylan's forehead. I felt his thin eyebrows and let my fingers trace the slope of his nose to the sharpness of its point, the circles of both nostrils, and the meeting point of his thin lips. I ran my finger between his lips then downward to his chiseled, prickly chin. I was memorizing his face with my fingers so I could keep it with me after he left me.

Dylan woke. We made love again.

Lying there, ten minutes after finishing, I was still quivering. My entire body was smiling. I hadn't felt this happy since the first time I played a Fender Strat guitar. I wanted to lay in our shared silence with my mouth open and lap up the moment in big meaty lumps of time.

"That was un-fucking-believable!" Dylan announced.

"Shhh, baby."

"I mean, the only thing that could possibly be better than that sex is death," Dylan said.

His analogy disturbed me. Dylan didn't know everything about my past, all the friends I've lost from drugs, the baby who died inside me. He may not have meant it like that, but I still didn't like it.

"What's that crap supposed to mean?" I asked.

"What it means is I've never experienced anything more fulfilling than sex with you, and I'm pretty sure nothing will top it in this life. I have no idea what happens after death, but that unknown is the only thing that could possibly be as amazing."

It was the most beautiful thing anyone had ever said to me.

"Skye, I need to ask, do you think it's us? Or do you think it's the drugs?"

"Whatever it is, I'm in love with *it*," I said. It was my first hint at the fact that I loved him. I was hoping he'd reciprocate. He didn't.

Dylan put his arm around me; his chest was still rising and falling faster than normal. "I want to know it's us and not the drugs. I want to know this intensity won't come and go with the buzz," Dylan said, looking at my face but not my eyes.

I knew Dylan had something more he wanted to say. I knew I wasn't going to like it. "What are you trying to ask me, Dylan?"

"I've smoked pot all my life. I love pot. But I've never used anything harder than weed until I met you. I'm not blaming you. I mean, I practically made you give me my first taste of heroin, and honestly, I'm glad I did it. It's opened doors of thought within me. The dope, along with you, has inspired me to write again. I haven't done that in forever. However, I'm concerned. I love what we have, and I want to know we can maintain this intensity without the drugs. Otherwise, it can't be sustained. We can't do this forever—we'll become addicted."

Dylan was lying to himself. He was trying to convince himself heroin was some casual habit with me. I'd never told him I wasn't an addict, and he'd been with me enough to know, but he was in a bit of denial about it. People believe what they want to believe. Dylan wanted this just to be a phase for me. I wanted to be able to give him what he wanted.

But I knew I couldn't.

"Dylan, what you're saying is sweet, but—"

"Besides all that, I'm worried about you. You've been high—"

"Stop, Dylan. I don't need a lecture."

"I'm the last person in this world to give a lecture. I just want us to stop using. At the rate we've been using, I'm worried I'll become a junkie. Maybe you have it under control, but I this is new to me, and I don't know if I can keep it under control."

"Dylan, I care for you, and that has nothing to do with drugs. I enjoy getting high with you, but if you need me to give it up, with you, for you, then I will. I'll do it because I love you."

I knew I was lying as I was saying it. "

Dylan

"Thank you, Skye."

"And?" Skye asked.

"And, I know we can make this work."

"Dylan, I just told you I love you."

"Skye, I feel strongly for you, and I want to say it back to you, but when I say those words to you I want to be positive it's going to be forever. That's why I want us to stop using." I couldn't tell Skye I loved her until I knew I could trust her never to do to me what Allison and Melinda had. I couldn't survive that again.

"My feelings are real," Skye said.

"How can you be sure? Whenever we're together, we're high. I want you to be sober when you tell me you love me. Do you understand?"

Skye stood, grabbed her pants, and began dressing. "Yeah, I understand. We'll get sober and then figure out how we really feel about each other."

"Skye, come on."

Skye got up, pulled her shirt over her head, stuck her underwear in her pocket, and made for the door.

"Where are you going?"

"I'm going to get sober, just like you said. Call me in a few days. We can go to dinner and a movie like normal people. We'll talk stupid bullshit talk just like all the other stupid fucking people out there. Then maybe afterward we can go home and fuck, and then you can decide whether or not you love me!" Skye slammed the bedroom door and then the front door. I watched through the window.

I walked to the window and opened it. "Skye!"

She ignored me.

"Skye! You know I'm right about this!"

She walked right up to the open window and said, "Yeah, Dylan, you win. I know you're right. We need to get sober and discover the truth before we get more involved."

My nosey neighbor from two doors down was standing on Ocean Front Walk behind Skye and was staring at my nakedness. I made eye contact with her then Skye noticed her. She turned to face the woman.

"Haven't you ever seen a penis before? Get out of here!" Skye yelled, then she turned back to face me. "Dylan, you're the only man I've said I love you besides my father. He did horrible things to me, and it really fucked me up. But you know what? This hurts worse!"

Skye stared at me, waiting for a response. I'm certain she said what she did for some kind of shock value. Women sometimes do that—they guilt a man into doing what they want. I didn't know what to do with the information she'd just given me—what had her Dad done to her?

I said nothing, and Skye walked away, in tears. I should have chased her, but I didn't. Instead, I put on a pair of shorts and walked down to the end of the beach where sand meets water and sat to watch the setting sun. Above me, the sky was freckled with hundreds of tiny blue-stained clouds with slashing pink streaks. Beneath me, the wet sand was cool and hard-packed. The water rushed to my toes and retreated back again, over and over, endless like my thoughts. I gazed out to the definitive point where the blue water's edge meets the sky. The horizon was disheartening, not the colors, but the finality of it.

Here I am at the edge of the world. On the other side of the ocean is nothing but more people with problems like mine. They're looking back across the ocean toward me in search of answers. There are no answers out there, just a lot of salt.

A weird feeling of melancholy was becoming me. I went back inside, took off my shorts, and smoked a bowl. T.J. came home; he was wearing the bottom half of his full-body cell phone costume. The weirdness of it was a little too much to deal with while still under the lingering spell of heroin, now tinged with marijuana and heartache.

"Jesus, Dylan! Could you put on some clothes please?"

"Jesus, T.J.! Could you get some self-respect please? Why are you still working a job that turns you into a walking corporate advertisement?"

"Because I need the money. I'm not having another classic Dylan style argument with you while you're naked. Go put on some clothes!"

I got up with the intent of putting on a pair of shorts. Halfway to my room, a piercing noise ripped through me. It felt like a thousand crooked, rusty heroin needles were pushed into my skull and then twisted in circles. I marched over to the stereo, hit eject, pulled out the disk, and snapped it in half.

"Dude, what the hell is wrong with you? I just bought that today!" T.J. cried.

"It's shit."

"Christina Aguilera was classically trained," T.J. said. "You're a music snob," he said under his breath. "You owe me fourteen dollars."

I walked into my room, grabbed a twenty, and returned. "Here. Keep the change. Best twenty bucks I've ever spent."

T.J. put it in his pocket. "What makes you the authority on music?" he asked. "You can't even play your guitar. And please put on some clothes!"

"I may not be musically gifted, but I can hear, and fake pop bullshit makes my sense of hearing feel like a curse."

"Please, dude, you're grossing me out—put on some clothes. And close the blinds. Everyone on Ocean Front Walk probably thinks we're gay lovers."

"Fuck them."

"Dude, c'mon," T.J. begged.

I went in my room, shut the door, and shot up the last of the heroin. A wonderful calm came over me. The first time I ever smoked pot I knew I'd never stop. Despite what I'd told Skye, trying heroin even once was a mistake. There was no reason to ever think I'd be able to be casual with it. I was so drawn to Skye I practically begged her to share with me. I did it partly because I thought it would make her feel more strongly about me, but mostly because I was curious.

Out in the common area, T.J. had turned on the television and was watching American Idol, which was fucking with my high. I opened my door to address him, "Are you serious?"

"Are you seriously still naked?"

"Let me ask you something, T.J. Did you vote for president?"

"No."

"Did you vote in the local elections this year?"

"I'm not speaking another word to you until you get dressed."

"You won't vote for your government, but you vote for American Idol every damn week." On the television, a mother hugged her daughter and yelled, *My baby girl's the next Whitney*, while proudly pointing at the camera like a two-year-old who just made doo-doo in the toilet. If she meant that her daughter would be the next crack-addicted Hollywood loser, then she might have been on to something. "Please turn it off."

Without taking his eyes off the television, T.J. said, "Clothes! Put. Them. On. Now! And stop bugging me."

"Stop bugging me," I said, mimicking T.J. "You sound like you're eleven. You're a grown man who spends his free time watching reality television and collecting baseball cards."

"I've been collecting cards since I was a kid. Some of my cards were my Pop Pops and are worth thousands of dollars."

"Thousands? That shit's worth thousands? Sell them!"

"Asshole. Those cards are all I have left from my Pop Pop."

"So sweet."

"Why are you being such an asshole?"

"Why are you being such a—nevermind. Look, I'm in a shit mood. I got in a big fight with Skye."

"What happened?" T.J. asked.

I went to my room and got dressed. When I came back out, I gave him the shell of the story. I left out the parts about the heroin, but I told him of my failure to reciprocate Skye's *I love you.*

"I won the argument, though," I said.

"Well, congratulations on winning the argument... So, what'd you win?"

I'd won nothing.

I didn't know what Skye's father had done to her, but it was obvious that she'd been hurt deeply and often. Skye had done her best to survive. She'd picked up the pieces of her life and had glued her broken self back together. I'd just smashed her back to bits.

Ron

Sonny the Chin patted me down when I entered the suite. "Great seats," I said to Zantini and Orlando.

"Fughetaboutit," Orlando said.

We watched the first four-and-a-half innings of the game like old pals; not a word of business was spoken. The Dodgers were beating the lowly Pirates, six to one, and the atmosphere was relaxed.

"Trust. That's the most important thing between a pitcher and catcher. It's also the most important thing in any business arrangement," Mr. Zantini said as the Pirates took the field in the middle of the fifth.

"I agree," I said.

"I'm glad. But we don't know you, and we don't trust you. You need to earn my trust."

"Okay. How?"

"Shut your friggin' spaghetti hole. I don't talk business in public. Now, watch Beltre knock this one out of the ballpark." Pitch. Swing. Home run. Zantini grinned. I wondered if he'd paid off the pitcher or something.

After the game, we went to Orlando's limo. I'd never been inside a limo.

"Listen, Ron," Orlando said, using my first name. Zantini was seated silently at Orlando's side. Zantini was an intimidating man, but when Orlando was speaking, he became wallpaper; it was obvious who the boss was. "To gain my trust, you need to do a job for me," Orlando continued.

"Yes sir. What job?" I asked. I was nervous he'd ask me to whack somebody.

"The key to being a successful businessman is to never get greedy. A greedy man will sell out his partner for pennies. Are you a greedy man, Ron?"

"No, sir."

"Good."

I was tinkering with all the buttons on the roof like I had some kind of nervous twitch. I turned on the mood lighting and the stereo by accident.

"Quit fucking around. This isn't a date, you asshole," Orlando said.

"Sorry."

"A man needs to have high self-respect. If you don't believe you're worth somethin', then you ain't worth nuthin'. A man who has no self-respect can't be trusted because if he doesn't respect himself, he can't respect others." Do you have self-respect, Ron?"

"I do."

"Good. Now prove it."

"How?"

"Shut up and I'll tell you."

"I—"

"Shut up! In one week, you're going to deliver a package to an associate of mine in Fresno. I can't tell you what's in the package, but if you're caught with it, you'll go to jail for a very long time. So drive safely. He'll give you money for the package. You bring the money back to me, after taking a fair cut for your work. You decide how much. Don't be greedy, but don't deny yourself what you are entitled too for your work. Capice?"

"Capice," I said, surely mangling the word.

"Great. Come by the restaurant one week from today."

"Thank you very much for this opportunity," I said. The Chin opened the door for me to get out.

There was at least a fifty-percent chance I'd end up dead or in jail by the end of this deal. But I had to do it for Amber and Kimberly. Amber was living life as a stripper constantly look over her shoulder for the man who raped her, and that's no way to go through life. I have never fully understood my feelings for Amber and Kimberly, and I'd stopped trying to figure it out; all I knew is I'd risk everything to make them happy.

T.J.

Some of my days are destined to be bad no matter what. Today was one of those days.

At a red light, in the opposite lane, two black guys in a tricked-out El Camino, hydraulics and everything, blasted rap music so loud that my brain rattled inside my skull. Two white guys in an equally tricked-out Ford F-150 pulled up next to them and tried to drown out the black guys with some white guy rap, Beastie Boys.

The white guys screamed with the music and pumped their fists in cadence with the bouncing front end of their truck. Then, like pure slapstick comedy, a coil shot off their left front wheel, cut through the air, and dented the door of the El Camino. The black guys jumped out, ready to fight. The light turned green, and people behind me began honking their horns, but I was laughing too hard to go.

"I got some Crazy Glue in the trunk if you need!" I hollered to the white guys.

"I'll Crazy Glue your fucking head to your ass, buddy!" the guy yelled back.

Intimidated, I drove off, laughing. I called Dylan. Whether he'd admit it or not, he was hurting from his fight with Skye, and I knew my story would cheer him up.

"Hilarious!"

"Yeah. Hey, have you talked to Skye yet?"

"No."

"So you haven't apologized?"

"Mind your own business, T.J."

I got off the phone with Dylan and called my buddy, Craig, in Pittsburgh, the friend that I went to Miami with. I was always the guy getting laughed at; now this was my funny story about someone else, and it was my right to share it. "And then all this steam started coming out of the engine," I said, embellishing.

I pulled into a 7-Eleven for gas. I entered, talking on the phone, grabbed some CornNuts, and paid for them and gas. I love CornNuts, original flavor. They've come up with all these new flavors like bar-b-que and pizza, but nothing beats the original flavor of the pure salted corn nut. Crunchy and tasty.

Driving away, enjoying my CornNuts, I called my buddy Todd. "Then the huge black guy got out of his car and peed on the white guy's truck—" I was mid-embellishment when my car started puttering.

"Todd, I'll call you back."

"IDIOT! IDIOT, IDIOT, IDIOT!!!"

The car was out of gas. I'd paid for gas but never actually pumped it into my car. Unbelievably, it was the second time I'd done that in the past month.

"STUPID FREAKING IDIOT!"

I'd become the butt of the joke, again. I'm the living incarnation of the "Humor in Life" section of *Reader's Digest*.

And for the third time in two weeks, I was forced to call AAA. It probably would've been cost effective for AAA to open up a separate division that just handled T.J. Martini's calls.

Before I was able to give the operator my coordinates on the 405, my phone died.

Typical.

I locked up my Neon, covered my mouth with a dirty T-shirt from the backseat, and hiked half a mile along the smoggy 405 to the next exit. I called AAA from a payphone, told them where my car was, and walked back to meet them. An hour later, the tow truck arrived.

"Again?" Fred the driver asked, laughing.

What are the freaking odds of getting the same tow truck driver twice in one month in a city of eight million people?

Fred towed me back to the 7-Eleven.

"Thanks, Fred."

"No problem," he said. He wrote down his cell number for me. "Call me direct next time," he said, chuckling. He was making fun, but I took the number anyway.

The 7-Eleven attendant teased me about my brain blunder, and then he let me get my gas. When a gas station attendant is laughing at your expense, you know your life is a joke.

As I was pumping, a ridiculously gorgeous woman pulled up at the adjacent pump. After unfolding out of her car, she stood about ten feet tall. She had to be a runway model. She approached me. I froze in confusion; women like her don't approach guys like me.

"Excuse me. My cell phone is dead, and I need to make a call. Can I borrow yours? It's local."

"Yes! Umm, I mean no. My phone's dead, too. Sorry."

A woman like that speaks to me about—actually, a woman like that has never spoken to me before, and I completely blew it. The supermodel moved on to the guy at pump six; they'd probably fall in love and make babies. Pissed, I got in my Neon, turned the key, put it in drive, and pulled out.

RIIIP! CRASH!

I'd forgotten to take the pump out of my gas tank.

"IDIOT! IDIOT, IDIOT, IDIOT!!!!"

I'm living proof that humans evolved from monkeys.

I considered fleeing the scene, but the attendant had my credit card info, so I didn't. Embarrassed, I went back inside and gave the hysterical laughing jackal my insurance information. I got back in my car and cursed the gods of karma. "Okay, I shouldn't have embellished the story, but are we not yet even?"

I made it home without further incident. I pulled into the parking space parallel to our garage, and with my foot on the brake, I reached for my day planner and saw my freaking cell phone charger on the passenger side floor mat. I'd gone through all that crap, and I had my freaking phone charger the whole time.

"STUPID IDIOT JERK-OFF!"

Disgusted, I threw my phone out the window. I immediately regretted my decision and got out of my vehicle to retrieve the phone before it got run over.

It took me about two seconds to notice my Neon idling toward a telephone pole; I'd never put it in park. I sprinted after it, but I wasn't moving fast enough to catch it. I looked down at my legs as if to remind them their purpose in life is to carry me as fast as I need them to, whenever I need them to. I caught up, grabbed the door, and tried to jump in. But then I tripped over Dylan's skateboard.

SMACK! I hit the ground.

SNAP! My right leg was run over by the rear tire of my Neon.

I lie on the ground, writhing in pain and watching my car jump over the curb, run through the fire hydrant, and bang into the telephone pole. The fire hydrant unloaded a rock-hard stream of water in my face.

I wished Dylan death by skateboarding accident.

Karma would probably get me for that, too.

Dylan

Sadness replaced euphoria as the heroin left me.

I'd been getting high on a regular basis. At first, it was only with Skye, then it was a weekend treat, then Wednesday pick me ups—it didn't take long until I was getting high almost every day. It doesn't take long to become a heroin addict. My first high was the best I'd ever felt, but eventually I came down, and I've been chasing that first high ever since. I've never quite replicated that first time. Every time you slam heroin you build tolerance to it; each time gets more expensive and less effective.

As I began coming down, I tried to drown that heavy sadness in alcohol; all it did was depress me more.

After getting off the phone with T.J., I called Skye's landline. She didn't answer. I got in my car and drove to her apartment in Palms. I needed to talk to her and get some things square with her, and I needed her to open up to me, and tell me about her dad. I needed to know what her last comment had meant. If we had any chance to find happiness together, then we had to share our pain, fight it together, and expel our demons instead of simply muting those demon voices beneath a blanketed heroin high.

I missed Skye badly, and there was a pathetic irony in that. I'd kept Skye at a distance so I wouldn't fall in love, so that once she was gone, I wouldn't miss her. Had I let myself love her, she may still be with me.

I got to Skye's in about half the time it should have taken. I knocked, but she didn't answer. "Come on, Skye. Open the door! I know you're in there! I want to apologize." I could hear her fumbling around. "Skye, open up!"

I was on edge and knew a quick boost of smack would calm my nerves. That's the direction an addict's thoughts always take him in.

"Open up, Skye!" I was pounding the door. Still, nothing. Silence. The kind of chaotic silence that happens ten seconds before the world explodes. Skye was inside, listening, choosing to ignore me, and I knew she was getting high. She was choosing drugs over me. I was furious and jealous. "Open up, Skye!" I pounded for about ten minutes and then gave up. "Forget it!" I yelled, got into my car, and hit the gas, arguing with myself as I drove away. "I won't let myself fall in love with a junkie," I told myself, lying, knowing full well I was already in love.

I screwed up with Skye by not reciprocating her pledge of love. But even if I hadn't screwed up that day, I would've eventually. The only thing to do now was medicate. I needed drugs. I needed to party, and I needed a meaningless lay; I needed to forget and move on.

I headed to the one place I could get all that, the Starr Club.

Skye

My body was fatigued, but my brain was wired. I wouldn't sleep until the sun came up and then started back down again.

Yesterday, I was out of smack, but I had plenty of blow. The first powdery line was raw adrenaline that filled my mouth with words that needed to be said. I decided to call Flora to let out my words. I'd lied to my best friend for too long. I'd confess everything to her and make things right. I called, but she wasn't home. I needed to share. It was the first time in my life that I'd ever felt this way, so I knew I needed to do it right away. I called Flora again; still no answer. So, I decided to call a crisis hotline.

"My father abused me, and I hate myself," I said. I went on and on, not even giving the person on the other end of the phone a chance to talk. I was purging myself, and for whatever reason, saying these things out loud made me feel marginally better.

Marginally.

After about two hours, my high began to close in on me. I did line after line, but it wasn't working. I'm not sure how much time passed, nine hours, six hours, fifteen hours, whatever. Time was immeasurable, bleeding into inanimate objects like the walls, the carpeting, and the air in the room. Eventually, gray morning light came in through the blinds and made the cocaine on the glass coffee table sparkle like snowflakes. It reminded me of growing up in Philadelphia, and I cried.

I picked up my guitar but felt too dead to make music. I popped a few Valiums to numb my inner deadness enough to sleep. It didn't work; still sleepless, I snorted another line, which intensified my depression.

The only way to beat this massive depression was to feed it more powerful drugs. I mixed my coke with baking soda, cooked it, and smoked it. Impromptu crack. I felt instantly better, but it didn't last for even a full moment. I smoked more, then more. I smoked until there was nothing left to smoke.

There was no stopping; I was out of control and falling towards rock bottom. The only other time I'd gotten this bad was when my baby and then my best friend, both died. I ended up in the hospital, and I think that's what I was subconsciously aiming for this time. I put a line of glue on my upper lip and took in a deep breath. I did this over and over until everything became nothing. I became physically lost while sitting in the middle of my living room. I was hallucinating and paranoid. I knew the spiders crawling on my wall weren't really there, but I couldn't make them go away. I closed my eyes, but I could still hear them. I rolled myself into a tight ball on the floor and covered my ears. My kitchen was out to get me: the pots and pans, the oven, the refrigerator—all of them were making noise and helping the spiders steal my sanity. I needed something. Then, a little tiny miracle happened. I remembered my emergency stash of coke. I dug it up and tried to get right.

That's what I was doing when Dylan started knocking on my door.

It had taken all my strength to tell Dylan I loved him. Part of me died when those naked words left my mouth. All Dylan had to do was tell me he loved me, too. It wouldn't have mattered if he were lying. Now, paranoid and hallucinating, I couldn't face him. To calm myself, I tried to think about the day we met. But I couldn't do it; my head was too congested with drugs and regrets and painful memories.

I wanted a time machine—

So I could go back in time and stop my father from whoring me out.

And I wanted my unborn child back in my belly.

I promise, God, I'll get sober if you give my baby back to me.

"Open up, Skye!" Dylan yelled, still pounding.

I began frantically cleaning up all drug evidence, even though I had no intention of opening the door.

Break down the door, Dylan. Rescue me.

"Open up!" he yelled. I peered at him through a sliver of space between the blinds. "Open up, Skye!" I let the blinds close all the way, picked up my pipe, and hit it hard. "Just forget it!" Dylan said.

Dylan peeled out of my driveway, and the hum of his voice resonated in my crowded head.

Dylan

A sex-saturated baseline smacked me in the face when I opened the door to Starr. Tabitha was on stage grinding her crack up and down the pole so violently I expected sparks to shoot out of her pussy.

I went to the ATM and withdrew everything I had. It wasn't much, but it would be enough.

"Dylan, what are you doing here?" Amber asked.

"Looking at naked women. You?"

"You don't look so good. You feel okay?"

"Tip-fucking-top. Is Tiffany here?"

"Why?"

"I want to see her."

"Yeah, she's here." Amber pointed to V.I.P. "Be careful. Okay?"

"Sure. I'll be careful. Thanks."

I sat at the bar, took in the sights, and waited. The club smelled of cheap perfume, cigarette smoke, and bad hygiene. The loud noise they called music was giving me a headache. I was here to forget about Skye, but I knew that it wouldn't work. I'm a writer, or am supposed to be, and writers, by nature, are hopeless romantics. I was cursed to feel pain and desire this lost love forever.

I made it through two Seven and Sevens and half a pack of cigarettes in half an hour, waiting on Tiffany; she still hadn't returned from the V.I.P. section. Smoking in bars is illegal in California, but at Starr they don't pay attention to laws. The *girls can touch you, but you can't touch them* rule was enforced with the same lack of tenacity.

When I worked at Starr, I knew girls who screwed customers in the V.I.P. booths for as little as a hundred dollars. Tiffany was one of these girls. Not only did the owner know about it, but he also profited because the girls used their prostitution money to buy drugs from him. These girls start using drugs for courage to dance naked for strangers. But the irony is that they get addicted, and now start fucking and sucking the customers so that they can buy more drugs. It's an endless circle that ultimately destroys them.

Honey was on stage when I ordered my third drink. She was thirty-two, but backstage, in real light, she looked older. Onstage, the lines in her face disappeared. Strip clubs use red light to silence pimples, stretch marks, scars, and ingrown pubic hairs and black light to reduce wrinkles and eye bags. Honey faced the crowd and had her backside against the pole, rubbing herself on it like a third grade boy trying to get off on the monkey bars at recess.

Honey had been dancing long before I ever worked at the club. She used to pay me twenty bucks to guard the door while she'd get a customer off in the bathroom. She was a master of the craft; it never took her longer than three minutes, and as dirty as that is, I'd seen much worse while working there. I saw doctors and lawyers smoking crack in bathroom stalls. I saw guy-on-guy action with strippers watching. I even saw a stripper shoot heroin into the vagina of another stripper.

Honey finished, and two girls I didn't know, Jersey and Rayne, took the stage together, and I tried to focus on them. I'd push out my sadness, and I'd push out Skye, replacing her with Jersey and Rayne.

"The leggy blonde's cute, huh?" Frank the bartender said about Rayne.

"She should change her stage name to Stripper Barbie," I replied.

"Her bright blue eyes do kinda make her look like a Barbie."

"You know, Mattel should make Barbies that are more representative of real-life women. Stripper Barbie, Junkie Barbie, Abused Barbie, Dominatrix Barbie, Lonely Housewife Barbie. That would be cool. Fuck that Malibu Barbie bitch."

"Yeah, fuck that bitch," Frank said, then laughed. "You want another drink?"

"Yeah."

The girl dancing with Stripper Barbie, Jersey, was dark as night. She had gang tattoos, braids, thick strong thighs, and solid dark eyes glazed with a hard wetness.

"The other one should change her name to Gangsta Barbie," I said.

"I'll drink to that," Frank said. We both did a shot, and then he mixed me a Seven and Seven.

Stripper Barbie and Gangsta Barbie looked sad and tired. I'd have felt sorry for them, but I lost my compassion for strippers long ago. I asked Gangsta Barbie for a lap dance after her stage performance, and she took me to a dark corner of the room. Her blackness made her nearly disappear in the dark.

"I'll start at the beginning of the next song," she said.

She folded her arms and looked through me as we waited. She had a flat belly, and her thick, muscular thighs touched each other halfway up, then curved away from each other just below her pussy, leaving a triangle though which stage-light pushed through.

The song began, and she wasted no time. She put her ass in my crotch and grinded on my unenthusiastic penis for the entire three-minute song. Afterward, she pulled her G-string aside, exposing her shaved mound to make room for my tip. I slid in two dollars, and she let go of the G-string. *Snap!*

Returning to the bar, I was upset I'd wasted seventeen dollars on that. None of this was doing anything to cure my depression or make me forget Skye. If anything, the slutty strippers, and the stench of the loser patrons was making everything worse. A young Mexican stripper sat down beside me and spread dark red lipstick on top of lips already thickly caked. Her heavy eyeliner looked like eyeglass frames.

"Hi," she said.

Not wanting to get coaxed into spending another seventeen dollars on a dance, I ignored her.

After an hour wait, Tiffany finally came out of V.I.P. She'd probably fucked some loser. "Tiff."

"Don't call me that here!" Tiffany shouted.

"Ohh, right. Sorry. *Brooklyn.* Can we talk?"

"What do you need?" Tiffany asked.

"You holding?"

"I'm holding these," she said, grabbing her small saggy breasts and shaking them at me. In the six years I'd known Tiffany, she'd transformed from a pretty, young, curvy, 125-pound black girl to an eighty-five-pound crack-whore. "I'm getting out of here in about an hour. You wanna party?" she asked.

"Yeah."

"You got money?"

"Some."

"Great. I know just the place. It'll be a good time. She ran her hand up my crotch and squeezed my manhood. "I'll be back in a minute," she said and disappeared.

Most of the girls at Starr worked there for a year or two, but some—like Tiffany, Honey, and even Amber—seemed handcuffed to the place. I knew Amber wanted a way out, a better life for her and her daughter. But I think Tiffany and Honey enjoyed the life.

Waiting, I watched another blonde dance. She took her top off and jiggled; her tits didn't budge. They were bad silicone implants. The newer saline implants have a more natural bounce; it's pathetic the kind of information you pick up when you hang around a place like this long enough. I was supposed to be an artist and a writer, and somehow I'd managed to waste most of my days working in various shitholes like this one.

Amber sat next to me. "So, what's been going on with you?" she asked. "I haven't seen you in forever."

"Nothing. Just having a drink. You?"

"Nothing new."

"How's Kimberly?" I strategically asked about her daughter

before she could pry deeper into my life.

"She's still the joy of my life."

"And how's your roommate-slash-lover. What's her name?"

"Her name's Beth, and she's not my lover. She's good. She's seeing a guy, Kelly, whom she met on a dating game show."

"Oh shit! I think I saw part of that episode. I knew that the girl looked familiar."

"Are you serious? Dylan Slade watches reality television? I wouldn't have believed it if I didn't just hear it."

"I wasn't watching. My roommate, T.J., loves that crap. I just saw part of it."

"Sure."

"You ready to go?" Tiffany asked, appearing beside me. She gave Amber a nasty look. They'd never gotten along.

"Yeah, let's go. I'll talk to you later, Amber. Good to see you again."

"Dylan." Amber held onto the sleeve of my T-shirt as I started walking away. "Watch yourself."

"Watch yourself, Amber," Tiffany said, mocking her. Tiffany grabbed my other arm, and pulled me away from Amber and out the door.

"What do you want to do?" Tiff asked as we walked to my car.

"Get loaded," I said, getting in the passenger seat.

"With?"

"Heroin if you can. Or whatever. Anything will do."

"Heroin? Jeez Dylan, when did you start messing with the Cheeba?"

"Just Drive."

"You're not a cop are you?" she asked, trying to be funny. I didn't laugh. "I don't know if I can get you tar, but I can get you high one way or another."

We headed east to a shady area somewhere between Compton and Watts. We turned down a quiet alley without street lights. I'd been to this part of town before but never at night. For whatever reason, I wasn't intimidated. I probably should've been.

"You'll be the only white person in this joint. Some of the brothers will get tense and territorial when they see a black girl roll in with a white dude in their neighborhood. So be cool."

"Yeah, whatever. Let's go."

"Give me a hundred," she said, and I did.

"Okay, let's go," she said.

I'd only seen crack houses in movies. This crack house was infinitely worse. There was trash everywhere, dead rats in the hall, and an overwhelming smell of feces. People were scattered throughout the house in zombie-like trances, more inanimate than alive.

There were security cameras that monitored the outside activity, which surprised me. Regardless, they were worthless—nobody was manning them; everyone was too stoned. An entire army dressed in hot pink fatigues wearing cowbells around their necks and blowing trumpets could have been doing the electric slide outside, and I don't think any of these crackheads would have noticed.

A woman sat in the middle of the floor, crying into her hands and cursing about her backstabbing friends. Two black guys stood above her talking to each other, both speaking at the same time. The darker one talked about a run-in with the cops, and the other guy was talking about his *fucking-bitch-ass-prostitute-whore-ass-wife*. Neither was listening to the other.

The whole scene was unreal. It was the anti-Grand Canyon. When I first saw all the greens, reds, and yellows of the Grand Canyon and the river that wound through, I was overwhelmed by its awesomeness. It was surreal. This situation in the crack house had the same surreal awesomeness, but not the grandeur. Just being in this environment was starting to make my depression spiral out of control.

I wanted to hold Skye so badly. I wanted her to comfort me.

I needed to get high.

Tiff approached an anorexic-looking black guy who fell asleep between every other sentence. They spoke. I have no idea how she made any sense of his babble. Tiff handed him cash; he gave her a couple bags, and then he stepped backward toward the couch. His bare foot squashed in a fat piece of shit, and then he sat down without noticing what he'd just stepped in. I wondered if it was human shit or dog shit... I didn't see any dogs.

"Here you go," Tiff said, handing me a dime bag.

Seconds later, my problems became ancient history.

I closed my eyes and let the calming tide of the heroin pull me into the sea on a raft of goodness. Then, a strong-scented cloud enveloped me. I opened my eyes. It was Tiffany's crack smoke.

Everyone has two or three momentous life decisions that will affect the rest of their lives. This was one of those decisions for me.

"What does crack feel like?" I asked. I was feeling good, but not as good as I wanted to be feeling. The dime bag wasn't quite enough to shutdown my inner voice. Skye was still lingering; I had to push her all the way out.

"Wanna hit?" Tiff asked.

"Can I crush it and snort it?" I asked. I thought by snorting the crack I'd somehow be different than these crack-smoking crackheads. Addicts always find a way to separate themselves from the other junkies.

Tiffany didn't respond to my question. "Tiff—you hear me?"

"What?" Her lips again wrapped around the glass pipe.

"Can I crush it?"

"It's better if you smoke it."

Crack is cocaine based. This crack looked gray and more dangerous than chalky-white cocaine. I wanted to try, but I didn't have the courage. I noticed a large black man eyeing me. I felt intimidated.

"Let me hit it," I said after Tiff took the pipe out of her mouth.

I hit it hard. Icy hot smoke seared my lungs. It felt like a cold knife scrapping along the inner lining of my throat. I desperately needed to cough, but I tried not to. That created excruciating pressure inside my head and eyes. I let the air out, and then took in a breath of fresh air, then another. My third breath was the finest air I've ever tasted. My lungs no longer burned, and the tip of my tongue was buzzing with razor sharp wit. I needed to talk; I needed to talk a lot, and so I did. I talked and talked and talked to everyone in the room. Thoughts came too quickly for my mouth to keep up, but I certainly tried. The only time my mouth stopped talking was to hit the icy hot pipe again. And again. And again. I didn't understand why the others seemed catatonic and depressed. I felt incredible. I felt massive.

I was Superman. Spider-Man. The Green Hornet.

I hit the pipe again.

I was invincible. I was energy. I was a lifetime of orgasms packaged in a body of muscle and strength.

"Hey, slow down a little," Tiffany suggested. I knew she wanted it all for herself.

I slipped my hand between her brown thighs and kissed her

puckered mouth.

Amber

Dylan looked despondent when he left the club; it scared me. I called Ron, he picked me up, and we took off in his old Pinto.

Ron sipped his coffee loudly. "Ouch! Damn that's hot."

Loud sippers are as annoying as soup slurpers. Ron is both.

Ron sucked down another spoonful and then randomly asked, "Amber, why don't you go back to school?"

"What? Where is that coming from?"

"I know you don't want to be a stripper forever."

"How do you know, maybe stripping is my biggest passion in life."

"Amber," he said, rolling his eyes in the way an older sibling would.

"I'm not going back to school. I failed."

I spread the blame around for my failure in school. I blame work, my teachers, and my responsibility to care for Kimberly. But none of those were the real reason. I failed because nursing bored me.

Ron took another loud sip from his coffee. "You'd pass if you quit dancing and focused completely on school," he said.

"You already know I applied a second time and didn't get accepted, so why are we even discussing this?"

"There are other schools you can apply to. You've got to go for it. You're the smartest person I know."

"That's not saying much about the people you know," I said.

"Seriously, Amber. You could make it if you gave up the dancing and studied more."

We hit a bump; the car bounced a little, and Ron spilled coffee on himself. Poetic justice.

"Ouch! Shit!"

I laughed. I hoped the distraction would be enough for him to drop the conversation. It wasn't. He wiped himself off and continued, "Seriously, why not quit dancing tomorrow and get back in school? What's stopping you?"

"What's stopping me? Oh, I don't know. Bills maybe?"

At the red light, Ron pressed his nose to the glass, looked out the window, and scratched his head. Then he looked back at me. "I could help out with the bills; you'd pay me back once you became a nurse."

"Thanks, but no way. Make a left at the next intersection," I said when the light turned.

"You should let me loan you money."

"You don't have any money, and I don't want to talk about it anymore." I wasn't happy about being a stripper, but it's what I was. Stripping is the only thing I'd ever been good at and the only thing I could do to put Kimberly through college. "Go south on Long Beach Boulevard."

"I'm going to find a way to help you, Amber."

"I owe some bad people some serious cash. You couldn't help me even if I let you, which I won't."

"Who do you owe?"

"Doesn't matter." And was the end of that. He didn't ask another question. He knew me well enough to know I was at my boiling point with the conversation.

Tyrone, my "boss" from my days as a drug running mule, had just gotten out of jail. He'd come to Starr with his boys. I saw him before he saw me, and I left immediately. Tyrone must've gotten one of the dancers to tell him where I lived. I'm certain it was Tiffany; that whore would sell her daughter for a couple bucks. The next day, Tyrone showed up at my place. I saw him coming and Kimberly and I hid in the attic. He banged on the door a while and then left.

But he'd be back.

He left a note on my door. It read—

One thousand dollars a week.

Compensation for crimes against me.

Leave it in the mailbox of the deserted house on 52nd and Normandie

After banging on my door, I watched Tyrone go through my trash, and I'm nearly positive that he got my social security number from a bill. If I moved, he'd find me. If I went to the cops, and even if I were able to put Tyrone behind bars, someone in his well connected drug pushing army would avenge his incarceration, and Kimberly and I would end up dead. There is no way to fight people who don't obey laws and who don't care if they end up dead. I had no choice but to pay him.

"Turn down that alley," I said.

The dark alley was narrow and cluttered with garbage, some of which we couldn't even see. Ron ran over something, hopefully it was only a speed bump, and both our heads bounced and hit the car's ceiling. Ron cursed as he spilled coffee on himself again.

"This is crazy," he said.

The mouth of the alley opened into another street, and I saw the house. A rusted-out Cadillac sat on cinder blocks in the driveway.

"Pull up alongside this house," I directed.

"Why aren't there any street lights in this neighborhood?"

"Because there's nothing good to see in this neighborhood at night."

"How'd you know about this place?"

"Tiffany told me about it." I was lying. I'd known Tiffany when I was running drugs for Tyrone, and I used to find Tiffany here. Having that information to hold over her was part of the reason she hated me so much.

"I don't know about this place, Amber."

The house looked straight out of a horror movie. Half shattered glass panes sat in every window like broken teeth. On the lawn were empty bottles, discarded pipes, and used needles. The fecund smell of old urine, blood, and decay made me dizzy. I suggested to Ron he stay in the car, but he had to be the protective tough guy and demanded to escort me inside. Ron and I, hand in hand, moved quickly through the pitch black. I was frightened, but this was a feeling that I was familiar in dealing with. We walked up the stairs; Ron knocked, and when nobody answered, we let ourselves in.

"Oh my God!" I said.

Dylan was unconscious and doubled over with drool hanging from the corner of his mouth. A crimson red thread ran down his forehead; he must've fallen. His shoes were gone, and Tiffany was nowhere in sight.

Dylan

I was awakened by the burning hell inside me. Someone had

removed my insides with an ice cream scooper and filled the empty space with lava.

I felt disoriented; I'd been pulled out of time and randomly placed back in it. I was unable to get my bearing, but I knew I needed to find a bathroom. I tried to roll out of bed, but my head was pounding too hard. Then I noticed the lines piercing my flesh, holding me fast to the bed.

I'm in a hospital.

With no time to spare, I turned my head to the side and emptied my stomach all over my pillow. And after my stomach was empty, the fun really began. Dry heaves. My body convulsed, my innards contracted. I couldn't breathe or call out for help. Eventually, between heaves, I was able to press the call button. Two minutes later, the nurse arrived. She gave me a shot of something which made everything start melting into soothing, tepid, blue liquid.

"You gave us quite a scare last night, Dylan," my nurse said. Her nametag read Flora.

"I don't remember."

"Thank your friend Amber. If she hadn't found you, you'd be dead."

"What happened?"

"We pumped your stomach, but you put a lot of drugs into your system, and you're going to feel this way for a few days."

"Great," I said. My insides tried to ball up again, but the medicine she'd given me wrestled that feeling into submission, and slowly, I faded out.

When I woke a couple hours later, Nurse Flora was tending to my IV.

"Can I get some water?" I asked.

"We can't give you anything by mouth because you might throw it up and choke on it. You're getting fluids through your IV.

"That sucks. I could really use a glass of water. How do I look?"

Flora handed me a small mirror. I was disgusting. My lips were cracked and bloody, and my eyes were sunken in and bloodshot with dark circles around them.

"Can I get another shot of whatever you just gave me to help me relax?"

"I'm sorry, but you can't get any more meds right now," Flora said on her way out the door.

The flickering light from the television hurt me. I didn't see the remote, so I shut my eyes. My body was cramping again. I needed water. The muscles in my arms and legs fucking hurt. I could feel my blood moving through my head, and my blood hurt. My blood was poisoned, and my body was hot and angry, and it was going to eject all my poisoned blood through my nose and ears and eyeballs. I needed something to numb the pain. I needed a pain shot, or a beer, or a joint, or a whack of heroin. Then the dry heaves started again, and I thought I was going to die. I hit the call button over and over until Nurse Flora returned.

"I need another shot."

"I can't give you one for another two hours."

"I swear I'm going to die if you don't give me a shot."

"You're not going to die."

"I'm going to fucking die."

Flora smiled and walked out on me.

Flora

"Juan, it's been over for years. What don't you understand? You need to move on!" I said to old Doctor Juan Salazar. He just wouldn't give up on us. "I understand you hurt. I understand that something hurt you in your childhood and still gives you pain, but we've all had broken childhoods. We all have demons. You've just got to move on." I was doing my best to remain patient.

"Nurse Garcia, please report to station two," my supervisor announced over the intercom. Station two was Juan's station. He used his authority to force me to talk to him. Had I not felt my job was in jeopardy I'd have reported this as sexual harassment of some kind.

I was having a shit day. I had eight patients at once, which is more than a nurse should have. And when I finally got a fifteen-minute break, I spent all of it on the psych ward arguing with Juan. It was the eighty-billionth time we'd had the same conversation since our break-up. Juan was becoming frightening. I didn't want to involve the authorities, but I would if I had to.

I returned to my workstation. "Ms. Garcia, you're late from break again," my supervisor said.

"I know. I'm sorry."

"This can't keep happening. This is a hospital, not a fast food joint. We need to be able to depend on our employees."

"It won't happen again."

"You have a new patient in Room 220. He's post-op open reduction internal fixation of the right femur."

I was late and didn't have time to check his chart before I went in to introduce myself.

"Hi. I'll be your nur—"

"Whoa. Hi. Umm, I need a sponge bath."

Unbelievable. T.J. Martini. I hadn't seen him since the New Year's Eve when I saw him sucking face with Skye.

"Wow, what a surprise. T.J. Martini. Small world."

"It's great to see you, Flora, but I wish the circumstances were different. I'm so—"

"Surprised?" I said, finishing his sentence.

"Yeah. You know, tomorrow's my thirtieth birthday. This is an early present."

"Well, happy birthday. This is a lousy way to spend it."

"Tell me about it. I've wanted to ask you something. Do you know Dylan? He's your friend Skye's boyfriend."

"Yeah, I know him. He's my patient also."

"Wait. What?"

"A friend brought him in. He had heroin, crack, and alcohol in his system. He's pretty messed up, but I think he's going to be okay. He got here quick enough we could still help him. He's really lucky."

"Are you serious! He's such a dick… I hope he's okay," T.J. said.

I can't explain why, but I began to feel bitter about T.J. kissing Skye on New Year's Eve.

T.J.

"I was just joking about the sponge bath; I do need one, but I don't want it from you. I mean, not that I wouldn't want a sponge bath from you because I would. I just mean—forget it. This morphine drip is messing with my head."

I had a needle buried in my forearm and attached to a machine that would pump me full of morphine when I pushed the button. I hit it again. Every time I pushed the button, it was like an injection of fluffy air that made me float with the clouds.

"So, Flora, how've you been?"

"Good. You?"

Flora murdered the stereotype of the fat, chain-smoking nurse. She was more of the cliché naughty nurse costume on Halloween.

"I'll be back in a second," Flora said. Flora left the room and took all of my oxygen with her. I'd have sold my soul to O.J. Simpson for another shot at her.

I remembered how beautiful Flora looked on our singular date, a zillion years ago. She wore a thin, silky, black blouse, through which her nipples playfully poked out of. She was the sexiest girl I'd ever been on a date with, and doing what I do, I fell flat on my face.

Flora came back. "I haven't checked your H&P. Can you brief me on what happened?"

"Shame on you, nurse. Skipping out on your homework," I said. She smiled. "I was at home, having a beer and watching the football game. At halftime, I went outside for the mail, and I saw a little girl chase after a soccer ball into the street. A big car was headed right at her. The driver must have been digging in the glove compartment or something because he wasn't watching the road. So, I just reacted, you know. There was no time for thinking. I just followed my inner male instinct to protect. I ran across the road, pushed the girl out of the way, and then, once I knew she was safe, I jumped out of the way of the car. Unfortunately, I caught my foot on the side of the curb, twisted in a funny way, and broke my leg in the fall. And you know the fucked up thing? After all that, after risking my life for the little girl, her mother is suing me for pushing her daughter. Can you believe that? Unbelievable!"

"Wow," Flora replied.

"I'll tell you what, the nerve of some people!"

"The nerve."

"I should sue her for my damn broken leg," I said.

"You'd probably win."

"I'm sure I would."

"Next time, you should just let the little girl get run over."

"Oh, no. I could never do that."

"So, I guess you missed the end of the game."

"What game?" I asked.

"The football game you were watching. You know, T.J., I always thought football was played in the fall and winter," Flora said.

"Oh, um, maybe it was basketball. You know, this morphine is really strong."

"T.J."

"Yes?"

"What happened to your leg?"

"I got out of my car with it still in drive. It started idling away. I chased after it, tripped on a skateboard, and the back wheel of my car ran over me."

"I'm sorry to hear that."

"Then why are you laughing?"

"I'm sorry. T.J., I can't be your nurse—"

"Why?"

"It's not appropriate because I know you personally. But it's good to see you. I'll wheel you to see Dylan later."

"But—"

Flora left. I wanted her to stay. *Oh well.* Morphine drip. *Ahhh.* I closed my eyes and went on a euphoric flight through the far away galaxy of Planazarian, accompanied by a dozen naked Filipino angels that all looked remarkably similar to Flora.

Flora came back a few hours later and plucked me from my fantasy. "T.J., wake up!" She looked upset

"I didn't do it!" I yelled, startled.

"I'm taking you to see Dylan, right now. Get out of bed quick."

I got up on one leg, sat in the chair, and Flora whisked me away. I thought she'd told me Dylan was okay. Why is she in such a rush? Something's going on. This is going to be gruesome, phlegm and blood everywhere. There's probably a priest reading him Last Rights. No, Dylan wouldn't have a priest. Dylan's going to die, and his family probably doesn't even know he's in the hospital. I should call them. *Shit. Where's his family from?* After all this time of living with the guy, and all I know about him is he smokes a lot of pot, dresses like a freak, and steals girls I find first.

T.J., you dick! I'm a dick. Dylan's dying, and I'm acting bitter about Skye. *Selfish dick!*

Flora pushed me down the hall at a high rate of speed. Her breaths were quickening, which excited me.

Maybe Dylan tried to kill himself. I hope Dylan doesn't need one of those speeches about how everyone loves him and he's too young to die— *You have too much going for you to kill yourself, Dylan.* I really don't want to give that speech. He did this because of one little fight with his girlfriend. That's bullshit.

"Flora, what's going on? What's wrong?"

"Nothing's wrong with Dylan, but I can't get a hold of Skye. She's turned her phones off. I think this may have something to do with Dylan's condition. I need to go find her."

We got on the elevator. Sure, I was worried for Skye, but that didn't stop me from hoping the elevator would get stuck. Flora and I would be trapped on the elevator for hours; I'd hold her and calm her; we'd share my morphine. The cable holding up the elevator would make frightening sounds like it was snapping. Terrified, Flora would dig her fingers into my back. I'd kiss her forehead. *Everything's going to be okay, Flora.* She'd bury her face in my shoulder, and her hair would smell like dandelions. She'd look up at me, and our eyes would meet, a tear in hers. *I don't want to die as a virgin,* she'd say. I'd smile. We'd kiss, make love. The cable would snap and, united, we'd plummet to our deaths.

Beautiful.

Let's go," Flora said as the elevator opened.

"Those two sure had one hell of a fight the other night," I said. "Let's never fight like that."

Oh shit, I can't believe I just said that.

Wait, they had a fight? A bad one?" she asked.

"Yeah, I'm sorry. I assumed you knew," I said in an apologetic tone. Flora turned two shades of peeked. I'd upset her. Luckily for me, she didn't notice my idiotic comment about us never fighting—as if there ever would be an 'us'.

"You want some of my morphine?"

Flora was about to drop me off in Dylan's room, but before she could, I grabbed the wheel, and we came to an abrupt halt.

"Flora, I'm not normally this forward or this brave with women, and I know I totally messed up our first date, but I like you, and I want to take you out again," I said.

She didn't respond, but she did allow herself a smile.

"So will you let me take you out on a date?"

"I'm not allowed to date my patients, T.J. Martini," she said.

"What about after when I'm not your patient anymore?"

"I don't know. You should ask me then," she said, now smiling and blushing. "The timing is a little inappropriate, don't you think?"

"Sorry," I said. I'm a blusher; there's nothing you can do when you're blushing; the more you fight it, the more the color bleeds out. The fact Flora was a blusher as well made me feel close to her. I couldn't wait to ask her out.

"Bye T.J." She pushed me into Dylan's room and left without even saying hi.

"Hi. You must be T.J.," said the old guy in the corner.

"Yes, sir."

"I'm Dylan's father, Terry."

"Hi," I said.

Dylan's father was nothing like I expected. He wore a suit and matching tie. Dylan didn't even own a tie.

An extremely sexy girl came out of the bathroom. "This is Dylan's sister, Katie," her father said.

Katie nodded.

Wow. Hello, Dylan's sister.

"Nice to meet you, Katie."

"Nice to meet you, too."

"I'm going to go get a soda," Katie said and left.

I watched her sashay her way out of the room. Stop that, T.J.! You're not that guy. Don't be that guy!

Dylan looked horrible. His face was empty and pale like a daytime moon. His eyeliner was smeared like that of a woman who'd been crying after being dumped. His cheeks were as sunken as those of the malnourished children in charity advertisements. *For the price of a cup of coffee, you can save this child's life.* I made a mental note to give to one of those charities after I got well.

Katie came back.

I should sit by her. No! Stop it, T.J. What's wrong with you? It's the morphine. I can't focus. I hope I don't get addicted. I'll end up pretending to be a heroin addict so I can get methadone. I'll sit around all day popping methadone and watching stupid movies.

Actually, that doesn't sound too horrible.

On the television, Potsie and Ralph Mouth were arguing. It was the *Happy Days* episode when they get an apartment together and use a ribbon to divide the apartment into halves. Ralph had to use the bathroom, but it was on Potsie's side of the apartment, and he wouldn't let Ralph use it. I laughed out loud, which agitated Dylan's father.

"Hey, T.J.," Dylan said, waking up.

"Hey, buddy. How you feeling?"

"I feel like I OD'd and almost died, but other than that, I'm cool."

"He's still got his sense of humor," said Katie. "And he's still an asshole, too." Katie's voice was as soft as a down comforter. I wanted to roll up in her voice and take a nap.

"T.J., this is my sister, Katie, and my father, Terry. They flew in from West Virginia." *West Virginia, that's where they're from. I remember him mentioning West Virginia. I think.*

"We already met T.J. while you were playing the role of the passed-out junkie," Katie replied.

I wonder how old Katie is. She must be his younger sister. She's got to be at least twenty-one. I'm sure she's twenty-one. She's at the stage when girls like to go out and get drunk and go home with random guys. I wonder how long she's in town. Maybe she'd like to go out for a drink down by the beach tonight. She probably doesn't get to the beach much. I bet she'd like that. I bet she'd like to hang at my beach pad. I should ask her. I wonder how old she is.

"How olll— err. How was the drive?" I asked Katie.

"Not fun. We were too worried about the asshole."

"You gave us a real scare, Dylan-boy," I said.

"Don't ever call me that again," Dylan said.

"Sorry. You know I broke my leg by tripping over your skateboard. Once you get well, I'm suing your butt." I said then looked at Katie. She laughed. I made her laugh.

I'm in.

Katie is so cute. I've got to ask if she's twenty-one.

"Hey, Katie—"

"Shhh—" Katie shushed me. "Dylan' just fell asleep."

"That quick?"

We listened to the quiet hum of the television while Dylan slept. I mostly tried to avoid looking at Katie, but I didn't have the self-discipline. When Katie looked at me, I'd avert my eyes.

"What happened to you?" Katie asked, in a sexy whisper.

"Um, well, I broke my leg tackling a mugger."

"Really?"

"Yeah… it was nothing though. I saw this huge black guy grab some poor old ladies purse and then take off running. I chased him down, jumped on his back, and tackled him. I got the purse back, but I broke my leg when we fell to the ground."

"Wow, you're a real life hero," she said, and I tried not to let my head explode from the excitement of the compliment.

"No, I was just doing what any good citizen would have. Honestly, it embarrasses me. Let's not talk about it."

I turned my attention back to the television, but I could feel that Katie's eyes were still on me. I tried my best to contain my smile. I hit the morphine. Warmth washed over me. I grabbed the remote control, turned up the volume, and changed stations. On one of the movie channels, a sexy woman dressed in a sequined gown and high heels was chasing after some thug. He was getting away, but she kicked off her heels and, despite an awkward running motion, she was gaining ground on him. The girl in the sequined gown caught the criminal from behind, slapped the gun out of his hand, jumped on top of him, and punched him out with one swing. Katie and I watched the entire hour program in what felt like tortuous silence. In reality, the silence was likely the only thing that saved me from saying something stupid. With my heroic story, she viewed me as a stud. Keeping my mouth shut was my best chance at preserving that point of view.

Skye and Flora appeared in the doorway. I immediately felt guilty for flirting with Katie. Skye looked ten years older than she had a few days ago and Flora looked concerned, like she knew that chaos was about to explode. Dylan was still sleeping. Katie saw Skye and sat up tall in her chair. She looked pissed. I wondered what she was thinking. I wondered how sexy her lips would look moving to the cadence of anger.

"Hey, everyone," Flora said, trying to sound cheerful.

Anticipating an uncomfortable confrontation, I hit the morphine again and tried to disappear.

Skye

I'd hit an all-time low, which for me, is impressive. I was so desperate to keep some kind of high going that I buried half my face in a brown paper bag and sucked up paint fumes. My brain became a lump of meat at that point. I was inhaling when Flora came into my apartment through a window I'd left open.

"Get cleaned up. I'm taking you to see Dylan," she shouted from down the hallway. I stashed the paper bag before she found me, but I'm sure she knew what I was doing.

"Hey, Flora," I said when she came in. And that's about the only thing I remember. The paint fumes hit me hard and everything faded to white noise.

I have no idea how Flora did it, but somehow she managed to get me into the car. I was beginning to gather my thoughts about the time we pulled up to the hospital

"No," I said, when Flora parked the car. "I'm not up for this."

"Well, you don't have a choice." Flora got out, walked around to my side of the car, grabbed my arm, and pulled me out. I was secretly glad she was being assertive. Somebody had to take control of me.

Inside, Flora got me a candy bar and a Coca-Cola from the vending machine. I wasn't hungry, but I knew my body needed something. She took me to Dylan's room and said that she'd help me get in rehab after our visit. I didn't bother putting up an argument.

"Hi, this is Skye," Flora said, when we entered the room.

"Oh…" a man who looked like his dad said. It was obvious that he didn't want me there. "Dylan's been in and out of consciousness all day long. Mostly out. But the doctor said he'll be okay."

I kept my eyes focused on the floor. I couldn't bare to look at either Dylan's dad or his sister. The room was saturated with his contempt for me, and the muted yellows and browns of the hospital room made the vibe even more ugly.

Dylan looked horrible. He was pale. His eye shadow was smeared down his face into the deep caverns of his cheeks. Tubes came in and out of him like an arcade game. I felt a hollow culpability for Dylan's situation. I was to blame for all this. I wanted to weep, but I was too mad at myself to cry. I wanted to run away, but I was too tired.

"Dylan doesn't deserve this. It should be me in a coma, not him," I whimpered.

"Everything happen for a reason, Skye," Flora said.

"Everything happens for a reason?" I said, chuckling, trying to contain my anger. Everything happens for a reason? Everything happens for a goddamned reason!" I pounded my fists against the closet door; the sound was hollow, and I could relate. "What's the fucking reason, Flora?"

"Calm down," the dad said.

"What are you going to tell me next, Flora? Huh? There's a lesson to be learned in this? Life goes on? What's the reason this happened to Dylan?"

"I don't know, Skye."

"Tell me, Flora."

"Fuck you," the girl said, softly.

"Fuck you!" I fired back, half crying and half screaming.

"Don't talk to my daughter that way! You want to know the reason this happened? You're the reason!"

His words hung between the walls of the room, echoing off the air.

"Thank you. You're right. It is my fault!"

"Be positive, Skye. He's going to get better," Flora said.

I started laughing. Laughing hurt even more than crying. I couldn't stop laughing. I had no idea why I was laughing: fatigue maybe. Tears ran out of my eyes and down my cheeks; their acidity stung my skin.

I grabbed Flora and held her as tightly as I could. "You and your G.D. positive attitude, Flora." At that moment, Flora's hug was the only thing I had in the world, and I was scared to let her go.

I was wasted and paranoid, and being around Dylan's father and sister was the absolute worst place for me. I feared that once Flora unwrapped my arms from hers, that I would spontaneously combust. I had to get out of there before that happened; I couldn't tolerate being in room another second. It's not that I didn't want to stay with Dylan, because I did, but I just couldn't. Flora sensed that.

"We've got to go and take care of some things, but we'll be back later," she said, pulling me out of the room.

"Don't hurry back," Dylan's sister said.

Outside, I waited for Flora to pull up with the car. The sun's rays slanted sharply, casting an oblong shadow that stretched nearly halfway across the road. Flora pulled up; I got in, and she took me to my place. Once there, we talked. Actually, Flora talked. She talked about getting me into rehab, getting well, Dylan, etc., etc., but all the while she talked, my mind drifted toward thoughts of death, wondering if there was a way to speed up time, to make life go by faster. After a couple hours, I faked falling asleep, so that Flora would leave. After she did, I began plotting to get my next fix.

I'm the real deal—a self-absorbed, drug addicted cunt.

Dr. Juan Salazar

I love the way the colors are separated by the practical little divider walls. The bloody red beets separate from the brown rice, separate from the green beans, separate from the dull, grayish meat. I need these boundaries. I get angry if my yellow beans violate the boundaries of my green brussel sprouts. I rarely eat the food, but I'm a fan of the presentation.

My appreciation for the lunch tray may be odd, but it fit, because everything about me is odd. For so many years, I pretended to be someone else. I hid beneath the mask of an educated doctor who was an upstanding member of the church and community. When Flora was in my life, I was able to be somebody normal without having to wear these masks. Now that she's gone; it's as if she was never there.

The yellow pad of butter melted in my mashed potatoes. I mixed them, trying to get them to the perfect consistency. I was about to take my first bite when Flora entered the cafeteria. I'd managed to leave her alone for the past three days; I knew she needed some space because of her friend's troubles. But I couldn't do it any longer; I needed to talk to her. I watched her in line. She got her food and sat alone at one of the round tables. I picked up my tray and pulled up a chair next to her.

"Hi, Flora."

"Juan, it's not a good time for this."

I spoke softly so others wouldn't hear. "Flora, please. I know you're upset today, but just hear me out for a couple minutes."

"How many times do I have to tell you I wasn't happy with you? When are you going to grasp that? I mean, what do you want? Do you want me to be with you even though I don't want to be?"

"You could be happy with me."

"I can't be happy if I'm loving you out of obligation. We've been over this a thousand times," she said. She was staring at me hard, being much more forward and confrontational than she typically was.

"What did I do wrong?" I asked.

"You loved me too hard. I felt smothered and stopped feeling like a person around you."

"I wasn't trying to smother you. I just liked having you around."

"Juan, I'm seeing somebody else now."

Terror ripped through me. "Who?"

"Doesn't matter."

"What's his name?" I asked. I could feel the blood surging to my head. My vision was becoming strained.

"His name is T.J. He used to be a patient here."

"How can you do this?"

"Let go, Juan."

"I don't know how."

"Let go, Juan. I'm serious. Let go of me right now!"

I didn't realize I'd grabbed her arm. And when she demanded I let go, my grip tightened. I don't know why; it wasn't a conscious decision. As I squeezed, Flora yelled, her anger smashed her English into tiny little pebbles and it crumbled. She spat out swear words and threats in a fury of Tagalog.

"I'm sorry, Flora," I said, but I didn't let go of her. I knew once I let go, I'd never see her again.

Everyone in the cafeteria was watching when Flora smacked me. I felt dizzy and sick and confused. I tried to tie together the loose strings in my brain and form a thought. I tried not to die from the realization that I'd lost her.

She smacked me again, this time hard enough to break free from my grip. "Get help, Juan," Flora said, then left.

My hands covered my face to cloak my tears, but I couldn't contain my sobbing, and it became a whole body cry. An orderly helped me to my office, and I locked the door when he left. I cried until I became so dehydrated I was crying air. I lied there, on the floor, too empty to care about germs. I spotted a tear in my khaki pants; it was in the shape of a heart. With a black pen, I outlined it and added some anatomically correct veins and arteries in an intricate spider web pattern.

The human heart is complex.

Flora was the validation for my existence. I was a dependant leech latched on to her honey-colored skin. When Flora broke up with me, the possibility that she would no longer think of me was unbearable.

I'd made Flora fear me partly because at least I'd be on her mind, which was better than being forgotten by her.

She finally pushed me completely away. Soon, she'd forget about me all together. I needed to move forward with my life, but how could I move forward if I spent every second thinking about Flora? I struck my head on the linoleum floor, hoping Flora would ooze out.

"Dr. Salazar, Mr. Brody is waiting to see you," Sheila, the chain-smoking seal like nurse, announced over my speaker phone for the third time in ten minutes.

"Cancel all my appointments," I responded.

"What should I tell them?"

"Whatever."

"Do you need anything?" she asked.

"No, Sheila."

I spent three hours lying on my office floor, staring at a brown water mark on the Styrofoam ceiling. The water mark looked like a penis, a microphone, and then a knife. When it began to look like Flora's silhouette, I decided it was time to go home.

At home, I began drinking heavily. I sat at my piano and played a lonely song that sounded a lot like Flora's absence. I played it over and over until my hands were shaking too badly to continue. I sat on my Italian leather sofa with a bottle of Jack Daniels, and watched *The Wizard of Oz*. I'd seen the movie a couple hundred times. I liked it because I've related to the lion since the day I let my best friend, Tamara, be raped.

I continued drinking. I drank until I couldn't feel my feelings anymore, and sometime before the end of the movie, I passed out.

Skye

Flora had been over to check on me about three different times in the past two days, and every time I'd sent her home.

"I'm too tired for company," I'd say.

Flora would leave, and I'd slam more dope.

My body finally crashed sometime yesterday. I slept hard, but I'm not sure for how long. I couldn't decipher reality from dream.

Pain in my leg eventually woke me. My leg was blue. It felt like bees were living inside it. It was throbbing and burning and freezing, and there were thousands of bees attacking me with their painful little stingers.

I shook my limb until the color began to return. Fifteen minutes later, the stinging had calmed enough that I could limp to the kitchen and feed my starving body. After eating, I fell back asleep.

The next time I woke, my body needed more dope. I had no money, so I pawned my stereo. I scored a gram in Venice. I cooked a small shot, just enough to take the edge off. I wanted to be back at my apartment for my big blast, so that I could kick back and listen to the sounds of the planets in orbit while relaxing in peace. So, I took my score home and slammed a huge shot, but instead of it leading me into a nebulous calm, it created the desire for me to go see Dylan.

So, I did.

I found Dylan at his place. He'd just gotten out of the hospital. We were alone. Before I could tell him what I needed to say, he opened up to me. "Skye, I want to say something about the other night."

"Shh—" I said, pressing my finger to his lips.

At some point during my drug binge, I wrote a love song for Dylan. I wanted to sing it for him, but at the moment I didn't have it in me to do so. Eventually, I would. I'd sing it every day, as loud as I could, with as much heart as I could. And when my voice blew out, I'd use my last breath to tell Dylan how much I loved him, and it wouldn't matter if he said it back.

"But—" he started, but I stopped him again.

"Don't say a word, Dylan. Everything that happened is my fault. I'm sorry for everything, and I'm going to get clean for you."

And I meant it. I would quit. I had enough heroin to get me through the day, and then I'd be done forever. I'd said that a thousand times before, but this time I meant it.

Kimberly

"What are you doing to Tubby?" Jonathon asked me.

"Uh, I was just wrestling with him. Here, take him." I handed him his stupid doll.

Truth is I was rubbin' with his stupid doll. Since I was real little, I liked to tickle myself down there. I called it rubbin' cause that's what it was. I'd rub on the monkey bars at school, I'd rub on the edge of my mattress, and I'd rub on stuffed animals or my pillow. My favorite was to sit in the tub and turn the faucet on and let the water hit me down there. That wasn't really the same as rubbin' but it felt good.

Once, in second grade, I got caught rubbin' at school and was sent home. We were having recess inside cuz it was raining. My friends were playing Heads Up Seven Up, but I didn't feel like it. I played by myself with some dolls behind the coat rack. I found this really big, thick coat with a furry hood; it was Susie's coat. I put one of my dolls inside the hood to make a crib for her. The fur felt nice, and it made me want to put it between my legs. So I did. Mrs. Sniderson caught me, and she was mad. She called Mom. Mom told me it was a normal thing to do, but I should never do it with other people's stuff or where they could see because it was private. Thank goodness she didn't never tell Susie.

After I had my first period, I read a book about puberty, and it taught me about stuff like masturbation, but I still called it rubbin' because that's what it was. When I think back to the second grade, I get a little embarrassed about all that.

"Why were you wrestling with Tubby?" Jonathon asked.

"For exercise."

I was afraid Jonathon would tell Auntie Beth, she'd tell Mom, and then I'd be in trouble for using his stupid doll.

"You wanna wrestle?" Jonathon asked, and then he smacked me upside the head with a pillow. I grabbed a pillow and cracked him. We went back and forth, hittin' each other. We was laughin' and runnin' around and swingin' them pillows like crazy, and I swear it was the most fun I had in forever. Then, not before too long, one of the pillows exploded. It was like we was in one of them funny old black and white movies where the whole room is covered in feathers from a pillow fight. Feathers was flying around all over the place, and we couldn't stop laughing. And the more we laughed, the more them feathers flew around the room. And got me to thinkin' maybe birds are really happy and laugh a whole bunch, and maybe the laughing helps them fly.

But I only thought that for a few seconds before I realized how silly it was.

Jonathon and I eventually settled down, cleaned up the mess, and put all the feathers in a plastic grocery bag. I took the bag across to the park because I knew Mom would never see it there and also because I wanted to go see the flowers.

"Don't tell momma nuthin' about this," I said to Jonathon before leaving.

Dr. Juan Salazar

"I'm sorry. I'm sorry for harassing you, for scaring you, and causing you pain. I'm sorry for being a lousy lover and for being a freak. And I promise not to bother you anymore. You're the only good thing has ever happened to me. I'm grateful for our time together."

I was drunk, dialing Flora over and over, filling up her message service every time until the service cut me off. I'd call back, apologize for babbling, then babble some more.

Because of yesterday's drinking binge, I woke up today with a monster headache. So, I called in sick and started drinking again. Jack Daniels, straight from the bottle. The hair of the dog or whatever. I didn't take my meds, and with that, and the J.D., the freak in me was unleashed. I left Flora about a dozen messages as I polished off the liquor during another viewing of *The Wizard of Oz*.

After I ran out of booze, I decided to walk my drunken butt to the park across the street. I'd watched children play there for years, but I'd never actually gone there. Parks are breeding grounds for viral plagues, so I avoid them. But today I'd have welcomed a plague. The world could use a good viral cleansing, an accelerated natural selection period, and I'd be first in line.

The late spring air was thick with pollen, and it felt good on my face. The dense, gray clouds to the east appeared to be rolling away. Approaching the garden, my olfactory senses were massaged by the soft scent of spider orchids, tulips, and rosemary. The scents reminded me of the fresh flowers Gina always wore in her hair.

I lay down next to a bush with beautiful little flowers on it. I opened my mouth and let its fragrance wash over my tongue, soak through my body, and bleed into my veins. It was invigorating. I closed my eyes to focus on the aroma; the sun penetrated the thin red tissue of my eyelids, and I could see the blood inside them. When I opened my eyes, I noticed the flower's color was the same shade of ripe blood-red as the inside of my eyelids. The flower's color was so dense that it seemed ready to drip from its petals.

A black and yellow bumblebee buzzed around a rose on the next nearest bush. The bee explored its innards. I stuck my finger into the heart of a rose. It was soft and kind, and I took stole a petal and rolled it between my fingers, back and forth and around in circles. It was so vulnerable that I couldn't resist. I had to destroy it. I closed my hand and mashed it in my palm. For whatever reason, I found this exciting and became marginally aroused. I opened my hand and examined the petal's damp and cool viscera.

I took another petal from the flower. I opened my mouth, placed the petal on my tongue, and closed my mouth and eyes. It was cool with a bold taste, but it wasn't overwhelming. I breathed in deeply through my nose and let the petal sit on the lap of my tongue for a minute, and then I swallowed it. This beautiful flower, soon, its stem would wilt, its petals would curl into a tiny blood-red heart, the color would drain to brown, and the petals would flake off and die.

Everything worth loving eventually leaves me and dies.

The bee buzzed around my head. Annoyed, I swatted at it.

It stung me.

"Are you okay, mister?"

I turned to find a lovely young girl behind me. She was wrapped in a cloud of pink and yellow, a play skirt hemmed above her knees.

"I'm okay. I just got stung by a bee."

"You need to pick the stinger out. Then put an ice cube on it so it don't swell up, then put honey on it so it heals faster," said the girl with pigtails.

"Do you want me to pull it out?" she asked.

"Yes, please," I said.

She came toward me. Her knees were too large for her thin legs, and her gait was pigeon-toed.

"Show me," she said.

I gave her the underside of my wrist. She took my arm in her soft hands and massaged the underbelly of my wrist. Her touch was kind. "I see it. Okay, now close your eyes, and I'll pull it out."

"Okay." I pretended to close my eyes, but I was watching her. I inhaled as she got closer. The air was an intoxicating mixture of the rose's plumage and the sacred flower of a young girl.

She reeked of puberty.

She yanked it out. The pricking sensation felt good. I opened my eyes, and she proudly displayed the stinger between two long, thin fingers.

"Hold out your hand," she said. I did. She extended her hand toward mine. Tiny sun-stained hairs lay on the back of her perfect brown hand. She placed the stinger in my empty palm and smiled. It was the first good moment I'd had since Flora left me. This girl was a sign from God that loving was good, in any form. Maybe I was not a sinner; maybe the world was wrong about love, not I.

"Thank you."

"You're welcome. Put some ice on it when you can."

"Yes, ma'am. May I ask you your name?"

"I'm Kimberly. And I think I know you. Aren't you that doctor I saw at Brotman hospital?"

"I don't know. Am I?"

"Yeah, you're him. I was with my mom visiting a sick friend, and I saw you there, in the cafeteria. I'm good with faces."

"I guess you are. I'm Juan," I said. I extended my hand, and Kimberly shook it. "Where are your friends, Kimberly?"

"I came here alone."

"Your mother allows that?"

"Yeah, we don't live far."

"Sit down with me?" I asked.

"Why?"

"To talk. There's nothing else to do."

"I guess I could for a while," she responded. Kimberly sat down, picked a flower from the garden, and put it in her hair. It was so beautiful that it caused me to die a little bit.

"You have very long fingers. Do you play the piano?" I asked.

"No. Why?"

"Beautiful long fingers like yours are made for the piano."

"Really?" she asked. Then she waved her hand in front of her face to analyze it.

"I have a piano. Would you like to play it?"

"I don't know how."

"I can teach you."

"My mom wouldn't approve of me going to a stranger's house," Kimberly said; she was looking at me with curiosity, the same way Gina used to.

"But I'm not a stranger. I'm the doctor you saw from the hospital. Besides, I owe you a favor for helping me with the stinger… Hey, do you like pumpkin pie?"

"Duh. Who doesn't?"

"Good question. Well, I baked a fresh pie this morning." It was my first lie to her. Immediately, I felt guilty. "Well, I didn't actually bake

293

one. I bought it two days ago, but it's in the refrigerator, and it's really good."

"I don't know."

"You can call your mother from my apartment and tell her where you are."

"Umm, Doctor. You kinda smell."

"Juan. Please call me Juan."

"You smell, Juan."

"I know. It's kinda good, though. I mean, I didn't shower today because I called in sick from work so I could come to the park and lie with the roses, and I'm glad I did," I said.

"Really?"

"Yes. I love flowers."

"I come here all the time. Roses are my most favorite."

A bubble of rainwater fell on Kimberly's little nose. I'd been so consumed with Kimberly I hadn't noticed the storm moving in from the east.

"Come on, Kimberly. Let's go play the piano before we get soaked."

"Okay, but only for a short while."

"Deal."

It started raining harder, and we began to run. I tried to hold Kimberly's hand across the street.

"I'm ten. I'm old enough to walk myself across the street," Kimberly said and shook her hand free from mine. She was younger than I thought.

We made it to my place, but we got wet along the way. Kimberly's tiny puffy pubescent nipples were poking through her T-shirt. She took off her wet shoes; her toes were darker than most of her, and her little toenails had the remains of pink nail polish. I would have done just about anything to kiss her tiny wrinkled damp feet. Kimberly asked for the phone and called her mom. I feared her mother would make her leave, but she didn't answer, and Kimberly left a message.

I cut Kimberly a piece of pie; her manners were perfect. She unfolded a napkin and set it on her lap; she chewed with her mouth closed and said please when she asked for another piece. Like me, Kimberly ate the pie portion out of the crust and discarded the rest. We were much alike. The pie was rich and sweet, and afterward, I didn't feel the need to wash the dishes; I didn't even bother to wash my hands. I felt liberated from my compulsions. Only Flora had ever been able to take me to that place before.

"I need to be home for dinner soon," Kimberly said. "Can we play piano now?"

"Let's go," I said.

We sat on the piano bench, I showed her how to place her hands and taught her a simple progression. She nailed it in just a couple of tries.

"Will you play me something," she said.

"Okay." I played a nursery rhyme I thought she'd recognize. Kimberly sang along— "The itsy bitsy spider went up the water spout. blah blah blah. I'm not six, play something good." I laughed. She had moxie.

Inspired, for the first time in a long time, I broke out a song I wrote in college. Kimberly swayed from side to side as I played.

"I love it," she said after I finished.

Kimberly's praise was more special than anyone's had ever been.

"Teach me," she insisted.

"Well, you're not quite ready to learn that, but put your hands on top of mine, and you can feel it."

Kimberly reached over, but her short arms didn't reach my hands.

"If you sit between my legs it will work better."

"That's not proper."

"Suit yourself, but it's the only way you're gonna learn."

"Umm, okay, I guess you're right." Kimberly wedged her tiny behind between my wanting thighs, and her buttocks kissed the underside of my hardness. Kimberly didn't react negatively to it. This was me, finally accepting who I was. This would become her coronation into adulthood. She wanted it as badly as I.

We toyed around with the keys. Kimberly was a natural. I knew she felt the flow of the music through my hands. Then, I slid my hands off the piano. I placed one hand on her thigh, just below the hem of her skirt. I placed my other hand on the nape of her neck, and slowly slid it down to her breast. Kimberly's hard nipple pressed back against my fingertips.

Then, I felt her breath tighten. "Stop it!" she said, jumping up.

"What's wrong? I thought—"

Kimberly ran out the door.

"Come back," I yelled after her.

Kimberly loved me; I could feel it. This was real, and now it was gone before I had it. Kimberly ran from me because that's what society has conditioned her to do. I couldn't live this life anymore.

I washed my hands eleven times. I stripped naked and took a scalding hot shower; the burning pain was necessary. To distract myself from the pain, I thought about Tamara and how, when we were kids, I ruined her life by leaving her with those drunken college perverts. I thought about all those that I'd hurt.

The scalding water ran over me, and I scrubbed hard, but I couldn't get clean; I'd never be clean.

After eleven minutes, I got out of the shower and gently toweled off. I caught a glimpse of myself in the mirror. I was falling apart. I looked unkempt and disgusting. I shaved my face, plucked my eyebrows, trimmed my nose hairs, shaved my head, and yanked the hair from my ears.

I put on my best suit, walked to the roof of my apartment complex, and prepared to jump.

Just before I leapt, I had a vision of Flora, dressed all in white. She looked perfect.

Flora

I expected a splat or thud, a loud cry, anything other than the muffled *oomph* that was barely a whisper louder than silence.

As I approached his body, the stench of released bowels overwhelmed me. I looked down on the body that had been Juan's; I didn't know what to feel.

I was much calmer than a person should be under such circumstances. I was void of feelings, like an eggshell after it's cracked and emptied. It took half a second to form any thought; my first one was—

Not again.

Juan's chest slowly rose and fell. His body was trying to hang on. I called 911, but I knew it was too late.

Six inches away from Juan's mouth lay something pink. I stared at it until I realized what it was. It was the tip of his tongue; he'd bitten it off in the fall. The rest of his tongue hung limply from the corner of his mouth, blood pooling around his open mouth. A few feet away, ants were collecting in the growing puddle.

This morning when I got home from T.J.'s, I found my answering service filled to capacity with frightening messages from Juan. I headed to his place to give him one final warning before I pressed charges for harassment and got a restraining order.

I caught sight of Juan mid-fall. The impact was directly on his head; there was an audible snap as his head bent backwards against his spine and nearly separated from his body. His body folded over and he collapsed into a limp pile of twisted flesh. Instinctively, I ran to him, to hopefully save him. When I saw the left side of his head was missing, my thoughts fell silent. His left side had no forehead, no eyebrow, and no eye. There was just an empty cavity where his face should've been. Some clumped brain matter rested on the sidewalk as wet streams of blood ran through the smaller pieces of brain and around the bigger chunks. The pool of blood around Juan grew, ran to the soles of my shoes, and trickled into the cracks of the sidewalk. It filled the cracks and spilled onto the green grass.

Juan's remaining eye was still open. It didn't look sad or happy or confused or even real. It looked like an eye plucked from a doll and stuck into his head. Juan wasn't a person now. He was a pile of flesh with stolen doll eyes; he was a bleeding sore that stained my shoes.

I stood in stillness and silence, staring.

The rise and fall of Juan's chest stopped. I waited for the ensuing chaos to begin. I listened for the cries of women and children. There was nothing; nobody cries for people like Juan. I didn't even cry. This was the second time I'd witnessed the death of someone I'd loved—the first being the reason I fled from the Philippines to America.

Eventually, someone must have called 911, because an ambulance came. I told them what I knew, and then I left, my bloody footprints coloring the sidewalk in crimson red with each step.

And I wondered if my tears would come.

June 2003

Skye

In the ten days since I'd promised Dylan I'd get sober, the longest I stayed straight was forty-eight hours. When withdrawal kicked in, when the goose bumps and skin crawls began, when my stomach began to turn, getting high seemed like a better idea than suffering.

Yesterday, Dylan recommended, for the millionth time, that I go to rehab.

Fuck rehab.

The therapists will crack my head open and spill the ugly crap all over the examination table. They'll run my brain through their mental strainer in an attempt to take out the painful parts, and then they'll cram what's left back inside me. They'll pull my heart out of my chest and show it to me, like that cult leader from *Indiana Jones and the Temple of Doom*, so I can see all its wretched flaws. I don't want that. Rehab is bullshit! My pain can't be taken out of me, and even if it could be, where the hell would leave me? *Who would I be without my pain and anger?*

"We should go to rehab. Together," Dylan offered.

"I'm not doing rehab," I said. The twelve steps don't work. The meetings are just an excuse for addicts to whine about their pathetic lives. If anything, the meetings themselves become the addiction. Once an addict, always and addict.

"Maybe rehab will be a positive surprise to you," Dylan argued.

"No."

"I want you to quit," Dylan said. He knew I was still using. My pinprick-sized pupils gave away I was blasted out of my mind.

"No rehab."

"Then you're going to detox at home. I'll help you. If I did it, you can," he said, smiling. I wanted to beat smile off his face.

"Dylan, I respect you stopped using, but your little addiction is child's play compared to mine."

"I didn't know it was a contest," he said.

"I don't think you can help me, Dylan."

"I'm willing to try. Are you?"

"I don't know. I guess so," I said, terrified. The truth be told, I wasn't ready. But I'd swallow my fears and take a shot if it meant keeping Dylan in my life.

"Great. I know you can do this," Dylan said, and then he hugged and kissed me. Then, he sat back and examined me. "Did I give you this skirt?" he asked.

"No, you've never given me a skirt."

"Oh. Well, I should have given it to you. You look beautiful in it."

"I love you, Dylan."

"I love you, too," Dylan replied, casually, as if he had said it a thousand times before. He hadn't; this was the first time. And with those words, something within me came unglued, and for the first time, I felt compelled to open my closet and bare my skeletons.

Dylan

Skye teared up, and I knew something big was about to happen. She started talking, her voice quivering, and her cadence fast. When she started talking, I knew instantly that she was finally about to tell me about her father. She talked and I listened, never once interrupting, just staring into her eyes, and trying to comfort her.

Skye's story was more horrific than anything I could have imagined. I sat and listened stoically, but inside I was shocked and a bit afraid. After going through all of that trauma, what made me believe I could possibly help her? After she finished, I couldn't think of one helpful thing to say. So, instead of giving her empty words, I held her. I stroked her. I ran my fingers from the top of her head down to the end of her.

"We're going to make it," I said.

Skye smiled. "Are you sure you want to do this? I mean, this is going to be hell. I'm going to call you all kinds of names, lie to you, and probably hit you. Do you really want to go through all that?"

"Yes."

"You understand that I'm pretty fucked up, damaged goods, right?. I'll never be totally normal."

"Normal people are boring," I said.

Skye smiled. "I want to try to get sober, Dylan. For the both of us. But I'm scared."

I kissed her, we made love, and I told Skye I loved her over and over.

Skye

The next two days were the two most pain filled days of my life. I'd felt physical hell that I never before could have imagined. Living on the streets, I've seen people stabbed, beaten, burned, and none of that was even close to being as physically torturous as what I felt in these two days.

More than once the idea that death would be less horrific, had crossed my mind.

Dylan was by my side the entire time. He was amazing. I hit him, called him every name in the book, and threatened him. It had to be far worse for him than he had anticipated and I wondered if he was having second thoughts. I was grateful to have him, but it didn't change the fact that I was dying; I really just wanted him to go away, so that I could make a call and get high again. Had I the strength, I would have hit him in the head with a bat and knocked him unconscious so that I could escape. I loved Dylan with every ounce of me, but I'd gladly have traded him in for a singular hit; that's how bad it was.

My skin crawled every time anything touched me. When I tried to shower, the water felt like tiny razor blades on my skin. In bed, I felt bugs crawling all over me. My sweat pooled on the mattress. I was on fire, but my hands and feet were frozen. The slightest whiff of food made me vomit, and every sound was amplified a thousand-fold inside my head like war.

And this felt like vacation compared to what the first two days had been.

Dylan came in the room with a Valium. He tried to hug me. I pushed him away.

"Why'd you do that?" Dylan asked.

"My skin is crawling like fuck. Don't touch me."

"Okay."

"Why don't you make yourself useful and go score me some smack."

"You're joking, right?"

"Yeah, sure. Whatever. Thanks for the Valium."

"It's going to be okay, Skye."

"Fuck off!" I yelled.

After I swallowed the Valium, Dylan handed me some Doloxene.

I wanted to sleep, but my body wouldn't let me. I was hot and cold, sweaty and shaking and shivering. Bugs crawled all over me. Bugs everywhere. My clothes felt wrong so I took them off. Eventually, the Valium helped me fall asleep. Briefly. An hour later, my painful body was trying to wake me. I tried desperately to hold onto sleep to avoid the pain. I could avoid it if I just stayed asleep. *I just won't open my eyes.*

While squeezing my eyes shut as hard as I could, my stomach

started to rumble. I held my breath to prevent the unavoidable. It didn't work. I began dry heaving.

"Are you okay?" Dylan asked. His question must have been rhetorical. "Get some clothes on, Skye. You're shivering."

Dylan grabbed the T-shirt I'd cast on the floor and threw it over my shoulders. The shirt, coated with my sweat, felt cold and disgusting.

My dry heaves continued all night. I never fell back to sleep.

The next morning, I found myself slumped over the basin in the corner of the room throwing up the Saltines I ate at some point. I didn't remember when, in fact, I didn't remember getting up and going to the basin. I'd been hallucinating and blacking out on and off, all night. Most of my blackouts lasted only an hour or so, but there was one 12 hour period when everything was lost. I have no idea what happened but I'm sure I was a horrific bitch to Dylan.

Dylan woke and came over to wipe the sweat from my back. His touch felt good. It was the first time anything felt good, and I felt I'd gotten a brief reprieve from hell.

"Skye, I'm proud of you. You're probably almost through this. A couple more days, and it should be over," he said, handing me a couple pills to swallow.

"I want a whack."

"Your body wants it, but you don't."

"How the fuck do you think you know what I want?"

"I don't. I'm sorry," he said.

"I dreamt I was in a warehouse full of smack and picks. I ran around grabbing smack and hitting up every vein I could find. It was the first time in the past week I felt decent."

"It's going to get better."

I threw up; this time, liquid came out. Along with the pills I'd just taken. Then, I felt it trying to come out the other end. I spent the next ninety minutes shitting blood, pissing fire, vomiting blood, sweating acid, and wishing for death.

Later, when Dylan went to the bathroom, I snuck a few extra Valium, chasing them with two shots of 151. I still couldn't sleep, but the alcohol and Valium eased my pain. But a few hours later, a horrible current of electricity started pumping through my head. My brain went sideways on me, and my head was pulsating. I began hallucinating again and was seriously convinced that some microscopic alien life form was breeding inside me.

"Dylan, I need help," I said softly. My voice was too hoarse from yelling to speak up. Even if I could physically yell, at this point, the vibration of sound might have killed me. "Dylan," I whispered again.

He didn't respond. He was sleeping. Had I the energy, I would have gotten out of bed and ingested a container of Drano. Not to kill myself, but to kill the alien life breeding inside me. I was a danger to myself and to Dylan.

Ron

I completed Orlando's *trust earning* Fresno job and elected to pay myself seven hundred and fifty dollars from the ten grand I brought back to him. That amount seemed like it was a fair cut without going so low I'd disrespect myself, as Orlando had warned. Thankfully, Orlando seemed okay with my decision.

I passed the test. But they weren't through with me just yet. Orlando had Zantini give me a second, more difficult test. It was starting to seem as though Orlando was using me as an errand boy and had no real interest in my original proposal.

"My friend bet an undercard featherweight fight at the MGM Grand," Zantini said to me last month. Even though Orlando was the boss, all jobs went through Zantini in Vegas; Orlando's name was no good there. "Tony Fanilli's a heavy favorite over Bernard Taylor. You're going to bet on Taylor and get Fanilli to take a third-round dive."

The bet was twenty-five grand. The payoff for a third-round knockout would be one hundred thirty-five large. Zantini paid me two thousand, and he gave me eighty-five hundred to bribe Fanilli—half paid before the fight and half after.

I smelled danger. There were too many variables and way too many things that could go wrong. If Vegas bookies discovered I was connected to Orlando, they wouldn't take the bet, and Orlando would probably kill me. If Fanilli backstabbed me and didn't take the dive, I was instructed to break his legs. That or worse would happen to me. There was absolutely no way I could break Fanilli's legs; I wasn't the violent type. Besides, Fanilli would kick my ass. If Fanilli double crossed me, like Bruce Willis had Ving Rhames in *Pulp Fiction*, my plan was to flee to San Francisco and convince Amber to meet. She didn't realize it, but I'd endangered her and her daughter just by associating myself with these sick people. Once you cross these people, they don't stop coming for you until they've gotten everyone you care about.

I was in deep with Orlando and his gang. I was scared shitless and starting to regret my decision to go to him in the first place, but I was too involved to back out.

The long drive to Vegas probably would've been four hours of mental anguish and paranoia were it not for the stifling desert heat and the lack of a functional air conditioner in my car. To make matters worse, there's not one damned interesting thing to see between the two cities—except for giant thermometer in Baker that confirms it really is as hot as it feels. The thermometer read 112 degrees. My sweat was sweating.

As I passed the monument, I had a rare stroke of brilliance. To increase the odds of Fanilli cooperating with the dive, I doubled the offer on the back end. Then, I wagered my two grand on a third-round knockout to come up with the extra money. If he took the dive, I'd win enough to bank two thousand and pay Fanilli his share. My new proposal would make it stupid for Fanilli to fuck me because, as the favorite to win, an eighty-five hundred dollar bet on himself would yield only four grand more—less than what I'd give him. I don't know why Zantini didn't offer him more money in the first place. Maybe he was testing my intelligence, or maybe he just hadn't seen the double cross in *Pulp Fiction.*

Anyway, Fanilli went down in the *first* round, two rounds too early, and I think I saw my own ghost.

"Five. Six. Seven," the ref counted.

"Get up, you idiot!" I said.

Fanilli got up, but I could tell he was out cold on his feet. He was wobbling and then stumbled and fell as he approached his opponent. I couldn't believe the ref didn't stop the fight. Maybe he was on the take, too. Actually, come to think of it, he probably was.

Miraculously, Fanilli made it to the end of the round. He came to the corner, and his trainer started yelling all kinds of fighter speak, trying to motivate him.

"Just stay away. Don't let him hit you this round," I yelled, fearful he'd go down early.

Fanilli played defense the entire second round; he was exhausted, but he made it through the round without getting knocked out. At the start of the third round, he came out of his corner, threw a windmill, whiffed, and collapsed without being hit. He went down for the count. Fanilli didn't take a dive; he got his ass kicked.

I left money in an envelope in his locker. I cashed in my betting ticket and bought Kimberly a giant stuffed white tiger. It cost me half my winnings, but I'd be rich soon enough.

Back in Los Angeles, Zantini and Orlando were pleased with my passing of the second test. They were ready for my master plan.

I sat and listened as Zantini dictated the rules of the big night. "You fuck this up, you don't know me, you never met me, you never heard of Orlando," he said. "You rat me out, fughetaboutit," he added, sliding two fingers across his throat—a threatening gesture I've seen in every mob movie.

I tried not to wet myself, but I'm fairly sure a little got away from me.

"Now disappear," Zantini said. That was the last thing he ever said to me. I never saw him or Orlando again.

It was time to go to work and execute the biggest score of my life.

The director called a wrap, and everyone left the set.

It was the final week of shooting. The movie was shit. Maria Orlando had movie-star looks, but only porn-star acting abilities.

"See you tomorrow, Ron," Maria said.

What?

Maria had never used my name before. Why now? What made today special? Did she know? Was I being set up?

There were new faces on set today. Who were they? Spies? Cops? Feds? I considered blowing off the job and leaving town. But I couldn't. Orlando would have me found and killed.

"Bye, Maria. You were great today!" I said.

While packing up, I made sure all the film was unloaded from the cameras. I was told by the Hammer, who was told by Jew Boy, who was told by Zantini that Mr. Orlando would be pissed if anything ruined his daughter's work of art. I didn't have the guts to tell him his daughter's work didn't qualify as art.

We finished and started heading home. I made certain the security camera got a clear shot of me leaving. Then, I walked around the building, put on my Ronnie Reagan mask—an idea I stole from *Point Break*—and entered through the props room back door, which I'd unlocked during lunch. I went to Stage 39 and unlocked the storage room and waited while the guards armed the alarm and changed shifts. Then, I disarmed it. Disarming alarms was one of the few legitimate criminal talents I possessed.

I sat in the pitch-black storage room with nothing to do but wait and think. My thoughts were lousy company. I thought about Amber. I thought about the irony of my return to crime being my most noble act.

It was only a few hours, but the isolation made it feel like days. I thought about prison and how I tried to pass time without thinking. Eventually, my imagination always found the memory of black man on top of my mom.

Orlando's truck arrived on schedule around three a.m., and his men unloaded large props onto a mechanical dolly and drove it inside. They'd unload the props in the prop room and drive past the camera room, and I'd open the door and put a camera inside the small trunk of the dolly. They'd drive the dolly back into the truck, take out the camera, and load more props.

Wash, rinse, repeat.

They did this until we'd confiscated more than a million dollars worth of cameras. The guards outside, who were watching the loading and unloading, never suspected. When Orlando's men brought in the next-to-last batch of props, I squeezed into the dolly's trunk, and I climbed out inside the truck.

Tomorrow, when the guards reviewed the security tapes to determine who stole the cameras, they'd see President Reagan sneaking in through an unattended door.

It was simple. I couldn't believe it was that simple.

Skye

Three days later, the pain and the anxiety hadn't gotten too much better. Dylan tried everything to ease my suffering, but addicts who are in as deep as I rarely make a full recovery, and part of that is because of how physically impossible it is to survive the withdraw.

As much as anything, I was amazed that Dylan was still sticking around. When this was over, and as soon as I could stop hating him for the hell he was putting me through, I would reward him and eternally love him like no woman had ever loved a man before.

I smoked a cigarette. I smoked another. I smoked and smoked and smoked. But no matter how much I smoked, it wasn't enough. My withdrawal pains lessened some, but they were still there, and I felt empty. I needed to get fucked up. I had nothing.

I needed something.

Anything.

Dylan wouldn't give me any more Valium. Dylan wouldn't give me anything. I hated Dylan for that. I needed something to fill my emptiness.

I grabbed some short hairs on the back of my neck. I pulled. The pain filled me. I needed more. I pulled harder and harder until some hair came out. Stinging pain shot down my spine. I grabbed more short hairs, a bigger clump. I pulled slow and hard and felt the roots, one by one, coming out of the back of my neck. It hurt. And the pain, which was something, was better than nothing. I grabbed more hairs. I pulled. Pain. They came out. A couple blood droplets rolled down the back of my neck.

I was crying when Dylan came in.

"What's wrong," he asked.

I'm a drug addicted, human landfill of emotional pain.

"I need Valium."

Dylan put his arms around me and squeezed. I was sweaty and sticky and hot, and I didn't want him hugging me, so I didn't hug back. Dylan ran his hands up and down my back.

"You're bleeding, Skye."

"I know."

September 2003
T.J.

I only had thirty-five dollars to my name, so I stopped at McDonald's for a cheeseburger to fill up, so that later, on my date with Flora, I could save money by eating something light.

I was at Flora's for our third date, she was upstairs getting beautiful. The day I was discharged from the hospital, I asked her out before even leaving the premises. She said no, and I was dejected, but about a month later, she actually called me, and we went out. But on our date I still had the cast on, so it limited us. Today, my cast was removed, which opened the window of possibility for sex. At least a sliver.

However, I worried that if I somehow miraculously ended up in bed with Flora, that my hairy leg would disgust her. When the cast was cut off, my leg looked like a skinny Wookie. Or a Chia Pet. *Chi-chi-chi-chia!*

I was having anxiety about my hairy leg when my stomach ulcers started acting up from the cheeseburger. After the chicken-suit episode in

1999, I should have known better than to ever eat something from a fast food joint. My stomach was grumbling; the grumblings became rumblings, and I knew I was in trouble.

"You almost ready?" I yelled up the stairs, politely, but with urgency.

"You're early. Give me about fifteen," Flora said.

I had a little time to spare, so, I went to her guest bathroom and resolved my problem quickly. I flushed. A few sprays of air freshener, and I figured that the problem was solved. But then the water level in the toilet began to rise rather than fall. The toilet was clogged, and I had to react quickly to avoid disaster. As the water approached the toilet's rim, I flipped the lid off the water tank and yanked the chain to stop the water. The chain snapped.

This is bad.

A flash flood was inevitable. Water rolled over the toilet rim onto the tips of my shoes. I backed up about five feet to the bathroom door, and the water followed me. Then, much to my horror, one of my droppings cusped the rim, fell to the slick tile, and surfed the wave toward me. Reacting like Alex Rodriguez on a routine grounder to short, I scooped it up and underhand tossed it back at the toilet in one continuous and impressive athletic motion.

Swish!

Now damage control. I grabbed two bath towels off the rack and threw them on the floor to stop the dirty water before it could soil the living room rug. I soaked up as much water as the two towels would hold, then grabbed two more and two more after that.

My cuffs were soaked with shit water, and my shoes were soaked through to my socks. *Squish, squash, squish* with each step. I washed my hands, took off my shirt and socks, and began blow drying them. I knew Flora would be ready soon, so I could only do a half-assed job. I put on my half-dry clothes, threw Flora's wet towels over her shower door, sprayed air freshener on my cuffs, and tried to look relaxed, sitting on the couch.

I still was unable to flush the toilet, so my leavings were still in it. There was nothing I could do about it unless I somehow got some time alone in there after our date. I had no idea how I could make that happen. If Flora went in the bathroom before I could get in there, I'd just have to deny everything because I'm fairly certain clogging a girl's toilet, before you've been intimate, is a deal breaker. I hoped, if she did beat me in there, that her wet nasty face towels would dry before she used them.

I should tell her; it's the right thing to do.

"You ready to go?" Flora asked, coming out of her bedroom.

"I sure am. You look amazing, Flora."

"Duh," she replied and then giggled. "Hey, were you blow drying something? I swear I heard the blow dryer."

"Umm, ahh, yeah. I was blow drying my hair."

"Oh. That's weird—why didn't you do that at home? Anyway, I hope you didn't use the toilet. It's not working."

"Nope!"

Now that Flora knew I was in her bathroom I couldn't deny that I'd been the one to leave the turd in her toilet. I had to get back in there!

Flora

We stepped out of the car and the dense smell of diesel fumes, fried foods and children's vomit assaulted me.

T.J. and I moved hand-in-hand along the dirt walkway in search of an appealing snack while the carnival serenaded us with a choir of lights and sounds. Candy red, disco white, emerald green, and citrus yellow flashed off the canopies of the food tents and carnival rides. Our ears were filled with mismatching carnival sounds: rock music from the salt and pepper shakers, rap music from the roller coaster, cheers from the carnival games, and clinks and clanks of all the other rides.

I hadn't been to a carnival in years. I hoped the noise and smells and excitement would be effective in distracting me from thinking about Juan. Recently, I'd been doing everything I could to keep my mind and body occupied so I didn't have time to think about Juan.

"Can we go on the Ferris wheel?" I asked.

"Sure," T.J. said. He went to get tickets while I waited in line.

T.J. returned, chewing through a balloon of pink cotton candy.

"I'm excited. I haven't been on a Ferris wheel in years!" I said

We climbed aboard; the ride started, and we rose high above the bright lights and loud music, and everything below us got smaller. When we were at the peak of the wheel, the ride stopped, and momentum caused our car to teeter.

"It's beautiful up here," I said.

"Look," T.J. said, pointing with his sticky, pink fingers. The quarter moon was perched atop the ocean's horizon, making the water sparkle like glitter.

"Beautiful," I replied.

T.J. looked at me, paused, then smiled. I kissed his lips, and he blushed. A light breeze parted my hair, and I shivered.

"Cold?" T.J. asked.

"A little."

T.J. put his arm around my shoulder, resting his hand on the back of my neck with his index finger touching a spot behind my ear that almost never gets touched. It felt nice.

T.J.

After my pre-date cheeseburger, and the carnival activities, I still had two dollars and eleven cents left. Every second spent around Flora was absolutely thrilling, and I was sad our date was coming to an end as I drove her home. I wished I had more money so I could ask her to go out for a drink.

"I had a great time. Let's do it again soon?" I asked, pulling to the curb outside her house.

"I had fun, too. Hey, it's only eleven. Do you want to come in for a—"

"Yes!" I felt Flora liked me a little, but I never expected her to invite me in. I had already resigned to the fact she would go home alone, find the turd, and our relationship would be over forever. This was a fantastic change in events.

"Okay, great. Pull into my driveway."

And I did.

And we had a drink.

And then we had sex!

"Holy Good Lord! What just happened?!" I exclaimed, very excited, elated, exhausted, baffled, confused, scared, happy, and drenched. I felt euphoricasized, a new adjective for a new feeling.

"Sorry, I—that's embarrassing," Flora said, panting.

"Don't apologize. That was the sexiest freaking thing I've ever lived through, heard about, or seen. And to think I had something to do with it just blows my mind!" *I'm the biggest stud in the world! I'm the Hank*

Aaron of the bedroom! I'd just made her squirt like a super soaker! "You know, I read about this in *Playboy*, but I thought it was fiction."

Flora wiped some of her juice off my face. "Well, it's real."

"How often does this happen?" I asked.

"Umm, well, I've only ever slept with five guys."

"But how often does *THIS* happen?"

"Every time I touch myself."

"Wow. How about with men?"

She was blushing. I made a girl blush with my sexual prowess! "You're the first guy that's made me do that," she said.

I'm Joe Namath! I'm Wilt Chamberlain! I am T.J.!

"Wow! Do I get a prize for that?"

"Stop talking. You're ruining our moment," she said.

I had ten thousand more questions to ask. I'd only been with three women before Flora, and, consequently, I had the sexual confidence of a clam. This experience turned me into a Great White.

"My girlfriend is a female ejaculator," I said, not meaning to say it out loud.

"You want me to be your girlfriend?"

"Well… kinda."

"Kinda?"

"Yes, I want you to be my girlfriend. Badly."

"Good. Then you're my boyfriend. My new boyfriend, T.J. Tacey Jonco Martini."

Flora said my name, and for the first time ever, I liked the way it sounded. Flora was beautiful and smart, and she ejaculated, and now she was officially my first real girlfriend.

"Can I tell my friends you're a female ejaculator?"

"No."

"Please?"

"No," she said, firmly.

"K."

"T.J.—you want to do it again?"

Flora asked me! A woman had never asked me to do it.

I began kissing her to get my libido warmed up, but then I

realized I was still aroused: no refractory period. I'd always needed at least a fifteen-minute intermission regardless of what porn I watched while loving myself.

I kissed Flora deeply. I put my hand under her wet butt and gave it a firm squeeze and then put myself inside her. We had amazing sex for many minutes. It was intense and athletic. My lungs were burning, and my heart was pounding so hard I feared it would shoot up my esophagus and out my mouth.

"Oh, God!" Flora said.

"Am I hurting you?"

"Ahhh! Ahhh! Ahhhhhh!" she screamed, and then—

Swoosh!

"Awesome!" I yelled.

When Flora climaxes, every muscle in her vagina contracts simultaneously. The contraction ejects everything in there, including me, as well as a pint of juice. I've heard men describe women's scent in a foul way like, *her pussy smells like fish*. I had never experienced that, and I thought it was a horrible thing to say. But she definitely smelled like fish. In fact, her juices smelled like a whole freaking ocean.

And I loved it!

Flora's wonderful and arousing aroma followed me into the bathroom. But I still had a semi-erection, and ended up getting quite a bit of urine on the wall and the floor. By the time I got back in bed, Flora was sleeping. Her nose was crinkled and her mouth was turned up, almost like she was smiling, and I wondered what she was dreaming. She had the sheet tucked under the crease where her light brown breasts swelled from her torso, and pushed up from each breast was a dark-brown button nipple. I stared at her for as long as I could, but the physical nature of the studly sex I'd just given her had taken a lot out of me. My eyes were heavy, and I ended up falling asleep. It was the best sleep of my life...

"What if she can't conceive?" I asked Mr. Elephant. He didn't respond, so I asked the Mr. Giraffe.

"Hmm. Good point. Maybe we should allow four of every animal on the ship, just in case" said Mr. Giraffe.

"We won't be able to accommodate that many animals," replied Mr. Elephant. His voice was much squeakier than I thought an elephant's would be.

"T.J.!" said Mrs. Kangaroo. She was jumping up and down behind the elephant, trying to get my attention.

"Maybe we need two arks," Mr. Giraffe said.

"T.J.!" Mrs. Kangaroo yelled again. "T.J.! You're talking in your sleep."

"Huh?" I woke up. It took me a second to remember where I was.

"You were talking crazy," Flora said. "What were you dreaming about?"

"Ohh. I was dreaming you and I were the human couple on Noah's Ark before the big flood."

"Then wouldn't it be called T.J.'s ark?" Flora asked.

"Yeah. I guess it would. Weird dream. I think that ridiculously great sex we had threw my whole system out of whack."

"Maybe if we do it again, it will get you straight again."

"You think?"

"Can't hurt to try."

I grabbed Flora around the waist; she giggled and squirmed and slipped out of my grasp like a wet bar of soap. She rolled across the bed and shot me a seductive grin as if to say, *come and get me.* I did. I wrapped my scrawny arms around her. Flora kissed my lips. I felt a little self-conscious about my mid-morning breath, but Flora kissed me with such passion I was able to let go of my sexual insecurities. Again we had sex, and again there was screaming and multiple spraying orgasms.

Cue the marching band's fight song.

Cue the harps and angelic choir.

"We're going to have to invest in some new linens if we keep this up," Flora said, using the pronoun we. "I really like you, T.J."

"I really like you too. Flora, I should tell you that I'm not like a super-smooth guy or anything—"

"No, really?"

"You've developed quite a sophisticated American sarcastic wit," I said, and Flora laughed. "I don't always say the right thing, I'm rarely the cool guy, I'm not poetic, athletic, or smart, and I'm a bit of a klutz—"

"Jeez. What the heck am I doing with a guy like you?" Flora asked.

"I just want you to know all this from the beginning. That way you won't be disappointed later when you find out what a dork I am."

"You're right. You are a dork. You're a big dorky geeky clumsy man with a disproportionately skinny and hairy right leg."

"I was hoping you wouldn't notice that."

"How could I not notice? I have friction burns all over my inner thigh from it."

"Sorry."

"Your skinny hairy leg is sexy, just like the rest of you, you big dork."

It was the perfect thing for her to say.

"Goodnight, Flora."

"Goodnight, T.J."

Flora laid her head on my chest and fell asleep in seconds, and I faded to sleep with her...

"Sir, how'll we feed everyone?" Mr. Octopus asked me.

"First of all," I said, addressing Mr. Octopus and his bride, "I don't recall inviting you on board. You guys can swim. Get off my ark!"

Still, Mr. Octopus made a valid point. How would I feed all the animals? Would Mr. Lion get hungry and eat Mr. and Mrs. Gazelle? Would Mrs. Coyote eat Mr. and Mrs. Cat? Would I eat Mrs. Cow? What about the excrement? Mr. Elephant alone eliminates more than two hundred pounds of feces a day. How would we clean it all?

Poop. Poop. *Poop!*

"Holy crap!" I awoke.

Flora

I woke from the first earth-shattering wet dream I'd had in years to find T.J. had left me. He hadn't even left a note.

I was sad, maybe slightly heartbroken. When the reality of Juan's death hit me, I felt like some giant parasite had eaten all my organs, including the part of the brain that controls emotion. Juan and I had been broken up forever, and I never loved him. But since his suicide, I'd felt hollow and detached. T.J. was something of a mental repairman for all my dilapidated parts. And I don't think he even had a clue.

About a month after rejecting T.J., I was feeling down and lonely. I called him up, and I'm glad I did. T.J. made me laugh a lot, and laughing felt healthy and healing;. When I was immersed in a good laugh, I felt like I was purging my body of all the dreg holding me down. I didn't tell T.J.

about Juan and his suicide because I didn't want to have to talk about it. I just wanted to move past it like it never even happened, fill up the empty spots with something new. When T.J. entered me last night, I felt full, all patched up. But now he's gone. T.J. was the last person in the world I'd expect to run off like that.

I went downstairs to get a glass of water.

I was surprised and delighted to find him. "T.J., what are you doing?" T.J. was naked in my living room with an armload of my bathroom towels.

"I'm just, you know, tidying the place up a bit," he said.

Skye

I'd gotten sober. I'd been sober for three months.

My butt was comfortably wedged in the couch's contoured furrow T.J. and Dylan had worked so hard to form. My feet were propped on a secondhand glass coffee table, which was tinted with various-colored rings from the bottoms of glasses left there too long. A Samuel Adams mug, which had been sitting on the table since the first time I'd been to their place, had apparently sealed itself to the glass.

I had the radio tuned to Indy 103.1. One of my favorite songs played, *Your Birthday Present* by The Good Life. I sat in the classic Al Bundy position, one hand on the clicker, the other comfortably down my pants. I had the television muted, and the muted MTV video looked ridiculous. Half-naked women sat in the back seat of a bouncing car driven by some rapper dude, one handed. His other hand held a gun. Then, the video cut to a pool party scene with half naked women. I took a drag off the cigarette rested between my lips, removed my hand from my pants, and stubbed the cherry out. I was bored out of my mind.

Boredom is a loaded gun sticking in my ribs, urging me to buy drugs.

Fight it, Skye.

I changed stations. I smoked another cigarette. I changed stations.

The television flickered lights like lasers at a rave. Click, click, click. I changed channels looking for something to distract me. Nothing worked. I wanted to get high.

Fight it.

Jane Says came on the radio. I shut off the television and danced.

> *Jane says,*
> *Have you seen my wig around?*
> *I feel naked without it.*
> *She knows*
> *They all want her to go*
> *But that's okay man—she don't like them anyway.*
> *Jane says,*
> *I'm going away to Spain when I get my money saved*
> *I'm gonna start tomorrow*
> *I'm gonna kick tomorrow*

I tilted my head back, spread my arms out, and danced in circles. See Jane dance, see Jane use drugs, see Jane die.

Jane Says was written by *Jane's Addiction*. The band's name, and the song, come from a friend to the band, Jane, whom was a lover of music and someone they loved, but whom could never beat her habit, and ultimately died of an overdose.

I understood Jane. I practically was Jane.

The music filled my head, but it didn't replace my boredom. My desire to get high was never completely gone, but today it was worse than usual. I was on the tightrope of sobriety, and I was losing my balance.

I called Dylan. I needed Dylan on the couch with me to restore my balance.

No answer.

I lit another cigarette.

I called T.J.

No answer.

I called Flora. Nothing.

Looking through the small inventory of phone numbers in my cell phone, I came to Amber in the D section because I had her saved as Dylan's Amber. We'd met a few times, and I didn't know her well, but I knew Dylan trusted her, and I was short on friends of my own.

"Hi, Amber. It's Skye, Dylan's friend." I wondered why I said friend rather than girlfriend.

"I know it's you. I have you programmed in my phone," she said, which made me more at ease about calling her.

"So, how've you been?" I asked.

"Good. You?"

"I'm good. So, what are you up to?"

"On my way to pick up Kimberly from school. You?"

"Umm, not a whole lot I guess, just bored."

"Oh," Amber said, followed by a heartbeat of silence. "Did you need something?"

"Umm, actually, well—I don't know how to say this so I'll just come out with it. I'm alone at Dylan's, and I'm, umm, I'm falling off the wagon."

"Don't do it, Skye. Dylan would be so upset. Look, stay put. I'll pick up Kimberly and drop her off with Beth's dads, and then I'll be over. Can you hang in there for half an hour?"

"I honestly don't know," I said. I'm sure I sounded pathetic, but I was telling the truth. I was scared.

"I'm assuming you called Dylan."

"Yeah."

"Give me one second. I'm going to see if Beth can get out of work and pick up the kids. I'll call you right back."

Amber hung up.

I sat back down, changed the channel. It was *Permanent Midnight*. Ben Stiller was shooting up. I changed the channel: drugs were in the news. I changed stations again, a "this is your brain on drugs" commercial was on. My phone rang.

"Amber?"

"I'll be there in ten minutes. Sit tight."

"Thank you, Amber."

Ten minutes I'd survive. I turned up the TV's volume and kept flipping. *Pulp Fiction* was on HBO. I watched. Harvey Keitel, The Wolf, instructed John Travolta and Samuel Jackson how to clean up the blood, brain, and guts from the back seat of their car before Tarantino's wife, Bunny, got home. By the time they'd finished cleaning, and Tarantino was hosing them off in the backyard, Amber arrived. Mission accomplished.

"Hey, doll," Amber said with a big smile on her face. She checked my pupils, and gave me a strong hug.

"Thanks for coming," I said.

"Don't mention it. I have a surprise for you, Skye. It's exactly what you need right now." I hoped she brought a beach ball-sized bag of junk and the world's biggest spoon to cook it in. "Grab an overnight bag and pack three days' worth of clothes."

316

"Huh?" I asked.

"I said, go grab an over—"

"I heard you. Why?"

"We're going away for a few days!"

"Oh, thanks, Amber, but I can't." I considered the possibility she might be selfishly using my desperation to get in my pants. I immediately felt like a jerk for thinking that.

"Why? Are you working?" she asked.

"No."

"Got important plans?"

"No."

"Playing a gig?"

"No."

"Then you can go."

"But, I—"

"No buts. You need to get your mind off things, drugs specifically, so we're going," Amber said.

"What about your daughter?"

"Taken care of. Beth's going to watch her."

"What about work?"

"I'm a stripper. I think they'll survive without me. Anyway, I need the time off."

"But we barely know each other. Why would you do all this for me?" It was a legitimate question.

"For one, you're a friend of Dylan, and he and I have been through a lot. And two, it's not just for you—you'll understand better when we're there."

"Umm—"

"Stop trying to think of an excuse and go pack. I left Dylan a message about where we're going."

"And where's that?"

"I can't tell you. If I tell you, you won't want to go."

"Oh, sounds great."

"That came out wrong. You'll think it sounds like a dumb idea, but when we get there, trust me, it's exactly what you need."

"Tell me."

"Just get your bag."

"What should I pack?" I asked.

"Couple pairs of shorts, bathing suit, tank tops, T-shirts, a sweatshirt, and athletic shoes."

"Are we doing a triathlon?"

"And bring your guitar," Amber said.

"How much money do I need?"

"A few bucks. Hurry up. We need to beat the 405's four-hour rush hour."

I packed, and in less than twenty minutes we were on the road. We headed north on the 405 then took the 5 to the 99. We could've been going to San Francisco or Big Sur. San Francisco was the easiest city in America to get drugs. Big Sur was exploding with psychedelic mind-altering drugs as well as spiritual, existential mind-fuck experiences.

Why would she take me there?

North of the grapevine, we got into industrial farming areas. Miles and miles and miles of garlic, cotton, and apples. The garlic scent was so strong I could taste it. I wanted to eat it. I wanted to fill my emptiness with garlic. Lots and lots of garlic.

Amber told me a story about a horse in Northern Florida where she grew up, or something. Her eyes got a little glassy, and I think she was trying to open up to me, but I hadn't heard much of what she'd said. I wasn't interested; there isn't a more self-involved person in the world than a junkie who's itching for a fix. I just wanted to get high. A resourceful junkie like me could find junk in less than fifteen minutes when we stopped for gas and food, and I feared I would.

I turned on the radio, and we sang a few oldies together.

"Dylan told me about your beautiful voice, but I had no idea," Amber said. "I can't wait to hear you play your own songs tonight."

Singing kept my mind busy for a little while, but soon I was obsessing over drugs again. To distract myself, I decided I'd ask Amber personal questions about being a lesbian, and the challenges it presented to her as a mother. But I didn't know how to start the conversation tactfully, so I didn't. The desire to ask her grew inside me mile after mile. Eventually, my desire to ask, was strong on it's own to distract my thoughts enough to whittle away at my massive craving.

We passed through Fresno, stayed on the 99, and it hit me.

"Yosemite? We're going to Yosemite!"

"It's about time you figured it out."

"I've never been there."

"You'll love it."

I doubted I'd be able to score smack in Yosemite. But I could always try.

Amber

It was ten-thirty by the time we got close to Yosemite, and my thoughts were still in Los Angeles with Kimberly, Beth, and oddly, Ron.

Despite my mild homesickness, it was good to get away from my life for a little while. Tyrone was up my ass for money, and there was no way to escape him. At least if Kimberly and Beth were staying at Beth's parents, then I could feel that everyone was safe. But I felt like Tyrone's re-emergence was a product of bad Karma from the year I spent slinging drugs to addicts. Even if it wasn't, this penance was necessary. I hoped God was watching.

We entered the long tunnel that cuts through the mountain. The air was damp, and I was getting claustrophobic, the tunnel was so long and narrow that it made me fell like the mountain would cave in on us and bury us for all eternity.

"Cover your eyes, Skye."

"Why?"

"Because on the other side of this tunnel is one of the most breathtaking views on earth, and I want you to see it all at once."

Skye closed her eyes. I looked at her. Beneath the yellow glow of the tunnel lighting, she looked leathery and worn.

"Can I look yet?"

"Not yet. Not yet. Not yet....Okay, hold it... now!"

Skye opened her eyes, and her face lit up when she saw the view. "Wow! It's stunning! It's a big beautiful mirage. Wow! I just want to eat it up and keep it inside me!"

"Nice description," I said.

Ron

I tasted blood. I touched my lip, it was still bleeding. Above me, the yellow plaster ceiling moved in a circular pattern like water down a toilet. There were red stains in the corner of the ceiling. Could it be blood?

I got up and went to the breadbox-sized window. I grabbed its bars and peered through. Palm trees were being blown by a heavy wind, and I pressed my face between the bars to feel the fresh air. Unfortunately, the garbage bin below the window spoiled the romance. It felt much too familiar.

Yesterday, I got "laid off" by the studio for "financial reasons." But my per diem was less than what the producers kept in their petty cash jar. Finances weren't the reason they let me go, but they had no evidence to pin the robbery on me, so getting rid of me was the way they chose to deal with the ex-con.

If I'd gotten the money from Orlando, I wouldn't care about being laid off, but I didn't have it yet, and getting laid off made me fell like a loser. After, I went to Tammie's, a bar in Mar Vista, and got wasted. I'm not sure exactly when things went from a yelling match to a fist fight, but it was sometime after I'd lost two hundred dollars over five successive games of pool. After the last game, I called the guy and his friend's *fathead fucking losers who had nothing better to do than play pool all night in a shitty-ass redneck bar with their reject dumbass friends*. A beating ensued, and by the time the cops arrived, I was laying on the floor bleeding. I was the only one still present to arrest.

While in the holding cell, I feared my prior record would get me stuck behind bars longer than I should be for a bar fight. But worse than that, when Orlando learned I'd been arrested, he'd likely put even more distance between us. The odds of me getting the money were getting slimmer.

After all the time I'd spent behind bars in my life, I couldn't stand being boxed up. At home, I always kept my doors and windows open; I needed to feel the air on my face as a reminder of my freedom. I loved my freedom; I valued my freedom, and now, because I'd been careless, it was at risk.

As usual, I fucked up everything.

Amber

I was eating a bowl of oatmeal when Skye came over from her tent. "Good morning," she said.

"How'd you sleep?" I asked.

"Not too well. I couldn't fall asleep without a mattress, and this morning the sun turned my tent into a toaster oven."

"Sorry to hear. I have an air mattress in my tent. You can have it tonight."

"That's sweet, Amber, but you've already done too much for me. I couldn't take it. You know, I don't think I ever realized how much I dream in a night. Last night, I kept waking up every five minutes, so I remember a lot of them. I had some weird dreams."

"Like what?"

"I dreamed Dylan and I overdosed together, died, and went to hell, where we popped pills with Marilyn Monroe and Elvis and shot dope with Kurt Cobain. I even gave Marilyn an enema to relieve constipation."

"That's weird. But kinda cool."

"No kidding. Hey, where's the bathroom?"

I pointed to a tree. Skye frowned and hiked off. An eagle flew over the top of the tree, circled, and descended. Its shadow ran over me, and as the eagle descended, it's shadow got smaller and smaller until it met its shadow on the ground where it landed, about fifty yards from me. I called Skye, but by the time she emerged, the eagle had taken off. Its shadow growing as it lifted.

"The air out here is so—"

"Refreshing?" I said, finishing Skye's sentence.

"Yeah. I've gotten so used to the smog in Los Angeles, I've stopped noticing it. Now that it isn't here, it's like, wow, so this is what air is supposed to be like," Skye said.

There was only one cloud; it looked like Abraham Lincoln in his stovepipe hat. The light breeze carried Abe's cloud in front of the sun, which tinted Abe yellowish-red. The breeze continued, carrying the cloud past the sun, and I tried to stare at the naked sun, just to see if I could.

"Let's go, doll," Skye said, rubbing SPF 45 into her chalk-white skin.

"You're cheery this morning," I said.

"The air makes me feel good."

A gob of sun block sat on Skye's cheekbone. I rubbed it in with my thumb. Her face didn't feel as soft as it should for a girl her age.

I grabbed my backpack, and together we made our way to the Yosemite Falls. There was nothing to hear but our footsteps, which were calming. We passed between magnificent redwoods and aromatic eucalyptus then stomped over fallen sequoia branches. There were countless sequoias thousands of years old standing next to baby saplings. In another thousand years, many of these trees would remain, long after my grandkids' grandkids had passed. We weaved through the family of trees to where the mountain began to ascend. Skye and I began our climb, athletic and strong, women in nature, free and resilient. Five minutes later I was drenched in sweat and could feel the air thinning with each of my breaths. I tried to keep my breathing quiet so Skye wouldn't notice. I wanted her to think I was in better physical condition than she because I was drug free.

"We got any more water?" Skye asked at the mile marker.

"No, you drank both bottles on the last break. If you carried your own pack, we'd still have some."

"I would've brought a backpack had someone told me where we were going before we left the house."

"Good point."

My throat was parched, too, and my stomach was growling. We were inadequately prepared.

"Can we stop for a smoke break? I'm going to have a heart attack unless I get a cigarette."

I acted annoyed, but my legs were heavy and my feet were screaming, and I wanted a break too. I couldn't decide whether the balls of my feet or the bottoms of my heels felt worse, but I knew if I dared to take off my shoes and spread my toes apart, the screaming ache would be relentless. I considered suggesting, for Skye's sake, that we turn back, but I knew if we did, we'd have accomplished nothing, and we'd be more depressed than we were before we came here.

I was contemplating our situation when an elderly couple passed us. It was so hot I wanted to strip naked, but the elderly couple was dressed in matching teal sweatsuits.

Why are old people always cold?

A minute later, we got up and picked up our pace in an attempt to overtake the elderly couple. We climbed and climbed, tired, sweaty, fatigued, and growing weaker by the minute, but we kept fighting. We rounded a blind corner and the magnificent Yosemite falls were in sight.

Our final destination was only two hundred yards away—straight up. We stopped, sucked in a breath of air, looked at each other in an expression of team unity, and went for it. We grunted and clawed our way up. It took serious sweat and determination, and thought it nearly killed us both, we made it. At the top, we found the teal-wearing elderly couple seated on a bench overlooking the falls. They looked relaxed and comfortable, like they were out for a Sunday stroll, while Skye and I were struggling to catch our breath.

"Wow! The falls are unbelievable," Skye said. The view was beautiful and powerful. The two mountain peaks formed a V through which a river ran before falling off the mountain. It took millions of years for the river to carve V into the mountain, and in another million years, the water would steal away more earth, flattening it entirely.

"What do you think will end the world? A hole in the ozone layer or another ice age?" I asked.

"That's a depressingly random question considering the beautiful scene I'm looking at right now."

"Maybe. Yeah, I guess so. But what do you think?"

"Neither. Nuclear war will end it," Skye said.

"I don't even want to think about that."

"You brought it up," Skye said.

"After life ends, do you think the earth will replenish? Do you think evolution will start all over again?" I asked.

"Earth begat life once already, why not again? I'd guess yes," Skye said. "It's kind of weird we're even talking about this."

"Yeah, it is," I said. "But you can't help contemplating our existence and mortality when looking at the grandeur of this place."

"Maybe Earth has gone through this cycle of life hundreds of times already," Skye suggested.

"Maybe."

"I was here for the last cycle," joked the elderly man in teal. "And let me tell you, this whole universe, all the planets, the stars, everything, it's all nothing but a fleck of dust on a carbonation bubble in one of God's beers. Someday, the whole thing is just going to pop," he said and smiled. "So, what does it really matter what happens to little old Earth?"

"Really? You think? I always suspected the universe was a soap sud in the supreme being's bathtub," Skye said.

"You suspected wrong," the old man laughed.

The elderly lady smiled at me. I smiled back. Her hair was thin and gray, and her smile was wrinkled. The elderly man walked to the fence that read *do not cross*; he glanced back at his wife then folded his body to crawl under it. Then he stood to take a picture of the falls.

His wife laughed. "He's showing off for you girls."

"I'm impressed," Skye replied.

"Arnold, you're an idiot. You're going to slip and fall."

"Stop being a nag, Helen."

Arnold, the old man, could've gotten just as good of a picture from behind the fence. He went under the fence to agitate his life long bride. I guess you do those kinds of things after a hundred years of marriage.

Trees grew out at an angle from the mountain, which continued upwards, touching the sky. I would've been happy to watch one of Yosemite's sequoias grow from seedling to maturity. The crystal clear waterfall flying off the mountain seemed so pure; maybe this was the last clean place in the world. I tried to focus on a single drop of water as it ran over the cliff and fell. I counted until it hit bottom. It took exactly eleven seconds. Then I wondered how long it would take me to hit bottom, and an odd, uncomfortable feeling came over me. I worried I might jump. I didn't want to jump; I had no intention of jumping, but I worried some odd impulse might overtake my body and toss me off the mountain. Sometimes I get like that; I lose control of my internal impulses.

"Look how the rock looks when the water runs over it. See where hole in the rock is?" Skye pointed at the top of the falls. "The water runs over it and retreats the same as the ocean's tide. It makes the rock look like it's swelling and collapsing, almost like it's breathing."

Skye was right. "Maybe that's the wounded arrhythmic pulse of Yosemite. Maybe it is breathing. Maybe the rock's alive. I mean, what defines life anyway?"

"I don't know," She responded.

Skye was a cool, artistic girl who happened to be a little crazy—in ways we were a lot alike. Together, Skye and I, high above the Earth, with only twelve inches of rock separating us from a deadly fall, were forced to trust each other. Skye could push me; I could push her. Who'd know? It's amazing how often we blindly trust in one another.

Skye

What if I pushed Amber off the mountain right now?

She'd fall, scream, curse. *Splat!* She'd be a dark stain on a jagged rock. Those are the kinds of thoughts going through my head. Amber put herself in a position where she had to trust me with her life, and that made me feel good about myself for some reason.

Amber and I soaked up the view, and some rest, for a couple hours, and then began our hike down. The giant waterfall was one of the most fascinating things I'd ever seen. I understood why people travel thousands of miles to see it. The sound of the water rushing off the mountain and crashing into rocks below was pacifying, and at the same time, its grandness was terrifying. It reminded me of the song *Momentary Lapse of Reason* by Pink Floyd—soothing soft music but lyrically frightening.

"Amber, thanks so much for bringing me here."

"You're welcome."

In took a while to get down, and Amber commented that the descent after a climb is always anti-climatic. Back at the campsite, we got a fire going and grilled chicken while watching the sun drop, kiss the mountain tops, and disappear behind them, leaving a hazy red glow behind.

After dinner, we drove to the famed Glacier Point to sleep above the world and under the stars. The road was long, winding, foggy, steep, and narrow. There were no street lights, and it got dark in a hurry. Amber zipped up the mountain, gripping the edges of the curved road. I gripped my seat so tightly I nearly tore through the pleather. The steep angle at which we ascended made me feel as if we were chasing after the full moon. The road was too dark and foggy to see the two deer that jumped in front of us, and we were on top of them before Amber was able to jerk the wheel. Our car fishtailed. Amber turned the wheel again, and we fishtailed the other way. I was halfway through a *Hail Mary* before I realized we hadn't fallen off the mountain. I'm not Catholic, or religious at all, but I became religious in that moment. I guess it's like they say, *there's no atheists in a foxhole.*

By the time we finally got to the top of the mountain, my stomach was in a knot the size of the famous Half Dome. I had to use a toilet, but the only one was an outhouse that stood alone in the middle of the dark night. I had no choice but to use it. It was horrific inside, and I feared something would crawl out of the toilet and attack me. I hovered, held my breath, did my business, and I swear I could've counted to at least four before I heard it hit anything. It was surely the deepest well of human waste in the entire world. Running out of oxygen, I finished quickly, cleaned myself, and then burst out, gasping for the fresh Yosemite air.

Amber's plan was for us to hike to the lookout area, lay down, and observe the stars. I don't think she'd thought it out very well; the path to get to the lookout was completely dark, and we didn't have a flashlight. We stumbled over the quarter-mile path, but we arrived without injury.

"You first, rookie," Amber said at the foot of the lookout.

I took ten short steps, and with each step, the view below became exponentially more beautiful. Below us, a thousand campfires flickered like fireflies on a summer's night; we were surrounded on all sides by wilderness, and the sky was brightly lit by a trillion flittering stars. We were entirely isolated, far away from the stresses of real life, and completely removed from my world of drugs. There at the edge of the world, Amber lay down two blankets, and we nestled between them. I was tired, and for once, I'd earned my fatigue; it wasn't a result of abuse.

I wanted to lay there on the edge of the world forever. I felt I could fall into a sleep so deep that my dream would be a destination rather than a transitory phase I passed through on my way to the next day. I closed my eyes, took in a breath, and at that moment, I became aware of Amber's soft arm touching my forearm. Her skin felt nice, and a faint desire to kiss Amber came over me, but I didn't act on it. Together, we lay side by side silently. Relaxed and satisfied with my day, I let my imagination explore.

"What would you do if you saw an alien spaceship?" I asked.

"Wave."

"What if it landed right here?"

"I guess I'd say hello," Amber said.

"What if the aliens told you Earth wasn't real. It was just a tiny experiment being conducted by something greater, and the experiment was going to be over in a week, and our planet would be destroyed? What would you do? Who would you tell?"

"Umm, Skye, you just summarized *The Hitchhiker's Guide to the Galaxy*."

"Really?"

"Yes, really."

"Sounds like a cool book," I responded.

Amber was great to talk to; she was a creative thinker. Society resists original thinkers like her. Historically, most geniuses were misunderstood, mocked, and persecuted for their ideas in their own time. Gandhi, Galileo, and Jesus come to mind. Sometimes I feel misunderstood. I'm not a genius, and I'm not trying to compare myself to Gandhi or Jesus, but I can relate to the loneliness that comes with being misunderstood. I wonder if those guys ever turned to drugs to kill their inner loneliness. Probably not. Dylan was the only person who understood me and helped numb the loneliness. Amber understood that Dylan and I had something special, and I was close to throwing it all away with one stupid slip up. Amber was saving me, and I loved her for it, but ultimately what she was doing would be in vain.

No matter what I do, I'll always be an addict. On Glacier Point, I'm far away from reality. There in Yosemite, four hundred miles from my problems in Los Angeles, I had no desire to taste a drug, no desire to lash out in anger. I'm far from the home where my father abused me and the streets where my baby died. But I can't live on Glacier Point. I'll have to return to my real life as a recovering junkie. At least, in living the junkie life, I know how I'll die, which gives me one less thing I have to live in fear of. But maybe misery and fear are the whole point of existence; maybe earth is a reality television disaster God created for amusement.

Maybe God is just like the rest of us—a bored reality television junkie.

My leg fell asleep, and I tried to adjust my position. I accidentally kicked a stone off the cliff; it bounced repeatedly off the slanted mountain, chipping at its surface and taking pieces away with it.

I'm that stone. I deform those I come in contact with and take them down with me in my fall. I won't change. Fifty years from now, I'll still sit when I pee, I'll still smell the same when I sweat, my fingers will still understand the sexual desires of a guitar, and I'll still be a substance abuser who, as a child, was whored out by her father.

"BRO-KEN," I said.

"What?"

"I'm broken, Amber. I'm broken, and everyone who tries to put me back together ends up cutting themselves on shards of me. I appreciate you are trying to help me, but you shouldn't bother with me."

"Broken, huh?"

"Yeah. Broken," I replied.

"Well, I've got news, love. We're all broken. We've got broken hearts, we come from broken homes, we've got broken bodies, broken dreams, broken governments, broken faith, broken memories. We're all broken people living broken lives in a broken world. Life isn't easy. Nobody gets through it without scars. I've got mine. So you've got a little drug problem, whatever. Your problems are only as big as you make them."

"You can't say that. You haven't been where I have."

"No, I haven't, but I've lived, and anyone who's lived has been broken."

"Some of us have been battered more than others."

"Yeah, I know. For example, have you ever heard of Jim MacLaren?" Amber asked.

"Jim who?"

"Jim MacLaren."

"No."

"Jim was a six-foot-five, three hundred pound football player at Yale. One day, he was on his motorcycle on his way to his girlfriend's, and he got smacked by a forty-ton bus—"

"I don't need to hear some inspirational survival story, Amber."

"Yes you do. You need to know that you're not the only one who's had hurdles to overcome; so don't interrupt me. Anyway, Jim was found dead on the scene. The police even chalk-lined where his body had fallen. Eight days later, he woke up in a hospital missing half his left leg. He didn't remember the accident and didn't realize he was lucky to be alive. He was depressed about his leg. He developed a cocaine habit to cope—"

"Oh, Jesus—here we go. And how do you know about this guy? You don't exactly seem like a big football fan."

"I heard his interview on Oprah," she said, which made me laugh.

"Eventually, Jim was able to get off the drugs. He fought back, became a tri-athlete, and competed in the Iron Man. He beat eighty percent of the two-legged athletes. Ten years after his first accident, in the middle of a triathlon, Jim got hit by a truck. It broke his neck and turned him into a quadriplegic—"

"Holy shit. What are the odds of that happening twice?"

"Jim started doing blow again, only now he was so pathetic he needed someone else to shovel the shit into his nose. He felt he had nothing to live for and was content to do coke until his heart exploded—"

"I can relate to that," I said.

328

"That's bullshit, Skye! You've got Dylan, and you've got great friends, and you've got all this beauty surrounding you." Amber threw her hands up in the air then spun around in a circle as if to show me something I didn't see. "And Jim knew learned that his self-pity was bullshit, too, so he beat it. Jim fought his addiction. He got his second PhD, and now he tours the country to help troubled youth. After an event he spoke at, Senator John Kerry approached him and said it was inspiring a man could be such a motivational personality while confined to a wheelchair. Jim turned to the Senator and said to him, *'Don't kid yourself. We're all in wheelchairs.'* Those are words to live by."

"Is a true story?"

"Are you suggesting that Oprah's a fake?" she asked. This time we both laughed.

"Well, Jim what's-his-face is a stronger person than me."

"Maybe he is. But you're missing the point. The point is we're all in wheelchairs. We're all broken. We all need to help ourselves and help each other. You're wheelchair is drug addiction."

"I guess."

"You definitely aren't the first drug addict in the history of the world. Others have been where you are, and they've gotten well. You can get well, too, but the first thing you've got to do is stop pitying yourself. Stop being a victim.

"Maybe I do pity myself, but sometimes that's about all I've got the strength to do."

"Fair enough. But you're going to get well, and I'm going to help."

"Why do you even care?" I asked.

"Who said I do?" she asked then winked.

"Most of my life, I've felt alone and unwanted. I appreciate what you're doing." I felt my eyes welling up, like I might cry.

"You're making too big a deal of it. I'm just practicing to fill Oprah's chair one day," Amber said, trying to keep a straight face. She held her face ridged for as long as she could, but it yielded to a smile.

I started laughing. Amber did, too. My laugh echoed inside me and came out of me feeling like music. It must've been contagious because Amber let out a hearty belly laugh and a bit of a snort, which made us laugh even harder. I wasn't sure why I was laughing, but it felt wonderful. It was and the kind of beautiful moment I'd think about ten years from this and smile.

I wished I could bottle my laughter and use it later, whenever I wanted, to help glue my broken pieces back together.

November 2004
Flora

We got word, from the Philippines, that my dad was sick. So, without telling me, T.J. sold his baseball cards to some guy named Kelly who wanted to buy them for his girlfriend's kid, named Jonathon. T.J. used the money to buy us tickets to the Philippines. It was the kindest thing anyone had ever done for me. However, I wasn't ready to go back home, and when T.J. presented me with the tickets, a cold tsunami of fear and guilt washed over me.

It was a fifteen-hour flight to Cebu, Philippines. I had the window seat. I laid my head on T.J.'s bony right shoulder. His round belly would've been more comfortable, but I couldn't contort my body to get my head there. Regardless, the amount of Valium I'd ingested would've been enough to put an elephant to sleep, maybe two elephants. And I needed it; my brain was so wired with anxiety that I felt as though I'd never sleep again.

Landing was exhilarating. We bounced a little when we hit the runway. T.J. squeezed my hand. Once we were safely stopped, he relaxed, but my turbulent heart was not prepared to deal with my family and the inevitable confrontation with my past.

We took a two hour bus ride to Maya, which was brutally hot. The landscape was plush green. I'd nearly forgotten how beautiful the Philippines are. I'd also forgotten the intolerable humidity. In Maya, I suggested we take a boat to Malapascua Island for a short stop off before going to my father's home.

"Isn't your dad expecting us soon?" T.J. asked.

"It'll be okay to stop," I said. I was stalling. I needed more time to get my head straight.

As is typical, I got my way with T.J., and we went to the island.

"This place is so beautiful. It's like movie. What's the name of that movie?" T.J. asked.

"Umm—"

"*The Beach*," he said. "This reminds me of *The Beach*. I love the scene where Leonardo DiCaprio stabs the shark in the head. And that little Italian girl was smokin' hot. Great movie."

330

"Yeah, good movie, but the girl was French, and the movie was filmed in Thailand."

"Well, whatever. It reminds me of this place. Exotic."

The beaches on Malapascua are clean, pure, quiet, and completely unlike the beaches of Los Angeles. Here, there are no billboards for cell phones or fast food chains, and there are no cigarette butts rolling in with the waves. They don't treat the sand like it's the world's biggest ashtray. Today, like every day in the Philippines, the beach air was thick. The sunshine reflected off the ocean's small ripples which made it look like the ocean was glazed with millions of sparkling, diamonds. Kids playfully splashed around, and adults basked in the sun.

When I was a child, my family went to Malapascua once every couple of years for a short vacation; that's all we could afford. On vacation, we never ate out; we stayed at the cheapest place we could find, and we didn't do anything that wasn't free. Still, I remember those trips as the happiest times of my life. I suppose, at my young age, life had yet to desensitize me to simple pleasures.

Hand in hand, T.J. and I stepped ankle deep into the water; it was perfect, a comfortable temperature neither cool nor warm: the exact temperature where you get that warm tingle that you only get when standing within six inches away from your new lover.

T.J. pointed at our reflection in the ocean water. "Is the water here always so calm?" T.J. asked.

"Yeah, there's hardly ever any waves. I think it's because of all the surrounding islands, but I'm not sure."

We waded up to our knees and then our thighs. In Los Angeles, when you get waste deep, the cold water sends an electric current of shock through your genitals that moves into the belly, up the torso, and into the head and arms that causes them to wildly flail out of control. *Oooo! Oooo, oooo!*

"I can't believe how pleasant the water is. I'd be freezing my balls off in the Pacific right now," T.J. said.

"This is the Pacific, dorko."

T.J. laughed at himself. He'd done a lot more of that recently—he'd learned to laugh at the silly things he said and did rather than getting red-faced and embarrassed. I like to think I had something to do with his transformation.

I kissed T.J. on the cheek and said thank you, maybe for the first time since he told me about the trip. He was pleased with himself for the sacrifice he made to bring me here. He didn't tell me he sold his baseball cards, but I knew he had.

In the past, I've always discouraged people from doing anything nice for me. I don't like favors. When someone does something kind, they're rewarded with the feeling of martyrdom while the recipient of the deed is left with a noose around the neck. The martyr always has one hand on the loose end of the noose, ready to tighten it. *Remember when I did thing for you? Remember? You owe me.* A favor never goes without mentioning. I wanted to believe T.J. was above this, but if he was, he would be the first in the history of the world.

We started walking out of the water. I could've stayed in the surf all day, but I couldn't put off the inevitable; I had to go face my father. On our way back to the beach, a couple young children caught sight of the white boy, T.J., and made him the target of their horseplay. They splashed him and giggled. T.J. laughed and splashed back. I joined in the splash fight, and before I knew it, T.J. was picking up kids and throwing them in the ocean. We spent another half an hour playing, and splashing. It was refreshing and inspiring. So inspiring, in fact, that after playing with the kids, we walked down the beach to a rocky area, and with nobody else in sight, we made love.

We'd spent so much time at the beach, the day was starting to end. I had successfully put off the visit to my dad for nearly the entire day. After making love, we got dressed and made the trip to my dad's. I swear my leg didn't stop twitching the entire way.

"Hey, Daddy," I said when we walked in.

My dad took me in his arms and hugged me. Then he let me go and pinched my nose, just like he did when I was a little kid. Daddy's always been a nose pincher. He was always pinching and pulling and trying to elongate our noses to be more like white women's. He was so fanatical about noses that, on New Year's Eve, when the clock struck midnight, he'd have my sisters and I pinch our noses and jump in the air, hoping in the new year our noses would grow longer and our bodies taller. After all these years, I still jump and pinch at midnight on New Year's Eve.

"I so happy you're here," Daddy said, lying in bed. He hugged me again. I wasn't any more comfortable hugging him now than I was ten years ago.

"It's been a long time Cackoy, Daddy," I said. We called him Cackoy because of his love of *sabong*, which is cock fighting. Mother swore he loved his cocks more than his own children, and when she got mad at him, she'd put a knife to a cock's throat and threaten to kill it.

It was obvious Daddy was ill. He wasn't sick enough that he was going to die immediately, but it was very possible that this visit to the Philippines could be my last visit with him. So,, I need to relish every moment, and try to make this visit count. I don't want to be one of those people with regrets about my relationship with my father. I'd let him pinch away at my nose, and I'd giggle accordingly. I'd hug him firmly even though it felt awkward. I'd play the role of the beloved long-lost daughter to the father who has missed her for so long. Some of my feelings would be real and some contrived, but I'd be convincing.

We spent the evening bedside my father. My dad talked in his broken English to be polite. However, if T.J. went to the bathroom or stepped out, my Dad would revert to Tagalog. My Tagalog had crumbled under the weight of my American English, and we were able to communicate more efficiently in English.

"Can you gets me a beer, Buena?" he asked. Dad nicknamed me Buena, which meant good-luck girl. I never felt like good luck to anyone, especially my family.

"You shouldn't be drinking, Cackoy."

"Just one."

"Fine." T.J. came with me to the kitchen. "Hey, T.J., would you run down to the market and get some chicken? I'm going to make chicken tinolang manok for

dinner."

"Umm, how do I get to the market?"

"Just tell the tricycle driver to take you to the market. They know where it is."

"You want me to ride a tricycle there?"

"A tricycle is a motorcycle with a sidecar. That's how we get around here. I told you all this before."

"Oh, yeah. Maybe after the market, I'll go to the bar and sing karaoke with those hooba hooba stripper girls you told me about.

"Knock yourself out." T.J. knew I needed some alone time with Daddy. What he didn't know is I didn't really want the alone time.

I kissed T.J. goodbye, grabbed a San Miguel, and gave the beer to Dad. He wrapped his lips around it. Dad's face looked old to me, partially because I hadn't seen him in almost seven years, and partially because he was ill.

T.J. wasn't gone two minutes when Daddy brought up the inevitable. "Buena, You remember when you little brother, Deang, pill you bed with seaweeds to get you back for pulling down his shorts in pront of girl he likes?" Daddy asked. He still did the Filipino thing of mixing the P sound with the F sound like I used to.

"Yeah, I remember." I could barely remember Deang's face. It's funny how the memory selectively erodes.

It was early in January of 1997, and we were celebrating *Sinulog*, the Filipino celebration of Santo Niño, the baby Jesus. We spent all day at the parade and went home for a big dinner. I sat at the main table with my father, my mother, and my sisters Inez, Meela, and Ate Joida.

Our live-in cousins sat at a small table outside. Though they are family, they didn't have our financial security; so, in exchange for a place to live and food to eat, they worked as our servants. This is common where I'm from; in the Philippines, you either have servants or you are one.

Mother was yelling for my thirteen-year-old brother, Deang, to come down for dinner. Mother, a staunch Catholic, wouldn't allow us to eat until everyone sat to say grace. Mother sent cousin Elmie to get him. Elmie returned and said Deang's door was locked and he wasn't responding. Ate Joida, Inez, Meela, Deang, and I all shared a room and slept together on a giant mattress. We had a lock for the room, but it was pointless because our parents had a key. Though they rarely used it, just knowing they had it was usually enough to scare us from doing anything we shouldn't be.

"I'll go get him," Mother said; agitated, she marched upstairs. Meela, our nosey twelve-year-old sister, followed closely.

Mother knocked three times, but Deang didn't answer. So, she put the key in the lock and opened the door. As reported later by Meela, Mother found her only son lying on his back, headphones blaring 'evil American rapper music' in his ears so loud Mother could hear it. Deang had a towel under his butt, his feet were propped up on the wall, his eyes were shut, and he was ramming a carrot stick in and out of himself.

"Deang!" my mother shrieked, at the top of her lungs. We all heard her from downstairs, and I knew that her world had just turned upside down.

Deang's music was so loud that he still couldn't hear her. So, to stop Deang's horrible mortal sin against his own body, Mother put one hand over her eyes, approached Deang, and shook him. Deang reflexively jerked the vegetable out of his body and simultaneously yanked the bed sheet over himself, thus launching his walkman into orbit, which hit Mother in the face and broke her nose. In Deang's hand, was the carrot stick.

334

Half of it.

After six long hours in the waiting room, a nurse finally put Deang on a gurney and took him through the swinging doors. We waited behind with dozens of injured people and other families. There was moaning and blood and people doubled over, hugging themselves and trying to contain their pain. One guy was impaled with a fire poker that went under his collarbone and out the other side just above his shoulder blade, and even he had to wait half an hour. Healthcare, in the Philippines, or any other third world country, is not to be coveted.

It didn't take them long to get the remainder of the carrot out of Deang; they sent him home that night. He was physically okay but mentally wrecked. My sisters and I vowed never to make fun of Deang about it. I knew I'd never be able to enjoy carrot sticks, but that was a small price to pay compared to the humiliating hell Deang would live.

We knew that life at home would be uncomfortable for a while, but Mother took mortification to a new level on the very first night. She invited Father Miranda over for dinner. It seemed like an awkward time for company, but I assumed she thought company would be a welcomed distraction. I assumed wrong.

At dinner, Mother set a plate of carrot sticks in front of Deang. She told Father what Deang had done and begged him to pray for her son, and to rid him of the demons of the Sodomites. Father Miranda, stunned and embarrassed, prayed quickly. Deang, humiliated, hung his head and listened in silence. Tears began to stream down his face. The rest of us, including Dad, sat in silence, not knowing what to do. After finishing his prayer, Father Miranda made up some excuse about having to go to the hospital for someone's last rights, and he left our home before he even touched his meal.

The next morning, on my way too school, I saw Deang in his favorite climbing tree. I waved to him, but he didn't see me. Then, I noticed the noose around his neck. I wanted to call to Deang, to say something to keep him from doing it, but my mouth was empty. I opened it to scream, but nothing came out. Deang fell from the tree, and I heard his neck snap.

I instantly detached myself emotionally. I had to; otherwise, I would have lost my sanity.

I moved toward Deang, getting as close as I could without touching him. I looked in his eyes; he looked like a stranger. His left eye was red and strained and pushed halfway out of his head. Tears, not yet dry, ran down his cheek. His tongue hung limply from his mouth, drool ran over his chin, and his body swayed in tiny circles.

I walked away. Then I started running. Ten minutes later, I had a complete panic attack. I lost consciousness and woke in the hospital.

For years, I hated Deang. I hated myself for not stopping him. I hated my father for not intervening at dinner. And I hated Mother for provoking him. About a week after it happened, I began saving every peso I could get my hands on. As soon as I had enough, I left for America.

Two months after I left, Mother killed herself.

"Cackoy?"

"Yes, Buena?"

"I miss Deang."

"I miss him, too."

"Daddy," I said.

"Yes, Buena?"

"I was there."

"What?"

"I was there. I was there when Deang killed himself. I saw it."

"I knows this, Buena."

"You know? How?"

"I always knows. Meela wasn't very par behind you dat day. She saw, too."

"Why haven't you ever said anything?"

"It wasn't por me to say. It was por you to say when you ready. Buena. Deang death was not your fault, neither was Mother's. There was nothing you could do."

"I know, Daddy."

"Don't say, *you know*. Believe it in you's heart."

Dad hugged me. His hug did for me exactly what a father's hug should do for his prodigal daughter. I didn't expect it would. I didn't expect I'd feel anything; I didn't think I was capable. Everything felt like it was locked up inside me too deeply to surface. But Daddy hugged me, and the tears I'd held back for seven years fell. Tears for Deang, for Mother, and even for Juan; the tears all came at once, and we cried, together, for what felt like an hour.

"Mahal Kita, Daddy."

"I love you too, Buena."

We hugged again. The hug felt natural for the first time since

Deang left. Finally, the burden of my horrible secret was lifted. Daddy and I talked and cried about Deang for hours; I told Dad about Juan, and we talked about Mother.

"Keep Deang alive in your heart and on your lips. Deang only gone if we forget him," Dad said.

Later, I told T.J. the whole story for the first time. Telling my secret, of being witness, was much easier the second time. In fact, I wished I'd confessed long ago. T.J. listened attentively, and his eyes welled up every time I cried. T.J. is a good man. He'd lived such a squeaky clean life, I couldn't imagine how he'd ended up with someone as screwed up as me.

After a couple days, we returned to Malapascua Island, but this time it felt different. I was relaxed, re-birthed. In the dark, we made love out in the ocean. The release of my orgasmic fluids into the sea was a cleansing. I ejected some anger and hatred. I forgave my mother and Deang and Juan and God and myself.

Then T.J. asked, "will you marry me?"

I was afraid to let another person get close to me. Everyone who gets close to me ends up dead, and that is just a fact. But my love for T.J. was strong, and it conquered the rational side of me.

"Yes! I will! I'll marry you today and every day for the rest of my days."

"All I need is once."

December 2004
Skye

Yosemite with Amber changed my life. It didn't happen overnight, but I was able to take Amber's message, and learn to stop being a victim. It wasn't so much the Jim MacLaren story as it was the idea that someone like Amber, who was not much more than a casual acquaintance, could exercise real love for me and could treat me with the respect I never gave myself; her kindness gave me hope.

It was always a struggle to stay sober, but I managed, and I grew a little stronger and felt a little more loved, every day. On Christmas Eve, Dylan and I were at Flora's to celebrate the holiday.

"Thanks for having us, Flora. Not having family on the holidays kind of sucks," I said as she let us in.

"I know how that feels. I left my family in the Philippines, and I've made a new family here from the people I love."

Dylan, T.J., and I were the only white people at Flora's party. The rest, all sixteen of them, were Filipino. They were nurses and nurse assistants Flora had bonded with when she first came to America. These people, strangers to her, loved her and took care of her, and became her family away from home.

"Fix yourselves a plate," Flora said, pointing at the kitchen table, which was loaded with various dishes. "First we eat, then we play white elephant, and then we karaoke," Flora said.

The gathering felt nice. I usually spent Christmas alone, crying and getting high. Two years ago, on Christmas Eve, I rented *Henry: Portrait of a Serial Killer,* drank a gallon of eggnog, ate a frozen TV dinner, shot some primo heroin, and passed out before midnight.

"What's this?" Dylan asked.

"Adobo," T.J. responded.

"What's adobo?"

"It's chicken, cooked in sugar, soy sauce, and some kind of magical Filipino vinegar. It's the best chicken you'll ever taste," T.J. said. T.J. thoroughly enjoyed sharing his knowledge of Filipino culture. He was head over heels for Flora.

Dylan took a bite. "Wow, that's good." Juice dripped from his newly grown thin goatee, which was silly looking. "What about this dish?" Dylan asked.

"Pansit. It's like Filipino chow mien," T.J. said.

"This?"

"Dinuguan,"

"What's that?"

"Just eat. It all so good. My many favorite," said Clarissa, one of Flora's friends. Clarissa, like most of the others there, spoke broken English. They probably spoke Tagalog at these get-togethers, but tonight, for us, they stumbled through their English, which was sweet.

Dylan fixed a healthy plate of adobo and pansit and filled a separate bowl with dinuguan. His enthusiasm for the food was pleasantly surprising.

"This deno-gwan is pretty good, Flora. What exactly is it?" Dylan asked.

"It's pork."

"What's the sauce?"

"Blood."

I wish I had a camera to capture Dylan's face. He spit the dinuguan back into the bowl, sat it down, and nonchalantly stepped outside. The Filipinos burst into laughter.

I followed Dylan out the door. He was smoking.

"Are we on goddamn Fear Factor or something?" Dylan asked.

"I don't know. Do they eat dinuguan on Fear Factor? I don't watch those crappy reality shows," I said, mocking him.

Dylan exhaled a thick white cloud of smoke that turned red as it rose into the Christmas lights above the door.

After a few cigarettes, we went back inside for the white elephant game. Flora explained: everyone puts a wrapped gift under the tree. Each person pulls a number, and then gifts are picked in numerical order. After someone opens a gift, they have the option of trading it for somebody else's gift.

I pulled an ice cream maker. I liked it, but Meeko snatched it from me and left me with bed linens. T.J. snatched the linens and gave me a gift certificate to a sporting goods store. I couldn't understand why a guy would trade for linens, but T.J. said he had his reasons. Flora laughed, and I assumed it to be a sick little sex joke between them. The game was cheesy, but fun, and the Filipinos were a riot, laughing and shouting the entire game.

"These Filipinos sure know how to make noise," Dylan whispered.

"You have no idea," T.J. responded.

They spoke in high-pitched sounds that resembled an off-key flute. Everyone talked at once, creating a thick carpet of sound. Nobody made much effort to listen. Occasionally, someone yanked a thread out of the conversation and weaved it into something entirely new that had nothing to do with what the first person was talking about. It was total chaos. I imagine most large families are cacophonous, but this was my first exposure to such.

After I finished my second helping of food, Flora's friend, Pea, forced a third plate down my throat. I ate it and then slipped away on my own. I watched *It's a Wonderful Life* on TNT. I was able to enjoy the story without feeling sorry for myself for the first time since I was a young kid. Back then, I always wanted to be one of the girls who jumped in the swimming pool when the retractable gymnasium floor opened during the dance; they all looked so happy. I wanted to be happy.

James Stewart's character, Jimmy, was offering to lasso the moon for Donna when a platoon of Flips barged in the room. Flora turned off the television and announced—

"Karaoke time!"

Everyone applauded

"They're addicted. Literally. And the worst part is they're all terrible singers," T.J. said.

"Tonight, I be the best Filipino Idol ever!" Ruthie declared.

Everyone applauded. Dylan rolled his eyes. Ruthie stood about four-foot-eight, weighed about eighty pounds, and had no chest or hips. From behind, it was hard to tell if she was a boy or girl. She took the microphone and stumbled through Nancy Sinatra's *These Boots Are Made for Walkin'*. She was horrible, and my music snob of a boyfriend, Dylan, looked like he was going to have a panic attack.

"A few nights ago, I woke up at like three a.m. to go to the bathroom. I heard a cat whining downstairs, but we don't have a cat," T.J. said to Dylan and I. "I followed the sound. It led me to Flora. She was sitting by the television, singing the *Wind Beneath My Wings* into the karaoke machine. I asked her to come back to bed three times, and three times she ignored me. I made the mistake of trying to snatch the microphone from her. I'm lucky to still have all my fingers," he said.

Karaoke continued. A girl named Delia did a Whitney Houston number. Joseph did *I Will Survive*. Barry did Sister Sledge's *We Are Family* then the Village People's *YMCA*. That was the last straw. T.J. interrupted.

"Skye, you've got to sing some karaoke and rescue us from this Filipino Asian annihilation on American music," T.J. said.

"Yes, Skye, sing!" Flora exclaimed.

I'd pretty much given up music. I'd decided music and drugs were too tightly woven together, and I wouldn't be able to do one without the other. I'd sacrificed music to stay sober. I hadn't sung in front of a crowd for almost two years. I know Flora's party wasn't exactly a sold out concert show, but, still, the idea of singing again, in front of people, seemed monumental. I didn't know if I could do it. But they left me no choice.

"Which song you sing?" One of the girls, Tamisha, asked. "Here, you pick." She handed me the karaoke play list.

I looked through the list but didn't see anything I wanted to sing. "I don't really know any of these," I said, lying.

340

"Great, just do a cappella. That would be even better," Flora said.

"We no have dis song," Tamisha said.

"No, baby, a cappella means singing without music," Flora explained.

Flora handed me the microphone. She saw the anxiety on my face; she knew this next step in my growth, as simple as it may have seemed, was one I couldn't do on my own. So, she started singing—

"I saw Mommy kissing Santa Claus

Underneath the mistletoe last night."

I took the microphone from her and took over the song. It felt good. Really good. After I finished the song, I was rewarded with a standing ovation. One of the girls, Miranda, hugged me, and I cried the happiest tears I think I'd ever cried. Everyday I was growing and healing; it was time to take the next step. I had to start making music again. I had to learn to separate music and drugs.

"That was the most prettiest song I ever hears! You like Celine Dion."

Dylan coughed, holding back a laugh. The others were clapping; it was just a silly little thing, but it felt good. It was the best holiday moment of my life.

We hung around for a couple more hours; everyone took turns at the karaoke— even the music snob, Dylan—it was a wonderfully festive evening. Later, people started filing out, and nearly every person hugged me and thanked me for singing. I felt more love, and received more hugs, than any girl could ask for.

When it was just Flora, T.J., Dylan, and I remaining, we started cleaning up. Dylan and Flora disappeared for a moment, leaving T.J. and I at the sink scrubbing dishes.

"Where did they run off to?" I asked after about five minutes.

Two seconds later, they appeared together in the doorway. They were holding a new guitar with a bow wrapped around it.

"For you," Dylan said, extending the guitar to me.

I embraced the guitar; I was so awestruck by their act of love I couldn't form words. I hugged the guitar and cried, and then I put it down and embraced them.

"You're a musician. Make music," Flora said.

"We love you," Dylan added. "I know you can do this, and I know you can do it sober. I believe in you. We believe in you."

Dylan was right. I'm a musician. I'd been sober in the past year, and I'd been in love, but my life still wasn't right. I could never be right unless I was making music. I couldn't let my fears and my addiction control who I was anymore.

I'd never escape my childhood demons, and my battle with drug addiction would go on as long as I lived. The only difference is now I have an army of friends fighting with me.

June 2005
Dylan

"On the tenth count, a lesser charge. We the jury find the defendant not guilty," I heard as I came out of my bathroom.

"I knew he was innocent," Kelly said.

"Just because they found him not guilty doesn't mean he's innocent," Amber responded.

Flora and T.J. were getting married, and we were all pitching in to help. Flora was bursting with excitement while she addressed the invitations. T.J. added the RSVP card, I added the return envelope, Dylan sealed it, Ron added the return address labels, and Beth added the postage.

"It's black, it's white, yeah, yeah, yeah!" Ron sang, doing his best Michael Jackson, which wasn't very good.

"Don't make it racial, Ron," Amber said.

"I wasn't. I'm just singing," Ron said. "But as long as we're on the subject, I think the verdict was racially motivated."

"That's bullshit!" Skye said.

"Don't tell me it's bullshit. America's been afraid to convict a black celebrity since the Rodney King riots."

"Objection. The prosecution is speculating," Amber said.

"I'm not speculating. I'm stating facts," Ron replied.

"Can't we all just get along?" asked Flora. Everyone laughed.

Ron continued, "Let's run down the list. We'll start with today. Michael Jackson, not guilty. Kobe was found not guilty of rape. Jason Williamson, Snoop Dogg, and Ray Lewis were found not guilty of murder. O.J. freaking Simpson was found not guilty for Christ's sake!" Ron said. "Then we have Martha Stewart: white, guilty. Wynona Ryder: white, guilty—"

"Robert Blake: white, *not* guilty," Beth said.

"Look, Ron, you're half right, half wrong," I said. America doesn't refuse to convict black celebrities. It refuses to convict *celebrities*. Period. Let's face it, celebrities are the high priests of our society. They're above the law. And, disturbingly, they're the ones who set the standards for America's children."

"True," Amber replied as she stuffed another wedding invitation.

T.J. added an RSVP card to the invite and said, "M.J. was found not guilty, and we should give him the benefit of the doubt. We don't know what really happened. And if he makes another record, I'll buy that one, too. He's the King of Pop."

"Celebrities give you a boner," I replied.

"Not true. I'm just entertained by them."

"You and your celebrity-idolizing E-Network watching buddies are the easy sells of this society. You run out and spend your money on the newest corporate crap just because some stupid celebrity endorses it. You're fascinated by fame, regardless of circumstance."

"Celebrities are fascinating. What's wrong with taking an interest in their lives?" T.J. asked.

Amber interceded, "It's not taking an interest that's wrong, it's the celebrity worship. If Osama Bin Laden could hit a baseball four hundred feet or rip a killer guitar riff, people would throw rose petals at his feet. American's have no moral perspective when it comes to choosing their heroes."

I agreed with Amber. "Thank you for a rational, intelligent statement, Amber," I replied.

"Blow it out your butt, Dylan!" Amber responded. "I don't need your endorsement to validate me. You talk down to people. You may be intelligent and witty, but it doesn't make you better than anyone else."

"Thank you for noting my intelligence."

Whack!

Amber

"Ouch!" Dylan yelled. He'd gotten whacked in the side of the face with a wadded up wedding invite.

"T.J., don't do that, we don't have any invitations to spare," Flora commanded.

343

"Yeah, dork," Dylan added.

"Why do you have to be such a sarcastic dick all the time?" T.J. asked Dylan.

"Because without my bitterness and sarcasm, I've got nothing. I'm nobody," he said. I don't think anyone could tell if he meant it. Dylan can be hard to read at times.

Dylan's nails were painted orange to match his secondhand, orange bridesmaid's gown that he'd bought for the singular purpose of dressing for this festive occasion. He purchased an orange gown because it matched the tacky orange invitations that we were stuffing in assembly-line fashion at T.J. and Dylan's dirty beach pad.

As a group, we'd only all known each other a short while, and this was probably only the third or fourth time we'd hung out as a gang. Regardless of how new it all was, I loved our gatherings. These new friends felt like family to me. We were all the same, and we all had issues. We'd all been broken, and spending time together gave us a sense of community—at least it did for me; it made me feel less alone. I hoped we could all remain tight and get together frequently. Besides Beth, I'd never had real friends, and this felt good.

The five o'clock news ended, and thankfully so did our Michael Jackson discussion. *The Golden Girls*, one of the worst sitcoms in history, started. T.J. laughed at all the stupid one-liners.

"Why do you laugh at that shit, T.J.?" Dylan asked.

Dylan and T.J., the two I'd known the longest beside Beth, were constantly at each other. They lived together and obviously loved each other, but they were complete opposites and fought like an old married couple. It was usually funny, but sometimes it got annoying.

"I laugh because it's funny. Don't ask stupid questions," T.J. said to Dylan.

"It's not funny, and that's not why you laugh."

"Really? Then why do I laugh?"

"Because you're conditioned by the laugh track. You're like one of Pavlov's dogs." T.J. barked *Arf! Arf! Arf!* "Did you know most of the people you hear laughing on those tracks were dead before *The Golden Girls* were ever made?" Dylan asked.

"Is that so?"

"Most of those laugh tracks were recorded in the fifties," Dylan said,.

"That's kind of gross in a weird way," Ron said.

Dylan lit a cigarette and changed the channel. Dylan's place smelled like a cigarette graveyard. It disgusted me. "Yep. Look, the same dead people laughing at jokes on *The Golden Girls* are laughing at the jokes on *Family Ties, Cheers,* and *Seinfeld.*"

"Nobody cares, Dylan!" T.J. said.

"I'll drop another elbow on your head if that's what it takes to knock some sense into you," Dylan fired back.

"Honey, hold these," T.J. said, handing Flora his stack of RSVP cards. "I'm about to put an ass whooping on this cross-dressing freak."

After a single puff, Dylan mashed the fiery end of his cigarette into the mountain of butts in the ashtray and jumped to his feet. T.J. started shadow boxing the air.

Flora rolled her eyes. "Sit down, T.J., or I'll be the one to drop an elbow on your head. You guys can be gay with each other after this job is finished. Now, get back to work."

"Wow. Guess she told you," Dylan chuckled.

Flora shot Dylan a look. "You want one of these?" she asked, touching her pointy elbow.

Dylan laughed and pulled his barely smoked cigarette out of the ashtray. He tried to light it, but his lighter was spent. Dylan smoked so much the white walls of his place had turned a cancerous yellow, and there were holes burned into his black pleather couch in the places he's passed out while smoking. Dylan tossed his dead lighter, grabbed a pack of matches, lit the cigarette, and blew out the match. The sulfur smell from the matches triggered my ugly memory, and made me ill.

"You okay, Amber?" Flora asked.

"I'm okay. Thanks."

Ron looked at me, and he knew. I worried he'd say something confrontational. Ron's a great guy, but he gets very defensive of me. I pretend to get mad when he gets that way, but it feels good to have someone that cares that much.

"Could you put that out, Dylan? Not everyone in here wants to smell your cigarette smoke," Ron said.

"Sorry," Dylan said. He stubbed out his cigarette and then sat down on the floor, his legs flayed in a V.

"Drafty in here huh, Webster?" I asked Dylan.

"Umm. No," Dylan replied.

"If you're going to dress like a woman, then please, for us ladies, try to sit like one," I said. At this point, a normal guy would blush and cross his legs. Of course, a normal guy wouldn't be wearing a bridesmaid's gown.

"Why'd you call me Webster?" Dylan said, unfazed.

"Figure it out for yourself, smart guy."

"Seriously, Dylan, nobody wants to see that little thing. Put that ugly thing away! I'm sick of having to see your nasty genitals every time I'm over here," Flora commanded.

"I'm comfortable with my body. The human body is not something to be ashamed of," Dylan said.

"It is when it's that tiny," T.J. said. Everyone laughed. An invitation fired across the room and hit him in the head. I'm not sure who threw it.

"My penis is six and a half inches, which is very average," Dylan said. If nothing else, the guy is stubborn.

"Seriously, Dylan. Your penis is the ugliest thing I've ever seen. It looks like a hundred-year-old tortoise halfway out of his shell." Flora said, and we all erupted into laughter.

Dylan seemed unembarrassed. I'm a stripper, and I was embarrassed for him. You'd think, at this point, Dylan would get up and go put on some pants, but he didn't.

"Listen Sharon Stone," Flora began, cracking us up. "From now on, the new rule is when I'm in your house, you cover your shit up," Flora said; it was the first time I'd ever heard her swear. "And seriously, why does it look like that?" she asked.

We all erupted in laughter. That was part of what was so great about being this group; we were able to tease each other without anyone taking it personally. We were always laughing. After a day with this group, and a few good hearty laughs, I always felt normal.

"Not that it's your business, but my penis looks like that because I, like my parents, do not believe in circumcising," Dylan said, finally crossing his legs.

"Why not?" asked T.J.

"It's unnatural."

"It's not sanitary. You should get it snipped," Ron said.

"First, the sanitation argument for circumcising is just propaganda. Circumcisions were started as a way to keep boys from masturbating, but it didn't work. For some reason, we continue to circumcise anyway. It's no different than the female genital mutilation they do in Africa that American activists lose their shit over," Dylan replied.

"Not true," I said. "Female genital mutilation in Africa is inhumane."

"And so is male genital mutilation. It serves no functional purpose beyond aesthetics. And did you know the foreskin has 22,000 erotic nerve endings. The clit has only 8,000. So, in reality, a male circumcision is more brutal and cruel than a clitorectomy."

"Twenty two thousand erotic nerve endings? Really?" Ron asked.

"I'm just stating facts."

"Wow, now I kinda want mine back," T.J. said. Again, we all laughed.

"Still, it's ugly," Kelly said.

"Well, whatever. All I know is when I have sex, I have a lot more feeling than you do," Dylan said.

"Yes, but it's ugly," Flora said.

"And he walks, a free man" Beth said, changing the subject, pointing to Michael Jackson on the television. M.J. was leaving the courthouse.

"I can't believe he got off," Kelly said.

"I'm telling you, he got off because he's black," Ron said.

"That's bullshit!" I said.

"Hey, you guys know the moonwalk?" Flora wisely interrupted. Flora was the cutest thing ever, and though she was twenty-three, she didn't look old enough to get married without parental consent. She moon-walked across the room. It was the saddest moonwalk I'd ever seen. "Shamoan!" she yelled, standing on her tiptoes, the fingers of one hand pointing in the air and the other hand resting across her belly, like Michael.

Flora moon-walked back to where she started. "You're a dork, Flora," T.J. chirped.

"Takes one to know one, baby. Shamoan!"

"You tell him, Flora!" I cheered. I found Flora fascinating. She seemed so carefree and playful, but there was a deeper darkness layered beneath her childlike demeanor. There was something perverse and interesting behind her eyes. Some of us had shared our demons with each other; some of us hadn't yet done so. Flora hadn't yet shared with me, but the demons were there, and I hoped that at some point she would feel close enough to me to share.

"Shamoan!" Flora yelled again, moon-walking back across the room.

"Okay, my turn," I said. I got up and gave it my best shot. One by one, we did our version of the moonwalk. It was the most fun I had in years. On our own, we were all broken individuals; as a group, we were powerful. We were all threads of a tightly woven family.

It was nice to belong to something positive.

T.J.

"She's beautiful and sweet. You're a lucky man," Kelly whispered to me.

My smile was so big and proud you'd think Flora was the Sistine Chapel and I'd just painted her. I've never been the lucky guy before. I've always been the guy reeking of envy.

"You know, I might not be engaged if it weren't for meeting you, Kelly."

"So I guess you have me to thank for this," he said, smiling.

"Maybe. But I'm pretty sure that your purchase of those baseball cards from me helped your relations with Beth's son, Jonathon. So, we're even."

"Fair enough, even considering that you jacked up the price on me with a lie about Flora's dad needing money for a kidney transplant. Not cool." Kelly looked up at our yellow-stained ceiling. He appeared to be in deep thought. "It's funny how life works. The night I met my miserable, cheating, ex-wife, Reece, I lied and told her the scar on my back was from donating a kidney. Karma's weird, huh?"

"It sure is."

Selling my baseball card collection to Kelly, a complete stranger at the time, made the trip to the Philippines possible. Meeting Kelly again, through Amber and Beth, was some kind of weird cosmic magic. Life is full of the type of coincidences that artists fall in love with, and the coincidences surrounding our group were more than accidents. We needed each other to thrive and be happy, and that's why the Universe brought us together.

Flora did another pathetic moonwalk. She didn't notice when the left strap of her tank top fell off her shoulder, exposing the lacy brown cup of her bra. It made me want to kiss her. But first I'd linger in the moment and allow it to tease me.

Flora sat down on the loveseat in a shadow-filled corner of the room. She giggled as Dylan was the next to moon walk. The blinds above Flora were raised barely an inch, letting in a splinter of light that illuminated her eyes.

I walked to her and let my hand disappear behind her back. I pulled her shoulder strap up then gently ran my fingers across her bare shoulder. She turned her head back and smiled at me.

She loves me.

September 2005
Kelly

I was leaving church and stopped outside to talk to the preacher. With T.J. and Flora's wedding coming up I'd been thinking a lot more about Beth and I, and I wanted an outside opinion about our relationship.

I approached our preacher, Paul, and after exchanging some polite courtesies, I delved into the subject. "See, Paul, I just don't know what the problem is. She's smart, attractive, and she's the kindest person I've ever known. She's a great mother, and she treats my son well, but—"

"But what?" Preacher Paul asked.

"But, I don't know. Sometimes I think I love her. But—"

"But?"

"But sometimes our relationship lacks that passionate, raw, sexually fueled chemical thing."

"And?" Paul asked. I wasn't sure if he was urging me to hurry up or what. He was looking over my shoulder as if he had somewhere else to go.

"And, well, I want that."

"We all want that. I want that," Paul said.

He was looking past me again. I turned and looked over my shoulder and saw what had him distracted. It was his ridiculously sexy girlfriend, the actress, my ex-patient, Maria Orlando. "You have that."

"Kelly, there are guys who would kill for a woman like Beth. If you don't feel you're passionate about her, then you owe it to her to let her go so she can find someone who will be. Or, maybe you should consider the possibility you're just afraid of commitment because of what happened with your ex-wife."

"Maybe," I said. It wasn't exactly the kind of earth shattering revelation I was hoping to get from him.

"Think about it."

"I will."

"And try to come to church more than twice a year."

"Yeah. Thanks, Paul," I said. Paul shook my hand and then went to Maria. I couldn't help but ache with envy as I watched him hug her.

Did my envy mean I was unhappy with my situation? Or was it that I was just afraid of commitment? What could I do about it? How could I move forward with love if my past had my heart on lockdown?

I thought about love on the drive to Reece's. Teddy must have been waiting by the window because he came running out before I had the car in park.

"It's time to go back to work full-time, Kelly. We need the money!" Reece shouted out the door.

Typically, I'd fight back. Today, I simply left.

"Don't ignore me! You loser!"

A man once told me a joke about his wife. He said she didn't give head, but she gave great headache. It's a crude joke, but it was the perfect anecdote for Reece. Reece is poison. Every time I wash her out of me, the cuts start to scab over and heal, but then she rips the wounds open, and claws her way back in. For the sake of my relationship with Beth, I couldn't allow Reece's words to affect me anymore.

I knew that my feelings for Reece had always been more about infatuation with her beauty than love, but knowing that didn't make it hurt any less. On the very day I caught her with Jackson's penis in her mouth, I knew it would hurt every day until I found new love to fill the enormous hole she'd created. Then I found Beth, but still the hole was there. Reece had broken my ability to love.

Once we got to my place, Teddy and I played one-on-one wiffle ball in the back lot of my apartment complex. Brady, our dog, was our all-time fielder. Points were awarded based on the length of a hit.

Teddy was a competitive little guy and a good athlete—quick and strong. At seven years old, he was by far the best player on his pee-wee league baseball team, which was made up mostly of eight- and nine-year-olds. I couldn't understand why the coach had him batting eighth in the order and playing right field. It was obvious he should've been a cleanup-hitting shortstop.

Teddy got his athleticism from my side of the family. Luckily, Reece gifted him with his looks, which was the only genetically valuable trait she had to offer.

"Home run, Dad!"

"Bull! It was not. Brady caught it!" I said.

"Bull! It bounced before he caught it."

"Bull!"

"You're cheating, Dad!"

"You're cheating!"

We played ball all afternoon. It felt good. We were stars; we were competitors; we were better than the rest of the world. We were athletes of skill and endurance who could play wiffle ball for days on end. Wiffle ball all day and all night, stopping only to rest and feed and use the bathroom.

Unfortunately, our game had to end.

"We've got to get going pretty soon," I said as the sun started cresting the horizon.

"Back to Mommy's?"

"Yeah."

"How come I'm not staying with you this weekend?"

"I told you, Teddy, I have to work at the nursing home this weekend to make some extra money to help Mommy with the bills."

"I wanted to hang with you and Beth all weekend."

"Yeah, I wanted that too," I said.

"Do you love Beth?" Teddy asked. I wasn't expecting such a question, but Teddy never ceased to amaze me with his seeking of information.

"I don't know," I replied.

"Dad, let's look into this. Do you not love her or do you love her but fear telling her because you're afraid of getting hurt again? Do those feelings sit inside you and burn in the pit of your stomach, making you sick with anxiety? Is that why you drink a little too much? Are you worried if you try to express the gargantuan feelings of love that have built up inside you that maybe Beth won't love you back? Or maybe she'll love you back and create a perilous situation in which you'll fall deeper and deeper, helplessly, into a bottomless crater of love? Is it, Dad? Are you worried the love will start to push all other emotions out of you and you'll be incapable of any cerebration or emotion other than love? Are you scared that as you continue to gorge on this love Beth will eventually stick a pin in your overinflated head, and it'll pop, exploding into a billion tiny, rancorous pieces? All love and potential for love will escape from you and disappear into a chasm of regret and render you neutered and impotent. Is what keeps you up at night, Dad?"

"I'm not sure, Teddy," I replied.

"Dad, are you worried at some point you may subconsciously sabotage your relationship with Beth because of fear Beth will leave you much in the way your mom did? Do you want to marry Beth to make sure she stays, or are you afraid marriage will create a possibly calamitous situation in which you'd fail again as a husband? Are you worried you'll be a terrible stepfather to Jonathon? Do you worry our stitched-together family would be a fraudulent union that's merely pretending to be legitimate? That we'd be a fabricated, malevolent concoction, a group of strangers parading around as a family like every day is Halloween. Is it, Dad?"

"I don't really know exactly how I feel—"

"Poor Dad," Teddy said, patting me on the head.

"Dad, are you worried if you love Beth as much as you fear you may love her it could lessen the amount of love you'll have left for me? Do you worry you have only a set amount of love to give, and you've already wasted most on loving a mother who you never met? Are you afraid if you love Beth you'll lose your individuality and originality and become merely *the guy in love with Beth* much in the same way you were just *the guy married to Reece*? Are you afraid you'll forget about all the other things you love like music and sports? Are you afraid of losing those things, or are you placing more value on them than you should because you need an excuse not to fall in love? Are you untrusting of your own instincts, which failed you before? Or is it Jonathon?
Are you too bothered about Jonathon being the son of King Jackson that you don't know if you could be fair to him? Is that it, Dad? Every time you look at Jonathon, you see King Jackson then you see King Jackson's nakedness in Reece's mouth. Is that the problem, Dad?"

"You shouldn't talk about your mother that way."

"Dad, are you confused about pretty much everything in life? Everything you ever thought you knew? Do you think all the decisions you've made have already fucked me up beyond repair long before I even hit puberty? Do you wonder how you could've done everything—the whole kit and kaboodle, the whole ball of wax, the whole shebang—

differently over this long onerous pilgrimage of life? Do these things trouble you?

"Sometimes."

"Do you worry that it's already too late to start a new marriage? That you and Beth will grow old and lonely even though you're married and living in the same house? Do you fear you'll get comfortable in life and become a gray, patriarchal, overtaxed, weary, bitter, and cynical old man? Are you terrified you'll be married but sleep in a separate bed from Beth, speak to her only when you need a second helping of mashed potatoes or when you need her to bring another beer as you grow fatter in your La-Z-Boy? Do you worry you and Beth will stop listening to each other? You'll no longer hear when Beth says *I love you*? That maybe you won't hear it when she scolds you for leaving the toilet seat up for the umpteenth time? Are you afraid all you'll have to look forward to are Sundays when you go to the YMCA and play chess with the other geezers who are trying to escape their wives too? Is this what worries you, Dad? Are you afraid with each passing day you'll become less desirable and a bigger disappointment to Beth, breaking down all her faith, the confident idealism and the lusty love she longed to share with you? Is it, Dad?"

"I think so."

"Which part?"

"All of it."

"So, back to my original question, do you love Beth?"

"I think so."

"Yes or no, Dad. There's no *I think so* with love. You do or you don't."

"Then I do."

"Are you sure?" he asked.

"Positive," I said.

"Sorta-positive or positive-positive?"

"Definitely sorta-positive positive."

"Well, I guess that's good enough for now. The point is, there's always something that will make you question your decisions. Sometimes you just have to block everything out, and move forward on instinct. It's the only way to heal."

"I think you're right, Teddy. You're such a smart young boy."

Actually, all Teddy said was he really liked Beth and I should stop being a chicken-sissy-pants and tell Beth how much I like her. But his tone and facial expressions suggested the rest.

Later, after I took Teddy back to Reece's, I spent half my night looking at old photo albums of Reece and me. My thoughts chased my memories like Brady chases his tail. I went around in circles for hours and then, in typical movie fashion, I burned every photo.

It was my cleansing before my new beginning.

Beth

My life was becoming more and more routine and predictable.

Every Tuesday through Saturday, I'd wake at six a.m., pee, shower, dress, open the door for the sitter, kiss Jonathon goodbye, and leave for work. I'd head south on La Cienega, stop at the newsstand on the corner of La Cienega and Venice, and exchange good mornings with Kapil, the owner. I'd give him four dollars for a newspaper and a large coffee with two creams and three sugars, and Kapil would give me exactly fifty-eight cents back. I'd head west on Venice Boulevard, make a left on Duquesne Avenue, and a right on Culver Boulevard. I'd start to feel small and insignificant next to the huge building-sized posters of the Hollywood celebrities lining the side of the Sony building. I'd think about Jonathon, Kelly, Amber, my dads, war, death, social injustices, whatever, everything, nothing. Life couldn't be more routine if I lived in a house full of monks.

Nothing ever happens.

Today, after I let the sitter in and kissed Jonathon goodbye, something happened.

Kelly was standing on the porch. I don't know how long he'd been standing there. He gave me a large cup of coffee, two creams, three sugars, and the morning paper.

"I love you," he said. It was the first time a man, other than my dads, had ever said those words to me.

"I love you too, Kelly."

Jackson

I don't think I felt anything even close to love for Beth. I don't think I've ever felt love for anyone, even myself.

But I wanted her in my life. I wanted her and my son to be my family.

I drove to Beth's with the intention of making it work. I would take care of her and our son, and in return they would kill my loneliness.

I pulled up outside Beth's. There was a man there. He hugged her and gave her flowers.

Family is worth fighting for. Getting to know my son was worth fighting for.

But loneliness is painful, and I was tired. It took all the strength I could muster to even drive to Beth's. And When I saw the way Beth hugged that man, the way she loved him, I lost the small amount of fight that resided within me.

I grabbed a handful of little oval white pills from my pocket and swallowed them dry, waited a while for that warm purple light to fall upon me, and then I drove away.

Amber

It was the night before T.J. and Flora's wedding, and we were in a hotel room in Palm Springs. The room's beige walls were decorated by boring Ansel Adams lithographs. The brown carpet was worn thin and splattered with stains. The heavy dark curtains flapped lightly against the window, blown by the pressurized, cold air from the air conditioner. The small television hummed, and its reds and purples and greens flickered on the walls. The running toilet blended with the air conditioner and television, completing the orchestra of background noise. The pillows were lumpy and overstuffed, and the mattress was too firm. And when I thought about the thousands of lonely businessmen who masturbated to twelve-dollar adult films in this bed, I became disgusted.

The room was not sexy.

But I felt sexy for the first time in my life.

My entire body felt like a giant, engorged clitoris.

Beside me lay the man with the beautiful green eyes, green like the rolling hills of the safe places I'd never been. The man who was everything I loved and everything I hated lay beside me in silence. I wanted Ron to kiss me.

Why? Is this curiosity? Is this real? What is this? Should I kiss him? What if I kiss him, and there's no chemistry? What if I kiss him, and it's everything? Then what?

Ron and I were going to Flora and T.J.'s wedding together as friends . We shared a room because neither of us really has money to waste. We were supposed to have two queen beds, but instead we'd gotten a king. I'd shared a bed with Ron on two previous occasions, and it wasn't a big deal. I scratched his back; he played with my hair; we made half-hearted jokes about sex, but it never escalated. Nor had I wanted it to. Until tonight.

Ron's pinky finger was touching the top of my hand, and it felt nice.

I'm terrified.

Tonight, Ron's beautiful green eyes were inviting me in, and I wanted to go.

I began to question everything I thought I knew about myself.

Ron

If I don't kiss Amber now I'll explode.

Our plutonic *understanding* was no longer enough. I needed more. I needed more than engaging conversation a couple of nights a week on her tacky pink couch while watching a stupid movie. I needed more than sharing a bed as friends. I had to make a move, regardless of consequence; hopefully, she wouldn't slap me.

I'd been stressed recently. Until just a week ago, I was sure Orlando had stiffed me on my money. But just when I'd completely given up on the money completely, he contacted me via mail. Inside an envelope with no return address, there was a key— *#208A*—and a bank address. I hadn't yet gone to retrieve the money because I'd been feeling like someone was following me; in fact, I was almost positive that someone was following me. It may have been the feds, or even one of Orlando's men. Regardless, I'd wait to retrieve the money until it felt safe, even if took months.

Despite my stress, I was also in good spirits because I knew that I could outsmart this secret agent. I'd get my money and I'd finally be able to say to Amber, "you can quit stripping. I'm taking care of you now."

That would be soon, maybe a few weeks down the road. But at the moment I had more pressing needs to tend to.

I have to kiss her.

I took in two deep breaths and announced my intentions.

"Amber, I'm going to kiss you."

Amber didn't respond.

I could feel my heart pulsating in my throat. I rolled left, put my hand on Amber's cheek, parted my lips, and placed them on her mouth just long enough to taste her. I pulled back, expecting her to say something, but instead her long lashes reached for my face, and she kissed me back.

Amber

It was so masculine and strong and so unlike what I was used to in a kiss. It was wonderful and alarming and long, but not long enough. I felt his hardness pressing against my bare thigh as he kissed me.

And I wanted all of him.

But I was nervous and feared my body would seize up.

Please kiss me again, Ron. Kiss me again and again and again until I'm not afraid anymore.

Ron kissed me, then his hand disappeared beneath the covers. He tugged at my shorts, testing my boundaries. I reached down and pulled his shorts to his ankles. Ron touched me. I was wet. He parted me with his fingers.

Don't do it, Ron. Not yet. I'm not ready. I can't do this.

Ron entered me.

And I let go of hearty, opalescent tears.

Ron

All those years of longing were finally satisfied in one raw and honest moment.

I knew it was Amber's first consensual experience with a man. I expected her to experience pain, but she didn't. It was good, like a first experience should be but rarely is. Everything felt easy and natural, like we were just doing what we are programmed to do.

We moved together like long time lovers. Amber had an orgasm in just a couple minutes, and then a second orgasm ten minutes later. It wasn't because I'm an amazing lover or because she was incredibly sensuous. It was because the two of us, collectively, were a perfect union in bed.

After forty-five minutes, we rested silently with fingers interlaced while gazing aimlessly at each other, trying to catch our breath. If that isn't beautiful, then nothing is. We lay, paralyzed by pleasure, for exactly twelve minutes. I know it was twelve minutes because it was midnight when we stopped making love and twelve-twelve when we started again. We made love over and over; we'd rest, sleep, wake up, and make love again. It was the best night of my life.

By the time the morning's gray light penetrated the room through a sliver of space between the vertical curtains, we were exhausted and fully requited

Amber's face rested on my chest. When she exhaled, her breath caressed my chest for a brief second before dissipating through the room. Our air was so sinful and hot, it would've melted the wings of our guardian angels if they were watching.

Amber

"Everything I ever need is here in this bed," Ron said. It was corny and beautiful. I wanted to capture his words, frame them, and hang them in the room in place of the lithographs.

"That was the most perfect thing I've ever been part of," he added.

I smiled.

"Are you sure you're a lesbian?" Ron asked.

"Right now, I'm not sure of anything."

Things would be different between us. I didn't know how we got to this point or where it was going. My heart was in so many places all at the same time.

Flora

Five nights ago, T.J. and I went to see the indie film, *Me, You and Everyone We Know*. It was our final date before our lifetime union. Afterward, we went at it like a couple of teenagers who had just discovered sex. We made love well into the early morning hours, storing up orgasms so we could survive without each other until the wedding.

After we finished, when our heads weren't swirling with thoughts, we tried to sleep. Since the day T.J. proposed, I'd been working on my fear of getting close to someone. I can't say I didn't still have reservations, but I was ready to take the chance.

Today, our wedding day, I was craving T.J. We'd been apart for four nights. After a lifetime with your heart locked up in solitary confinement, you'd think that four days would be easy, but it wasn't. Once the body tastes the euphoria of love, it becomes addicted.

I stepped out of the shower; my wet hair was thick and stuck to my body like boiled noodles on the bottom of the pot. I cracked open the bathroom door to let some steam escape. I wiped the mirror and began the process of building my hair into a glamorous tower. I spent over an hour combing, drying, curling, piling, and spraying. My straight Filipino hair required a gaggle of pins to hold it in place.

T.J.

I must refute the misconception that brides and grooms are too busy to enjoy their own wedding day.

The soon-to-be Mrs. Flora Martini stood, barefoot in the sand, a hundred feet away from me. She looked beautiful in her inexpensive, secondhand dress. I have no idea who wore the dress first, but the seamstress must've had Flora in mind when she threaded the first needle. Anything more beautiful than Flora wearing that dress would be deadly.

I'm marrying the most beautiful girl in Los Angeles.

It was a perfect day to be married on a California beach. The sun was beginning to set, and the clouds reflected reds and purples across the sky. Skye strummed her guitar gently playing *Collide*, by Howie Day. Flora began taking her final steps as a single girl. I shot a smile toward my mother, and she began crying; my father gave me a big thumbs-up. When my father met Flora last week, he said he was impressed I'd scored such a special girl. For the first time, it felt like I'd earned my father's respect. I wished that Flora's dad could be there; his death had been hard on Flora, but at least they'd had the chance to patch up their relationship.

Flora moved towards me. Her cadence was slow and metered, one foot crossing directly over the other, her hips billowing from side to side, and her eyes locked on mine. I expected to be nervous, but I wasn't; I was eager. At a traditional wedding the groom is expected to keep his thoughts pure, but this wasn't a traditional wedding, Flora wasn't your typical girl, and I hadn't seen her in five days, so making love was heavy on my mind. From thirty feet away, I could smell her sex like she was straddling me. In that moment, I wanted Flora more than ever; it took all my will to keep from grabbing her, throwing her over my shoulder, and running away.

Flora took her spot by my side, and I kissed her cheek. Everyone's eyes were on her; she was the show. I was merely a backdrop dressed in a monkey suit.

The preacher started, "We are gathered here today."

He carried on about the sacred union of marriage, the importance of keeping God in ones marriage, blah, blah, blah; whatever, I wasn't paying much attention. My head was dizzy from doing mental cartwheels; I was as excited as I'd ever been. After the preacher finished, Skye sang a song, a reader read a bible passage, our friends cried, and then Flora started her vows, *'for richer and poorer, in sickness and health'*, whatever; it didn't matter much what she said, everything I needed to know was in the way she was looking at me.

Flora and I are happy together. We understand each other. We love each other. What else matters? Maybe I should have been pondering the gravity of the situation, but I was too distracted in bliss. The priests can discuss the importance of God in the marriage, and the intellectuals can debate the significance of a vow; in the meantime I'll be busy making love to my beautiful bride.

We'll be one of those rare couples, fifty years from now, sitting at the head of a banquet dinner table in some fire hall somewhere, gathered with a hundred friends and family to celebrate our golden anniversary. A young, struggling couple will approach us and ask us our secret. I'll say, *there's no secret—there's just love.*

"You may kiss your bride," the preacher said.

So, I did. I kissed my bride, and then I took her hand. I'd never let go.

Skye

Everyone cried when they exchanged vows.

Everyone but me.

I was too dead inside to feel anything.

The reception in the hotel lobby was joyous. People were dancing and laughing and enjoying the alcohol and cake and the beautiful decorations. Flora approached Dylan and me. We were sitting with an empty chair between us.

"Are you guys having fun?" Flora asked.

"Yeah," I said.

"You look beautiful," Dylan added.

"Thank you."

Flora pulled me onto the dance floor. She executed a 1980s spin-move that was as adorable as everything else about her. She giggled and hugged me. The photographer snapped shots of us dancing and hugging, and I imagined Flora, years later, looking at the pictures with her kids.

"Who's that one?" her gorgeous daughter would ask, pointing to the picture of the two of us; me trying to look sober.

"That's Skye. She was my best friend. She's dead now," Flora would say, and then she'd cry because that's the kind of person Flora is.

Flora took my hands, pushed me away, pulled me in, dipped me, and laughed.

"I'm happy for you," I said.

"Thanks, Skye. We've got to get together soon. I've been so busy planning this wedding that we haven't seen much of each other," Flora said. She spun me. "How've you been?"

"Great. Really great," I said, lying, not wanting to spoil her wedding day with the truth.

Flora looked like a dream in her off-the-shoulder empire gown. It looked like something from Vera Wang or some other designer whose dresses cost tens of thousands. But knowing Flora, she probably got her dress at some secondhand store, while still managing to look more beautiful than every Hollywood celebrity.

"Are you sure you're doing okay?" Flora asked, her smile yielding to a motherly look of concern.

Flora, the constant guardian of goodness, the bright-eyed girl with the perfect smile and flawless skin, Flora, the bride, was concerned about me on her wedding day. Her selflessness made me feel even guiltier.

"Yeah, everything's great," I said, and smiled as big as I could.

There was no reason to tell her Dylan and I had broken up yesterday; that we were pretending to be a couple today so we wouldn't ruin the wedding. I decided to dump him after he caught me shooting up. I loved Dylan, but I would never change, and I knew I had to let him go to save him.

Flora twirled me, brought me back, twirled me the other way.

"When we get back from the honeymoon, the four of us will have to get together."

"Sounds great," I said.

I didn't want to tell her I'd probably be somewhere in Venice or West Hollywood or on fucking Pluto, trying to lose myself, trying to fill my veins with as much dope as I could squeeze into them.

"Can we get you dancing with the groom's father?" the photographer asked, tugging at Flora's arm.

The photographer wanted Flora as badly as every other guy who's ever met her. It was obvious.

"Thank you for the dance," Flora said.

She smiled and winked and kissed me on the forehead.

Goodbye kisses hurt.

"Flora. I love you. You know that, right?" I asked.

"Aw, of course I do, Skye. I love you, too. You're my best friend."

Now that Dylan and I were over, Flora was the only thing I had.

But that wasn't enough.

"See you later," she said.

"Bye," I said.

I watched Flora dance and laugh with T.J.'s dad, making him feel as special as she makes everyone feel.

Since I decided to get sober, every day had been a constant struggle. Most of them I've won, but the victories had always been nominal because deep inside I'd always be incapable of change.

I've tried; I've fought with everything I have, and I've surrounded myself with good people. Despite my friends and despite Dylan's love and support, I've learned there's only one relationship in my life that will last until the end.

I walked back to the table and grabbed my purse. Dylan stared down at his feet.

He was hurting. I'd hurt him.

I took my purse and my dope, the one true love of my life, and we went to the ladies room.

Dylan

The problem with loving someone is you expose your naked self, putting yourself out there to be hurt. I'd been hurt by love before, but the others were pin pricks in comparison to the fleshy heart Skye inflicted on me.

Skye took her purse and made for the ladies room; I knew exactly what she was going there to do.

I sat at the table and tried to mind my own business. I tried to stop loving her. But I couldn't. Love had its claws deep inside me, down to the bone. I knew I could never help Skye, but I also was incapable of giving up. She was my muse, the blood in my veins, my reason for existing.

Ten minutes after Skye went to the restroom, I knew she wanted me to leave her alone.

But I couldn't.

I went into the ladies room to stop her. I found Skye on the floor in one of the stalls. She was full of dope and starring at the ceiling, crying.

"Go away," she said when she saw me.

I bent down and took her in my arms. "I will never go away."

Skye didn't resist. She put her arms around me, buried her face in my chest. "You need to stop loving me. I'll ruin you."

I pulled her in tighter, and together we wept.

Ron

We knew we'd be showing up late, and we felt bad, but not bad enough to rush through our early afternoon sex.

We missed the beach wedding altogether, and when we finally went downstairs for the reception, it was halfway over. I wanted to run around telling all our friends what had happened. I wanted to tell them I loved Amber, but I wasn't going to steal the spotlight from T.J. and Flora. Besides, I think our friends could tell what happened just by looking at my face.

"Where have you two been?" Beth asked Amber, smiling.

"Wow, Ron, you've got quite the healthy glow. What's gotten into you?" Kelly asked, teasing.

Amber and I took our seats, and as I scanned the room, the first person I noticed was Maria Orlando. I became alarmed. Why was she here? The wedding gathering was small, just a dozen friends of their closest friends and a few family members, and as far as I knew, she wasn't friends with T.J. or Flora.

I know she knows.

Anxiously, I searched for the man who'd been following me. He was there; I didn't see him, but I knew it. I searched for someone suspicious looking. I didn't know who exactly was following me; maybe one Orlando's men, or maybe the feds, but I knew someone was, and whoever it was, Maria Orlando was in on it. Maybe he was tucked behind the long satin curtains or under the bridal table..

Where are you?

The preacher approached Maria and kissed her. Why? Was he the man who'd been following me? I felt I'd seen him before but couldn't place him. *Was he someone I knew from prison? From the hospital?* He was familiar in the way that a forgotten childhood friend is. His long nose, his high cheekbones—I knew them. His name was hidden somewhere in my head with all the other names and faces from over the years.

"Are you okay, Ron?" Amber asked.

"Not really."

"What's wrong?" she asked me.

"See her over there? She's Maria Orlando, the actress. I worked with her and she was nasty to me. I don't like her," I said, not wanting to reveal the whole truth.

Amber didn't respond. "Amber?" I turned my attention toward her to get her attention.

Her face was white.

"Amber?"

"It's him," Amber mumbled, trembling.

"Him who?"

She grabbed my arm, and pulled me in tight. "Why now?" Her voice was quivering. She was afraid.

"Amber, what is it?"

She put her hand on my chest and pointed toward the preacher. "He raped me."

Rage went through me. I reacted before I could think. I charged the preacher, steak knife in hand.

Amber yelled, "Ron! Don't!"

"Die rapist!" I swiped at his face. I wanted to cut out the eyes that watched my lover as he raped her. He ducked. I missed his eyes, but the knife caught his ear, slicing it from his head. Stunned, he bent over to pick it up. Then he covered the hole in the side of his head with his hand. Blood ran between his fingers and down his forearm. The fucking scumbag glanced at Amber, which fueled me with hatred. We locked eyes.

"Drop the knife!" somebody yelled.

I lunged at Paul again, and this time I drove the knife into his chest. Empowered by Amber's anger, my mother's anger, and the anger of all women who'd ever been raped, I pushed the blade into his chest all the way to the handle.

He fell.

Chaos exploded around me. People ran. I couldn't pick out Amber's voice from the tidal wave of screams. Maria Orlando picked up the rapist's head from the floor and held him in her lap. I was standing over his bleeding body, which would soon be an empty corpse. I felt an immeasurable surge of power. His life force was leaving him and entering me. He was wheezing for air, not yet dead, and already I wanted to kill him again. I stood over him, staring, hating.

Amber, too weak to stand, crawled toward me and curled her body around my leg.

"I love you so much, Amber."

Amber's mouth began to quiver. I knew she loved me, but I wanted to hear her say it. She didn't have the strength. She looked up and silently mouthed, *I love you, too.* Smiling, I bent over and kissed her on the lips. I turned away. Amber tried to cling on, but I stepped out of her grasp. I knew I was now in danger, and I couldn't expose her to it.

I'm 100% certain Amber knew what would happen next.

Whoever was following me had me now; I knew it. I wasn't planning on getting away; I couldn't get away. There were a thousand witnesses. Amber could never be mine again as she had been last night. I preferred death to a lifetime of conjugal visits. I walked outside so Amber wouldn't have to watch me die.

Paul

Today was redemption day. Today was my penance for my sins from long ago.

My body temperature was cooling; I felt a growing physical distance between my flesh and the intangible portion of me.

I would die soon.

I wondered how God would receive me.

My hand held my detached ear. I looked at it and almost

chuckled. What irony. In losing my ear, I finally had something in common with my idol, the preacher and artist, Van Gogh.

I grabbed the handle of the knife still sticking out of my heart. I closed my eyes and pulled. Blood poured out in waves and began to congeal when it hit the floor. My pain was lessening, almost gone; it wouldn't be long.

"Please hold me," I asked my new wife, Maria.

"I am," she said, trembling.

Cradling me, protecting me, Maria's hair fell over our faces and sheltered us in privacy for my final moments. I looked at her face and, for the last time, I wished again I could paint it. Maria smiled her broken crooked smile, and I looked in her eyes and was comforted. I would die while roaming the vast open meadows in her eyes.

My vision narrowed. Everything became darker until there was nothing but blackness. The blackness started coursing through my veins the way death creeps through a morgue at night.

Then I swallowed the last bittersweet taste of air meant for me in this world.

Maria

I cried, but mostly I was confused. Why had this happened? That horrible man called Paul a rapist before he stabbed him. Was that true? Paul was my rock, my salvation and sanity all rolled up in one. His love was a ribbon around my heart that I could hold for safety as I crawled through the terrifying maze of life.

But now Paul was dead.

My husband is dead!

I held his limp body and wailed. The pain was immeasurable, it was absolute, it felt like I'd been stabbed in the heart with him.

Paul had always been a tortured soul.

Now he's free of his demons.

But where does that leave me?

Ron

I'd walked away from Amber knowing we'd made love for the last time. I walked away knowing I'd saved Amber. She'd never have to dance again, and the man she feared was dead.

I walked toward the door hoping for a reprieve. When I opened the door, I knew that wasn't going to happen. "Drop the knife, put your hands behind your head, and lie flat on your stomach!" yelled a cop. He stood behind a patrol car, his partner nearby.

Going back to prison was not an option. I did the only thing I could. I raised my knife and charged.

He fired a shot.

I felt nothing. I kept charging.

A second shot.

The bullet burrowed through my thigh, and I crashed to the ground. I tried to stand up, but couldn't.

I'd been hit. Twice. There, on the ground, I began to feel the pain. Razor-sharp, searing heat.

So this is what it feels like to be shot.

Both shots had connected—the first in my flank, the second in my thigh. I struggled to my feet.

"Don't shoot!" I heard Amber yell from behind me.

I couldn't turn back and look at her; I'd lose my nerve.

"I love you forever, Amber!" I yelled. I ignored the violent throbbing pain in my thigh, raised the knife overhead with both hands, let out a final guttural scream, closed my eyes, and ran full speed at him.

"Drop the weapon," he yelled.

"Don't you shoot him!" Amber cried, hysterically.

He fired again.

Amber

Ron dropped, and my heart fell out of me. I ran to him. I took him in my arms and focused on the life force behind his eyes; it was dwindling. Ron was letting go.

"Look at me, Ron!"

Ron's green eyes were becoming distant. Terrified, I stayed focused on his beautiful eyes, trying to bring the life back into them; my efforts were in vain. The depth in his green eyes became two shallow, reflective pools that took my gaze and reflected it back to me, unchanged.

Ron was gone.

Ron

Death didn't happen like I expected it to. There was no Grim Reaper, no chorus of angels, no army of demons. And my life didn't flash before my eyes. Death was the color of softness, a delicate green under a thin film of baby powder. There was nothing but soft random thoughts and pictures, drifting through me like a child's breath blowing through a dandelion after making a wish. And as I died, Amber held me. She was crying puddles of love around me. I wanted to soak up her love and smuggle it with me to wherever I was going next.

So I did.

They say everyone dies alone.

But I know that's just a lie they say to scare you.

April 2006
Amber

It had been six months since Ron's passing, and I was only just beginning to heal. The smell of simmering onions filled the kitchen as I took them off the stove and added them to my marinara sauce. While stirring pot, for the millionth time, I looked up and read the poem on the wall that Ron had written in his journal. Before Ron died, he had made out a will; I was his sole beneficiary. His journals were the one thing I had that allowed me to hear his voice, over and over, anytime I wanted. In life, Ron was private about his writing. He'd written things in those journals that he wanted to share with me but didn't know how to. In these journals was a confession about Ron's prison history and his original plan to take advantage of me. I didn't get mad when I read these things; I mean, the man gave his life in the name of love. Love changed Ron and his love helped heal my wounds. Reading his journals allowed Ron and me to bond in ways I didn't believe two people could bond when separated by life and death. My favorite passage from his journal was framed on our wall:

> *Walls move tighter on me by the hour;*
> *I want to break out, but have no power.*
> *What if what we see is all we've got,*

A world full of filthy everlasting rot.
We must endure and be strong;

We must continue to move on.
Keep walking.
Keep walking.

Haunting memories I keep inside me;
Childhood nightmares only I can see.
Her screams echo against cement walls;
I'm cursed forever to hear her calls.
Pleas for help sounding dead and alone,
I will save her and take her home.
And she'll keep walking;
We must keep walking.

Maybe there is a celestial being,
and to the pain it will bring meaning.
Soothe our wounds and temper our hate,
Bring us peace before too late.
May love find a soul in need;
Give me the strength to proceed,
To keep walking,
Keep walking;

Despite our broken selves.

The love of my life died six months ago. I will always miss him, but he will never be too far.

Ronni kicked me. It must have caught me in the lung because it knocked the breath out of me. Ronni had the strength and attitude of her daddy. I sang to her, and it seemed to soothe her. She settled within me, and I pictured Ronni, inside my uterus, humming along with me.

"What time is dinner, Mom?" Kimberly asked.

"Soon, love. Go get ready. Everyone's coming over."

"Okay, Mom," Kimberly said. Despite all the chaos I'd put my daughter through, she was becoming quite a strong and healthy young lady, and for that I was grateful.

Ron died trying to save me, and I'm sure if he had it to do over, he would do the same thing again. Ron did save me, but it wasn't what he did at the wedding or the money; it was his love. It took me years to deal with my pain and allow myself to be loved and to love.

From this lesson in love, I realized that I needed to express my love to Kimberly every single day, and my love had to be pure and truthful. So, I told Kimberly the truth about her father. And though Kimberly was hurt; she didn't turn against me. She's a stronger and better person than I am.

Tonight, Kelly, Beth and their kids, as well as T.J., Flora, and Dylan were coming over for dinner. We'd been getting together twice a month since the tragedy. Skye was coming for a while, but now she was back in rehab again. Together, we shared our painful stories, we cried, we laughed, we hugged, we loved one another, and we pulled strength from one another. We all wanted to bring Skye back, especially Dylan, but we couldn't force it; it would happen in her own time.

I hosted the biweekly gatherings because I loved being in the home Ron had given me. Ron left me enough money for the house, Kimberly's college, and a dance studio where I taught jazz and ballet to children; I had enough left to give Beth money for a down payment on her home. And though I was eternally grateful for all those things, I'd trade it all in for just one more night with him.

"Oh, wow," I said. Ronni kicked inside me again. This time she got a kidney.

I couldn't wait to bring Ronni into the world. And I prayed every night my lover's daughter would be blessed with his beautiful green eyes.

I know no matter what I do as a parent, eventually both Ronni and Kimberly will be hurt by this world. All I can do is teach them what I have learned. I've learned that we all get hurt and we all end up broken; to heal, we must allow ourselves to be loved, and we must keep walking.

Appendix A
Broken's Characters

Skye is a homeless teenage musician who dreams of unattainable rock stardom. Abused as a child, she's turned to drugs to help erase the memories and pain.

Amber is young black mother who's been forced to resort to unsavory means in order to take care of her daughter, Kimberly. They've run to Los Angeles to escape a dangerous man from Amber's childhood.

Ron is an ex-con who was raised to resent black people. He has moved to Los Angeles to start over.

T.J. is an out of work actor who fails auditions by day and wears a hamburger suit outside a burger joint at night. T.J. needs to make it on his own in Los Angeles to prove his father wrong.

Dylan is a pseudo-intellectual-Chuck Palahniuk wanna-be, and a cynic. He wants to be a writer, but he has no muse, nor inspiration.

Flora is a Filipino immigrant who's fled to America to escape the horrific tragedy that her family endured.

Beth is a lonely, overweight girl. She was raised by two gay men and consequently she has trouble relating to the opposite sex.

Dr. Juan Salazar is a psychologist who was sexually scarred as a child, and has become more disturbed than all of his patients.

Kelly is a lonely Physical Therapist who's unhappy with his career and wants nothing more out of life than companionship.

Jackson is a retired professional football player who became addicted to pain killers after a career ending injury. Jackson, who inherited his father's corporate empire, seems incapable of love.

Paul is preacher who fled the east coast for Los Angeles to atone for the sins of his dark past.

Kimberly is the young daughter of Amber who struggles through life without a father figure.

Maria is an actress and the daughter of a major mafia boss. She struggles with her physical image and is bulimic.

Reece is an aging model whose career has never taken off. Reece dreams of finding fame and wealth.

The author, J. Matthew Nespoli, can be contacted at MattNespoli@hotmail.com

Acknowledgements

First, I want to thank my bride, Rea, for always loving me and supporting me, even when it was not convenient. I love you. Thank you World Audience and Mike Strozier for working with me and publishing my novel. Thank you Kyle Torke for editing. Thank you to the photographers, Joel Silva and Melanie Morgan, for your work on the front and back covers. Thank you to my parents for raising me well. Thank you Potzie for the love you've shown to my family and for helping us market this book. And thank you to all of my friends and family whom I forced to read *Broken* before it was ready for publication.

Author Biography

Matthew has traveled the world and met many interesting people. He is hard at work on his second novel, *The Suck Monster*, a humorous memoir about fatherhood. Matthew resides in Hermosa Beach, CA, with his wife and newborn son. He owns, operates, and writes for a highly popular socio-political Web site: www.nakedwordsurfer.com. Matthew is passionate about writing and seeks to make it his full-time career. *Broken* is his debut novel.

LaVergne, TN USA
25 February 2011
217972LV00003B/6/P